JANE AUSTEN'S
MANUSCRIPT WORKS

D1256716

broadview editions
series editor: L.W. Conolly

JANE AUSTEN'S MANUSCRIPT WORKS

edited by Linda Bree, Peter Sabor, and Janet Todd

broadview editions

Library and Archives Canada Cataloguing in Publication

Austen, Jane, 1775-1817
    Jane Austen's manuscript works / edited by Linda Bree,
Peter Sabor, and Janet Todd.

(Broadview editions)
Includes bibliographical references.
ISBN 978-1-55481-058-1

    I. Sabor, Peter II. Todd, Janet M., 1942- III. Bree, Linda
IV. Title. V. Series: Broadview editions

PR4032.B74 2012   823'.7   C2012-905812-2

Broadview Editions
The Broadview Editions series represents the ever-changing canon of literature in English by bringing together texts long regarded as classics with valuable lesser-known works.

Advisory editor for this volume: Colleen Franklin

Broadview Press is an independent, international publishing house, incorporated in 1985.

We welcome comments and suggestions regarding any aspect of our publications—please feel free to contact us at the addresses below or at broadview@broadviewpress.com.

North America
Post Office Box 1243, Peterborough, Ontario, Canada K9J 7H5
2215 Kenmore Avenue, Buffalo, NY, USA 14207
Tel: (705) 743-8990; Fax: (705) 743-8353
email: customerservice@broadviewpress.com

UK, Europe, Central Asia, Middle East, Africa, India, and Southeast Asia
Eurospan Group, 3 Henrietta St., London WC2E 8LU, United Kingdom
Tel: 44 (0) 1767 604972; Fax: 44 (0) 1767 601640
email: eurospan@turpin-distribution.com

Australia and New Zealand
NewSouth Books
c/o TL Distribution, 15-23 Helles Ave., Moorebank, NSW, Australia 2170
Tel: (02) 8778 9999; Fax: (02) 8778 9944
email: orders@tldistribution.com.au

www.broadviewpress.com

Broadview Press acknowledges the financial support of the Government of Canada through the Canada Book Fund for our publishing activities.

Typesetting and assembly: True to Type Inc.,
Claremont, Canada.

PRINTED IN CANADA

Contents

Acknowledgements

This edition draws directly on two volumes of The Cambridge Edition of the Works of Jane Austen (Gen. Ed. Janet Todd [9 vols, Cambridge: Cambridge UP, 2005-08]): *Juvenilia*, edited by Peter Sabor (2006), and *Later Manuscripts*, edited by Janet Todd and Linda Bree (2008), which themselves reproduce Austen's texts directly from her manuscripts. The texts of Austen's juvenile writings and of "Lady Susan" are those of the relevant Cambridge volume, and the texts of "The Watsons" and "Sanditon" are reproduced from the line-by-line transcriptions in the *Later Manuscripts* volume. We are grateful to Cambridge University Press for giving us permission to draw on the Cambridge volumes in this way. We also wish to renew our thanks to those acknowledged in the two Cambridge University Press volumes. We are grateful to Leonard Conolly, Colleen Franklin, and Tara Trueman at Broadview for their careful and thorough reading of the manuscript. We are indebted to Hilary Havens for her energetic and expert research assistance.

Abbreviations

JA   Jane Austen

Johnson Samuel Johnson, *A Dictionary of the English Language*, 4th ed. (1773)

OED *Oxford English Dictionary Online* (www.oed.com)

Introduction

When Jane Austen died, at the age of 41, on 18 July 1817, she had published just four novels: *Sense and Sensibility*, *Pride and Prejudice*, *Mansfield Park*, and *Emma*. All had been issued in the last six years of her life, though *Sense and Sensibility* and *Pride and Prejudice* had first been drafted in the late 1790s. Within months of Austen's death, her family organized the publication of two shorter works of fiction, *Northanger Abbey* (another novel which had long been extant in draft form) and *Persuasion*, which she had been working on in 1815-16. In the "Biographical Notice of the Author" attached to *Northanger Abbey and Persuasion*—the first biographical account of Jane Austen, occupying just a few pages —Henry Austen praised his sister's imagination and wit, and also her "polish" in her life and in her writing: "Every thing," he wrote, "came finished from her pen." All her writings, he added, were worthy of publication.[1] The clear implication was that *Northanger Abbey* and *Persuasion* completed the Jane Austen oeuvre.

In fact, Austen left behind her a significant amount of other work in manuscript that she had carefully kept, sometimes in draft form and sometimes in fair copies, often over several house moves, and, in some cases, for more than twenty years. In the early 1790s, when still a teenager, she collected together into three exercise-book "volumes" her juvenile writings, now generally referred to as the Juvenilia; some time in or after 1805 (the date of the watermark on the paper), she wrote out, for preservation, a fair copy of a novella, "Lady Susan." An early draft of a novel, untitled and now generally referred to as "The Watsons," probably stems from the same period; and there remains her final novel, also untitled, but known as "Sanditon," written in the early months of 1817 and abandoned as her last illness took hold. Alongside these, there are twenty-two miscellaneous poems and charades that bear witness to her love of wordplay, and the amusing "Plan of a Novel" that satirizes the formula-fiction her juvenile work had already burlesqued so mercilessly. Finally, there are works that might or might not be by Austen, including some prayers, which were preserved by family members, and a

---

1 Henry Austen, "Biographical Notice of the Author," reproduced as Appendix 2 in Jane Austen, *Persuasion* (1817, ed. Janet Todd and Antje Blank [Cambridge: Cambridge UP, 2006]), p. 331.

play in her handwriting that reduces Samuel Richardson's massive novel *Sir Charles Grandison* (1753-54) to the equivalent of fourteen pages in a modern printed edition. There is no way of telling now what further work might have been lost or destroyed along the way, but enough remains to show Austen in a completely new light, in terms of both the range of her writing and her methods of creation.

This volume reprints the great majority of Austen's manuscript works, including more than half of her juvenile writings and all the later fictions—"Lady Susan," "The Watsons," and "Sanditon."[1] The subject-matter of these writings is similar to that of the published novels: there are the same preoccupations with genteel families in villages in the south of England, the same concerns about courtship, the same specific fears of what might happen to young women, however beautiful and intelligent, if their families are not wealthy enough to attract desirable husbands for them. But in every other respect, the manuscript writings come as quite a shock. From the brilliance of the juvenilia to the unexpected modernity of "Sanditon," they show Austen pushing the conventional boundaries of fiction in a way quite at odds with the published novels, exploring the implications of vulgarity and violence, experimenting with different styles and tones, practising and refining her arts of narrative, and adding a whole new dimension to her own comment about her writing as a "little bit (two Inches wide) of Ivory on which I work with so fine a Brush, as produces little effect after much labour."[2]

Work in Progress

Austen's unpublished stories and tales were well known within the family circle that meant so much to her. Many of her early writings were formally dedicated to family members, and the act of fair-copying must have been designed, at least in part, so that the work would be available for reading: Henry wrote in the "Bio-

---

1 For a scholarly edition of all of Austen's known manuscript writings, together with those for which claims for Austen's authorship have been made, see the two relevant volumes in *The Cambridge Edition of the Works of Jane Austen: Juvenilia*, ed. Peter Sabor (Cambridge: Cambridge UP, 2006) and *Later Manuscripts*, ed. Janet Todd and Linda Bree (Cambridge: Cambridge UP, 2008).

2 Austen to James Edward Austen 16 December 1816 (*Jane Austen's Letters*, 3rd ed., ed. Deirdre Le Faye [Oxford: Oxford UP, 1995], p. 323).

graphical Notice" that she "read aloud with very great taste and effect," and that her own works "were never heard to so much advantage as from her own mouth."[1] The manuscript works might be fragmentary, but they continued to resonate. In 1814, Austen wrote to her sister Cassandra that a particular travelling arrangement "put me in mind of my own Coach between Edinburgh & Sterling,"[2] alluding to the ending of "Love and Freindship," a tale written decades earlier; long after Austen's death, Cassandra recalled her sister's intentions for the unfinished tale of "The Watsons" (see p. 29).

Just as Austen went back to her earlier work to make fair copies, so she seems to have continued to tinker with the works she had left unfinished. These drafts are occasionally quite heavily corrected and, while some of the corrections are likely to have been part of the original drafting process, others were evidently made when Austen revisited her work at a later date. In "Catharine," for example, there is an odd juxtaposition between the powdering of a young gentleman's hair—a fading trend even in the 1790s—and the heroine's reading Hannah More's *Coelebs in Search of a Wife* (1809) and wearing a "Regency dress," so named for its popularity during the Regency of the future George IV, which began in 1811.

She did not, however, revise her spelling. It has recently been claimed that Austen was ill-educated or somehow incompetent as a novelist partly because of the vagaries of her spelling,[3] but this was a period when orthographic conventions were not as inflexible as they are today. Austen was not alone in spelling "ie" words as "ei": not only "freindship" (perpetuated in the title of one of her most brilliant juvenile writings), but also "greif," "neice," "beleive," etc. Other spellings that look unusual now— "expence," "agreable," "chearful"—were accepted alternatives in her lifetime: "stile" was used for "style," for example, throughout the first published edition of *Sense and Sensibility* (1811). Her punctuation is often careless, though mostly in first drafts. Her

1 Henry Austen, "Biographical Notice," *Persuasion*, p. 330.
2 Jane Austen to Cassandra Austen, 23 August 1814, *Jane Austen's Letters*, p. 270.
3 See articles in various English newspapers on 22 and 23 October 2010, including the *Daily Telegraph* article, "Jane Austen's famous prose may not be hers after all" (accessed online), all quoting interviews given by Kathryn Sutherland in connection with the launch of the Jane Austen Digital Manuscript project. This free-access online project offers facsimiles and transcriptions of a large proportion of the manuscript works.

use of the apostrophe is certainly inconsistent (though the angle of her handwriting sometimes makes the exact placing unclear), and she maintains the habit of occasionally emphasizing a noun by beginning it with a capital letter, an eighteenth-century practice rapidly becoming outdated during her lifetime. But rarely is there a fault in sentence construction, and her meaning is generally clear, while many of her revisions reflect her concern about finding exactly the right word or phrase.

The manuscripts show that Austen was not among those many writers who begin their fictions with names and locations in place. In "The Watsons," she revised her original idea of setting the narrative in the town of "L." in Sussex in favour of the town of "D." in Surrey only once she was some way into the manuscript. Consistency in the form of names is also not Austen's highest priority. Sharp-eyed readers of *Pride and Prejudice*—the most carelessly printed of Austen's finished novels—would have noted that the Bennet girls' aunt and uncle in Meryton are sometimes named "Philips" and sometimes "Phillips"; this inconsistency was almost certainly originally the author's. The librarian in "Sanditon" is variously Miss or Mrs. Whilby or Whitby; the family with whom Emma Watson attends the ball at "D." is Edwards or Edwardes, seemingly at random. The juvenilia and "Lady Susan," being fair copies, offer fewer variations, but, in "Lady Susan," the name of the protagonist's friend is visibly altered to "Alicia" only after the fair-copying had started, while in "Catharine" Austen decided, at some point when re-reading the manuscript, not only to formalize the original "Kitty" to "Catharine" on many more occasions than in the original (including in the title), but also to alter her surname from Peterson to Percival, though in both cases the corrections are made inconsistently.

Such fitful drafting exists alongside considerable precision in detail. We can see from a series of letters written by Austen in 1814 to her niece Anna, who was writing a novel, what a sharp eye Austen had for accuracy: "As Lady H. is Cecilia's superior, it w^d not be correct to talk of *her* being introduced; Cecilia must be the person introduced"; "They must be *two* days going from Dawlish to Bath; They are nearly 100 miles apart"; "Let the Portmans go to Ireland, but as you know nothing of the manners there, you had better not go with them. You will be in danger of giving false representations."[1] In Austen's own manuscripts, the

---

1   Austen's postscript to a letter from Mrs. Austen to Anna Austen Lefroy, ?mid July 1814, reproduced in *Later Manuscripts*, p. 214; Austen to

many corrections mostly adjust tone and nuance rather than changing fact or matters of social protocol, where her command is assured.

Austen's revisions do, however, illuminate the ways in which she must first have written her published fictions and how she must have worked on them to provide fair copies of her work. Even the small tales in "Volume the First" of the juvenilia imitate published books, beginning with dedications and finishing with the word most often used at the end of the novels of the time, "Finis." "Lady Susan" is largely epistolary, and the letters are reproduced with the formalities accorded to other letters in novels until the work's non-epistolary conclusion, justified by the narrator on the grounds that "This Correspondence, by a meeting between some of the Parties and a separation between the others, could not, to the great detriment of the Post office Revenue, be continued longer" (p. 265). The narrative concludes entirely "in character," with a witty and worldly flourish: "Whether Lady Susan was, or was not happy in her second Choice—I do not see how it can ever be ascertained—for who would take her assurance of it, on either side of the question?" (p. 267).

But it is perhaps by comparing "Catharine," the last of Austen's juvenilia and the tale most nearly approaching the realistic tone of her adult works, with "The Watsons," the novel she probably began writing in about 1804, that Austen's methods in writing her finished fictions can most clearly be approached. "Catharine" extends to about 16,500 words and "The Watsons" to 18,000—in other words, both came to a stop at the equivalent of about half-way through the first of the three volumes of Austen's full-length works. The openings of both "Catharine" and "The Watsons" are well in line with what we might expect from an Austen novel, and in fact there are considerable similarities between the two drafts: in the first, we have a bright young girl, Kitty (or Catharine), hampered by the overprotectiveness of her guardian and left isolated because her good friends the Wynne sisters have been dispersed on the death of their father, a country clergyman who had not been able to leave them well provided for; in the second, Emma Watson has been left isolated by the remarriage of the aunt who had previously designed Emma as her heir, and has returned unexpectedly to her family of

---

Anna Austen Lefroy, 18 August 1814, reproduced in *Later Manuscripts*, p. 218. See also Appendix A.

sisters, headed by her father, a country clergyman who is not going to be able to leave his daughters well provided for. At this point in *Mansfield Park*, for example, the Bertrams were only just visiting the Rushworths at Sotherton, while in *Emma*, Emma Woodhouse (and possibly the reader) is still under the impression that there is a budding courtship between Mr. Elton and Harriet Smith, while neither Jane Fairfax nor Frank Churchill—nor of course Mrs. Elton—have even made an appearance. So it is impossible to be sure how the narratives of "Catharine" and "The Watsons" would have developed. And of course Austen did not go ahead with either of them (though empty pages were available both at the end of "Volume the Third" and in the last booklet of "The Watsons").

What is perhaps most startling about both the fair-copy "Catharine" and the draft "Watsons" is that, despite a length equivalent to perhaps eight or nine chapters in one of the published novels, neither contains any chapter divisions. Moreover, there is very little paragraphing in either fragment. It is not always easy to determine where new paragraphs are intended in Austen's manuscripts (for example, the next line after a half-line of text may not be indented), but Austen's general practice is clear. "Catharine" contains about 140 paragraph divisions, many more than "The Watsons," but only because Austen decided, probably in the course of fair copying the earlier work, to start most speeches with a new paragraph, and a substantial proportion of both narratives—as with Austen's published novels—consists of conversation. Excluding the paragraphs prompted by opening or closing speech acts, "Catharine" has only five paragraph breaks and "The Watsons" three, together with two clear divisions in the text marked by a line. All this provides persuasive evidence that while Austen gave close attention to her phrase and sentence structure, she was not writing to the rhythm of either paragraphs or chapters.

The other notable difference in appearance between "Catharine" and "The Watsons" is in Austen's use of the dash as a form of punctuation. Much has been made by recent scholars of the use of the dash in women writers in general and in Austen in particular:[1] the dash is seen as more typical of female than of male expression, and its use in manuscript and published work

---

1 See, for example, Janine Barchas, "Sarah Fielding's Dashing Style and Eighteenth-Century Print Culture," *English Literary History* 63 (1996): 633-56.

has been scrutinized for possible evidence of censorship by male editors and compositors. So it is remarkable that Austen's fair-copy "Catharine" contains only about 150 dashes in all, with most of these occurring in the direct speech of female characters, while the draft of "The Watsons" contains more than 850. Some of these can be accounted for by Austen's tendency to split speeches with a dash in the absence of a new paragraph in the latter work, but the conclusion seems inescapable that Austen removed many of the dashes that proliferated in her drafts when she came to produce fair copies of her own work, either as a routine stage of formalisation or as a gesture towards the presentation of published texts.

Her practice in the later "Sanditon"—a longer fragment, at about 23,500 words—reflects the habits of an experienced professional author in one important respect: although a first draft, it is neatly divided into chapters, formalizing natural breaks in the narrative.[1] However, there are still only twelve paragraph divisions, and there are more than 1100 dashes, proportionately about the same as in "The Watsons." Evidently Austen, though now conforming to published-novel conventions in the larger divisions of her narrative, continued to favour continuous prose and the evocative dash in place of more formal punctuation when drafting her work.

Juvenilia 1: Outside Influences

Jane Austen's juvenilia are widely recognized as some of the most extraordinary writings ever produced by a child: whether or not Austen herself recognized how remarkable they were, she cared enough about them to copy twenty-seven items—including short fictions, dramatic sketches, verses, and a few non-fictional pieces—into three notebooks, to which she gave the mock-solemn titles of "Volume the First," "Volume the Second," and "Volume the Third," as though collectively they formed a three-volume novel, the format in which the four novels that she published in her lifetime would appear. It is probable that all the works contained in the notebooks were originally written between 1787 and 1793, that is, from the time when Austen was eleven years old until she was seventeen, although the works are

---

1 The rejected final pages of *Persuasion*, written in 1816 and the only surviving fragment of Austen's published novels, are also divided into chapters.

not copied in the order of their original composition: the latest date mentioned is 3 June 1793, placed at the end of the first volume after her poem "Ode to Pity," while the dedication to "Catharine," the last work in "Volume the Third," is dated August 1792.[1] The manuscripts are all fair copies, but they contain extensive revisions, deletions, and insertions: some pieces are very lightly altered, while others contain copious revisions. There are about a hundred changes, for example, in both "Love and Freindship" and "Lesley Castle."[2]

All but one of Austen's early writings has a dedicatee, either a family member or a close friend. Dedications are often written with fulsome compliment, and some dedicatees are honoured on more than one occasion. The links between the writings and their dedicatees are carefully calibrated. To her brother James, writer of a series of programmes for family theatricals, Austen dedicated "The Visit," the best of her comic plays. The outrageously inventive "Love and Freindship" is dedicated to Austen's glamorous and indomitable cousin, Eliza de Feuillide. "Evelyn," in which the insatiably grasping hero instantaneously acquires a new house and bride, was presented to Mary Lloyd, Austen's friend and neighbour, just as she was displaced from a local parsonage in favour of James Austen, who was about to acquire the house as well as a bride.

These dedications act as a reminder of how important her family and friends were to Austen's development as a writer, but they also, like many other effects in the juvenilia, mimic the features of the published fiction of the time. Even in her early teens, Austen was evidently an experienced reader of novels and a sharp observer of their prevailing faults. The fiction of the second half of the eighteenth century was dominated by the work of Samuel Richardson, whose three hugely popular novels, *Pamela* (1740-41), *Clarissa* (1747-48), and *Sir Charles Grandison* (1753-54), described, in vivid and intense detail, the trials of virtue—particularly in the person of a vulnerable young girl—under stress. It was said that Austen's "knowledge of Richardson's works was such as no-one is likely again to acquire,"[3] and Richardson was clearly a strong influence on her writings, but her attitude to his

---

1   For further detail on the dating of individual items in the juvenilia, see Peter Sabor's introduction to *Juvenilia*, particularly xxviii-xxix.

2   For a complete record of the changes in the juvenilia, see Peter Sabor's textual notes in *Juvenilia*.

3   James Edward Austen Leigh, *A Memoir of Jane Austen* (London 1870), pp. 109-10.

work seems to have changed over her writing life. In her last fiction, Austen describes one of her characters, Sir Edward Denham, as someone whose "fancy had been early caught by all the impassioned, and most exceptionable parts of Richardsons" so that in imitation of Richardson's most controversial villain, Robert Lovelace, "Sir Edward's great object in life was to be seductive," strongly implying that this was a wearisome outcome of poor literary judgement.[1] But the teenage Jane's response was less complicated: she clearly relished Richardson's lively ear for conversation, as well as his penchant for scenes of high emotional intensity, both traits further developed in the novels of Frances Burney, *Evelina* (1778), *Cecilia* (1782), *Camilla* (1796), and *The Wanderer* (1814), along with renewed emphasis on the social dilemmas of very young, genteel women who needed to find security through a good marriage.

Moreover, Austen was equally steeped in novels by writers much less talented than Richardson and Burney, whose work reflected more simplistically the age's seemingly inexhaustible fascination with emotional extremes and tortuous plot twists. Many of her juvenile writings are outright burlesques of the threadbare conventions of the sentimental novel, with its impossibly perfect heroes and heroines all equipped with a tremulous, self-absorbed, and entirely impractical sensibility. In "Frederic and Elfrida," we learn at the outset that the titular characters "loved with mutual sincerity but were both determined not to transgress the rules of Propriety by owning their attachment" (pp. 49-50). Austen embellishes the joke with Mozartian invention to the point where she even mocks the conventional novel heroine's modesty over naming a wedding day (Pamela Andrews' "No, pray, Sir, pray, Sir, hear me!—Indeed it cannot be to-day,"[2] in particular, echoes into the text), so that Elfrida remains engaged to her cousin for eighteen years while her parents, "knowing the delicate frame of her mind could ill bear the least excertion ... forebore to press her on the subject" (p. 57). In "The First Act of a Comedy," Austen punctures the fiction-writer's perennial problem—a problem more acute than ever, given the habit of eighteenth-century novelists of writing novels in letters—of how to fill in a back story:

---

1   "Sanditon," pp. 363, 364.
2   Samuel Richardson, *Pamela: or, Virtue Rewarded* (1740, ed. Albert J. Rivero, *The Cambridge Edition of the Works of Samuel Richardson* [Cambridge: Cambridge UP, 2011]), p. 301.

Pistoletta: Pray papa how far is it to London?
Popgun: My Girl, my Darling, my favourite of all my Children, who art the picture of thy poor Mother who died two months ago, with whom I am going to Town to marry to Strephon, and to whom I mean to bequeath my whole Estate, it wants seven Miles. (p. 151)

In "Love and Freindship," she mocks the hackneyed plot device of heroes arriving under assumed names and identities by the deadpan. "The noble Youth informed us that his name was Lindsay—. for particular reasons however I shall conceal it under that of Talbot" (p. 97). And the self-regarding implications of narratives revolving around the marriage chances of young, genteel heroines—narratives Austen herself would be writing within a few years—are laid bare in Margaret Lesley's account of the life she and her sister lead:

> never were two more lively, more agreable or more witty Girls, than we are ... We are handsome my dear Charlotte, very handsome and the greatest of our Perfections is, that we are entirely insensible of them ourselves. (p. 126)

In such observations as these, Austen goes far beyond mere burlesque to illuminate and satirise the whole set of assumptions underlying a literary genre with which she was so joyously familiar.

Juvenilia 2: Violence and Vulgarity

"She was formed for elegant and rational society ... Faultless herself, as nearly as human nature can be, she always sought, in the faults of others, something to excuse, to forgive or forget."[1] This description of Austen is irreconcilable with the evidence of the juvenilia, which shows that, as a teenager at least, Austen was merciless in exploiting the comic potential of human faults and failings and far from "elegant and rational" in her narrative interests. The juvenilia abound with illicit love affairs, adultery, bigamy, and bastardy, all recounted with relish rather than moral outrage: in "Love and Freindship," Lord St. Clair and his two youngest daughters have six illegitimate children between them;

---

1   Henry Austen, "Biographical Notice," *Persuasion*, pp. 328, 329.

in "Lesley Castle," Margaret Lesley mourns her beloved brother's unhappiness in marriage since "the Worthless Louisa left him, her Child and reputation a few weeks ago in company with Danvers and dishonour" (p. 125).

Moreover, there is a startlingly high level of violence in these stories and plays. Not only do various characters die of grief (with one young woman, Charlotte, in "Frederic and Elfrida," committing suicide), and endure gory accidents (being thrown from a horse and dying of a fractured skull in "Lesley Castle," or expiring, "weltering in their blood," after a carriage accident in "Love and Freindship"), but they are capable of very violent acts. The extreme example is perhaps Sukey Simpson in "Jack and Alice," who, after endeavouring to cut Lucy's throat, poisons her instead and is "speedily raised to the Gallows" (p. 73). But lesser acts of violence, many of them not at all elegant, abound. People kick each other out of windows ("Frederic and Elfrida"), cudgel their haymakers ("Henry and Eliza"), knock down a pastry cook ("The Beautifull Cassandra"), and are maimed after being caught in a steel trap ("Jack and Alice"). In "Henry and Eliza," children bite off their mother's fingers.

Petty theft—accompanied by preening self-congratulation, combined with outright contempt for the victim—is still more common. The heroine of "Henry and Eliza" steals fifty pounds from her "inhuman Benefactors" while remaining "happy in the conscious knowledge of her own Excellence" (pp. 74-75), while "Love and Freindship" contains an orgy of robbery: August steals money from "his Unworthy father's Escritoire"; Philander and Gustavus steal first from their mothers and then from their cousins, Laura and Sophia; Sophia, caught in the act of stealing a fifth banknote from another cousin, merely demands "in a haughty tone of voice 'Wherefore her retirement was thus insolently broken in on?'" (p. 111).

Not surprisingly, the creator of Lady Catherine de Bourgh in *Pride and Prejudice* excels in creating characters given to verbal abuse, but abuse in Austen's juvenilia has a startling rawness and vulgarity, as when Frederic and Elfrida, with their friend Charlotte, declare to the "amiable Rebecca" that "your forbidding Squint, your greazy tresses and your swelling Back ... are more frightfull than imagination can paint or pen describe" (p. 52). In some of the stories there is an almost Rabelaisian interest in food: "Lesley Castle" offers a remarkable study in obsession with menus; in "Evelyn," Mr. Gower has no sooner eaten his way through "The Chocolate, The Sandwiches, the Jellies, the Cakes, the Ice, and the Soup" than, not forgetting to pocket the rest, he enjoys "a most excellent Dinner and partook of the most exquisite Wines" (pp. 157-58). Alcohol features prominently, perhaps most notably in "Jack and Alice," where the Johnsons are said to have many good qualities despite being "a little addicted to the Bottle and the Dice," while the heroine herself is so incensed at being accused (with total justification) of being drunk that she has to be restrained from physically attacking her mentor, Lady Williams. The overall effect of reading such passages is rather like looking at the characters of the published novels through a crazy mirror, where in some alternative Austen universe the alter egos of Anne Elliot and Lady Russell from *Persuasion* come to fisticuffs. One thing the juvenilia make clear is that the "elegance and rationality" that Henry Austen claimed for his sister, and which are often said to be reflected in the published novels, were for Austen a conscious choice rather than an instinct, a narrowing down of creative options from a much wider span of possibilities than many of Austen's readers would have guessed.

Betweenities

The last of the juvenilia, "Catharine, or the Bower," shows a marked change of tone from the earlier narratives. Gone, for the most part, is the burlesque or satire of other novels, and gone, too, is the intention to play the story primarily for laughs. Instead, "Catharine" has much more in common, in approach, tone, and content, with the later manuscript narratives, and indeed with the published novels. Consider the opening sentence:

> Catharine had the misfortune, as many heroines have had before her, of losing her Parents when she was very young, and of being brought up under the care of a Maiden Aunt, who while she tenderly loved her, watched over her conduct with so scrutinizing a severity, as to make it very doubtful to many people, and to Catharine amongst the rest, whether she loved her or not. (p. 164)

It could be argued that too much is packed into this, and that Austen later learned that she could achieve more with less:

> Emma Woodhouse, handsome, clever, and rich, with a comfortable home and happy disposition, seemed to unite some of

the best blessings of existence; and had lived nearly twenty-one years in the world with very little to distress or vex her.[1]

The opening sentence of *Emma*, too, is more controlled in its tone, and more self-contained, in comparison with that of "Catharine," with its open appeal to the conventions of other novels (in this sense it has more in common with the opening of *Northanger Abbey*, a novel widely assumed to have been first drafted in the 1790s: "No one who had ever seen Catherine Morland in her infancy, would have supposed her born to be an heroine"[2]). But each sentence does its job in foregrounding the heroine and setting up the particular domestic and family situation that is going to be explored in the subsequent narrative, and, in some ways, the situation described in "Catharine" is the most complex and unusual of the three.

At 16,500 words, "Catharine" is by far the longest piece in the juvenilia, and it seems very unlikely that Austen would have thought that the few pages left in the exercise book would be sufficient to wind up a story that seems to be set up very much in the way of her full-length novels. The opening segment establishes Catharine Percival as living with her rich, bourgeois aunt, but as otherwise socially isolated. Mrs. Percival's distant relatives, the Stanleys, are visiting; Catharine hopes to find a new friend in Camilla Stanley (though Camilla's evident vanity and ignorance suggest this hope may be a mistaken one), and she embarks on what seems set to be misplaced romantic interest in Camilla's brother, Edward. The fragment ends as young Stanley is forced out of the house by Mrs. Percival, though it is not clear whether her protectiveness on this occasion will prove to have been justified.

What would have happened next? Austen talked to family members of the afterlives of some of her fictional creations—musing on whether Mr. Darcy would have allowed his wife's portrait to be painted, or discussing what might happen to the various inhabitants of Stanton in "The Watsons"—but there is no record of how "Catharine" might continue. She may indeed not have had any thought-through plan: this is apprentice work after all, and Austen might simply have felt it was a piece of writing

---

1   Jane Austen, *Emma* (1816, ed. Richard Cronin and Dorothy McMillan [Cambridge: Cambridge UP, 2005]), Vol. 1, ch. 1.

2   Jane Austen, *Northanger Abbey* (1817, ed. Barbara M. Benedict and Deirdre Le Faye [Cambridge: Cambridge UP, 2006]), Vol. 1, ch. 1.

worth keeping in its own right. Later, she shared the narrative with her nephew and niece, James Edward Austen (later Austen Leigh) and Anna Austen (later Lefroy); James Edward wrote a conclusion some time around 1815 or 1816 on the blank pages at the end of the notebook, but this is a feeble contribution, reducing "Catharine" to the level of the earliest of the juvenilia, and can be no indication of Austen's own thoughts on the matter beyond suggesting that she had little or no interest in continuing the narrative herself (James Edward's second attempt, made about 1845, is little better).[1]

"Lady Susan," on the other hand, is a complete work. It is generally thought to have been written in the mid-1790s, that is, within a couple of years of "Catharine." The novella exists only in a fair copy, which was probably made to circulate among friends and family rather than to send to a publisher; significantly, it was not chosen for publication alongside *Persuasion* and *Northanger Abbey* in 1817. In fact, it was with "Lady Susan" chiefly in mind that Austen's niece, Caroline Austen, wrote rather critically of Austen's "betweenities," which she defined as those works "when the nonsense was passing away, and before her wonderful talent had found it's proper channel."[2] The epistolary novella "Lady Susan" is thoroughly a "betweenity," probably in date of composition, and certainly in tone and genre. It has a skill, sophistication, realism, and length that set it apart from the juvenile works, together with a subject matter that separates it from the later published novels.

"Lady Susan" is a huge surprise to those who come to it from the published novels, though less so for those who read forward from the juvenilia. The eponymous heroine is the most finished portrait of clever and charming malice that Austen ever penned. A few earlier novels had shown mothers disliking their daughters and vying with them for lovers,[3] but Austen's economy of means and rejection of sentiment set her heroine apart. The closest parallels are in the juvenilia—Laura of "Love and Freindship" or Eliza of "Henry and Eliza"—but Lady Susan is given an inner life and an outer environment which together make her acts and atti-

---

1   See Appendix B for James Edward's continuations of "Catharine."

2   Caroline Austen to James Edward Austen Leigh, 1 April [1869], (National Portrait Gallery, RWC/HH, fos. 4-7), reproduced in *J. E. Austen-Leigh: A Memoir of Jane Austen and Other Family Recollections*, ed. Kathryn Sutherland (Oxford: Oxford UP, 2002), p. 186.

3   See, for example, Margaret and Susannah Minifie, *The Histories of Lady Frances S—, and Lady Caroline S—* (1763).

tudes more shocking and less comical than those of the heroines of the juvenilia.

In its general celebration of its heroine's amorality, it is less like any published English novel of the period than, startlingly, Choderlos de Laclos' *Les Liaisons dangereuses* (1782). Some critics have even argued that Laclos' novel must have influenced Austen's novella, pointing out that her attention could have been drawn to the novel, in French or in English translation, by her cousin Eliza, who had married a French count.[1] Whether or not this was the case, there may be some parallel to "Lady Susan" in this cousin herself. Eliza Hancock was a glamorous figure even before she married the Comte de Feuillide. In her racy letters, Eliza delights in her power over men and enjoys the game of social life. She relishes frippery and fashions, the ebullient wigs, hair styles, and outlandish jewelry of the 1780s and 1790s. In February 1794, Eliza's husband was guillotined and, in 1795-96, Eliza, visiting the Austens, flirted with two of Austen's brothers, James and Henry, at the same time. For marriage, James was the better bet, but Henry, ten years Eliza's junior, a dashing lieutenant in the Oxford militia, had compensating charms; in December 1797, Henry and Eliza were married. It is possible that this outcome led Austen to shelve a novella that could be said to be presenting her sister-in-law in a very hostile light.

Alternatively, it has been claimed that the reason Austen never (as far as we know) tried to publish the work was that "she knew how attractive she had made her masterly villainess."[2] Masterly Lady Susan is. Power and the social game are her obsessions, even more than sex and money, though she enjoys both. To control men who control power, she exploits the feminine weapons that society both admires and condemns, such as beauty, stylishness, skill, hypocrisy, sexual allure, and strategic use of sympathy, so that she both fulfils and profoundly mocks the conduct-book literature that teaches girls how to be modest and submissive while also catching and managing men. Above all, Lady Susan is an exploiter of language: she knows that eloquence and wit are the greatest assets a woman can have. She is capable of convincing the sensible but inexperienced young gentleman, Reginald, that she has been wronged by slander even in the face of direct evidence of her flouting of society's conventions—"Pro-

---

1 See, for example, Warren Roberts, *Jane Austen and the French Revolution* (1979; London Athlone P, 1995), p. 129.

2 Park Honan, *Jane Austen: Her Life* (London: George Weidenfeld & Nicolson, 1987; revised ed., London: Phoenix, 1997), p. 101.

priety and so forth" (p. 258), as she wonderfully pigeonholes them.

Excelling in energy and charm, Lady Susan plays people as she might play cards, and she enjoys the process of the game as much as the winning. She is a gambler in society, quite prepared to risk everything for a chance at a prize. In a classic book of Austen criticism, Marvin Mudrick argues that the society in which Lady Susan plays is unworthy of her, that her energy is superfluous in a patriarchal world, and that, as a result, she herself becomes a victim.[1] But she can only manoeuvre within the rules and conventions of the world she inhabits, and she does not regard herself as a victim—except as the mother of an inadequate daughter. At the end, though she does not gain what she most wants, she has kept her independence by marrying a rich fool, and is rid of her troublesome child.

Austen could not directly present sex in her work, but in the liaison between Lady Susan and Mr. Manwaring she comes as close to it as she can; and she is well aware of the power of sexual desire in keeping that affair alive (in stark contrast to the relationship with Reginald, in which—at least as far as Lady Susan is concerned—sexual feelings play no part). But beyond sexual enjoyment is sexual manipulation, which requires control of another's desire: "There is exquisite pleasure in subduing an insolent spirit" (p. 217). The clever operator, however, must beware of being besotted if she is to succeed in controlling, because love of control becomes as much an addiction as sexual desire. Lady Susan wants gratification and the power that desirability gives. She wishes men to respond completely and irrationally; the closer she gets to imposing her version of affairs on others, the more energetic and excited she becomes.

Perhaps the most startling aspect of Lady Susan is her robust attitude to motherhood—and this at a time when the state was much sentimentalized. Even now it is largely unacceptable to judge one's children so cruelly: "She is a stupid girl, and has nothing to recommend her" (pp. 215-16). Fathers relate to sons through inheritance: Sir Reginald sees his son as "the representative of an ancient Family" (p. 222). Pretending to the rival scheme of sentimental and fashionable attachment to her daughter, Lady Susan hypocritically delivers the feminine counterpart of this arrogant male ideal.

---

1 Marvin Mudrick, *Jane Austen: Irony as Defense and Discovery* (1952; reprinted Berkeley and Los Angeles: U of California P, 1968), pp. 129-38.

"Lady Susan" is written in the form of letters, concluding with a swerve to narrative commentary to wind up the action. Samuel Richardson, the great master of epistolary fiction, found that his creation, Lovelace, intended as the villain of *Clarissa*, was admired because the wit, eloquence, and flair of his voice had more powerful an effect than the actions he perpetrated. Perhaps Austen also felt that she needed to move readerly sympathies away from a too-convincing villain. And yet, though some of the narrator's words suggest a moral standard, others—for example, the cynical final remarks—are more in the outright mocking mode of the juvenilia: "For myself, I confess that *I* can pity only Miss Manwaring, who coming to Town and putting herself to an expence in Cloathes, which impoverished her for two years, on purpose to secure [Sir James], was defrauded of her due by a Woman ten years older than herself" (p. 267).

This dual effect will coalesce in the conclusion of *Northanger Abbey*, where moral and mockery are delivered together: "I leave it to be settled by whomsoever it may concern, whether the tendency of this work be altogether to recommend parental tyranny, or reward filial disobedience."[1] The Bluestocking hostess and woman of letters, Elizabeth Montagu, might consider that "Wit in women is apt to have bad consequences; like a sword without a scabbard, it wounds the wearer and provokes assailants,"[2] but, in a narrative context, it is hard for it not to triumph. The cold narrative eye that looks on at the end of "Lady Susan" has also the ebullience that marks the juvenilia; the combination is rarely present in the later novels and it shocks when it obtrudes even in modified form, as when the narrator of *Persuasion* seems to find amusing the incongruity of obesity and grief, or sentimental motherhood and worthless offspring.[3]

Epistolary fiction was, in fact, a dying form in England by the turn of the century, though it had been given momentary life by radical women writers of the later 1790s, such as Mary Hays in *Memoirs of Emma Courtney* (1796) and Mary Wollstonecraft in *The Wrongs of Woman* (1798). These works employed the form in a way quite different from the multi-vocal novels of Richardson, concentrating on a single voice expressing something rarely before allowed in literature, an apparently unmediated and tragic yearning for social and sexual freedom on the part of women,

---

1 *Northanger Abbey*, Vol. 2, ch. 16.
2 *The Letters of Elizabeth Montagu*, ed. Matthew Montagu (London, 1810), Vol. 3, pp. 96-97.
3 *Persuasion*, Vol. 1, ch. 8.

speaking directly to a new female audience of readers. Perhaps Austen became aware of these scandalous and much-derided novels, and pulled away from their transparent aims. Or, like the nation as a whole, she may simply have tired of the letter form, as suggested by a family tradition that she reworked an epistolary "Elinor and Marianne" into the third-person narrative of *Sense and Sensibility*. Austen never really experimented with the Richardsonian method of juxtaposing powerfully different and distinctive narrative tones: Lady Susan's is by no means the only voice in the novella, but it is the only one we care for.

The Unfinished Novels

The only manuscript material that remains from the texts of Austen's published novels are the two chapters from the end of the second volume of *Persuasion*, which she had rejected in favour of the version that appeared in print. The drafts of "The Watsons" and "Sanditon" therefore become enormously significant, not only in their own right, but as evidence of the way in which Austen created her fictions. These two unfinished works come from the beginning and end of Austen's life as an adult novelist. Austen's great-niece, Fanny Caroline Lefroy, wrote that "The Watsons" was written "somewhere in 1804,"[1] which fits with the watermarks of 1803 and 1804 on the paper. This took place after "Susan," the early version of *Northanger Abbey*, had been accepted for publication but before it was actually published (in fact the publisher never did bring "Susan" out and Austen recovered the manuscript only in 1816), and after *Sense and Sensibility* and *Pride and Prejudice* had been completed broadly in the form in which they were later published. By the early months of 1817, Austen was a skilled professional writer, one of the benefits of which was that she recorded her writing schedule more carefully, so we know that her last work of prose fiction, "Sanditon," was written between 27 January and 18 March of that year. The similarities and the differences between the two fragments are therefore significant as signs of Austen's mature writing practice.

Both were written in small notebooks made, probably by Austen herself, by folding and cutting larger sheets of paper. "The Watsons," after a start on some loose leaves, was mostly

---

1 *Is it Just?* (London, 1883), p. 277; the work is anonymous but generally accepted to be by Fanny Caroline Lefroy. Some recent critics have suggested a later dating, but the majority follow Fanny Lefroy's suggestion.

written in short booklets of eight pages; some pages run smoothly but others are heavily revised, and three sections were added on inserted paper, neatly affixed with a pin. Each of these adds dialogue, and one contains the heroine Emma's memorable response to the conversation of the fatuous Lord Osborne: "Female Economy will do a great deal my Lord, but it cannot turn a small income into a large one" (p. 302). By the time of "Sanditon," Austen was writing with more confidence, in three booklets of thirty-two, forty-eight, and eighty pages respectively (the text finishes half way through the third booklet) and, while there are still a large number of revisions, there are no additions or removals of a paragraph or more.

"The Watsons" extends to about 18,000 words (just a little longer than "Catharine") and it gives every indication of intending to be a full-length novel—indeed, it has been described as "a tantalizing, delightful and highly accomplished fragment, which must surely have proved the equal of her other six novels, had she finished it."[1] Austen skilfully sets up the dynamic of the Watson sisters needing to find husbands and the local society which offers limited choices for them. And in her heroine, Emma Watson, who "did not think, or reflect;—she felt and acted" (p. 288), Austen has begun to create a character who might well stand comparison with Elizabeth Bennet or Emma Woodhouse.

So, why did Austen stop writing the novel? She continued to tinker with it, and talked to her sister Cassandra of how the story would have continued:

> Mr. Watson was soon to die; and Emma to become dependent for a home on her narrow-minded sister-in-law and brother. She was to decline an offer of marriage from Lord Osborne, and much of the interest of the tale was to arise from Lady Osborne's love for Mr. Howard, and his counter affection for Emma, whom he was finally to marry.[2]

As far as we know, however, she never seriously returned to the narrative. The reason might well be autobiographical. In 1800,

---

1 Jane Austen, *Lady Susan, The Watsons, Sanditon*, ed. with intro. by Margaret Drabble (Harmondsworth: Penguin, 1974), p. 15.

2 James Edward Austen Leigh, *Memoir of Jane Austen* (2nd ed., London, 1871), p. 364. R.W. Chapman, Austen's first scholarly editor, commented on the reference to Lady Osborne, "Doubtless a slip for *Miss Osborne*. Lady Osborne was nearly fifty" (*The Works of Jane Austen*, vol. 6, *Minor Works* [Oxford: Oxford UP, 1954]), p. 363. The remark was

Austen's father, a clergyman of limited means, had retired with his wife and two unmarried daughters to the fashionable spa of Bath. On 21 January 1805, he died suddenly and his clerical income ceased; he left three grieving and considerably poorer women to depend largely on the charity of his sons, Austen's brothers. Perhaps she found it too difficult to continue for long with a story that was to deliver the death of a clergyman and the consequent poverty of his daughters. Supporting this argument, Marilyn Butler stresses that "The Watsons" seemed "the most depressed and bitter of [Austen's] fragments," conceived in resentment over "the arrogance and indifference of the comfortably rich and their meanness over sharing their resources when alive, or generally dispersing them after death."[1]

There may also be reasons within the story itself. The situation of the Watson sisters resembles that of the Bennets in *Pride and Prejudice*: too many girls and not enough money. But the Watson daughters are older, poorer, and with fewer realistic hopes. Unless Austen was planning a radical change from her mode elsewhere, economically viable marriages would need to have been found for most, if not all, of the sisters, and it is quite hard to see how. Austen's nephew, James Edward, was thinking to some extent on these lines when he speculated that she might have realized, once into the story, that she had put her characters into too lowly a sphere of life. Rather snobbishly, he noted that "such a position of poverty and obscurity ... though not necessarily connected with vulgarity, has a sad tendency to degenerate into it"; he saw the subject-matter as "unfavourable to the refinement of a lady."[2] Austen ventured into lower-middle-class territory with Fanny Price's return to her confined home in Portsmouth (a variation on the theme of Emma's return to Stanton) but she left a clear escape-route for Fanny and for the narrative.

It seems possible that Austen was influenced in her depiction of Robert Watson and his vulgar wife by the novels of Frances Burney. In her first novel, *Evelina*, Burney had had a great comic success when she sent her heroine to stay with the ebulliently

---

removed in the 1969 edition of *Minor Works*, with revisions by B.C. Southam. There seems no reason to see this as a slip: after all, Lady Susan is twelve years older than Reginald De Courcy, a matter that upsets his family but that is not seen as likely to override the attraction he feels for her.

1 Marilyn Butler, "Jane Austen," *Oxford Dictionary of National Biography* entry (print ed. Oxford: Oxford UP, 2004).

2 Austen Leigh, *Memoir* (1871), p. 296.

vulgar Branghtons, and Austen enjoyed the relevant scenes: her niece Caroline remembered one occasion in which she had "take[n] up a volume of Evelina and read a few pages of Mr. Smith and the Brangtons [sic] and I thought it was like a play."[1] But the overall tone of Burney's novel is very different from that of Austen's published fictions and Austen may have come to question whether she wanted her own heroine to face the shaming powerlessness of poverty and the necessity of marriage as the only way out of it, within an extended comic setting.

The need to marry informs all the novels, and romantic comedies require a closing marriage. But the anxieties of the journey to this generic close are more unpleasantly presented in "The Watsons" than elsewhere, for women are reduced to competing for not very attractive husbands with the energy and duplicity men use to compete within business and the professions. The women do not consider the limited career opportunities tried, and described, by the feminist writer Mary Wollstonecraft, but those options shadow their lives as the consequences of defeat. Raised, like Fanny Price, in more affluent circumstances than the rest of her family, Emma suggests to her sister that she would rather be a teacher than marry a man she did not like. This material will be fully explored by Victorian writers in later decades, but Austen touches on the predicament when Elizabeth replies, with conviction: "I would rather do any thing than be a Teacher at a school ... *I* have been at school, Emma, and know what a Life they lead" (pp. 274-75).

The ending has especial poignancy. Emma has been ejected from the social and financial security of her aunt's house; the siblings from whom she hoped for companionship are vulgar and conniving, and even her kindly eldest sister Elizabeth lacks true sympathetic intelligence. With no room of her own, Emma retreats to tend her father, where she lapses into understandable self-pity:

> from being the Life and Spirit of a House, where all had been comfort and Elegance, and the expected Heiress of an easy Independance, she was become of importance to no one, a burden on those, whose affection she could not expect, an addition in an house, already overstocked, surrounded by infe-

---

1 Caroline Austen, *My Aunt Jane Austen: A Memoir* (1867), reproduced in *J.E. Austen-Leigh: A Memoir of Jane Austen, and Other Family Recollections*, ed. Kathryn Sutherland (Oxford: Oxford UP, 2002), p. 174.

rior minds with little chance of domestic comfort, and as little hope of future support. (p. 316)

W.H. Auden wrote of his shock to find Austen "Reveal so frankly and with such sobriety / The economic basis of society."[1] At the end of *Sense and Sensibility*, the narrator says of Elinor and Edward, "They were neither of them quite enough in love to think that three hundred and fifty pounds a-year would supply them with the comforts of life."[2] In "The Watsons," the lack of money with its consequent diminishing of space and confining of minds completely undermines the romantic notion of anything, even love, being a sufficient compensation. Here everything is calibrated and judged in financial and class terms: houses, clothes, domestic habits, and servants. Every action—even the choice of which board game to play after dinner—declares rank and the social direction within which a person is travelling; class hostility is barely concealed.

When she penned "The Watsons," Austen was living with the disappointment of the continuing non-appearance of a novel that had been accepted for publication;[3] she was unmarried and close to thirty. For A. Walton Litz, Emma Watson was "deliberately pictured as an isolated and sensitive person, cut off from all expectations and trapped in an alien world," her situation "an epitome of the dilemma faced by the free spirit in a limited world."[4] For whatever reason, Austen decided against taking Emma Watson on her journey back to social and financial security. Instead, she cannibalised the fragment for use in her other fictions. Various critics have identified in "The Watsons" "anteghosts ... of a Mrs. Elton, of an Elizabeth Bennet, of a Darcy"; the fragment has been

---

1 W.H. Auden, "Letter to Lord Byron," Canto 1, stanza 17.

2 Jane Austen, *Sense and Sensibility* (1811, ed. Edward Copeland [Cambridge: Cambridge UP, 2006]), Vol. 3, ch. 13.

3 The novel was "Susan," an early version of *Northanger Abbey*, for which the publisher Crosby & Co. had paid £10 in 1803. It was never published. In response to a letter from Austen in 1810, Crosby wrote that she could have the return of the manuscript for £10, which she could not afford. The money was eventually paid by Austen's brother Henry, who, once he had the manuscript in his possession, took great pleasure in informing Crosby that it had been written by the author of the by then very successful *Pride and Prejudice* (see Austen Leigh, *Memoir* [1870], pp. 170-72).

4 A. Walton Litz, *Jane Austen. A Study of Her Artistic Development* (London: Chatto & Windus, 1965), pp. 86-87.

described as "a sketch for *Emma*," a contribution to the revisions of "First Impressions" into *Pride and Prejudice*, a necessary antecedent to *Mansfield Park*.[1] Neatly encapsulating all these theories, Joseph Wiesenfarth described "The Watsons" as a "pretext" in which almost every element "makes its appearance in Jane Austen's canon in some finished fashion."[2] Perhaps, in the end, there was nothing left of "The Watsons" itself for Austen to come back to.

With "Sanditon," (the draft is untitled and there was a family tradition that she had intended to call it not "Sanditon" but "The Brothers") the situation was quite different, since here Austen ran out of time rather than inclination or invention. She wrote the 23,500-word beginning of the novel quickly, in two-and-a-half months, and despite the poignancy about the fragment, captured in the date Austen provided immediately below the last line of writing, "March 18" 1817, the day on which she stopped writing fiction because she was too ill to hold a pen, the fertility of her imagination until then shows little sign of flagging. And yet it is strange that a manuscript inevitably connected with Austen's illness and death (she died in July) should take as its prime satiric target questions of health and hypochondria. There are even poignant echoes of Austen's own situation, when Diana Parker—like her author on bad days—is hardly able to crawl from her bed to the sofa, because of "my old greivance, Spasmodic Bile" (p. 344). "I am more and more convinced that *Bile* is at the bottom of all I have suffered," Austen wrote to a friend on 24 January,[3] and she deliberately added the term "anti-bilious" to her manuscript where she listed the "antis" for which Sanditon air was claimed to be the cure.

Unlike the later published novels—*Mansfield Park*, *Emma*, and *Persuasion*—"Sanditon" is a work of gusto, of larger-than-life grotesques and of comic letters and scenes. In a curious way, this suggests a turn full-circle back to the juvenilia; in fact, some critics have seen "Sanditon" as having more in common with Austen's earliest writings than with the novels in between. It is clear from the revisions that Austen valued her characters' idiosyncracies, heightening rather than softening their eccentricities

1 Anne Thackeray, *Cornhill Magazine* 34 (1879): 159; R.W. Chapman, *Jane Austen: Facts and Problems* (Oxford: Clarendon P, 1948), p. 51; Mary Waldron, *Jane Austen and the Fiction of Her Time* (Cambridge: Cambridge UP, 1999), p. 26.
2 Joseph Wiesenfarth, "*The Watsons* as Pretext," *Persuasions* 8 (1986): 109.
3 Jane Austen to Alethea Bigg, 24 January 1817, in *Letters*, ed. Le Faye, pp. 326-27

with her changes, as when Diana's assurance that "I know where to apply" becomes "I could soon put the necessary Irons in the fire" or Susan is reported to have fainted, not upon "poor Arthur's sneezing," but on "poor Arthur's trying to suppress a cough" (ch. 5). In this tale of exaggeration—exaggerated claims, exaggerated confidence, exaggerated fears—Austen subtly but consistently works to exaggerate the language in which it is told.

Readers have relished the energy and novelty of the fragment, which seems to explore a world generations later than that of the early novels. Austen avoids the country-village setting that, only a few years earlier, she had told her niece was "the very thing to work on."[1] Instead, she chooses to set her characters in an evolving English seaside resort, a location of new and growing popularity in the early nineteenth century, and one much mocked by conservative writers of the time who disliked the growing fashion among the middle classes for tourism and travelling.

The subject was not an entirely new one. Austen had herself referred to Brighton as one of Lady Lesley's "favourite haunts of Dissipation" ("Lesley Castle") and Lydia Bennet, having imagined "the streets of that gay bathing place covered with officers"[2] elopes from there with Wickham. Mr. Knightley refers to Weymouth (the place where Frank Churchill and Jane Fairfax met, while on a party of pleasure) as one of the "idlest haunts in the kingdom."[3] Other writers, too, had found the new seaside resorts a suitable topic for literary work. William Cowper, said to be one of Austen's favourite poets, mocked the passion for diversifying a dull life by flying to the coast: "And all impatient of dry land, agree / With one consent to rush into the sea."[4] Deriding speculation more than the fad for sea cures and resort tourism, Thomas Skinner Surr, in *The Magic of Wealth* (1815), depicted "Flimflamton," created by a silly, rich banker, Flimflam, who makes his resort the "*magnet of Fashion*"; the mockery is of the "trafficking spirit of the times" that replaced decent gentry values with a new economy of credit, and it is a swift and sharp creative commentary as Napoleon's final overthrow ushered in new conditions of economic slump and opportunity. Austen (who had

1   "3 or 4 Families in a Country Village is the very thing to work on," Jane Austen to Anna Austen, 9-18 September 1814, reproduced in *Later Manuscripts*, p. 220.
2   *Pride and Prejudice*, Vol. 2, ch. 18.
3   *Emma*, Vol. 1, ch. 18.
4   Austen Leigh, *Memoir* (1871), p. 84; "The Retirement," in *Poems by William Cowper, Of the Inner Temple, Esq.* (London, 1782), p. 284.

direct experience of the ill effects of post-war uncertainties, having lost money in the crash of her brother Henry's bank in 1816) mentions the speculative impulse that drives Mr. Parker; however, she does not seem set to relate money and morality in the way of many contemporary critics who were uneasy about the new notion that consumerism was driving the economy in ways ultimately positive rather than pernicious. Her emphasis is more on people than systems: Lady Denham may be grasping and avaricious, but Mr. Parker, for all his speculative enthusiasm, remains a traditional gentleman in his care for those dependent on him.

The balance between old and new is a somewhat precarious one, however, as Austen shows with self-conscious symbolism in the dramatic opening—something new in itself in Austen's fictions—where the carriage taking Mr. and Mrs. Parker uphill in the wrong direction (and indeed in the wrong village entirely), overturns and they are rescued by Mr. and Mrs. Heywood, hospitable representatives of well-established country gentry. And yet, within a few days, Charlotte Heywood is quite happy to get into the mended coach and is as eager to be transported down the bad road to Sanditon—another double location, this time with old and new juxtaposed—as Catherine Morland was to go with the Allens to Bath.

Much is made of Charlotte's physical health, yet, in this novel, the "sick" characters are as shifting and energetic as the healthy. Invalidism is their profession. Mrs. Bennet used her nerves to control her family, as her husband was only too well aware; the Parkers delight in the state of illness itself, the paraphernalia of medicines, remedies, and treatments, as well as their own fascinating body parts. As John Wiltshire argues, invalidism here is no longer a private matter but "the pivot of economic activity"; it is the result of wealth, and a compromise formation between the possession of leisure and the need for outlet and activity. As a result the hypochondriacs' bodies "have become the grounds of inventiveness and energy, preoccupying their imaginations and becoming the source of sufficient activity to direct the conduct of every hour of the day."[1]

Marriage—so dominating in most of Austen's fictions from the outset—is pushed to the margin of interest in "Sanditon," at

---

1 John Wiltshire, *Jane Austen and the Body: "The Picture of Health"* (Cambridge: Cambridge UP, 1992), pp. 198-220; "Sickness and Silliness in *Sanditon*," *Persuasions* 19 (1997): 102.

least in these early chapters, as Austen opts instead to explore more general themes. Alongside issues of bodily sickness and health, there is a more familiar preoccupation with the propensity of weak-minded individuals to muddle up literature and life. Sir Edward Denham is a throwback to Austen's own early work: to the fiction-maddened girls of the juvenilia, to the would-be ladies' men, Edward Stanley in "Catharine" and Tom Musgrave in "The Watsons," and, more complexly, to the literature-loving Henry Crawford in *Mansfield Park* and Captain Benwick in *Persuasion*. But he is also a throwback in wider literary terms since, despite his extravagant praise of some recent Romantic poets, his main stimulant is Richardson's novels from the mid-eighteenth century, and he regards himself as "a dangerous Man—quite in the line of the Lovelaces" (p. 364).

Would he have succeeded in seducing Clara Brereton, and, if so, could he have retained any of the reader's sympathy? Would Charlotte and Sidney Parker have made a match? Would the hypochondriacal Parker siblings have been healed by the influence of old gentry, or would they have been shown to be genuinely ill? Would Sanditon have flourished as a seaside resort, and if so, how, and if not, what would have happened to the Parkers and the Denhams? Alas, though, as with "The Watsons," attempts have been made to complete the novel, none has been able to benefit from any knowledge of what the author had in mind for her characters and her themes.

"Posthumous Busybodies"

After Austen's death, most of her literary manuscripts were left with her loyal sister Cassandra; when Cassandra died in 1845, those manuscripts that she did not choose to destroy were fully dispersed around a wider family group. By this time, Jane Austen's fame was beginning to spread, as her novels came to be appreciated by a growing audience. In the 1860s, three of Austen's surviving nieces and nephews, James Edward Austen Leigh, Anna Lefroy, and Caroline Austen, agreed that a full-length memoir of their aunt was desirable, and that it should include a few examples of her unpublished work—not the prose fragments, but a small number of light verses written for the family. In this way, they proposed to control Austen's legacy as far as possible and reinforce the character they were giving of her, which was essentially that of a virtuous and pious Victorian lady.

In the first edition of the *Memoir*, Austen Leigh mentioned, but did not include, "an old copy-book containing several tales, some of which seem to have been composed when she was quite a girl" and a few works written later that were "not without merit, but which [Austen] considered unworthy of publication."[1] Initially reviewers approved of this act of reticence. *The Times* for 17 January 1870 noted that the family had unpublished manuscripts, "but have, very properly, declined to allow their publication"; the *Quarterly Review* agreed, arguing that a work which an author "has judged discreet to withhold from public view from a sense of its incompleteness, ought to be sacred from being pored over and printed by posthumous busybodies."[2] But theirs was a minority view: the reviewer in *The Athenaeum* quoted Austen's remark about writing on little pieces of ivory with much labour, and complained "But of this labour we hear scarcely anything."[3] Others clamoured to know exactly what the unpublished writings were and how they might see them. Austen Leigh's cousin, Lady Knatchbull (who, as the adolescent Fanny Knight, had spent much time with her aunt) threatened to publish her own copy of "Lady Susan."

In the end, Austen Leigh bowed to pressure, and in the second edition of the *Memoir* in 1871 cautiously presented some—though still not all—of Austen's "minor works." He amended his own reference to "an old copy book" to the more accurate "copy books" of "childish effusions," and he now printed one example of their contents, "The Mystery. An Unfinished Comedy." Regarding the more adult writings, he was more generous, appending "The Watsons" and "Lady Susan." "Sanditon"—or "The Last Work," as it was referred to in the *Memoir*—presented more of a problem. It was one thing to write indelicately in youth as Austen might have done with "Lady Susan," but quite another to be composing rollicking satire during a final illness. As a compromise, "Sanditon" was first brought into public view as a series of short studies of the three "original" characters whom Austen Leigh considered "ready dressed and prepared for their parts": Mr. Parker, Lady Denham, and Diana Parker. The sketches mostly used Austen's words, but tidied up and repunctuated.

"Sanditon" would not be published in full until R.W. Chapman's edition of 1925 (under the title "Fragment of a Novel").

---

1 Austen Leigh, *Memoir* (1870), pp. 59-60.
2 *The Quarterly Review* 128 (January and April, 1870): 199-200.
3 *The Athenaeum*, 8 January 1870: 53-54.

Those who wanted to see Austen's juvenilia in full had to wait even longer. The three volumes of juvenilia had passed down separately through different branches of the Austen family after Cassandra Austen's death. "Volume the Second" was published first, in 1922, while it was still in private hands; "Volume the First" was formally edited by R.W. Chapman in 1933. The publication of "Volume the Third," in 1951, completed the set. Three years later, Chapman included the contents of all three volumes, together with all Austen's other known literary manuscripts, in his volume, *Minor Works*, in The Oxford Edition of the Works of Jane Austen. The title is a questionable one. Austen's manuscript works might be minor compared with the achievements of the six published novels, but they contain within them flashes of the wittiest and most skilful writing, as well as numerous fascinating insights into the writing practice, of one of the world's major authors.

Jane Austen: A Brief Chronology

Dates for the manuscript works are tentative; see the Introduction and notes for further information.

1764	Rev. George Austen, rector of Steventon, marries Cassandra Leigh (26 April). Three children, James (1765), George (1766), and Edward (1767), are born.
1768	The Austens move to Steventon, Hampshire. Henry (1771), Cassandra (1773), and Francis (1774) are born.
1773	George Austen becomes rector of Deane, as well as Steventon.
1775	Jane Austen (JA) born at Steventon (16 December).
1779	Charles, the last of the Austen children, is born.
1781	JA's cousin, Eliza Hancock, marries Jean-François Capot de Feuillide, in France (winter).
1782	Austen family participates in amateur theatricals.
1783	JA's third brother, Edward, is adopted by Mr. and Mrs. Thomas Knight of Godmersham in Kent. Later he will take their name.
1785	JA and Cassandra attend the Abbey House School, Reading (spring).
1786	JA's fifth brother, Francis, enters the Royal Naval Academy in Portsmouth (April); JA and Cassandra leave school and return to Steventon (December). Between now and 1793, JA writes her three volumes of juvenilia.
1787	"Edgar and Emma," "Amelia Webster," "Frederic and Elfrida."
1788	Mr. and Mrs. Austen, JA, and Cassandra on a trip to Kent and London (summer). "Sir William Montague," "Memoirs of Mr Clifford," "The Mystery," "The beautifull Cassandra," "Henry and Eliza" (late December or early January 1789). Francis leaves the RN Academy and sails to East Indies and does not return until winter 1793 (December).
1789	"The Visit."
1790	"Love and Freindship" (13 June), "Jack and Alice," "The adventures of Mr Harley."
1791	JA's sixth and youngest brother Charles enters the

Royal Naval Academy in Portsmouth (July). "The History of England" (26 November), "Evelyn" (November-December), "The Three Sisters" (?December). Edward Austen marries Elizabeth Bridges (27 December); they live at Rowling in Kent.

1792   JA's eldest brother, James, marries Anne Mathew (27 March); they live at Deane. "Lesley Castle" (Spring), Contents page (6 May), "Catharine, or the Bower" (August), "A Collection of Letters" (autumn). Cassandra becomes engaged to Rev. Tom Fowle (?winter).

1793   Edward Austen's first child, Fanny, born (23 January). War between Britain and France (1 February). JA's fourth brother, Henry, becomes a lieutenant in the Oxfordshire Militia (8 April). James Austen's first child, Anna, born (15 April). "The female philosopher," "A Tour through Wales," "A Tale" (all between January and June). "A fragment," "A beautiful description," "The Generous Curate" (all 2 June). "Ode to Pity" (3 June, last item of JA's juvenilia).

1794   M. de Feuillide guillotined in Paris (22 February). Charles goes to sea (September). "Lady Susan"?

1795   "Elinor and Marianne." James's wife Anne dies (3 May). Tom Lefroy visits Ashe Rectory, and he and JA have a brief flirtation (December).

1796   JA starts writing "First Impressions" (October).

1797   James Austen marries Mary Lloyd (17 January). Rev. Tom Fowle dies of fever at San Domingo (February). JA finishes "First Impressions," and George Austen offers a JA manuscript for publication to Thomas Cadell, which is rejected sight unseen (August). JA begins rewriting "Elinor and Marianne" as *Sense and Sensibility*, and Mrs. Austen and daughters visit Bath (November). Henry Austen marries his cousin, the widowed Eliza de Feuillide, in London (31 December).

1798-99 JA writes "Susan" (later *Northanger Abbey*).

1800   George Austen decides to retire and move to Bath.

1801   Henry Austen resigns commission (24 January) and sets up as a banker and army agent. The Austen family leave Steventon for Bath (May).

1802   Peace of Amiens appears to end Anglo-France War

	(25 March). JA and Cassandra visit Steventon, and landowner Harris Bigg-Wither proposes to JA; she accepts but then declines the following day (December). JA revises "Susan" (winter).
1803	JA sells "Susan" to publisher Benjamin Crosby (spring). War with France recommences (18 May). The Austens visit Ramsgate in Kent and possibly the West Country (summer). The Austens visit Lyme Regis (November).
1804	JA starts writing "The Watsons." The Austens visit Lyme Regis again (summer).
1805	George Austen dies (21 January). Martha Lloyd joins Mrs. Austen and her daughters (summer). Battle of Trafalgar (21 October).
1806	Austen women visit Adlestrop, Stoneleigh, and Hamstall Ridware, before settling in Southampton in the autumn.
1808	Edward Austen's wife Elizabeth dies at Godmersham (10 October).
1809	JA tries to secure publication of "Susan" (April). Mrs. Austen, Jane, Cassandra, and Martha Lloyd move to Chawton, Hants (July).
1810	*Sense and Sensibility* accepted for publication by Thomas Egerton.
1811	JA starts planning *Mansfield Park* (February). *Sense and Sensibility* published (30 October). JA starts revising "First Impressions" into *Pride and Prejudice.*
1812	JA sells the copyright of *Pride and Prejudice* to Egerton (autumn).
1813	*Pride and Prejudice* published (28 January). JA finishes *Mansfield Park*, which is accepted for publication by Egerton.
1814	JA begins *Emma* (January). Napoleon abdicates and is exiled to Elba (5 April). *Mansfield Park* published (9 May).
1815	Napoleon escapes and resumes power in France (March). *Emma* finished (March). Battle of Waterloo ends war with France (18 June). JA starts *Persuasion* (August). Henry Austen takes JA to London; he falls ill (October). JA visits Carlton House, is invited to dedicate future work to Prince Regent (November). *Emma* published by John Murray and dedicated to the Prince Regent (December; title page 1816).

| 1816 | JA ill. Henry Austen buys back manuscript of "Susan," which JA revises (spring). First draft of *Persuasion* (July). *Persuasion* finished (August). |
| 1817 | JA starts "Sanditon" (January). JA too ill to work (18 March). JA goes to Winchester for medical attention (24 May). JA dies (18 July), and is buried in Winchester Cathedral (24 July). *Northanger Abbey* and *Persuasion* published together, by Murray, with a "Biographical Notice" added by Henry Austen (December; title page 1818). |

A Note on the Text

The texts for the juvenilia, "Lady Susan," and Austen's letters on fiction are reproduced from *Juvenilia*, edited by Peter Sabor (Cambridge: Cambridge UP, 2006), and *Later Manuscripts*, edited by Janet Todd and Linda Bree (Cambridge: Cambridge UP, 2008), in The Cambridge Edition of the Works of Jane Austen, which are themselves based on detailed study of the original manuscripts. For the texts of "The Watsons" and "Sanditon," where the Cambridge edition offers a line-by-line transcription and a reading text, the text for this Broadview volume is based on the line-by-line transcription, with further reference back to the original manuscripts.

A small number of editorial changes have been made: Austen's ampersands (&) are expanded to "and" except where the ampersand is clearly intended, as in the phrase "&c." Austen's underlinings are converted to the usual printed equivalent of italics. No alteration has been made to Austen's spelling and punctuation, except where in the case of punctuation the meaning is obscured. In "The Watsons" and "Sanditon," which exist only in draft form, numbers up to a hundred are written out and contractions of dates and names are expanded; where the spellings of names vary we have left the inconsistencies, but when expanding initials to names we have used the form that Austen favours most often.

Austen's handwriting is clear and legible, but there are some ambiguities in her manuscripts. Since her indentations are often extremely slight, it is not always clear where a new paragraph begins. Many initial letters of words fall somewhere between upper and lower case, while commas cannot always be distinguished from full stops. In all cases we have done our best to follow Austen's intentions as far as we can assess them.

We refer readers to the volumes in the Cambridge edition for further information on the manuscripts and their presentation.

Juvenilia

From Volume the First

Frederic and Elfrida

To Miss Lloyd[1]

My dear Martha

As a small testimony of the gratitude I feel for your late generosity to me in finishing my muslin Cloak,[2] I beg leave to offer you this little production of your sincere Freind[3]

The Author

Frederic and Elfrida
a novel.[4]

Chapter the First.

The Uncle of Elfrida[5] was the Father of Frederic; in other words, they were first cousins by the Father's side.[6]

Being both born in one day and both brought up at one school,[7] it was not wonderfull that they should look on each other with something more than bare politeness. They loved with

---

1 Martha Lloyd (1765-1843), with her younger sisters, Eliza and Mary, was a friend and neighbour of JA at Steventon. Martha, Mary, and their newly widowed mother rented Deane Parsonage from JA's father in the spring of 1789.

2 Cloaks made of muslin, a finely woven cotton, were fashionable in the late 1780s and early 1790s.

3 JA's usual spelling, as well as "beleif," "greif," "veiw," etc. See introduction, p. 13.

4 In *The Progress of Romance* (1785), Clara Reeve distinguishes the term "novel" from "romance": "The Romance is an heroic fable, which treats of fabulous persons and things.—The Novel is a picture of real life and manners, and of the times in which it is written" (Vol. 1, *Evening* vii). The distinction, however, was not yet a firm one, and despite its subtitle, "Frederic and Elfrida" combines novel and romance elements.

5 The first of many examples in the juvenilia of esoteric, polysyllabic names, mocking the convention in contemporary fiction of avoiding everyday names.

6 Frederic and Elfrida thus have the same surname, Falknor, as Elfrida signs herself in her letter to Miss Drummond. Had they been cousins on the mother's side, their surnames would have been different.

7 As improbable as the cousins being born on the same day, since children of their rank would have attended single-sex schools.

mutual sincerity but were both determined not to transgress the rules of Propriety by owning their attachment, either to the object beloved, or to any one else.

They were exceedingly handsome and so much alike, that it was not every one who knew them apart. Nay even their most intimate freinds had nothing to distinguish them by, but the shape of the face, the colour of the Eye, the length of the Nose and the difference of the complexion.

Elfrida had an intimate freind to whom, being on a visit to an Aunt, she wrote the following Letter.

To Miss Drummond

"Dear Charlotte"

"I should be obliged to you, if you would buy me, during your stay with Mrs Williamson, a new and fashionable Bonnet, to suit the Complexion[1] of your

E. Falknor."

Charlotte, whose character was a willingness to oblige every one, when she returned into the Country, brought her Freind the wished-for Bonnet, and so ended this little adventure, much to the satisfaction of all parties.

On her return to Crankhumdunberry (of which sweet village[2] her father was Rector) Charlotte was received with the greatest Joy by Frederic and Elfrida, who, after pressing her alternately to their Bosoms, proposed to her to take a walk in a Grove of Poplars which led from the Parsonage to a verdant Lawn enamelled with a variety of variegated flowers[3] and watered by a purling Stream, brought from the Valley of Tempé[4] by a passage under ground.

---

1 In the 1770s, the woman's cap became a large bonnet, a hat with a small brim, often tied with a ribbon beneath the chin. The fashionable colour for bonnets in the 1780s was pale, also the desirable colour for a woman's complexion.

2 Echoing the first line of Oliver Goldsmith's poem, "The Deserted Village" (1770): "Sweet Auburn, loveliest village of the plain." "Crankhumdunberry" is a mock-Irish name, comparable to the mock-Welsh "Pammydiddle" in "Jack and Alice."

3 To enamel is "to inlay; to variegate with colours" (Johnson); the landscape here thus resembles an artefact, such as a painted box or vase.

4 "Purling" (rippling or undulating) streams are a clichéd feature of poetry. JA's stream runs a most improbable underground course. Its source, the Valley of Tempé, is the valley in Greece between the moun-

In this Grove they had scarcely remained above 9 hours, when they were suddenly agreably surprized by hearing a most delightfull voice warble the following stanza.

Song.

That Damon[1] was in love with me
I once thought and beleiv'd
But now that he is not I see,
I fear I was deceiv'd.

No sooner were the lines finished than they beheld by a turning in the Grove 2 elegant young women leaning on each other's arm, who immediately on perceiving them, took a different path and disappeared from their sight.

Chapter the Second.

As Elfrida and her companions, had seen enough of them to know that they were neither the 2 Miss Greens, nor Mrs Jackson and her Daughter, they could not help expressing their surprise at their appearance; till at length recollecting, that a new family had lately taken a House not far from the Grove, they hastened home, determined to lose no time in forming an acquaintance with 2 such amiable and worthy Girls, of which family they rightly imagined them to be a part.

Agreable to such a determination, they went that very evening to pay their respects to Mrs Fitzroy and her two Daughters. On being shewn into an elegant dressing room, ornamented with festoons of artificial flowers,[2] they were struck with the engaging Exterior and beautifull outside of Jezalinda[3] the eldest of the

---

tains of Olympus and Ossa, celebrated for its beauty and formerly a shrine to Apollo.

1 Damon is a shepherd singer in Virgil's eighth Eclogue, whose name was adopted for rural lovers by English poets such as Milton and Marvell.

2 Dressing rooms, usually attached to bedrooms, were increasingly decorated as sitting rooms in the later eighteenth century, and used primarily by women spending their mornings indoors. The decoration here is ornamental carved woodwork in the shape of wreaths or garlands of flowers.

3 Jezalinda is an invented name that combines the Biblical Jezebel with "Ethelinde," the name of the eponymous heroine of Charlotte Smith's novel *Ethelinde, or the Recluse of the Lake* (1789).

young Ladies; but e'er they had been many minutes seated, the Wit and Charms which shone resplendant in the conversation of the amiable Rebecca, enchanted them so much that they all with one accord jumped up and exclaimed.

"Lovely and too charming Fair one, notwithstanding your forbidding Squint, your greasy tresses and your swelling Back,[1] which are more frightfull than imagination can paint or pen describe, I cannot refrain from expressing my raptures, at the engaging Qualities of your Mind, which so amply atone for the Horror, with which your first appearance must ever inspire the unwary visitor."

"Your Sentiments so nobly expressed on the different excellencies of Indian and English Muslins,[2] and the judicious preference you give the former, have excited in me an admiration of which I can alone give an adequate idea, by assuring you it is nearly equal to what I feel for myself."

Then making a profound Curtesy to the amiable and abashed Rebecca, they left the room and hurried home.

From this period, the intimacy between the Families of Fitzroy, Drummond, and Falknor, daily encreased till at length it grew to such a pitch, that they did not scruple to kick one another out of the window on the slightest provocation.

During this happy state of Harmony, the eldest Miss Fitzroy ran off with the Coachman and the amiable Rebecca was asked in marriage by Captain Roger of Buckinghamshire.[3]

Mrs Fitzroy did not approve of the match on account of the tender years of the young couple, Rebecca being but 36 and Captain Roger little more than 63. To remedy this objection, it was agreed that they should wait a little while till they were a good deal older.

Chapter the third.

In the mean time the parents of Frederic proposed to those of Elfrida, an union between them, which being accepted with

---

1 Rebecca's hair is unclean and soaked in pomatum, an oil-based dressing; apparently, she is also hunchbacked.
2 Muslin fabrics produced in English mills (often in Lancashire) were relatively inexpensive; those imported from India were more costly and generally considered superior.
3 A county in the south of England, east of Oxfordshire and north of JA's native Hampshire.

pleasure, the wedding cloathes were bought and nothing remained to be settled but the naming of the Day.

As to the lovely Charlotte, being importuned with eagerness to pay another visit to her Aunt, she determined to accept the invitation and in consequence of it walked to Mrs Fitzroys to take leave of the amiable Rebecca, whom she found surrounded by Patches, Powder, Pomatum and Paint[1] with which she was vainly endeavouring to remedy the natural plainness of her face.

"I am come my amiable Rebecca, to take my leave of you for the fortnight I am destined to spend with my Aunt. Beleive me this separation is painfull to me, but it is as necessary as the labour which now engages you."

"Why to tell you the truth my Love, replied Rebecca, I have lately taken it into my head to think (perhaps with little reason) that my complexion is by no means equal to the rest of my face and have therefore taken, as you see, to white and red paint which I would scorn to use on any other occasion as I hate Art."[2]

Charlotte, who perfectly understood the meaning of her freind's speech, was too goodtemper'd and obliging to refuse her, what she knew she wished,—a compliment; and they parted the best freinds in the world.

With a heavy heart and streaming Eyes did she ascend the lovely vehicle[3] which bore her from her freinds and home; but greived as she was, she little thought in what a strange and different manner she should return to it.

On her entrance into the city of London which was the place of Mrs Williamson's abode, the postilion,[4] whose stupidity was

---

1 Black patches, made of velvet, were supposed to resemble beauty-spots, and remained fashionable until c. 1790. Powder was used for colouring hair; pomatum kept hair plastered in place. White paint was applied to the neck and red paint (rouge) to the cheeks, but the use of both colours declined in the 1780s.

2 Rebecca is using the word in its sense of "artifice."

3 JA's note here, "a post chaise," explains why Charlotte's carriage is "lovely"; this was the most expensive and luxurious type of hired carriage. A post-chaise, using horses that were changed at posting stations, generally carried only two passengers and travelled rapidly, in contrast to the much cheaper and slower stage-wagon later used by Captain Roger and Rebecca. See p. 56.

4 The driver mounted on the "near" (left) horse of the team drawing the post-chaise. Postilions also served as attendants during a journey. A larger carriage, such as Captain Roger's and Rebecca's stage-wagon, would have a driver mounted on a box at the front of the vehicle. See p. 101.

amazing, declared and declared even without the least shame or Compunction, that having never been informed he was totally ignorant of what part of the Town, he was to drive to.

Charlotte, whose nature we have before intimated, was an earnest desire to oblige every one, with the greatest Condescension[1] and Good humour informed him that he was to drive to Portland Place,[2] which he accordingly did and Charlotte soon found herself in the arms of a fond Aunt.

Scarcely were they seated as usual, in the most affectionate manner in one chair, than the Door suddenly opened and an aged gentleman with a sallow face and old pink Coat, partly by intention and partly thro' weakness was at the feet of the lovely Charlotte, declaring his attachment to her and beseeching her pity in the most moving manner.

Not being able to resolve to make any one miserable, she consented to become his wife; where upon the Gentleman left the room and all was quiet.

Their quiet however continued but a short time, for on a second opening of the door a young and Handsome Gentleman with a new blue coat, entered and intreated from the lovely Charlotte, permission to pay to her, his addresses.

There was a something in the appearance of the second Stranger, that influenced Charlotte in his favour, to the full as much as the appearance of the first: she could not account for it, but so it was.

Having therefore agreable to that and the natural turn of her mind to make every one happy, promised to become his Wife the next morning, he took his leave and the two Ladies sat down to Supper on a young Leveret,[3] a brace of Partridges, a leash of Pheasants[4] and a Dozen of Pigeons.

---

1 "Voluntary submission to equality with inferiours" (Johnson): the term was thus used more positively than today.

2 A magnificently wide street, originally laid out by the Adam brothers, Robert and James, in 1778, and one of the most fashionable addresses in London. It was named after William Bentinck, the second Duke of Portland.

3 A young, and therefore tender, hare.

4 Two partridges and three pheasants. The list combines scarce, prized game (pheasants and partridges) with common game (hares and pigeons). The total of seventeen birds and a hare makes a very large supper for two young women.

Chapter the Fourth

It was not till the next morning that Charlotte recollected the double engagement she had entered into; but when she did, the reflection of her past folly, operated so strongly on her mind, that she resolved to be guilty of a greater, and to that end threw herself into a deep stream which ran thro' her Aunts pleasure Grounds in Portland Place.[1]

She floated to Crankhumdunberry where she was picked up and buried; the following epitaph, composed by Frederic Elfrida and Rebecca, was placed on her tomb.

Epitaph
Here lies our freind who having promis-ed
That unto two she would be marri-ed
Threw her sweet Body and her lovely face
Into the Stream that runs thro' Portland Place

These sweet lines, as pathetic as beautifull were never read by any one who passed that way, without a shower of tears, which if they should fail of exciting in you, Reader, your mind must be unworthy to peruse them.

Having performed the last sad office to their departed freind, Frederic and Elfrida together with Captain Roger and Rebecca returned to Mrs Fitzroy's at whose feet they threw themselves with one accord and addressed her in the following Manner. "Madam"

"When the sweet Captain Roger first addressed the amiable Rebecca, you alone objected to their union on account of the tender years of the Parties. That plea can be no more, seven days being now expired, together with the lovely Charlotte, since the Captain first spoke to you on the subject."

"Consent then Madam to their union and as a reward, this smelling Bottle which I enclose in my right hand, shall be yours and yours forever; I never will claim it again.[2] But if you refuse to

---

1 The narrow town-houses of Portland Place did not possess "pleasure Grounds," which would require extensive space, or a stream of any kind.

2 Smelling bottles, small and ornamental, contained smelling-salts, hartshorn, etc., which were used as restoratives in cases of faintness or headache.

join their hands in 3 days time, this dagger[1] which I enclose in my left shall be steeped in your hearts blood."

"Speak then Madam and decide their fate and yours."

Such gentle and sweet persuasion could not fail of having the desired effect. The answer they received, was this.

"My dear young freinds"

"The arguments you have used are too just and too eloquent to be withstood; Rebecca in 3 days time, you shall be united to the Captain."

This speech, than which nothing could be more satisfactory, was received with Joy by all; and peace being once more restored on all sides, Captain Roger intreated Rebecca to favour them with a Song, in compliance with which request having first assured them that she had a terrible cold, she sung as follows.

Song
When Corydon[2] went to the fair
He bought a red ribbon for Bess,
With which she encircled her hair
And made herself look very fess.[3]

Chapter the fifth

At the end of 3 days Captain Roger and Rebecca were united and immediately after the Ceremony set off in the Stage Waggon[4] for the Captains seat in Buckinghamshire.

---

1 A parody of the traditional choice between dagger and bowl. In Joseph Addison's *Rosamond an Opera* (1707), Queen Elinor, wife of Henry II, gives her rival Rosamond the choice of committing suicide by drinking poison from a bowl or being stabbed.

2 Corydon, like Damon (see p. 51, note 1), is a traditional name for a rustic lover in pastoral poetry, deriving from shepherds so named in the *Idylls* of Theocritus and the *Eclogues* of Virgil.

3 A dialect word from southern and south-western England for lively, gay, smart.

4 The cheapest, slowest, and least comfortable form of public transport, and thus especially inappropriate for newly-weds. Passengers sat on benches in this very large conveyance, drawn by ten or more horses, which would proceed at walking pace.

The parents of Elfrida, alltho' they earnestly wished to see her married to Frederic before they died, yet knowing the delicate frame of her mind could ill bear the least excertion and rightly judging that naming her wedding day would be too great a one, forebore to press her on the subject.

Weeks and Fortnights flew away without gaining the least ground; the Cloathes grew out of fashion and at length Capt. Roger and his Lady arrived to pay a visit to their Mother and introduce to her their beautifull Daughter of eighteen.

Elfrida, who had found her former acquaintance were growing too old and too ugly to be any longer agreable, was rejoiced to hear of the arrival of so pretty a girl as Eleanor with whom she determined to form the strictest freindship.

But the Happiness she had expected from an acquaintance with Eleanor, she soon found was not to be received, for she had not only the mortification of finding herself treated by her as little less than an old woman, but had actually the horror of perceiving a growing passion in the Bosom of Frederic for the Daughter of the amiable Rebecca.

The instant she had the first idea of such an attachment, she flew to Frederic and in a manner truly heroick, spluttered out to him her intention of being married the next Day.

To one in his predicament who possessed less personal Courage than Frederic was master of, such a speech would have been Death; but he not being the least terrified boldly replied,

"Damme Elfrida—*you* may be married tomorrow but *I* won't."

This answer distressed her too much for her delicate Constitution. She accordingly fainted and was in such a hurry to have a succession of fainting fits, that she had scarcely patience enough to recover from one before she fell into another.

Tho', in any threatening Danger to his Life or Liberty, Frederic was as bold as brass yet in other respects his heart was as soft as cotton and immediately on hearing of the dangerous way Elfrida was in, he flew to her and finding her better than he had been taught to expect, was united to her Forever—.

Finis.

Jack and Alice
a novel.

Is respectfully inscribed to Francis William Austen Esqr Midshipman on board his Majesty's Ship the Perseverance[1]

by his obedient humble

Servant The Author

Chapter the first

Mr Johnson was once upon atime about 53; in a twelvemonth afterwards he was 54, which so much delighted him that he was determined to celebrate his next Birth day by giving a Masquerade[2] to his Children and Freinds. Accordingly on the Day he attained his 55th year tickets[3] were dispatched to all his Neighbours to that purpose. His acquaintance indeed in that part of the World were not very numerous as they consisted only of Lady Williams, Mr and Mrs Jones, Charles Adams and the 3 Miss Simpsons, who composed the neighbourhood of Pammydiddle[4] and formed the Masquerade.

Before I proceed to give an account of the Evening, it will be proper to describe to my reader, the persons and Characters of the party introduced to his acquaintance.

Mr and Mrs Jones were both rather tall and very passionate,[5] but were in other respects, good tempered, wellbehaved People. Charles Adams was an amiable,[6] accomplished and bewitching

---

1 JA's fifth brother, Francis (1774-1865), one year her elder, served in the East Indies as a midshipman on the ship *Perseverance* from December 1789 to November 1791. "Esquire" was used as a courtesy title for gentlemen. Francis Austen was in his mid-teens when the dedication was written, but JA might have felt that his having left home and begun his naval career gave him the right to the title. A midshipman is a rank between that of the crew and the lowest commissioned officer.

2 A masked ball.

3 Printed tickets were issued for public masquerades, but would be inappropriate for a small, private ball such as this. The "ticket" here is probably a calling card, with an invitation written by hand.

4 Pammydiddle, a Welsh-sounding place name, is a composite word formed from "pam," a card game, and "diddle," to cheat or waste time.

5 Easily moved to anger.

6 An ambiguous word, meaning both "lovely" or "pleasing" and "pretending" or "shewing" love.

young Man; of so dazzling a Beauty that none but Eagles could look him in the Face.[1]

Miss Simpson was pleasing in her person, in her Manners and in her Disposition; an unbounded ambition was her only fault. Her second sister Sukey[2] was Envious, Spitefull and Malicious. Her person was short, fat and disagreable. Cecilia (the youngest) was perfectly handsome but too affected to be pleasing.

In Lady Williams every virtue met. She was a widow with a handsome Jointure[3] and the remains of a very handsome face. Tho' Benevolent and Candid, she was Generous and sincere; Tho' Pious and Good, she was Religious and amiable, and Tho' Elegant and Agreable, she was Polished and Entertaining.[4]

The Johnsons were a family of Love,[5] and though a little addicted to the Bottle and the Dice, had many good Qualities.

Such was the party assembled in the elegant Drawing Room of Johnson Court, amongst which the pleasing figure of a Sultana was the most remarkable of the female Masks.[6] Of the Males a Mask representing the Sun, was the most universally admired. The Beams that darted from his Eyes were like those of that glorious Luminary tho' infinitely Superior. So strong were they that no one dared venture within half a mile of them; he had therefore the best part of the Room to himself, its size not amounting to more than 3 quarters of a mile in length and half a one in breadth. The Gentleman at last finding the feirceness of his

---

1 Drawing on the traditional belief that only eagles could look at the sun.

2 A pet-form for Susan, itself a diminutive of Susannah.

3 The property settled on the wife at the time of her marriage for her use in the event of her husband's decease.

4 Although the sentence seems to be a model of Johnsonian symmetry, the three apparent antitheses are all false. "Candid" is used in the eighteenth-century sense of free from malice; not desirous to find faults.

5 The term derives from a pietistical sect, the "Family of Love," founded by Henry Nicholas in 1540, but by the eighteenth century it was used without religious implications.

6 Oriental costumes, combining aspects of Turkish and Persian clothing, were popular at masquerades. They allowed their wearers to dress in exotic, flattering costumes with gaudy displays of jewels. The Turkish dress of the Sultana—the wife or concubine of a Sultan—was a favourite among women. "Masks" here are masqueraders who carry masks for disguise, worn on or held in front of the face, although JA also uses masks for the objects themselves in this story.

beams to be very inconvenient to the concourse[1] by obliging them to croud together in one corner of the room, half shut his eyes by which means, the Company discovered him to be Charles Adams in his plain green Coat, without any mask at all.

When their astonishment was a little subsided their attention was attracted by 2 Domino's[2] who advanced in a horrible Passion; they were both very tall, but seemed in other respects to have many good qualities. "These said the witty Charles, these are Mr and Mrs Jones." and so indeed they were.

No one could imagine who was the Sultana! Till at length on her addressing a beautifull Flora[3] who was reclining in a studied attitude on a couch, with "Oh Cecilia, I wish I was really what I pretend to be", she was discovered by the never failing genius of Charles Adams, to be the elegant but ambitious Caroline Simpson, and the person to whom she addressed herself, he rightly imagined to be her lovely but affected sister Cecilia.

The Company now advanced to a Gaming Table where sat 3 Dominos (each with a bottle in their hand) deeply engaged, but a female in the character of Virtue[4] fled with hasty footsteps from the shocking scene, whilst a little fat woman representing Envy, sate alternately on the foreheads of the 3 Gamesters. Charles Adams was still as bright as ever; he soon discovered the party at play to be the 3 Johnsons, Envy to be Sukey Simpson and Virtue to be Lady Williams.

The Masks were then all removed and the Company retired to another room, to partake of elegant and well managed Entertainment,[5] after which the Bottle being pretty briskly pushed about by the 3 Johnsons, the whole party not excepting even Virtue were carried home, Dead Drunk.

---

1 The confluence of many persons or things to one place; the persons assembled.

2 Those wearing dominos. A domino was "an all-enveloping gown, Venetian in origin, its serviceable shape ideal for intrigue, love adventures, conspiracy etc.; it was often, but not always, black and worn by both sexes" (Aileen Ribeiro, *The Dress Worn at Masquerades in England, 1730 to 1790* [New York: Garland, 1984], p. 29).

3 The Roman goddess of flowers.

4 Abstractions such as Virtue, taken from Cesare Ripa's *Iconologia* (translated into English in 1709) and other printed sources, were popular masquerade characters, as were Peace, Plenty, Hope, Fortune, Temperance, Liberty, etc.

5 An elegant meal served to guests.

Chapter the Second

For three months did the Masquerade afford ample subject for conversation to the inhabitants of Pammydiddle; but no character at it was so fully expatiated on as Charles Adams. The singularity of his appearance, the beams which darted from his eyes, the brightness of his Wit, and the whole *tout ensemble*[1] of his person had subdued the hearts of so many of the young Ladies, that of the six present at the Masquerade but five had returned uncaptivated. Alice Johnson was the unhappy sixth whose heart had not been able to withstand the power of his Charms. But as it may appear strange to my Readers, that so much worth and Excellence as he possessed should have conquered only hers, it will be necessary to inform them that the Miss Simpsons were defended from his Power by Ambition, Envy, and Self-admiration.

Every wish of Caroline was centered in a titled Husband; whilst in Sukey such superior excellence could only raise her Envy not her Love, and Cecilia was too tenderly attached to herself to be pleased with any one besides. As for Lady Williams and Mrs Jones, the former of them was too sensible, to fall in love with one so much her Junior and the latter, tho' very tall and very passionate was too fond of her Husband to think of such a thing.

Yet in spite of every endeavour on the part of Miss Johnson to discover any attachment to her in him; the cold and indifferent heart of Charles Adams still to all appearance, preserved its native freedom; polite to all but partial to none, he still remained the lovely, the lively, but insensible[2] Charles Adams.

One evening, Alice finding herself somewhat heated by wine (no very uncommon case) determined to seek a releif for her disordered Head and Love-sick Heart in the Conversation of the intelligent Lady Williams.

She found her Ladyship at home as was in general the Case, for she was not fond of going out, and like the great Sir Charles Grandison scorned to deny herself when at Home,[3] as she looked

---

1 French for "general effect."

2 Both void of feeling and void of emotion or affection. JA is playing with both senses of the term.

3 An allusion to Richardson's novel, *Sir Charles Grandison*, and the praise bestowed upon the eponymous hero by a character in the novel, Harriet Byron, for refusing to comply "with fashions established by custom." Sir Charles "never, for instance, suffers his servants to deny him, when he

on that fashionable method of shutting out disagreable Visitors, as little less than downright Bigamy.

In spite of the wine she had been drinking, poor Alice was uncommonly out of spirits;[1] she could think of nothing but Charles Adams, she could talk of nothing but him, and in short spoke so openly that Lady Williams soon discovered the unreturned affection she bore him, which excited her Pity and Compassion so strongly that she addressed her in the following Manner.

"I perceive but too plainly my dear Miss Johnson, that your Heart has not been able to withstand the fascinating Charms of this young Man and I pity you sincerely. Is it a first Love?"

"It is."

"I am still more greived to hear *that*; I am myself a sad example of the Miseries, in general attendant on a first Love and I am determined for the future to avoid the like Misfortune. I wish it may not be too late for you to do the same; if it is not endeavour my dear Girl to secure yourself from so great a Danger. A second attachment is seldom attended with any serious consequences; against *that* therefore I have nothing to say. Preserve yourself from a first Love and you need not fear a second."

"You mentioned Madam something of your having yourself been a sufferer by the misfortune you are so good as to wish me to avoid. Will you favour me with your Life and Adventures?"

"Willingly my Love."

Chapter the third

"My Father was a gentleman of considerable Fortune in Berkshire;[2] myself and a few more his only Children. I was but six years old when I had the misfortune of losing my Mother and being at that time young and Tender, my father instead of sending me to School, procured an able handed Governess to superintend my Education at Home. My Brothers were placed at Schools suit-

---

is at home. If he is busy, he just finds time to say he is, to unexpected visiters" (Book 4, Letter 26). Conventionally, servants would use the phrase "not at home" to mean not available to visitors.

1   A deft pun on "spirits," employing the senses of alcohol and good cheer; Alice is "out of spirits" despite drinking spirits.

2   A county to the west of London, south of Oxfordshire, where Windsor Castle is located.

able to their Ages and my Sisters being all younger than myself, remained still under the Care of their Nurse."

"Miss Dickins was an excellent Governess. She instructed me in the Paths of Virtue; under her tuition I daily became more amiable, and might perhaps by this time have nearly attained perfection, had not my worthy Preceptoress been torn from my arms e'er I had attained my seventeenth year. I never shall forget her last words. 'My dear Kitty'[1] she said 'Good night t'ye.'[2] I never saw her afterwards" continued Lady Williams wiping her eyes, "She eloped with the Butler the same night."

"I was invited the following year by a distant relation of my Father's to spend the Winter with her in town.[3] Mrs Watkins was a Lady of Fashion, Family and fortune; she was in general esteemed a pretty Woman, but I never thought her very handsome, for my part. She had too high a forehead, Her eyes were too small and she had too much colour."[4]

"How can *that* be?" interrupted Miss Johnson reddening with anger; "Do you think that any one can have too much colour?"

"Indeed I do, and I'll tell you why I do my dear Alice; when a person has too great a degree of red in their Complexion, it gives their face in my opinion, too red a look."

"But can a face my Lady have too red a look."?

"Certainly my dear Miss Johnson and I'll tell you why. When a face has too red a look it does not appear to so much advantage as it would were it paler."

"Pray Ma'am proceed in your story."

"Well, as I said before, I was invited by this Lady to spend some weeks with her in town. Many Gentlemen thought her Handsome but in my opinion, Her forehead was too high, her eyes too small and she had too much colour."

"In that Madam as I said before your Ladyship must have been mistaken. Mrs Watkins could not have too much colour since no one can have too much."

"Excuse me my Love if I do not agree with you in that particular. Let me explain myself clearly; my idea of the case is this.

---

1 A pet-form of Catherine, Lady Williams's first name.
2 Dialect for "to you."
3 Fashionable people aspired to spend winter in London townhouses, and summer at their country houses. The London "Season" lasted until 4 June, when the King celebrated his official birthday.
4 Either naturally, from using too much rouge, or, as is the case with Alice Johnson, from excessive drinking.

When a Woman has too great a proportion of red in her Cheeks, she must have too much colour."

"But Madam I deny that it is possible for any one to have too great a proportion of red in their Cheeks."

"What my Love not if they have too much colour?"

Miss Johnson was now out of all patience, the more so perhaps as Lady Williams still remained so inflexibly cool. It must be remembered however that her Ladyship had in one respect by far the advantage of Alice; I mean in not being drunk, for heated with wine and raised by Passion, she could have little command of her Temper.

The Dispute at length grew so hot on the part of Alice that "From Words she almost came to Blows"[1] When Mr Johnson luckily entered and with some difficulty forced her away from Lady Williams, Mrs Watkins and her red cheeks.

Chapter the Fourth

My Readers may perhaps imagine that after such a fracas,[2] no intimacy could longer subsist between the Johnsons and Lady Williams, but in that they are mistaken for her Ladyship was too sensible to be angry at a conduct which she could not help perceiving to be the natural consequence of inebriety and Alice had too sincere a respect for Lady Williams and too great a relish for her Claret,[3] not to make every concession in her power.

A few days after their reconciliation Lady Williams called on Miss Johnson to propose a walk in a Citron Grove[4] which led from her Ladyship's pigstye to Charles Adams's Horsepond.[5]

---

1 An adaptation of a line ("From words they almost came to blows") in James Merrick's poem "The Camelion: A Fable after Monsieur De La Motte," in which a dispute arises over the colour of a chameleon.

2 "A disturbance, noisy quarrel, 'row,' uproar" (*OED*), which gives 1727 as the date of first use.

3 Red wine from Bordeaux, normally drunk by gentlemen.

4 A grove of citrus trees, fruit trees that flourish in temperate and sub-tropical regions but not found in England. JA here establishes a comic link between Charles Adams and Adam, whose citron grove appears in Milton's *Paradise Lost*, Book 5, line 22.

5 Two of the least picturesque parts of a country scene. Horseponds, used for watering and washing horses, were also traditionally used to punish offenders by ducking them.

Alice was too sensible[1] of Lady Williams's kindness in proposing such a walk and too much pleased with the prospect of seeing at the end of it, a Horsepond of Charles's, not to accept it with visible delight. They had not proceeded far before she was roused from the reflection of the happiness she was going to enjoy, by Lady Williams's thus addressing her.

"I have as yet forborn my dear Alice to continue the narrative of my Life from an unwillingness of recalling to your Memory a scene which (since it reflects on you rather disgrace than credit) had better be forgot than remembered."

Alice had already begun to colour up and was beginning to speak, when her Ladyship perceiving her displeasure, continued thus.

"I am afraid my dear Girl that I have offended you by what I have just said; I assure you I do not mean to distress you by a retrospection of what cannot now be helped; considering all things I do not think you so much to blame as many People do; for when a person is in Liquor, there is no answering for what they may do."

"Madam, this is not to be borne, I insist—"

"My dear Girl dont vex yourself about the matter; I assure you I have entirely forgiven every thing respecting it; indeed I was not angry at the time, because as I saw all along, you were nearly dead drunk. I knew you could not help saying the strange things you did. But I see I distress you; so I will change the subject and desire it may never again be mentioned; remember it is all forgot—I will now pursue my story; but I must insist upon not giving you any description of Mrs. Watkins; it would only be reviving old stories and as you never saw her, it can be nothing to you, if her forehead was too high, her eyes were too small, or if she had too much colour."

"Again! Lady Williams: this is too much"—

So provoked was poor Alice at this renewal of the old story, that I know not what might have been the consequence of it, had not their attention been engaged by another object. A lovely young Woman lying apparently in great pain beneath a Citron tree, was an object too interesting not to attract their notice. Forgetting their own dispute they both with simpathizing Tenderness advanced towards her and accosted her in these terms.

"You seem fair Nymph to be labouring under some misfortune which we shall be happy to releive if you will inform us what it is. Will you favour us with your Life and adventures?"

"Willingly Ladies, if you will be so kind as to be seated." They took their places and she thus began.

---

1 Conscious, aware.

Chapter the Fifth

"I am a native of North Wales and my Father is one of the most capital Taylors[1] in it. Having a numerous family, he was easily prevailed on by a sister of my Mother's who is a widow in good circumstances and keeps an alehouse in the next Village to ours, to let her take me and breed me up at her own expence. Accordingly I have lived with her for the last 8 years of my Life, during which time she provided me with some of the first rate Masters, who taught me all the accomplishments requisite for one of my sex and rank. Under their instructions I learned Dancing, Music, Drawing and various Languages, by which means I became more accomplished than any other Taylor's Daughter in Wales. Never was there a happier Creature than I was, till within the last half year—but I should have told you before that the principal Estate in our Neighbourhood belongs to Charles Adams, the owner of the brick House, you see yonder."

"Charles Adams!" exclaimed the astonished Alice; "are you acquainted with Charles Adams?"

"To my sorrow madam I am. He came about half a year ago to receive the rents of the Estate I have just mentioned. At that time I first saw him; as you seem ma'am acquainted with him, I need not describe to you how charming he is. I could not resist his attractions;"—

"Ah! who can," said Alice with a deep sigh.

"My Aunt being in terms of the greatest intimacy with his cook, determined, at my request, to try whether she could discover, by means of her freind if there were any chance of his returning my affection. For this purpose she went one evening to drink tea with Mrs Susan,[2] who in the course of Conversation mentioned the goodness of her Place[3] and the Goodness of her Master; upon which my Aunt began pumping[4] her with so much dexterity that in a short time Susan owned, that she did not think

---

1 North Wales was celebrated for the wildness of its mountain scenery and for its rustic peasantry. Tailors of any kind, let alone "capital," or excellent, ones, would be hard to find.

2 A lower servant, and thus referred to by her first name. An upper female servant was normally known by her surname, together with the honorific "Mrs."

3 Job, position; employment as a servant.

4 To pump someone is "to examine artfully by sly interrogatories, so as to draw out any secrets or concealments" (Johnson).

her Master would ever marry, 'for (said she) he has often and often declared to me that his wife, whoever she might be, must possess, Youth, Beauty, Birth, Wit, Merit, and Money. I have many a time (she continued) endeavoured to reason him out of his resolution and to convince him of the improbability of his ever meeting with such a Lady; but my arguments have had no effect and he continues as firm in his determination as ever.' You may imagine Ladies my distress on hearing this; for I was fearfull that tho' possessed of Youth, Beauty, Wit and Merit, and tho' the probable Heiress of my Aunts House and business, he might think me deficient in Rank, and in being so, unworthy of his hand."

"However I was determined to make a bold push and therefore wrote him a very kind letter, offering him with great tenderness my hand and heart.[1] To this I received an angry and peremptory refusal, but thinking it might be rather the effect of his modesty than any thing else, I pressed him again on the subject. But he never answered any more of my Letters and very soon afterwards left the Country. As soon as I heard of his departure I wrote to him here, informing him that I should shortly do myself the honour of waiting on him at Pammydiddle, to which I received no answer; therefore choosing to take, Silence for Consent, I left Wales, unknown to my Aunt, and arrived here after a tedious Journey this Morning. On enquiring for his House I was directed thro' this Wood, to the one you there see. With a heart elated by the expected happiness of beholding him I entered it and had proceeded thus far in my progress thro' it, when I found myself suddenly seized by the leg and on examining the cause of it, found that I was caught in one of the steel traps so common in gentlemen's grounds."[2]

"Ah cried Lady Williams, how fortunate we are to meet with you; since we might otherwise perhaps have shared the like misfortune"—

"It is indeed happy for you Ladies, that I should have been a short time before you. I screamed as you may easily imagine till the woods resounded again and till one of the inhuman Wretch's servants came to my assistance and released me from my dreadfull prison, but not before one of my legs was entirely broken."

---

1 It was a breach of propriety for a single woman to write a letter to a marriageable man, unless they were engaged. Proposing marriage to him compounded the offence.

2 Steel man-traps were placed on the grounds of private estates to catch trespassers, poachers, etc.

Chapter the sixth

At this melancholy recital the fair eyes of Lady Williams, were suffused in tears and Alice could not help exclaiming,

"Oh! cruel Charles to wound the hearts and legs of all the fair."

Lady Williams now interposed and observed that the young Lady's leg ought to be set without farther delay. After examining the fracture therefore, she immediately began and performed the operation with great skill which was the more wonderfull on account of her having never performed such a one before. Lucy, then arose from the ground and finding that she could walk with the greatest ease, accompanied them to Lady Williams's House at her Ladyship's particular request.

The perfect form, the beautifull face, and elegant manners of Lucy so won on the affections of Alice that when they parted, which was not till after Supper, she assured her that except her Father, Brother, Uncles, Aunts, Cousins and other relations, Lady Williams, Charles Adams and a few dozen more of particular freinds, she loved her better than almost any other person in the world.

Such a flattering assurance of her regard would justly have given much pleasure to the object of it, had she not plainly perceived that the amiable Alice had partaken too freely of Lady Williams's claret.

Her Ladyship (whose discernment was great) read in the intelligent countenance of Lucy her thoughts on the subject and as soon as Miss Johnson had taken her leave, thus addressed her.

"When you are more intimately acquainted with my Alice you will not be surprised, Lucy, to see the dear Creature drink a little too much; for such things happen every day. She has many rare and charming qualities, but Sobriety is not one of them. The whole Family are indeed a sad drunken set. I am sorry to say too that I never knew three such thorough Gamesters as they are, more particularly Alice. But she is a charming girl. I fancy not one of the sweetest tempers in the world; to be sure I have seen her in such passions! However she is a sweet young Woman. I am sure you'll like her. I scarcely know any one so amiable.—Oh! that you could but have seen her the other Evening! How she raved! and on such a trifle too! She is indeed a most pleasing Girl! I shall always love her!"

"She appears by your ladyship's account to have many good qualities," replied Lucy. "Oh! a thousand," answered Lady

Williams; "tho' I am very partial to her, and perhaps am blinded by my affection, to her real defects."

Chapter the seventh

The next morning brought the three Miss Simpsons to wait on Lady Williams; who received them with the utmost politeness and introduced to their acquaintance Lucy, with whom the eldest was so much pleased that at parting she declared her sole *ambition* was to have her accompany them the next morning to Bath,[1] whither they were going for some weeks.

"Lucy, said Lady Williams, is quite at her own disposal and if she chooses to accept so kind an invitation, I hope she will not hesitate, from any motives of delicacy on my account. I know not indeed how I shall ever be able to part with her. She never was at Bath and I should think that it would be a most agreable Jaunt[2] to her. Speak my Love," continued she, turning to Lucy, "what say you to accompanying these Ladies? I shall be miserable without you—t'will be a most pleasant tour to you—I hope you'll go; if you do I am sure t'will be the Death of me—pray be persuaded"—

Lucy begged leave to decline the honour of accompanying them, with many expressions of gratitude for the extream politeness of Miss Simpson in inviting her.

Miss Simpson appeared much disappointed by her refusal. Lady Williams insisted on her going—declared that she would never forgive her if she did not, and that she should never survive it if she did, and inshort used such persuasive arguments that it was at length resolved she was to go. The Miss Simpsons called for her at ten o'clock the next morning and Lady Williams had soon the satisfaction of receiving from her young freind, the pleasing intelligence of their safe arrival in Bath.

It may now be proper to return to the Hero of this Novel,[3] the brother of Alice, of whom I beleive I have scarcely ever had occasion to speak; which may perhaps be partly oweing to his unfortunate propensity to Liquor, which so compleatly deprived him

---

1   The famous spa town in Somerset, where JA herself would live with her family from 1801 to 1804, was still at the height of fashion in the 1780s and 1790s.
2   Ramble, flight, excursion, often used humorously.
3   Jack Johnson, who is named only in the title and who lacks even a speaking part.

of the use of those faculties Nature had endowed him with, that he never did anything worth mentioning. His Death happened a short time after Lucy's departure and was the natural Consequence of this pernicious practice. By his decease, his sister became the sole inheritress of a very large fortune, which as it gave her fresh Hopes of rendering herself acceptable as a wife to Charles Adams could not fail of being most pleasing to her—and as the effect was Joyfull the Cause could scarcely be lamented.

Finding the violence of her attachment to him daily augment, she at length disclosed it to her Father and desired him to propose a union between them to Charles. Her father consented and set out one morning to open the affair to the young Man. Mr Johnson being a man of few words his part was soon performed and the answer he received was as follows—

"Sir, I may perhaps be expected to appear pleased at and gratefull for the offer you have made me: but let me tell you that I consider it as an affront. I look upon myself to be Sir a perfect Beauty—where would you see a finer figure or a more charming face. Then, sir I imagine my Manners and Address to be of the most polished kind; there is a certain elegance a peculiar sweetness in them that I never saw equalled and cannot describe—. Partiality aside, I am certainly more accomplished in every Language, every Science, every Art and every thing than any other person in Europe. My temper is even, my virtues innumerable, my self unparalelled. Since such Sir is my character, what do you mean by wishing me to marry your Daughter? Let me give you a short sketch of yourself and of her. I look upon you Sir to be a very good sort of Man in the main; a drunken old Dog to be sure, but that's nothing to me. Your daughter sir, is neither sufficiently beautifull, sufficiently amiable, sufficiently witty, nor sufficiently rich for me—. I expect nothing more in my wife than my wife will find in me— Perfection. These sir, are my sentiments and I honour myself for having such. One freind I have[1] and glory in having but one—. She is at present preparing my Dinner, but if you choose to see her, she shall come and she will inform you that these have ever been my sentiments."

Mr Johnson was satisfied; and expressing himself to be much obliged to Mr. Adams for the characters he had favoured him with of himself and his Daughter, took his leave.

The unfortunate Alice on receiving from her father the sad

---

1 Mrs Susan, the cook.

account of the ill success his visit had been attended with, could scarcely support the disappointment—She flew to her Bottle and it was soon forgot.

Chapter the eighth

While these affairs were transacting at Pammydiddle, Lucy was conquering every Heart at Bath. A fortnight's residence there had nearly effaced from her remembrance the captivating form of Charles—The recollection of what her Heart had formerly suffered by his charms and her Leg by his trap, enabled her to forget him with tolerable Ease, which was what she determined to do; and for that purpose dedicated five minutes in every day to the employment of driving him from her remembrance.

Her second Letter to Lady Williams contained the pleasing intelligence of her having accomplished her undertaking to her entire satisfaction; she mentioned in it also an offer of marriage she had received from the Duke of —— an elderly Man of noble fortune whose ill health was the cheif inducement of his Journey to Bath. "I am distressed (she continued) to know whether I mean to accept him or not. There are a thousand advantages to be derived from a marriage with the Duke, for besides those more inferior ones of Rank and Fortune it will procure me a home, which of all other things is what I most desire. Your Ladyship's kind wish of my always remaining with you, is noble and generous but I cannot think of becoming so great a burden on one I so much love and esteem. That One should receive obligations only from those we despise, is a sentiment instilled into my mind by my worthy Aunt, in my early years, and cannot in my opinion be too strictly adhered to. The excellent woman of whom I now speak, is I hear too much incensed by my imprudent departure from Wales, to receive me again—. I most earnestly wish to leave the Ladies I am now with. Miss Simpson is indeed (setting aside ambition) very amiable, but her 2d Sister the envious and malvolent Sukey is too disagreable to live with.—I have reason to think that the admiration I have met with in the circles of the Great at this Place, has raised her Hatred and Envy; for often has she threatened, and sometimes endeavoured to cutt my throat.— Your Ladyship will therefore allow that I am not wrong in wishing to leave Bath, and in wishing to have a home to receive me, when I do. I shall expect with impatience your advice concerning the Duke and am your most obliged

&c &c—Lucy."

Lady Williams sent her, her opinion on the subject in the following Manner.

"Why do you hesitate my dearest Lucy, a moment with respect to the Duke? I have enquired into his Character and find him to be an unprincipaled, illiterate Man. Never shall my Lucy be united to such a one! He has a princely fortune, which is every day encreasing. How nobly will you spend it!, what credit will you give him in the eyes of all!, How much will he be respected on his Wife's account![1] But why my dearest Lucy, why will you not at once decide this affair by returning to me and never leaving me again? Altho' I admire your noble sentiments with respect to obligations, yet let me beg that they may not prevent your making me happy. It will to be sure be a great expence to me, to have you always with me—I shall not be able to support it—but what is that in comparison with the happiness I shall enjoy in your society?—t'will ruin me I know—you will not therefore surely, withstand these arguments, or refuse to return to yours most affectionately—&c &c

C. Williams"

Chapter the Ninth

What might have been the effect of her Ladyship's advice, had it ever been received by Lucy, is uncertain, as it reached Bath a few Hours after she had breathed her last. She fell a sacrifice to the Envy and Malice of Sukey who jealous of her superior charms took her by poison from an admiring World at the age of seventeen.[2]

Thus fell the amiable and lovely Lucy whose Life had been marked by no crime, and stained by no blemish but her imprudent departure from her Aunts, and whose death was sincerely lamented by every one who knew her. Among the most afflicted of her freinds were Lady Williams, Miss Johnson and the Duke; the 2 last of whom had a most sincere regard for her, more particularly Alice, who had spent a whole evening in her company and had never thought of her since. His Grace's affliction may

---

1   A pun on the economic and social connotations of the terms.

2   A critical age for girls, who were expected to "come out," or begin to take part in social activities, in their late teens. Sukey murders Lucy just as she is establishing herself in society and receiving desirable offers of marriage.

likewise be easily accounted for, since he lost one for whom he had experienced during the last ten days, a tender affection and sincere regard. He mourned her loss with unshaken constancy for the next fortnight at the end of which time, he gratified the ambition of Caroline Simpson by raising her to the rank of a Dutchess. Thus was she at length rendered compleatly happy in the gratification of her favourite passion. Her sister the perfidious Sukey, was likewise shortly after exalted in a manner she truly deserved, and by her actions appeared to have always desired. Her barbarous Murder was discovered and in spite of every interceding freind she was speedily raised to the Gallows[1]—. The beautifull but affected Cecilia was too sensible of her own superior charms, not to imagine that if Caroline could engage a Duke, she might without censure aspire to the affections of some Prince—and knowing that those of her native Country were cheifly engaged,[2] she left England and I have since heard is at present the favourite Sultana of the great Mogul[3]—.

In the mean time the inhabitants of Pammydiddle were in a state of the greatest astonishment and Wonder, a report being circulated of the intended marriage of Charles Adams. The Lady's name was still a secret. Mr and Mrs Jones imagined it to be, Miss Johnson; but *she* knew better; all *her* fears were centered in his Cook, when to the astonishment of every one, he was publicly united to Lady Williams—

Finis.

---

1 Hanged, the punishment for murder as well as for many lesser offences.
2 An allusion to the attachments of the Prince of Wales, later the Prince Regent (1811-20) and then George IV (1820-30), and of his younger brothers. George had secretly wedded Maria Fitzherbert, a widowed Catholic, in 1785. Frederick, Duke of York, was notorious for his many affairs, as were William, Duke of Clarence, and Edward, Duke of Kent. Three more princes—Ernest, Duke of Cumberland, Augustus, Duke of Sussex, and Adolphus, Duke of Cambridge—were still in their teens when "Jack and Alice" was written.
3 The European name for the emperor of Delhi. In becoming a Sultana, Cecilia assumes in life her sister Caroline's earlier masquerade role.

Henry and Eliza[1]
a novel.

Is humbly dedicated to Miss Cooper[2]
by her obedient Humble Servant
The Author

As Sir George and Lady Harcourt were superintending the Labours of their Haymakers, rewarding the industry of some by smiles of approbation, and punishing the idleness of others, by a cudgel, they perceived lying closely concealed beneath the thick foliage of a Haycock,[3] a beautifull little Girl not more than 3 months old.

Touched with the enchanting Graces of her face and delighted with the infantine tho' sprightly answers she returned to their many questions, they resolved to take her home and, having no Children of their own, to educate her with care and cost.

Being good People themselves, their first and principal care was to incite in her a Love of Virtue and a Hatred of Vice, in which they so well succeeded (Eliza having a natural turn that way herself) that when she grew up, she was the delight of all who knew her.

Beloved by Lady Harcourt, adored by Sir George and admired by all the World, she lived in a continued course of uninterrupted Happiness, till she had attained her eighteenth year; when happening one day to be detected in stealing a banknote of 50£, she was turned out of doors by her inhuman Benefactors.[4] Such a transition to one who did not possess so noble and exalted a mind as Eliza, would have been Death, but she, happy in the con-

---

1 The title alludes to JA's fourth brother Henry (1771-1850) and her cousin Eliza de Feuillide, née Hancock (1761-1813), who had married a French soldier, Jean François Capot de Feuillide, in 1781, at the age of nineteen. As early as August 1788, five years before her husband was guillotined in Paris in 1794, Eliza was expressing an interest in Henry, then a seventeen-year-old student at Oxford. They would eventually marry, in December 1797.

2 JA's cousin Jane Cooper (1771-98), who played the part of the lively heroine, Roxalana, in the Austen family production of *The Sultan*.

3 A conical heap of hay. "Foliage," normally referring to leaves, is an odd term to apply to hay.

4 Eliza's adoptive parents have in fact been lenient; stealing a considerable sum of money, such as fifty pounds, was still punishable by death.

scious knowledge of her own Excellence, amused herself, as she sate beneath a tree with making and singing the following Lines.

Song.

Though misfortunes my footsteps may ever attend
I hope I shall never have need of a Freind
as an innocent Heart I will ever preserve
and will never from Virtue's dear boundaries swerve.

Having amused herself some hours, with this song and her own pleasing reflections, she arose and took the road to M.[1] a small market town of which place her most intimate freind kept the red Lion.[2]

To this freind she immediately went, to whom having recounted her late misfortune, she communicated her wish of getting into some family in the capacity of Humble Companion.[3]

Mrs Willson, who was the most amiable creature on earth, was no sooner acquainted with her Desire, than she sate down in the Bar and wrote the following Letter to the Dutchess of F, the woman whom of all others, she most Esteemed.

"To the Dutchess of F."

"Receive into your Family, at my request a young woman of unexceptionable Character, who is so good as to choose your Society in preference to going to Service. Hasten, and take her from the arms of your"

"Sarah Wilson."

The Dutchess, whose freindship for Mrs Wilson would have carried her any lengths, was overjoyed at such an opportunity of

---

1 Supposedly an abbreviation for an actual market town. JA is playing with the convention in eighteenth-century fiction of disguising place names by their initials, as if to protect the identity of individuals living there. The names of characters, such as the "Dutchess of F." here, are also often disguised with initials or dashes for the same purpose of mystification.

2 A common name for taverns and inns.

3 Normally a position for a destitute gentlewoman. A companion was employed to entertain and assist another woman, such as a wealthy relative, in better circumstances.

obliging her and accordingly sate out immediately on the receipt of her letter for the red Lion, which she reached the same Evening. The Dutchess of F. was about 45 and a half; Her passions were strong, her freindships firm and her Enmities, unconquerable. She was a widow and had only one Daughter who was on the point of marriage with a young Man of considerable fortune.

The Dutchess no sooner beheld our Heroine than throwing her arms around her neck, she declared herself so much pleased with her, that she was resolved they never more should part. Eliza was delighted with such a protestation of freindship, and after taking a most affecting leave of her dear Mrs Wilson, accompanied her Grace the next morning to her seat in Surry.[1]

With every expression of regard did the Dutchess introduce her to Lady Hariet, who was so much pleased with her appearance that she besought her, to consider her as her Sister, which Eliza with the greatest Condescension promised to do.

Mr Cecil, the Lover of Lady Harriet, being often with the family was often with Eliza. A mutual Love took place and Cecil having declared his first, prevailed on Eliza to consent to a private union,[2] which was easy to be effected, as the dutchess's chaplain[3] being very much in love with Eliza himself, would they were certain do anything to oblige her.

The Dutchess and Lady Harriet being engaged one evening to an assembly,[4] they took the opportunity of their absence and were united by the enamoured Chaplain.

When the Ladies returned, their amazement was great at finding instead of Eliza the following Note.

"Madam"
"We are married and gone."

"Henry and Eliza Cecil."

---

1   The duchess's estate in Surrey, the county southwest of London.
2   With a common license from a bishop for a marriage in a church within his diocese, rather than after the publication of banns on three successive Sundays, as was otherwise required.
3   A chaplain could not authorize a private marriage without a license from a bishop. Since no such arrangement has been made here, the marriage is invalid.
4   A ball at the local Assembly rooms. Eliza, as a mere companion, has not been invited to attend.

Her Grace as soon as she had read the letter, which sufficiently explained the whole affair, flew into the most violent passion and after having spent an agreable half hour, in calling them by all the shocking Names her rage could suggest to her, sent out after them 300 armed Men, with orders not to return without their Bodies, dead or alive; intending that if they should be brought to her in the latter condition to have them put to Death in some torturelike manner, after a few years Confinement.

In the mean time Cecil and Eliza continued their flight to the Continent,[1] which they judged to be more secure than their native Land, from the dreadfull effects of the Dutchess's vengeance, which they had so much reason to apprehend.

In France they remained 3 years, during which time they became the parents of two Boys, and at the end of it Eliza became a widow without any thing to support either her or her Children. They had lived since their Marriage at the rate of 12,000£ a year, of which Mr Cecil's estate being rather less than the twentieth part,[2] they had been able to save but a trifle, having lived to the utmost extent of their Income.

Eliza, being perfectly conscious of the derangement in their affairs,[3] immediately on her Husband's death set sail for England, in a man of War of 55 Guns,[4] which they had built in their more prosperous Days. But no sooner had she stepped on Shore at Dover,[5] with a Child in each hand, than she was seized by the officers of the Dutchess, and conducted by them to a snug little Newgate[6] of their Lady's, which she had erected for the reception of her own private Prisoners.

No sooner had Eliza entered her Dungeon than the first thought which occurred to her, was how to get out of it again.

She went to the Door; but it was locked. She looked at the Window; but it was barred with iron; disappointed in both her

---

1 The mainland of Europe, but here signifying France, rather than the continent in general.

2 Henry Cecil's estate seems to be producing less than £600 per year. Henry and Eliza (like Eliza de Feuillide's improvident husband) have thus amassed huge debts.

3 A euphemism for unmanageable debt.

4 A fourth-rate warship, one carrying between fifty and sixty guns. The odd number of guns on JA's man of war is comically impossible: warships would carry an even number.

5 Seventy miles south-east of London, Dover was the closest English port to the Continent and the most popular route to France.

6 A private dungeon, named after the famous London prison.

expectations, she dispaired of effecting her Escape, when she fortunately perceived in a Corner of her Cell, a small saw and a Ladder of ropes. With the saw she instantly went to work and in a few weeks had displaced every Bar but one to which she fastened the Ladder.

A difficulty then occurred which for some time, she knew not how to obviate. Her Children were too small to get down the Ladder by themselves, nor would it be possible for her to take them in her arms, when *she* did. At last she determined to fling down all her Cloathes, of which she had a large Quantity, and then having given them strict Charge not to hurt themselves, threw her Children after them. She herself with ease descended by the Ladder, at the bottom of which she had the pleasure of finding Her little boys in perfect Health and fast asleep.

Her wardrobe she now saw a fatal necessity of selling, both for the preservation of her Children and herself. With tears in her eyes, she parted with these last reliques of her former Glory, and with the money she got for them, bought others more usefull, some playthings for her Boys and a gold Watch for herself.[1]

But scarcely was she provided with the above-mentioned necessaries, than she began to find herself rather hungry, and had reason to think, by their biting off two of her fingers, that her Children were much in the same situation.

To remedy these unavoidable misfortunes, she determined to return to her old freinds, Sir George and Lady Harcourt, whose generosity she had so often experienced and hoped to experience as often again.

She had about 40 miles to travel before she could reach their hospitable Mansion, of which having walked 30 without stopping, she found herself at the Entrance of a Town, where often in happier times, she had accompanied Sir George and Lady Harcourt to regale themselves with a cold collation[2] at one of the Inns.

The reflections that her adventures since the last time she had partaken of these happy *Junketings*, afforded her, occupied her mind, for some time, as she sate on the steps at the door of a

---

1 A gold watch was an expensive luxury item: exchanging a costly wardrobe for an equally costly fashion accessory is hardly a "fatal necessity."

2 Defined by Johnson as a "treat less than a feast," this assortment of cold meat, salads, etc., would not be sufficient for the Harcourts to "regale themselves."

Gentleman's house. As soon as these reflections were ended, she arose and determined to take her station at the very inn, she remembered with so much delight, from the Company of which, as they went in and out, she hoped to receive some Charitable Gratuity.[1]

She had but just taken her post at the Innyard before a Carriage drove out of it, and on turning the Corner at which she was stationed, stopped to give the Postilion an opportunity of admiring the beauty of the prospect. Eliza then advanced to the carriage and was going to request their Charity, when on fixing her Eyes on the Lady within it, she exclaimed,

"Lady Harcourt!"

To which the lady replied:

"Eliza!"

"Yes Madam it is the wretched Eliza herself."

Sir George, who was also in the Carriage, but too much amazed to speek, was proceeding to demand an explanation from Eliza of the Situation she was then in, when Lady Harcourt in transports of Joy, exclaimed.

"Sir George, Sir George, she is not only Eliza our adopted Daughter, but our real Child."

"Our real Child! What Lady Harcourt, do you mean? You know you never even was with child. Explain yourself, I beseech you."

"You must remember Sir George that when you sailed for America, you left me breeding."

"I do, I do, go on dear Polly."[2]

"Four months after you were gone, I was delivered of this Girl, but dreading your just resentment at her not proving the Boy you wished, I took her to a Haycock and laid her down. A few weeks afterwards, you returned, and fortunately for me, made no enquiries on the subject. Satisfied within myself of the wellfare of my Child, I soon forgot I had one, insomuch that when, we shortly after found her in the very Haycock, I had placed her, I had no more idea of her being my own, than you had, and nothing I will venture to say could have recalled the circumstance to my remembrance, but my thus accidentally hearing her voice which now strikes me as being the very counterpart of my own Child's."

---

1 An elegant euphemism; Eliza intends to beg from customers at the inn.
2 A pet-name for Mary Anne, the first time that Lady Harcourt is named.

"The rational and convincing Account you have given of the whole affair, said Sir George, leaves no doubt of her being our Daughter and as such I freely forgive the robbery she was guilty of."

A mutual Reconciliation then took place, and Eliza, ascending the Carriage with her two Children returned to that home from which she had been absent nearly four years.

No sooner was she reinstated in her accustomed power at Harcourt Hall, than she raised an Army, with which she entirely demolished the Dutchess's Newgate, snug as it was, and by that act, gained the Blessings of thousands, and the Applause of her own Heart.

Finis

The beautifull Cassandra.
a novel in twelve Chapters.
dedicated by permission to Miss Austen.[1]

Dedication.

Madam

You are a Phoenix.[2] Your taste is refined, Your Sentiments are noble, and your Virtues innumerable. Your Person is lovely, your Figure, elegant, and your Form, magestic. Your Manners, are polished, your Conversation is rational and your appearance singular. If therefore the following Tale will afford one moment's amusement to you, every wish will be gratified of

your most obediant
humble Servant
The Author.

The beautifull Cassandra.
a novel, in twelve Chapters.

Chapter the first.

Cassandra[3] was the Daughter and the only Daughter of a celebrated Millener in Bond Street.[4] Her father was of noble Birth, being the near relation of the Dutchess of ——'s Butler.

Chapter the 2d

When Cassandra had attained her 16th year, she was lovely and amiable and chancing to fall in love with an elegant Bonnet, her

---

1 Cassandra Elizabeth Austen (1773-1845), JA's elder sister, and as such known as "Miss Austen"; Jane, the younger daughter, was styled "Miss Jane Austen."

2 The bird that is supposed to rise with renewed youth from its own ashes: figuratively, "a person (or thing) of unique excellence or of matchless beauty; a paragon" (*OED*).

3 JA does not use her sister's name elsewhere in her fiction, but reserves it for the most indomitable of her heroines.

4 Milliners sold caps and hats, made trimmings and accessories for dresses, and acted as arbiters of fashion. Their shops were located in fashionable parts of London, such as Bond Street.

Mother had just compleated bespoke by the Countess of —— she placed it on her gentle Head and walked from her Mother's shop to make her Fortune.

Chapter the 3rd

The first person she met, was the Viscount of —— a young man, no less celebrated for his Accomplishments and Virtues, than for his Elegance and Beauty. She curtseyed and walked on.

Chapter the 4th

She then proceeded to a Pastry-cooks where she devoured six ices,[1] refused to pay for them, knocked down the Pastry Cook and walked away.

Chapter the 5th

She next ascended a Hackney Coach[2] and ordered it to Hampstead,[3] where she was no sooner arrived than she ordered the Coachman to turn round and drive her back again.

Chapter the 6th

Being returned to the same spot of the same Street she had sate out from, the Coachman demanded his Pay.

Chapter the 7th

She searched her pockets over again and again; but every search was unsuccessfull. No money could she find. The man grew peremptory. She placed her bonnet on his head and ran away.

---

1 Ice-cream and water ices, sold by pastry-cooks. The expense involved in producing ices and keeping them cool, using ice stored throughout the year in ice-houses, made them luxury items.
2 A coach available for hire. Hackney coaches were regulated by a central licensing office. A hackney-coach with two horses charged a shilling for one and a half miles.
3 An attractive, fashionable village, some four miles north of Bond Street, with fine views over London.

Chapter the 8th

Thro' many a Street she then proceeded and met in none the least Adventure till on turning a Corner of Bloomsbury Square,[1] she met Maria.

Chapter the 9th

Cassandra started and Maria seemed surprised; they trembled, blushed, turned pale and passed each other in a mutual Silence.

Chapter the 10th

Cassandra was next accosted by her freind the Widow, who squeezing out her little Head thro' her less window,[2] asked her how she did? Cassandra curtseyed and went on.

Chapter the 11th

A quarter of a mile brought her to her paternal roof in Bond Street from which she had now been absent nearly 7 hours.

Chapter the 12th

She entered it and was pressed to her Mother's bosom by that worthy Woman. Cassandra smiled and whispered to herself "This is a day well spent."

Finis.

---

1 The first of the great London squares, laid out in the early 1660s for Thomas Wriothesley, fourth Earl of Southampton.

2 Less large (i.e., smaller) than the widow's head. The smallness of the window is a sign of the widow's indigence: she is in an inexpensive upper-storey room, which would have narrower, lower windows than one on a lower storey.

The Visit:
a comedy in 2 acts

Dedication.
To the Revd James Austen[1]

Sir,

The following Drama, which I humbly recommend to your Protection and Patronage, tho' inferior to those celebrated Comedies called "The school for Jealousy" and "The travelled Man,"[2] will I hope afford some amusement to so respectable a *Curate*[3] as yourself; which was the end in veiw when it was first composed by your Humble Servant the Author.

Dramatis Personae

Sir Arthur Hampton
Lord Fitzgerald
Stanly
Willoughby, Sir Arthur's nephew

Lady Hampton
Miss Fitzgerald

---

1   JA's eldest brother (1765-1819), ordained as an Anglican priest at Oxford in June 1789. From 1782 to 1789, he directed a series of dramatic productions performed by the Austens at Steventon and wrote amusing prologues and epilogues for them: JA appropriately dedicates this comedy to her theatrically-minded brother. Paula Byrne speculates that "The Visit" was performed by the Austen family during the Christmas holiday, 1788-89, as a burlesque afterpiece to their production of James Townley's farce *High Life Below Stairs* (*Jane Austen and the Theatre* [London: Hambledon, 2002], pp. 13-14).

2   There are no records of eighteenth-century plays so titled. It is possible that they were comedies written for Austen family performances, either by James or by JA herself. "The School for Jealousy" might have been adapted from the libretto of an opera by Antonio Salieri, *La Scola de' Gelosi*, performed in London in March 1786. The titles may also allude to celebrated comedies by Sheridan, *The School for Scandal* (1777), and Goldsmith, *The Good-Natur'd Man* (1768).

3   Either of Stoke Charity or of Overton, the nearest town to Steventon, where James became curate in April 1790. A curate assisted a parish priest with his duties, or replaced him; Johnson defines a curate as "a clergyman hired to perform the duties of another."

Sophy Hampton
Cloe Willoughby

The scenes are laid in
Lord Fitzgerald's House.

Act the First
Scene the first a Parlour—
enter Lord Fitzgerald and Stanly

Stanly. Cousin your Servant.
Fitzgerald. Stanly, good morning to you. I hope you slept well
last night.
Stanly. Remarkably well; I thank you.
Fitzgerald. I am afraid you found your Bed too short. It was
bought in my Grandmother's time, who was herself a very short
woman and made a point of suiting all her Beds to her own
length, as she never wished to have any company in the House,
on account of an unfortunate impediment in her speech, which
she was sensible of being very disagreable to her inmates.
Stanly. Make no more excuses dear Fitzgerald.
Fitzgerald. I will not distress you by too much civility—I only beg
you will consider yourself as much at home as in your Father's
house. Remember, "The more free, the more Wellcome."[1]
                                                    (exit Fitzgerald)
Stanly. Amiable Youth!
    Your virtues could he imitate
    How happy would be Stanly's fate!
                                                    (exit Stanly.)

Scene the 2nd

Stanly and Miss Fitzgerald, discovered.[2]

Stanly. What Company is it you expect to dine with you to Day,
Cousin?
Miss F. Sir Arthur and Lady Hampton; their Daughter,
Nephew and Neice.

---

1 An allusion to Townley's *High Life Below Stairs*, in which Kitty declares:
   "Lady *Charlotte*, pray be free; the more free, the more welcome, as they
   say in my Country" (Act 2).
2 Revealed. The characters are in place when the curtain opens.

Stanly. Miss Hampton and her Cousin are both Handsome, are they not?

Miss F. Miss Willoughby is extreamly so. Miss Hampton is a fine Girl, but not equal to her.

Stanly. Is not your Brother attached to the Latter?

Miss F. He admires her I know, but I beleive nothing more. Indeed I have heard him say that she was the most beautifull, pleasing, and amiable Girl in the world, and that of all others he should prefer her for his Wife. But it never went any farther I'm certain.

Stanly. And yet my Cousin never says a thing he does not mean.

Miss F. Never. From his Cradle he has always been a strict adherent to Truth.

(Exeunt Severally)[1]

End of the First Act.

Act the Second.
Scene the first. The Drawing Room.
Chairs set round in a row. Lord Fitzgerald, Miss Fitzgerald and
Stanly seated.

Enter a Servant.

Servant. Sir Arthur and Lady Hampton. Miss Hampton, Mr and Miss Willoughby.

(exit Servant)

Enter the Company.

Miss F. I hope I have the pleasure of seeing your Ladyship well. Sir Arthur your servant. Yours Mr Willoughby. Dear Sophy, Dear Cloe,—

(They pay their Compliments alternately.)

Miss F. —Pray be seated.

(They sit)

Bless me! there ought to be 8 Chairs and these are but 6. However, if your Ladyship will but take Sir Arthur in your Lap, and Sophy, my Brother in hers, I beleive we shall do pretty well.

Lady H. Oh! with pleasure....

Sophy. I beg his Lordship would be seated.

Miss F. I am really shocked at crouding you in such a manner, but my Grandmother (who bought all the furniture of this

---

1 Characters leave the stage through different exits.

room) as she had never a very large Party, did not think it
necessary to buy more Chairs than were sufficient for her
own family and two of her particular freinds.

Sophy. I beg you will make no apologies. Your Brother is very
light.

Stanly, aside) What a cherub is Cloe!

Cloe, aside) What a seraph[1] is Stanly!

Enter a Servant.

Servant. Dinner is on table.

They all rise.

Miss F. Lady Hampton, Miss Hampton, Miss Willoughby.

Stanly. hands[2] Cloe, Lord Fitzgerald, Sophy Willoughby, Miss
Fitzgerald, and Sir Arthur, Lady Hampton.

(Exeunt.)

Scene the 2nd
The Dining Parlour.
Miss Fitzgerald at top. Lord Fitzgerald at bottom. Company
ranged on each side.
Servants waiting.

Cloe. I shall trouble Mr Stanly for a Little of the fried Cowheel
and Onion.[3]

Stanly. Oh Madam, there is a secret pleasure in helping so
amiable a Lady—.

Lady H. I assure you my Lord, Sir Arthur never touches wine;
but Sophy will toss off a bumper[4] I am sure to oblige your
Lordship.

Lord F. Elder wine or Mead,[5] Miss Hampton?

Sophy. If it is equal to you Sir, I should prefer some warm ale
with a toast and nutmeg.[6]

---

1 Two of the nine orders or "choirs" of angels; together with thrones,
   cherubim and seraphim form the triad closest to God.
2 Escorts, leads by the hand.
3 A coarse dish consumed by labourers, like the tripe and suet pudding
   that follow.
4 Drain a glass of wine filled to the brim, rather than sipping it in ladylike
   fashion.
5 Cheap domestic alternatives to French wine made, respectively, from
   elder berries and honey. They would be served by those of limited
   means and at rural entertainments, but never by people of fashion.
6 An invalid's drink, and thus especially inappropriate for the youthful
   and attractive Sophy Hampton.

Lord F. Two glasses of warmed ale with a toast and nutmeg.

Miss F. I am afraid Mr Willoughby you take no care of yourself. I fear you dont meet with any thing to your liking.

Willoughby. Oh! Madam, I can want for nothing while there are red herrings[1] on table.

Lord F. Sir Arthur taste that Tripe. I think you will not find it amiss.

Lady H. Sir Arthur never eats Tripe; 'tis too savoury for him, you know my Lord.

Miss F. Take away the Liver and Crow[2] and bring in the Suet pudding.[3]

(a short Pause.)

Miss F. Sir Arthur shant I send you a bit of pudding?

Lady H. Sir Arthur never eats suet pudding Ma'am. It is too high a Dish for him.[4]

Miss F. Will no one allow me the honour of helping them? Then John take away the Pudding, and bring the Wine.

(Servants take away the things and bring in
the Bottles and Glasses.)

Lord F. I wish we had any Desert[5] to offer you. But my Grand-mother in her Lifetime, destroyed the Hothouse[6] in order to build a receptacle for the Turkies with its' materials; and we have never been able to raise another tolerable one.

Lady H. I beg you will make no apologies my Lord.

Willoughby. Come Girls, let us circulate the Bottle.[7]

Sophy. A very good motion Cousin; and I will second it with all my Heart. Stanly you dont drink.

Stanly. Madam, I am drinking draughts of Love from Cloe's eyes.

---

1 Herrings preserved by being cured in smoke, considered inferior to fresh fish.

2 The entrails and giblets of calves, pigs, etc.; food for the poor.

3 A pudding made of flour and suet (animal fat), usually boiled in a cloth.

4 Suet pudding is not, of course, a "high" or rich dish.

5 Dessert, consisting of fruit and nuts, served at the end of a dinner, after the pudding.

6 A heated greenhouse in which fruits for dessert were cultivated: a much costlier and more prestigious structure than the "receptacle for the Turkies" that replaces it.

7 The custom of passing a bottle of wine around a dinner table after the meal, normally among men only, after women have adjourned to the drawing-room. Here, in contrast, the women are hearty drinkers, while neither Stanly nor Sir Arthur "touches wine."

Sophy. That's poor nourishment truly. Come, drink to her better acquaintance.

(Miss Fitzgerald goes to a Closet and brings out a bottle)

Miss F. This, Ladies and Gentlemen is some of my dear Grandmother's own manufacture. She excelled in Gooseberry Wine.[1] Pray taste it Lady Hampton?

Lady H. How refreshing it is!

Miss F. I should think with your Ladyship's permission, that Sir Arthur might taste a little of it.

Lady H. Not for Worlds. Sir Arthur never drinks anything so high.

Lord F. And now my amiable Sophia condescend to marry me.

(He takes her hand and leads her to the front)

Stanly. Oh! Cloe could I but hope you would make me blessed—

Cloe. I will.

(They advance.)

Miss F. Since you Willoughby are the only one left, I cannot refuse your earnest solicitations—There is my Hand.—

Lady H. And may you all be Happy!

Finis.

---

1 A simple, home-made wine, never served at a formal gathering.

From Volume the Second

Love and Freindship

To Madame La Comtesse De Feuillide[1]
This Novel is inscribed
by
Her obliged Humble Servant
The Author

Love and Freindship
a novel
in a series of Letters—.

"Deceived in Freindship and Betrayed in Love."[2]

Letter the First
From Isabel to Laura

How often, in answer to my repeated intreaties that you would give my Daughter a regular detail of the Misfortunes and Adventures of your Life, have you said "No, my freind never will I comply with your request till I may be no longer in Danger of again experiencing such dreadful ones."
Surely that time is now at hand. You are this Day 55. If a woman may ever be said to be in safety from the determined Perseverance of disagreable Lovers and the cruel Persecutions of obstinate Fathers, surely it must be at such a time of Life.

Isabel.

---

1 Austen's cousin Eliza de Feuillide; see p. 74, note 1.
2 The last line of an anonymous quatrain, published as a glee for three voices in *A Selection of Favourite Catches, Glees, &c. Sung at the Bath Harmonic Society* (1799):
  Welcome, the covert of these aged oaks;
  Welcome, each cavern of the horrid rocks;
  Far from the world's illusion let me rove,
  Deceiv'd in Friendship, and betray'd in Love.
A "glee" is an unaccompanied song for three or more voices, in which each voice takes a different part.

Letter 2d
Laura to Isabel

Altho' I cannot agree with you in supposing that I shall never again be exposed to Misfortunes as unmerited as those I have already experienced, yet to avoid the imputation of Obstinacy or ill-nature, I will gratify the curiosity of your daughter; and may the fortitude with which I have suffered the many Afflictions of my past Life, prove to her a useful Lesson for the support of those which may befall her in her own.

Laura

Letter 3rd
Laura to Marianne

As the Daughter of my most intimate freind I think you entitled to that knowledge of my unhappy Story, which your Mother has so often solicited me to give you.

My Father was a native of Ireland and an inhabitant of Wales; my Mother was the natural[1] Daughter of a Scotch Peer by an italian Opera-girl[2]—I was born in Spain and received my Education at a Convent in France.

When I had reached my eighteenth Year I was recalled by my Parents to my paternal roof in Wales. Our mansion was situated in one of the most romantic[3] parts of the Vale of Uske.[4] Tho' my Charms are now considerably softened and somewhat impaired by the Misfortunes I have undergone, I was once beautiful. But lovely as I was the Graces of my Person were the least of my Perfections. Of every accomplishment accustomary to my sex, I was Mistress.—When in the Convent, my progress had always exceeded my instructions; my Acquirements had been wonderfull for my Age, and I had shortly surpassed my Masters.

---

1 Illegitimate. Laura's mother thus could not take the surname of her aristocratic Scottish father.
2 A dancer in the ballet that was presented between the acts of an opera. Opera-girls were usually attractive and scantily clad and, like actresses, were sought after as mistresses by wealthy gentlemen.
3 In the sense of "full of wild scenery" (Johnson).
4 Usk is a picturesque river valley in south Wales; the river Usk flows north-south, through Monmouthshire.

In my Mind, every Virtue that could adorn it was centered; it was the Rendez-vous[1] of every good Quality and of every noble sentiment.

A sensibility too tremblingly alive[2] to every affliction of my Freinds, my Acquaintance and particularly to every affliction of my own, was my only fault, if a fault it could be called. Alas! how altered now! Tho' indeed my own Misfortunes do not make less impression on me, than they ever did, yet now I never feel for those of an other. My accomplishments too, begin to fade—I can neither sing so well nor Dance so gracefully as I once did—and I have entirely forgot the *Minuet Dela Cour*[3]—

Adeiu.

Laura

Letter 4th
Laura to Marianne

Our neighbourhood was small, for it consisted only of your Mother. She may probably have already told you that being left by her Parents in indigent Circumstances she had retired into Wales on eoconomical motives. There it was, our freindship first commenced—. Isabel was then one and twenty—Tho' pleasing both in her Person and Manners (between ourselves) she never possessed the hundredth part of my Beauty or Accomplishments. Isabel had seen the World. She had passed 2 Years at one of the first Boarding-schools in London; had spent a fortnight in Bath and had supped one night in Southampton.[4]

"Beware my Laura (she would often say) Beware of the insipid Vanities and idle Dissipations of the Metropolis of England; Beware of the unmeaning Luxuries of Bath and of the Stinking fish of Southampton."[5]

---

1 Austen signals Laura's affectedness by having her use a newly fashionable French term.

2 An allusion to Pope's *An Essay on Man* (1733-34): "Or Touch, if tremblingly alive all o'er, / To smart, and agonize at ev'ry pore" (Epistle 1, lines 197-98).

3 A court minuet; a formal dance, originally associated with the French court.

4 Unlike London and Bath, Southampton, a port and military town in Hampshire, on the south coast of England, had little claim to fashion.

5 The bad odours of Southampton were proverbial.

"Alas! (exclaimed I) how am I to avoid those evils I shall never be exposed to? What probability is there of my ever tasting the Dissipations of London, the Luxuries of Bath, or the stinking Fish of Southampton? I who am doomed to waste my Days of Youth and Beauty in an humble Cottage in the Vale of Uske."

Ah! little did I then think I was ordained so soon to quit that humble Cottage for the Deceitfull Pleasures of the World.

adeiu

Laura—

Letter 5th
Laura to Marianne

One Evening in December as my Father, my Mother and myself, were arranged in social converse round our Fireside, we were on a sudden, greatly astonished, by hearing a violent knocking on the outward Door of our rustic Cot.[1]

My Father started—"What noise is that," (said he.) "It sounds like a loud rapping at the Door"—(replied my Mother.) "it does indeed." (cried I.) "I am of your opinion; (said my Father) it certainly does appear to proceed from some uncommon violence exerted against our unoffending Door." "Yes (exclaimed I) I cannot help thinking it must be somebody who knocks for Admittance."

"That is another point (replied he;) We must not pretend to determine on what motive the person may knock—tho' that someone *does* rap at the Door, I am partly convinced."

Here, a 2d tremendous rap interrupted my Father in his speech and somewhat alarmed my Mother and me.

"Had we not better go and see who it is? (said she) the servants are out." "I think we had." (replied I.) "Certainly, (added my Father) by all means." "Shall we go now?" (said my Mother). "The sooner the better." (answered he.) "Oh! Let no time be lost." (cried I.)

A third more violent Rap than ever again assaulted our ears. "I am certain there is somebody knocking at the Door." (said my Mother.) "I think there must," (replied my Father) "I fancy the Servants are returned; (said I) I think I hear Mary going to the Door." "I'm glad of it" (cried my Father) "for I long to know who it is."

---

1 Pretentious and stilted terms to describe a family conversation in a rural cottage.

I was right in my Conjecture, for Mary instantly entering the Room, informed us that a young Gentleman and his Servant were at the Door, who had lossed their way, were very cold and begged leave to warm themselves by our fire.

"Wont you admit them?" (said I) "You have no objection, my Dear?" (said my Father.) "None in the World." (replied my Mother.)

Mary, without waiting for any further commands immediately left the room and quietly returned introducing the most beauteous and amiable Youth, I had ever beheld. The servant, She kept to herself.

My natural Sensibility had already been greatly affected by the sufferings of the unfortunate Stranger and no sooner did I first behold him, than I felt that on him the happiness or Misery of my future Life must depend.—

adeiu
Laura

Letter 6th
Laura to Marianne

The noble Youth informed us that his name was Lindsay—. for particular reasons however I shall conceal it under that of Talbot. He told us that he was the son of an English Baronet, that his Mother had been many years no more and that he had a Sister of the middle size. "My Father (he continued) is a mean and mercenary wretch—it is only to such particular freinds as this Dear Party that I would thus betray his failings—. Your Virtues my amiable Polydore (addressing himself to my father) yours Dear Claudia[1] and yours my Charming Laura call on me to repose in you my Confidence." We bowed. "My Father, seduced by the false glare of Fortune and the Deluding Pomp of Title, insisted on my giving my hand to Lady Dorothea.[2] No never exclaimed I. Lady Dorothea is lovely and Engaging; I prefer no woman to

---

1 Calling strangers by their Christian names is an outrageous breach of etiquette. Their names are also outlandish. "Polydore" was confined to romances and dramas, and "Claudia" was rare in the eighteenth century.

2 As a baronet, ranking below the lowest grade of the peerage, Sir Edward Lindsay would welcome a marriage between his son and Lady Dorothea; as the style of her name reveals, she must be the daughter of a duke, marquess, or earl.

her; but Know Sir, that I scorn to marry her in compliance with your Wishes. No! Never shall it be said that I obliged my Father." We all admired the noble Manliness of his reply. He continued.

"Sir Edward was surprised; he had perhaps little expected to meet with so spirited an opposition to his will. 'Where Edward in the name of Wonder (said he) did you pick up this unmeaning Gibberish? You have been studying Novels I suspect.' I scorned to answer: it would have been beneath my Dignity. I mounted my Horse and followed by my faithful William set forwards for my Aunts.

"My Father's house is situated in Bedfordshire, my Aunt's in Middlesex,[1] and tho' I flatter myself with being a tolerable proficient in Geography, I know not how it happened, but I found myself entering this beautiful Vale which I find is in South Wales, when I had expected to have reached my Aunts.

"After having wandered some time on the Banks of the Uske without knowing which way to go, I began to lament my cruel Destiny in the bitterest and most pathetic Manner. It was now perfectly Dark, not a single Star was there to direct my steps, and I know not what might have befallen me had I not at length discerned thro' the solemn Gloom that surrounded me a distant Light, which as I approached it, I discovered to be the chearfull Blaze of your fire. Impelled by the combination of Misfortunes under which I laboured, namely Fear, Cold and Hunger I hesitated not to ask admittance which at length I have gained; and now my Adorable Laura (continued he taking my Hand) when may I hope to receive that reward of all the painfull sufferings I have undergone during the course of my Attachment to you, to which I have ever aspired? Oh! when will you reward me with Yourself?"

"This instant, Dear and Amiable Edward." (replied I.). We were immediately united by my Father, who tho' he had never taken orders had been bred to the Church.[2]

adeiu
Laura.

---

1 Bedfordshire, a county to the northwest of London, is only some thirty miles north of Middlesex. Instead of travelling this distance south to his aunt's house, Edward has travelled about one hundred miles west to the Vale of Usk.

2 Laura's Irish father was presumably a Roman Catholic, as she was educated in a French convent. Despite being "bred to the Church," or raised in the Roman Catholic religion, he could not have conducted Laura and Edward's marriage ceremony since he is not a clergyman (he has not "taken orders").

Letter 7th
Laura to Marianne

We remained but a few Days after our Marriage, in the Vale of Uske—. After taking an affecting Farewell of my Father, my Mother and my Isabel, I accompanied Edward to his Aunt's in Middlesex. Philippa received us both with every expression of affectionate Love. My arrival was indeed a most agreable surprize to her as she had not only been totally ignorant of my Marriage with her Nephew, but had never even had the slightest idea of there being such a person in the World.

Augusta, the sister of Edward was on a visit to her when we arrived. I found her exactly what her Brother had described her to be—of the middle size. She received me with equal surprise though not with equal Cordiality, as Philippa. There was a Disagreable Coldness and Forbidding Reserve in her reception of me which was equally Distressing and Unexpected. None of that interesting Sensibility or amiable Simpathy in her Manners and Address to me, when we first met which should have Distinguished our introduction to each other—. Her Language was neither warm, nor affectionate, her expressions of regard were neither animated nor cordial; her arms were not opened to receive me to her Heart, tho' my own were extended to press her to mine.

A short Conversation between Augusta and her Brother, which I accidentally overheard encreased my Dislike to her, and convinced me that her Heart was no more formed for the soft ties of Love than for the endearing intercourse of Freindship.

"But do you think that my Father will ever be reconciled to this imprudent connection?" (said Augusta.)

"Augusta (replied the noble Youth) I thought you had a better opinion of me, than to imagine I would so abjectly degrade myself as to consider my Father's Concurrence in any of my Affairs, either of Consequence or concern to me—. Tell me Augusta tell me with sincerity; did you ever know me consult his inclinations or follow his Advice in the least trifling Particular since the age of fifteen?"

"Edward (replied she) you are surely too diffident in your own praise—. Since you were fifteen only!—My Dear Brother since you were five years old, I entirely acquit you of ever having willingly contributed to the Satisfaction of your Father. But still I am not without apprehensions of your being shortly obliged to degrade yourself in your own eyes by seeking a Support for your Wife in the Generosity of Sir Edward."

"Never, never Augusta will I so demean myself. (said Edward). Support! What support will Laura want which she can receive from him?"

"Only those very insignificant ones of Victuals and Drink." (answered she.)

"Victuals and Drink! (replied my Husband in a most nobly contemptuous Manner) and dost thou then imagine that there is no other support for an exalted Mind (such as is my Laura's) than the mean and indelicate employment of Eating and Drinking?"

"None that I know of, so efficacious." (returned Augusta)

"And did you then never feel the pleasing Pangs of Love, Augusta? (replied my Edward). Does it appear impossible to your vile and corrupted Palate, to exist on Love? Can you not conceive the Luxury of living in every Distress that Poverty can inflict, with the object of your tenderest affection?"

"You are too ridiculous (said Augusta) to argue with; perhaps however you may in time be convinced that...."

Here I was prevented from hearing the remainder of her Speech, by the appearance of a very Handsome young Woman, who was ushured into the Room at the Door of which I had been listening. On hearing her announced by the Name of "Lady Dorothea", I instantly quitted my Post and followed her into the Parlour, for I well remembered that she was the Lady, proposed as a Wife for my Edward by the Cruel and Unrelenting Baronet.

Altho' Lady Dorothea's visit was nominally to Philippa and Augusta, yet I have some reason to imagine that (acquainted with the Marriage and arrival of Edward) to see me was a principal motive to it.

I soon perceived that tho' Lovely and Elegant in her Person and tho' Easy and Polite in her Address, she was of that inferior order of Beings with regard to Delicate Feeling, tender Sentiments, and refined Sensibility, of which Augusta was one.

She staid but half an hour and neither in the Course of her Visit, confided to me any of her Secret thoughts, nor requested me to confide in her, any of Mine. You will easily imagine therefore my Dear Marianne that I could not feel any ardent Affection or very sincere Attachment for Lady Dorothea.

Adeiu

Laura.

Letter 8th

Laura to Marianne, in continuation

Lady Dorothea had not left us long before another visitor as unexpected a one as her Ladyship, was announced. It was Sir Edward, who informed by Augusta of her Brother's marriage, came doubtless to reproach him for having dared to unite himself to me without his Knowledge. But Edward foreseeing his design, approached him with heroic fortitude as soon as he entered the Room, and addressed him in the following Manner.

"Sir Edward, I know the motive of your Journey here—You come with the base Design of reproaching me for having entered into an indissoluble engagement with my Laura without your Consent—But Sir, I glory in the Act—. It is my greatest boast that I have incurred the Displeasure of my Father!"

So saying, he took my hand and whilst Sir Edward, Philippa, and Augusta were doubtless reflecting with Admiration on his undaunted Bravery, led me from the Parlour to his Father's Carriage which yet remained at the Door and in which we were instantly conveyed from the pursuit of Sir Edward.

The Postilions[1] had at first received orders only to take the London road; as soon as we had sufficiently reflected However, we ordered them to Drive to M——. the seat of Edward's most particular freind, which was but a few miles distant.

At M——. we arrived in a few hours; and on sending in our names were immediately admitted to Sophia, the Wife of Edward's freind. After having been deprived during the course of 3 weeks of a real freind (for such I term your Mother) imagine my transports at beholding one, most truly worthy of the Name. Sophia was rather above the middle size; most elegantly formed. A soft Languor spread over her lovely features, but increased their Beauty—. It was the Charectaristic of her Mind—. She was all Sensibility and Feeling. We flew into each others arms and after having exchanged vows of mutual Freindship for the rest of our Lives, instantly unfolded to each other the most inward Secrets of our Hearts—. We were interrupted in this Delightfull Employment by the entrance of Augustus, (Edward's freind) who was just returned from a solitary ramble.

Never did I see such an affecting Scene as was the meeting of Edward and Augustus.

---

1 See p. 53, note 4.

"My Life! my Soul!" (exclaimed the former). "My Adorable Angel!" (replied the latter) as they flew into each other's arms.— It was too pathetic[1] for the feelings of Sophia and myself—We fainted Alternately on a Sofa.[2]

Adeiu
Laura

Letter the 9th—From the Same to the Same

Towards the close of the Day we received the following Letter from Philippa.

"Sir Edward is greatly incensed by your abrupt departure; he has taken back Augusta with him to Bedfordshire. Much as I wish to enjoy again your charming Society, I cannot determine to Snatch you from that, of such dear and deserving Freinds— When your Visit to them is terminated, I trust you will return to the arms of your

Philippa."

We returned a suitable answer to this affectionate Note and after thanking her for her kind invitation assured her that we would certainly avail ourselves of it, whenever we might have no other place to go to. Tho' certainly nothing could to any reasonable Being, have appeared more satisfactory, than so gratefull a reply to her invitation, yet I know not how it was, but she was certainly capricious enough to be displeased with our behaviour and in a few weeks after, either to revenge our Conduct, or releive her own solitude, married a young and illiterate Fortune-hunter. This imprudent Step (tho' we were sensible that it would probably deprive us of that fortune which Philippa had ever taught us to expect) could not on our own accounts, excite from our exalted Minds a single sigh; yet fearfull lest it might prove a source of endless misery to the deluded Bride, our trembling Sensibility

---

1 "Affecting the passions; passionate; moving" (Johnson): a key term in the discourse of sensibility. The modern sense of arousing feelings of pity or sympathy was also becoming current.
2 An allusion to a stage-direction in the play-within-the play in Sheridan's burlesque drama, *The Critic* (1781): "They faint alternately in each others arms" (Act 3, Scene 1). Sheridan, in turn, is parodying the discovery scene in the second act of John Home's tragedy *Douglas* (1756).

was greatly affected when we were first informed of the Event. The affectionate Entreaties of Augustus and Sophia that we would for ever consider their House as our Home, easily prevailed on us to determine never more to leave them—. In the Society of my Edward and this Amiable Pair, I passed the happiest moments of my Life; Our time was most delightfully spent, in mutual Protestations of Freindship, and in vows of unalterable Love, in which we were secure from being interrupted, by intruding and disagreable Visitors, as Augustus and Sophia had on their first Entrance in the Neighbourhood, taken due care to inform the surrounding Families, that as their Happiness centered wholly in themselves, they wished for no other society. But alas! my Dear Marianne such Happiness as I then enjoyed was too perfect to be lasting. A most severe and unexpected Blow at once destroyed every Sensation of Pleasure. Convinced as you must be from what I have already told you concerning Augustus and Sophia, that there never were a happier Couple, I need not I imagine inform you that their union had been contrary to the inclinations of their Cruel and Mercenary Parents; who had vainly endeavoured with obstinate Perseverance to force them into a Marriage with those whom they had ever abhorred; but with an Heroic Fortitude worthy to be related and Admired, they had both, constantly refused to submit to such despotic Power.

After having so nobly disentangled themselves from the Shackles of Parental Authority, by a Clandestine Marriage,[1] they were determined never to forfeit the good opinion they had gained in the World, in so doing, by accepting any proposals of reconciliation that might be offered them by their Fathers—to this farther tryal of their noble independence however they never were exposed.

They had been married but a few months when our visit to them commenced during which time they had been amply supported by a considerable Sum of Money which Augustus had gracefully purloined from his Unworthy father's Escritoire,[2] a few days before his union with Sophia.

By our arrival their Expenses were considerably encreased tho' their means for supplying them were then nearly exhausted. But

---

1 An allusion to the title of a comedy by George Colman the elder and David Garrick, *The Clandestine Marriage* (1766).
2 A writing-desk with drawers.

they, Exalted Creatures!, scorned to reflect a moment on their pecuniary Distresses and would have blushed at the idea of paying their Debts.[1]—Alas! what was their Reward for such disinterested Behaviour! The beautifull Augustus was arrested and we were all undone. Such perfidious Treachery in the merciless perpetrators of the Deed will shock your gentle nature Dearest Marianne as much as it then affected the Delicate Sensibility of Edward, Sophia, your Laura, and of Augustus himself. To compleat such unparalelled Barbarity we were informed that an Execution in the House[2] would shortly take place. Ah! what could we do but what we did! We sighed and fainted on the Sofa.

Adeiu

Laura

Letter 10th
Laura in continuation

When we were somewhat recovered from the overpowering Effusions of our Greif, Edward desired that we would consider what was the most prudent step to be taken in our unhappy situation while he repaired to his imprisoned freind to lament over his misfortunes. We promised that we would, and he set forwards on his Journey to Town. During his Absence we faithfully complied with his Desire and after the most mature Deliberation, at length agreed that the best thing we could do was to leave the House; of which we every moment expected the Officers of Justice[3] to take possession. We waited therefore with the greatest impatience, for the return of Edward in order to impart to him the result of our Deliberations—. But no Edward appeared—. In vain did we count the tedious Moments of his Absence—in vain did we weep—in vain even did we sigh—no Edward returned—. This was too cruel, too unexpected a Blow to our Gentle Sensibility—. we could not support it—we could only faint—. At length collecting all the Resolution I was Mistress of, I arose and

---

1   The satire is directed at the wealthy, who were apt to leave debts to merchants, tradesmen, etc. unpaid for lengthy periods of time, whereas "debts of honour" incurred in gambling would be paid at once.

2   The seizure of goods, on the order of creditors; the goods would be sold and the proceeds used to pay outstanding debts. JA is punning on the word "Execution," juxtaposing it with "Barbarity."

3   The sheriff's officers, enforcing the execution of the creditors' writ.

after packing up some necessary Apparel for Sophia and myself, I dragged her to a Carriage I had ordered and we instantly set out for London. As the Habitation of Augustus was within twelve miles of Town, it was not long e'er we arrived there, and no sooner had we entered Holbourn[1] than letting down one of the Front Glasses[2] I enquired of every decent-looking Person that we passed "If they had seen my Edward"?

But as we drove too rapidly to allow them to answer my repeated Enquiries, I gained little, or indeed, no information concerning him. "Where am I to Drive?" said the Postilion. "To Newgate[3] Gentle Youth (replied I), to see Augustus." "Oh! no, no, (exclaimed Sophia) I cannot go to Newgate; I shall not be able to support the sight of my Augustus in so cruel a confinement—my feelings are sufficiently shocked by the *recital*, of his Distress, but to behold it will overpower my Sensibility." As I perfectly agreed with her in the Justice of her Sentiments the Postilion was instantly directed to return into the Country. You may perhaps have been somewhat surprised my Dearest Marianne, that in the Distress I then endured, destitute of any Support, and unprovided with any Habitation, I should never once have remembered my Father and Mother or my paternal Cottage in the Vale of Uske. To account for this seeming forgetfullness I must inform you of a trifling Circumstance concerning them which I have as yet never mentioned—. The death of my Parents a few weeks after my Departure, is the circumstance I allude to. By their decease I became the lawfull Inheritress of their House and Fortune. But alas! the House had never been their own and their Fortune had only been an Annuity on their own Lives.[4]— Such is the Depravity of the World! To your Mother I should have returned with Pleasure, should have been happy to have introduced to her, my Charming Sophia and should with Chearfullness have passed the remainder of my Life in their dear Society

---

1   Holborn, both a district of London and the name of a principal route by which travellers entered the City from the west. Laura has to look out for "decent-looking" inhabitants, since Holborn was not favoured by fashionable residents.

2   Carriage windows, which could be opened and closed.

3   The notorious London prison, which features in many eighteenth-century novels.

4   An annual return on capital, which ceased with the death of the recipients.

in the Vale of Uske, had not one obstacle to the execution of so agreable a Scheme, intervened; which was the Marriage and Removal of your Mother to a Distant part of Ireland. Adeiu.

Laura.

Letter 11th
Laura in continuation

"I have a Relation in Scotland (said Sophia to me as we left London) who I am certain would not hesitate in receiving me." "Shall I order the Boy to drive there?" said I—but instantly recollecting myself, exclaimed, "Alas I fear it will be too long a Journey for the Horses."[1] Unwilling however to act only from my own inadequate Knowledge of the Strength and Abilities of Horses, I consulted the Postilion, who was entirely of my Opinion concerning the Affair. We therefore determined to change Horses at the next Town and to travel Post[2] the remainder of the Journey. —. When we arrived at the last Inn we were to stop at, which was but a few miles from the House of Sophia's Relation, unwilling to intrude our Society on him unexpected and unthought of, we wrote a very elegant and well-penned Note to him containing an Account of our Destitute and melancholy Situation, and of our intention to spend some months with him in Scotland. As soon as we had dispatched this Letter, we immediately prepared to follow it in person and were stepping into the Carriage for that Purpose when our Attention was attracted by the Entrance of a coroneted Coach and 4[3] into the Inn-yard. A Gentleman considerably advanced in years, descended from it—. At his first Appearance my Sensibility was wonderfully affected and e'er I had gazed at him a 2d time, an instinctive Sympathy whispered to my Heart, that he was my Grandfather.

---

1 A journey of some 300 miles, from London to the Scottish border, was far more than hired horses would travel. Instead, as the postilion recommends, the horses would be left at a staging post, where fresh horses would be supplied.

2 A rapid but expensive means of transport. By changing horses at each stage the travellers could continue day and night, arriving in Scotland in about three days.

3 Both the coronet and the four horses, rather than two, are status symbols. The coronet, an emblem on the carriage in the form of a crown, indicates that the owner is a peer.

Convinced that I could not be mistaken in my conjecture I instantly sprang from the Carriage I had just entered, and following the Venerable Stranger into the Room he had been shewn to, I threw myself on my knees before him and besought him to acknowledge me as his Grand-Child.—He started, and after having attentively examined my features, raised me from the Ground and throwing his Grand-fatherly arms around my Neck, exclaimed, "Acknowledge thee! Yes dear resemblance of my Laurina and my Laurina's Daughter, sweet image of my Claudia and my Claudia's Mother, I do acknowledge thee as the Daughter of the one and the Grandaughter of the other." While he was thus tenderly embracing me, Sophia astonished at my precipitate Departure, entered the Room in search of me—. No sooner had she caught the eye of the venerable Peer, than he exclaimed with every mark of Astonishment—"Another Grandaughter! Yes, yes, I see you are the Daughter of my Laurina's eldest Girl; Your resemblance to the beauteous Matilda sufficiently proclaims it." "Oh!" replied Sophia, "when I first beheld you the instinct of Nature whispered me that we were in some degree related—But whether Grandfathers, or Grandmothers, I could not pretend to determine." He folded her in his arms, and whilst they were tenderly embracing, the Door of the Apartment opened and a most beautifull Young Man appeared. On perceiving him Lord St Clair started and retreating back a few paces, with uplifted Hands, said, "Another Grand-child! What an unexpected Happiness is this! to discover in the space of 3 minutes, as many of my Descendants! This, I am certain is Philander the son of my Laurina's 3d Girl the amiable Bertha; there wants now but the presence of Gustavus to compleat the Union of my Laurina's Grand-Children."

"And here he is; (said a Gracefull Youth who that instant entered the room) here is the Gustavus you desire to see. I am the son of Agatha your Laurina's 4th and Youngest Daughter."[1] "I see you are indeed; replied Lord St. Clair—But tell me (continued he looking fearfully towards the Door) tell me, have I any other Grand-Children in the House." "None my Lord." "Then I will provide for you all without farther delay—Here are 4 Banknotes

---

1 Laura's grandfather, Lord St. Clair, the Scottish peer first mentioned in letter the third, is thus found to have had four illegitimate daughters by Laurina, the Italian opera girl: Claudia, the mother of Laura; Matilda, the mother of Sophia; Bertha, the mother of Philander; and Agatha, the mother of Gustavus.

of 50£ each—Take them and remember I have done the Duty of a Grandfather—." He instantly left the Room and immediately afterwards the House.

Adeiu.
Laura.

Letter the 12th
Laura in continuation

You may imagine how greatly we were surprized by the sudden departure of Lord St. Clair—. "Ignoble Grandsire!" exclaimed Sophia. "Unworthy Grand-father!" said I, and instantly fainted in each other's arms. How long we remained in this situation I know not; but when we recovered we found ourselves alone, without either Gustavus, Philander, or the Bank-notes. As we were deploring our unhappy fate, the Door of the Apartment opened and "Macdonald" was announced. He was Sophia's cousin. The haste with which he came to our releif so soon after the receipt of our Note, spoke so greatly in his favour that I hesitated not to pronounce him at first sight, a tender and simpathetic Freind. Alas! he little deserved the name—for though he told us that he was much concerned at our Misfortunes, yet by his own account it appeared that the perusal of them, had neither drawn from him a single sigh, nor induced him to bestow one curse on our vindictive Stars. —. He told Sophia that his Daughter depended on her returning with him to Macdonald-Hall, and that as his Cousin's freind he should be happy to see me there also. To Macdonald-Hall, therefore we went, and were received with great kindness by Janetta the daughter of Macdonald,[1] and the Mistress of the Mansion. Janetta was then only fifteen; naturally well disposed, endowed with a susceptible Heart, and a simpathetic Disposition, she might, had these amiable Qualities been properly encouraged, have been an ornament to human Nature; but unfortunately her Father possessed not a soul sufficiently exalted to admire so promising a Disposition, and had endeavoured by every means in his power to prevent its encreasing with her Years. He had actually so far extinguished the natural noble Sensibility of her Heart, as to prevail on her to accept an offer from a young Man of his Recommendation. They were to be married in a few

---

1 Matilda, Lord St. Clair's eldest daughter, married a Scotsman named Macdonald, the former owner of Macdonald-Hall. Their son, Sophia's cousin, is the current owner.

Months, and Graham, was in the House when we arrived. *We* soon saw through his Character—. He was just such a Man as one might have expected to be the choice of Macdonald. They said he was Sensible, well-informed, and Agreable; we did not pretend to Judge of such trifles, but as we were convinced he had no soul, that he had never read the Sorrows of Werter,[1] and that his Hair bore not the least resemblance to auburn, we were certain that Janetta could feel no affection for him, or at least that she ought to feel none. The very circumstance of his being her father's choice too, was so much in his disfavour, that had he been deserving her, in every other respect yet *that* of itself ought to have been a sufficient reason in the Eyes of Janetta for rejecting him. These considerations we were determined to represent to her in their proper light and doubted not of meeting with the desired Success from one naturally so well disposed, whose errors in the Affair had only arisen from a want of proper confidence in her own opinion, and a suitable contempt of her father's. We found her indeed all that our warmest wishes could have hoped for; we had no difficulty to convince her that it was impossible she could love Graham, or that it was her Duty to disobey her Father; the only thing at which she rather seemed to hesitate was our assertion that she must be attached to some other Person. For some time, she persevered in declaring that she knew no other young Man for whom she had the smallest Affection; but upon explaining the impossibility of such a thing she said that she beleived she *did like* Captain M'Kenzie better than any one she knew besides. This confession satisfied us and after having enumerated the good Qualites of M'Kenzie and assured her that she was violently in love with him, we desired to know whether he had ever in anywise declared his Affection to her.

"So far from having ever declared it, I have no reason to imagine that he has ever felt any for me." said Janetta. "That he certainly adores you (replied Sophia) there can be no doubt—. The Attachment must be reciprocal—. Did he never gaze on you with Admiration—tenderly press your hand—drop an involantary tear—and leave the room abruptly?" "Never (replied She) that I remember—he has always left the room indeed when his visit has been ended, but has never gone away particularly abruptly or

---

1 Goethe's epistolary novel, *The Sorrows of Young Werther*, had been hugely popular and influential since its first publication in 1774. Its hero, hopelessly in love with Lotte, who is engaged to another man, personifies sensibility and delicate feelings. Eventually, he commits suicide.

without making a bow." "Indeed my Love (said I) you must be mistaken—: for it is absolutely impossible that he should ever have left you but with, Confusion, Despair, and Precipitation—. Consider but for a moment Janetta, and you must be convinced how absurd it is to suppose that he could ever make a Bow, or behave like any other Person." Having settled this Point to our satisfaction, the next we took into consideration was, to determine in what manner we should inform M'Kenzie of the favourable Opinion Janetta entertained of him. —. We at length agreed to acquaint him with it by an anonymous Letter which Sophia drew up in the following Manner.

"Oh! happy Lover of the beautifull Janetta, oh! enviable Possessor of *her* Heart whose hand is destined to another, why do you thus delay a confession of your Attachment to the amiable Object of it? Oh! consider that a few weeks will at once put an end to every flattering Hope that you may now entertain, by uniting the unfortunate Victim of her father's Cruelty to the execrable and detested Graham.

"Alas! why do you thus so cruelly connive at the projected Misery of her and of yourself by delaying to communicate that scheme which has doubtless long possessed your imagination? A secret Union will at once secure the felicity of both."

The amiable M'Kenzie, whose modesty as he afterwards assured us had been the only reason of his having so long concealed the violence of his affection for Janetta, on receiving this Billet[1] flew on the wings of Love to Macdonald-Hall, and so powerfully pleaded his Attachment to her who inspired it, that after a few more private interviews, Sophia and I experienced the Satisfaction of seeing them depart for Gretna-Green,[2] which they chose for the celebration of their Nuptials, in preference to any other place although it was at a considerable distance from Macdonald-Hall.

Adeiu—

Laura—

---

1 Note.
2 A town in southern Scotland, just north of the border. Because Lord Hardwicke's Marriage Act of 1753, which required parental consent for marriages between those under 21, did not apply to Scotland, Gretna Green had become a favourite destination for eloping couples. It is, of course, ludicrous for Janetta and M'Kenzie to get married there, since they are already in Scotland and thus have no need to elope at all.

Letter the 13th
Laura in Continuation

They had been gone nearly a couple of Hours, before either Macdonald or Graham had entertained any suspicion of the affair—. And they might not even then have suspected it, but for the following little Accident. Sophia happening one Day to open a private Drawer in Macdonald's Library with one of her own keys, discovered that it was the Place where he kept his Papers of consequence and amongst them some bank notes of considerable amount. This discovery she imparted to me; and having agreed together that it would be a proper treatment of so vile a Wretch as Macdonald to deprive him of Money, perhaps dishonestly gained, it was determined that the next time we should either of us happen to go that way, we would take one or more of the Bank notes from the drawer. This well-meant Plan we had often successfully put in Execution; but alas! on the very day of Janetta's Escape, as Sophia was majestically removing the 5th Bank-note from the Drawer to her own purse, she was suddenly most impertinently interrupted in her employment by the entrance of Macdonald himself, in a most abrupt and precipitate Manner. Sophia (who though naturally all winning sweetness could when occasions demanded it call forth the Dignity of her Sex) instantly put on a most forbiding look, and darting an angry frown on the undaunted Culprit, demanded in a haughty tone of voice "Wherefore her retirement was thus insolently broken in on?" The unblushing Macdonald without even endeavouring to exculpate himself from the crime he was charged with, meanly endeavoured to reproach Sophia with ignobly defrauding him of his Money ... The dignity of Sophia was wounded; "Wretch (exclaimed she, hastily replacing the Bank-note in the Drawer) how darest thou to accuse me of an Act, of which the bare idea makes me blush?" The base wretch was still unconvinced and continued to upbraid the justly-offended Sophia in such opprobious Language, that at length he so greatly provoked the gentle sweetness of her Nature, as to induce her to revenge herself on him by informing him of Janetta's Elopement, and of the active Part we had both taken in the Affair. At this period of their Quarrel I entered the Library and was as you may imagine equally offended as Sophia at the ill-grounded Accusations of the malevolent and contemptible Macdonald. "Base Miscreant! (cried I) how canst thou thus undauntedly endeavour to sully the spotless reputation of such bright Excellence? Why dost thou not suspect *my* innocence as soon?"

"Be satisfied Madam" (replied he) "I *do* suspect it, and therefore must desire that you will both leave this House in less than half an hour."

"We shall go willingly; (answered Sophia) our hearts have long detested thee, and nothing but our freindship for thy Daughter could have induced us to remain so long beneath thy roof."

"Your Freindship for my Daughter has indeed been most powerfully exerted by throwing her into the arms of an unprincipled Fortune-hunter." (replied he)

"Yes, (exclaimed I) amidst every misfortune, it will afford us some consolation to reflect that by this one act of Freindship to Janetta, we have amply discharged every obligation that we have received from her father."

"It must indeed be a most gratefull reflection, to your exalted minds." (said he.)

As soon as we had packed up our wardrobe and valuables, we left Macdonald Hall, and after having walked about a mile and a half we sate down by the side of a clear limpid stream to refresh our exhausted limbs. The place was suited to meditation—. A Grove of full-grown Elms sheltered us from the East—. A Bed of full-grown Nettles from the West—. Before us ran the murmuring brook and behind us ran the turn-pike road. We were in a mood for contemplation and in a Disposition to enjoy so beautifull a spot. A mutual Silence which had for some time reigned between us, was at length broke by my exclaiming—"What a lovely Scene! Alas why are not Edward and Augustus here to enjoy its Beauties with us?"

"Ah! my beloved Laura (cried Sophia) for pity's sake forbear recalling to my remembrance the unhappy situation of my imprisoned Husband. Alas, what would I not give to learn the fate of my Augustus!—to know if he is still in Newgate, or if he is yet hung.[1]—But never shall I be able so far to conquer my tender sensibility as to enquire after him. Oh! do not I beseech you ever let me again hear you repeat his beloved Name—. It affects me too deeply—. I cannot bear to hear him mentioned, it wounds my feelings."

"Excuse me my Sophia for having thus unwillingly offended you—" replied I—and then changing the conversation, desired

---

1 An exaggerated fear. If Augustus had been found guilty of stealing a "considerable Sum of Money" (p. 103), he could have been hanged. He has, however, been arrested as a debtor, not as a thief; his creditors, not his father, have brought charges against him.

her to admire the Noble Grandeur of the Elms which Sheltered us from the Eastern Zephyr.[1] "Alas! my Laura (returned she) avoid so melancholy a subject, I intreat you—Do not again wound my Sensibility by Observations on those elms—. They remind me of Augustus—. He was like them, tall, magestic—he possessed that noble grandeur which you admire in them."

I was silent, fearfull lest I might any more unwillingly distress her by fixing on any other subject of conversation which might again remind her of Augustus.

"Why do you not speak my Laura? (said she after a short pause) I cannot support this silence—you must not leave me to my own reflections; they ever recur to Augustus."

"What a beautifull Sky! (said I) How charmingly is the azure varied by those delicate streaks of white!"

"Oh! my Laura (replied she hastily withdrawing her Eyes from a momentary glance at the sky) do not thus distress me by calling my Attention to an object which so cruelly reminds me of my Augustus's blue Sattin Waistcoat striped with white! In pity to your unhappy freind avoid a subject so distressing." What could I do? The feelings of Sophia were at that time so exquisite, and the tenderness she felt for Augustus so poignant that I had not power to start any other topic, justly fearing that it might in some unforseen manner again awaken all her sensibility by directing her thoughts to her Husband.—Yet to be silent would be cruel; She had intreated me to talk.

From this Dilemma I was most fortunately releived by an accident truly apropos;[2] it was the lucky overturning of a Gentleman's Phaeton,[3] on the road which ran murmuring behind us. It was a most fortunate Accident as it diverted the Attention of Sophia from the melancholy reflections which she had been before indulging. We instantly quitted our seats and ran to the rescue of those who but a few moments before had been in so elevated a situation as a fashionably high Phaeton, but who were now laid low and sprawling in the Dust—. "What an ample subject for reflection on the uncertain Enjoyments of this World, would not that Phaeton

---

1 A soft, mild, gentle wind or breeze.

2 That is, à propos; to the point, timely.

3 With their large wheels and high centres of gravity, gentlemen's phaetons were more readily overturned than other carriages. Since they were also favoured by young, fast drivers, they were especially likely to be involved in accidents. The lower, more stable kinds were favoured by ladies.

and the Life of Cardinal Wolsey afford a thinking Mind"![1] said I to Sophia as we were hastening to the field of Action.

She had not time to answer me, for every thought was now engaged by the horrid[2] Spectacle before us. Two Gentlemen most elegantly attired but weltering in their blood was what first struck our Eyes—we approached—they were Edward and Augustus— Yes dearest Marianne they were our Husbands. Sophia shreiked and fainted on the Ground—I screamed and instantly ran mad—. We remained thus mutually deprived of our Senses, some minutes, and on regaining them were deprived of them again—. For an Hour and a Quarter did we continue in this unfortunate Situation—Sophia fainting every moment and I running Mad as often—. At length a Groan from the hapless Edward (who alone retained any share of Life) restored us to ourselves—. Had we indeed before imagined that either of them lived, we should have been more sparing of our Greif—but as we had supposed when we first beheld them that they were no more, we knew that nothing could remain to be done but what we were about—. No sooner therefore did we hear my Edward's groan than postponing our Lamentations for the present, we hastily ran to the Dear Youth and kneeling on each side of him implored him not to die—. "Laura (said He fixing his now languid Eyes on me) I fear I have been overturned."

I was overjoyed to find him yet sensible—.

"Oh! tell me Edward (said I) tell me I beseech you before you die, what has befallen you since that unhappy Day in which Augustus was arrested and we were separated—"

"I will" (said he) and instantly fetching a Deep sigh, Expired—. Sophia immediately sunk again into a swoon—. *My* Greif was more audible. My Voice faltered, My Eyes assumed a vacant Stare, My face became as pale as Death, and my Senses were considerably impaired—.

"Talk not to me of Phaetons (said I, raving in a frantic, incoherent manner)—Give me a violin—. I'll play to him and sooth him in his melancholy Hours—Beware ye gentle Nymphs of Cupid's Thunderbolts, avoid the piercing Shafts of Jupiter[3]—

---

1 Thomas Wolsey, the powerful cardinal and archbishop who cherished papal aspirations during the reign of Henry VIII. His fall from favour and disgrace were frequently used to exemplify the dangers of pride.

2 Horrifying, a favourite term in Gothic fiction.

3 Laura is muddled in her madness. Cupid, the god of love, should have the shafts or arrows, and Jupiter the thunderbolts.

Look at that Grove of Firs—I see a Leg of Mutton—They told me Edward was not Dead; but they deceived me—they took him for a Cucumber—" Thus I continued wildly exclaiming on my Edward's Death—. For two Hours did I rave thus madly and should not then have left off, as I was not in the least fatigued, had not Sophia who was just recovered from her swoon, intreated me to consider that Night was now approaching and that the Damps began to fall. "And whither shall we go (said I) to shelter us from either"? "To that white Cottage." (replied she pointing to a neat Building which rose up amidst the Grove of Elms and which I had not before observed—) I agreed and we instantly walked to it—we knocked at the door—it was opened by an old Woman; on being requested to afford us a Night's Lodging, she informed us that her House was but small, that she had only two Bedrooms, but that However we should be wellcome to one of them. We were satisfied and followed the good Woman into the House where we were greatly cheered by the Sight of a comfortable fire—. She was a Widow and had only one Daughter, who was then just Seventeen—One of the best of ages;[1] but alas! she was very plain and her name was Bridget[2].... Nothing therefore could be expected from her ... she could not be supposed to possess either exalted Ideas, Delicate Feelings or refined Sensibilities—She was nothing more than a mere good-tempered, civil and obliging Young Woman; as such we could scarcely dislike her—she was only an Object of Contempt—.

Adeiu

Laura—

Letter the 14th
Laura in continuation

Arm yourself my amiable Young Freind with all the philosophy you are Mistress of; Summon up all the fortitude you possess, for Alas! in the perusal of the following Pages your sensibility will be

---

1 Cassandra Austen was then aged seventeen and five months, having celebrated her seventeenth birthday in January 1790.

2 An allusion to Richard Steele's *The Tender Husband* (1705), in which the heroine, Bridget Tipkin, finds her name objectionable. In place of Bridget, or its hated abbreviation Biddy, she favours "a Name that glides through half a dozen tender Syllables, as *Elismonda, Clidamira, Deidamia*; that runs upon Vowels off the Tongue, not hissing through one's Teeth or breaking them with Consonants" (Act 2, Scene 2).

most severely tried. Ah! what were the Misfortunes I had before experienced and which I have already related to you, to the one I am now going to inform you of! The Death of my Father my Mother, and my Husband though almost more than my gentle Nature could support, were trifles in comparison to the misfortune I am now proceeding to relate. The morning after our arrival at the Cottage, Sophia complained of a violent pain in her delicate limbs, accompanied with a disagreable Head-ake. She attributed it to a cold caught by her continual faintings in the open Air as the Dew was falling the Evening before. This I feared was but too probably the case; since how could it be otherwise accounted for that I should have escaped the same indisposition, but by supposing that the bodily Exertions I had undergone in my repeated fits of frenzy had so effectually circulated and warmed my Blood[1] as to make me proof against the chilling Damps of Night, whereas, Sophia lying totally inactive on the Ground must have been exposed to all their Severity. I was most seriously alarmed by her illness which trifling as it may appear to you, a certain instinctive Sensibility whispered me, would in the End be fatal to her.

Alas! my fears were but too fully justified; she grew gradually worse—and I daily became more alarmed for her.—At length she was obliged to confine herself solely to the Bed allotted us by our worthy Landlady—. Her disorder turned to a galloping Consumption[2] and in a few Days carried her off. Amidst all my Lamentations for her (and violent you may suppose they were) I yet received some consolation in the reflection of my having paid every Attention to her, that could be offered, in her illness. I had wept over her every Day—had bathed her sweet face with my tears and had pressed her fair Hands continually in mine—. "My beloved Laura (said she to me a few Hours before she died) take warning from my unhappy End and avoid the imprudent conduct which has occasioned it ... Beware of fainting-fits ... Though at the time they may be refreshing and Agreable yet beleive me they will in the end, if too often repeated and at

---

1 Knowingly learned medical discourse, drawing on theories of the circulation of the blood developed by William Harvey in the seventeenth century.

2 Rapidly developing lung disease, or tuberculosis. It was a common fate for sensitive heroines, for whom it was considered appropriate; it made its victims pale and interesting, fading away rather than dying in a more unpleasant manner.

improper seasons, prove destructive to your Constitution ... My fate will teach you this ... I die a Martyr to my greif for the loss of Augustus ... One fatal swoon has cost me my Life ... Beware of swoons Dear Laura.... A frenzy fit is not one quarter so pernicious; it is an exercise to the Body and if not too violent, is I dare say conducive to Health in its consequences—Run mad as often as you chuse; but do not faint—".

These were the last words she ever addressed to me ... It was her dieing Advice to her afflicted Laura, who has ever most faithfully adhered to it.

After having attended my lamented freind to her Early Grave, I immediately (tho' late at night) left the detested Village in which she died, and near which had expired my Husband and Augustus. I had not walked many yards from it before I was overtaken by a Stage-Coach, in which I instantly took a place, determined to proceed in it to Edinburgh, where I hoped to find some kind some pitying Freind who would receive and comfort me in my Afflictions.

It was so dark when I entered the Coach that I could not distinguish the Number of my Fellow-travellers; I could only perceive that they were Many. Regardless however of any thing concerning them, I gave myself up to my own sad Reflections. A general Silence prevailed—A Silence, which was by nothing interrupted but by the loud and repeated Snores of one of the Party.

"What an illiterate villain must that Man be! (thought I to myself) What a total Want of delicate refinement must he have, who can thus shock our senses by such a brutal Noise! He must I am certain be capable of every bad Action! There is no crime too black for such a Character!" Thus reasoned I within myself, and doubtless such were the reflections of my fellow travellers.

At length, returning Day enabled me to behold the unprincipled Scoundrel who had so violently disturbed my feelings. It was Sir Edward the father of my Deceased Husband. By his side, sate Augusta, and on the same seat with me were your Mother and Lady Dorothea. Imagine my Surprize at finding myself thus seated amongst my old Acquaintance. Great as was my astonishment, it was yet increased, when on looking out of Windows, I beheld the Husband of Philippa, with Philippa by his side, on the Coach-box,[1] and when on looking behind I beheld, Philander

---

1 An elevated seat in front of the stage-coach on which the driver sat; it was not intended for passengers.

and Gustavus in the Basket.[1] "Oh! Heavens, (exclaimed I) is it possible that I should so unexpectedly be surrounded by my nearest Relations and Connections"? These words rouzed the rest of the Party, and every eye was directed to the corner in which I sat. "Oh! my Isabel (continued I throwing myself, across Lady Dorothea into her arms) receive once more to your Bosom the unfortunate Laura. Alas! when we last parted in the Vale of Usk, I was happy in being united to the best of Edwards; I had then a Father and a Mother, and had never known misfortunes—But now deprived of every freind but you—"

"What! (interrupted Augusta) is my Brother dead then? Tell us I intreat you what is become of him?"

"Yes, cold and insensible Nymph, (replied I) that luckless Swain your Brother, is no more, and you may now glory in being the Heiress of Sir Edward's fortune."

Although I had always despised her from the Day I had overheard her conversation with my Edward, yet in civility I complied with hers and Sir Edward's intreaties that I would inform them of the whole melancholy Affair. They were greatly shocked—Even the obdurate Heart of Sir Edward and the insensible one of Augusta, were touched with Sorrow, by the unhappy tale. At the request of your Mother I related to them every other misfortune which had befallen me since we parted. Of the imprisonment of Augustus and the Absence of Edward—of our arrival in Scotland of our unexpected Meeting with our Grandfather and our cousins—of our visit to Macdonald-Hall—of the singular Service we there performed towards Janetta—of her Fathers ingratitude for it.... of his inhuman Behaviour, unaccountable suspicions, and barbarous treatment of us, in obliging us to leave the House.... of our Lamentations on the loss of Edward and Augustus and finally of the melancholy Death of my beloved Companion.

Pity and Surprise were strongly depictured in your Mother's Countenance, during the whole of my narration, but I am sorry to say, that to the eternal reproach of her Sensibility, the latter infinitely predominated. Nay, faultless as my Conduct had certainly been during the whole Course of my late Misfortunes and Adventures, she pretended to find fault with my Behaviour in

---

1 The back compartment on the outside of a stage-coach, intended primarily for luggage. The coach is thus grossly overloaded, with nine passengers in all, including five inside the coach and two beside the driver. It was designed to carry four to six people.

many of the situations in which I had been placed. As I was sensible myself, that I had always behaved in a manner which reflected Honour on my Feelings and Refinement, I paid little attention to what she said, and desired her to satisfy my Curiosity by informing me how she came there, instead of wounding my spotless reputation with unjustifiable Reproaches. As soon as she had complyed with my wishes in this particular and had given me an accurate detail of every thing that had befallen her since our separation (the particulars of which if you are not already acquainted with, your Mother will give you) I applied to Augusta for the same information respecting herself, Sir Edward and Lady Dorothea.

She told me that having a considerable taste for the Beauties of Nature, her curiosity to behold the delightful scenes it exhibited in that part of the World had been so much raised by Gilpin's Tour to the Highlands,[1] that she had prevailed on her Father to undertake a Tour to Scotland and had persuaded Lady Dorothea to accompany them. That they had arrived at Edinburgh a few Days before and from thence had made daily Excursions into the Country around in the Stage Coach they were then in, from one of which Excursions they were at that time returning. My next enquiries were concerning Philippa and her Husband, the latter of whom I learned having spent all her fortune, had recourse for subsistance to the talent in which, he had always most excelled, namely, Driving, and that having sold every thing which belonged to them except their Coach, had converted it into a Stage[2] and in order to be removed from any of his former Acquaintance, had driven it to Edinburgh from whence he went to Sterling[3] every other Day; That Philippa still retaining her affection for her ungratefull Husband, had followed him to Scotland and generally accompanied him in his little Excursions to Sterling. "It has only been to throw a little money into their Pockets (continued Augusta) that my Father has always travelled in their Coach to veiw the beauties of the Country since our arrival in Scotland—

---

1   William Gilpin's recently published *Observations, Relative Chiefly to Picturesque Beauty, Made in the Year 1766, On Several Parts of Great Britain; Particularly the High-Lands of Scotland* (1789).

2   A coach has two seats and can hold up to six people; a stage is a carriage used for public transport, with fees charged according to the distance travelled.

3   Stirling, a town in central Scotland, is some 36 miles northwest of Edinburgh, then the largest and most important Scottish city.

for it would certainly have been much more agreable to us, to visit the Highlands in a Postchaise than merely to travel from Edinburgh to Sterling and from Sterling to Edinburgh every other Day in a crouded and uncomfortable Stage."[1] I perfectly agreed with her in her sentiments on the Affair, and secretly blamed Sir Edward for thus sacrificing his Daughter's Pleasure for the sake of a ridiculous old Woman whose folly in marrying so young a Man ought to be punished. His Behaviour however was entirely of a peice with his general Character; for what could be expected from a Man who possessed not the smallest atom of Sensibility, who scarcely knew the meaning of Simpathy, and who actually snored—.

Adeiu
Laura.

Letter the 15th
Laura in continuation.

When we arrived at the town where we were to Breakfast, I was determined to speak with Philander and Gustavus, and to that purpose as soon as I left the Carriage, I went to the Basket and tenderly enquired after their Health, expressing my fears of the uneasiness of their Situation. At first they seemed rather confused at my Appearance dreading no doubt that I might call them to account for the money which our Grandfather had left me and which they had unjustly deprived me of, but finding that I mentioned nothing of the Matter, they desired me to step into the Basket as we might there converse with greater ease. Accordingly I entered and whilst the rest of the party were devouring Green tea[2] and buttered toast, we feasted ourselves in a more refined and Sentimental[3] Manner by a confidential Conversation. I informed them of every thing which had befallen me during the course of my Life, and at my request they related to me every incident of theirs.

---

1 Improvements to roads and coaches made travel into the Highlands of Scotland increasingly popular in the later eighteenth century.

2 Tea roasted as soon as it has been gathered, and thus not allowed to ferment.

3 Not recorded in Johnson's Dictionary, this became a fashionable word in the mid-eighteenth century and a key part of the discourse of sensibility, emphasizing the importance of "sentiments" (feelings and emotions), rather than rational thought.

"We are the sons as you already know, of the two youngest Daughters which Lord St. Clair had by Laurina an italian Opera-girl. Our mothers could neither of them exactly ascertain who were our Fathers; though it is generally beleived that Philander, is the son of one Philip Jones a Bricklayer and that my Father was Gregory Staves a Staymaker[1] of Edinburgh. This is however of little consequence, for as our Mothers were certainly never married to either of them, it reflects no Dishonour on our Blood, which is of a most ancient and unpolluted kind. Bertha (the Mother of Philander) and Agatha (my own Mother) always lived together. They were neither of them very rich; their united fortunes had originally amounted to nine thousand Pounds, but as they had always lived upon the principal of it, when we were fifteen it was diminished to nine Hundred. This nine Hundred, they always kept in a Drawer in one of the Tables which stood in our common sitting Parlour,[2] for the Convenience of having it always at Hand. Whether it was from this circumstance, of its being easily taken, or from a wish of being independent, or from an excess of Sensibility (for which we were always remarkable) I cannot now determine, but certain it is that when we had reached our 15th Year, we took the Nine Hundred Pounds and ran away. Having obtained this prize we were determined to manage it with eoconomy and not to spend it either with folly or Extravagance. To this purpose we therefore divided it into nine parcels, one of which we devoted to Victuals, the 2d to Drink, the 3d to House-keeping, the 4th to Carriages, the 5th to Horses, the 6th to Servants, the 7th to Amusements the 8th to Cloathes and the 9th to Silver Buckles.[3] Having thus arranged our Expences for two Months (for we expected to make the nine Hundred Pounds last as long) we hastened to London and had the good luck to spend it in 7 weeks and a Day which was 6 Days sooner than we had intended. As soon as we had thus happily disencumbered ourselves from the weight of so much Money, we began to think of returning to our Mothers, but accidentally hearing that they were both starved to Death, we gave over the design and determined to engage ourselves to some strolling Company of Players, as we

---

1 A maker of women's corsets ("stays").

2 A house of a reasonable size, including the Austens' rectory at Steven-ton, would typically contain two parlours: a common one, to which visi-tors would be admitted, and a private room, reserved for family use.

3 Expensive items for fastening shoes, worn by the wealthiest and most fashionable gentlemen.

had always a turn for the Stage.[1] Accordingly we offered our Services to one and were accepted; our Company was indeed rather small, as it consisted only of the Manager his Wife and ourselves, but there were fewer to pay and the only inconvenience attending it was the Scarcity of Plays which for want of People to fill the Characters, we could perform. —. We did not mind trifles however—. One of our most admired Performances was *Macbeth*, in which we were truly great. The Manager always played *Banquo* himself, his Wife my *Lady Macbeth*, I did the *Three Witches* and Philander acted *all the rest*. To say the truth this tragedy was not only the Best, but the only Play we ever performed; and after having acted it all over England, and Wales, we came to Scotland to exhibit it over the remainder of Great Britain. We happened to be quartered in that very Town, where you came and met your Grandfather—. We were in the Inn-yard when his Carriage entered and perceiving by the Arms to whom it belonged, and knowing that Lord St. Clair was our Grand-father, we agreed to endeavour to get something from him by discovering the Relationship—. You know how well it succeeded—. Having obtained the two Hundred Pounds, we instantly left the Town, leaving our Manager and his Wife to act *Macbeth* by themselves, and took the road to Sterling, where we spent our little fortunes with great *eclat*.[2] We are now returning to Edinburgh in order to get some preferment[3] in the Acting way; and such my Dear Cousin is our History."

I thanked the amiable Youth for his entertaining Narration, and after expressing my Wishes for their Welfare and Happiness, left them in their little Habitation and returned to my other Freinds who impatiently expected me.

My Adventures are now drawing to a close my dearest Marianne; at least for the present.

When we arrived at Edinburgh Sir Edward told me that as the Widow of his Son, he desired I would accept from his Hands of four Hundred a year. I graciously promised that I would, but could not help observing that the unsimpathetic Baronet offered it more on account of my being the Widow of Edward than in being the refined and Amiable Laura.

---

1   A deft pun on the senses of the word stage, the theatrical stage and the stagecoach, in which the two actors have just taken a "turn."

2   French for flamboyance and conspicuousness, or "to great effect."

3   Advancement, employment.

I took up my Residence in a romantic Village in the Highlands of Scotland, where I have ever since continued, and where I can uninterrupted by unmeaning Visits, indulge in a melancholy Solitude, my unceasing Lamentations for the Death of my Father, my Mother, my Husband and my Freind.

Augusta has been for several Years united to Graham the Man of all others most suited to her; she became acquainted with him during her stay in Scotland.

Sir Edward in hopes of gaining an Heir to his Title and Estate, at the same time married Lady Dorothea—. His wishes have been answered.

Philander and Gustavus, after having raised their reputation by their Performances in the Theatrical Line at Edinburgh, removed to Covent Garden, where they still Exhibit under the assumed names of *Lewis* and *Quick*.[1]

Philippa has long paid the Debt of Nature,[2] Her Husband however still continues to drive the Stage-Coach from Edinburgh to Sterling:—

Adeiu my Dearest Marianne—.

Laura—

Finis

June 13th 1790

---

1 William Thomas Lewis (c. 1746-1811) and John Quick (1748-1831), two celebrated comic actors at Covent Garden, one of the two principal London theatres. They were at the height of their fame when "Love and Freindship" was written.

2 Died, a clichéd euphemism.

Lesley Castle

To Henry Thomas Austen Esqre[1]—.

Sir

I am now availing myself of the Liberty you have frequently honoured me with of dedicating one of my Novels to you. That it is unfinished, I greive; yet fear that from me, it will always remain so; that as far as it is carried, it Should be so trifling and so unworthy of you, is

another concern to your obliged humble

Servant

The Author

Messrs Demand and Co—please to pay Jane Austen Spinster the sum of one hundred guineas on account of your Humbl. Servant.

H.T. Austen.

£ 105.0.0[2]

---

1 JA's fourth brother (1771-1850), who completed his BA at Oxford in the spring of 1792.
2 A mock-note, signed by Henry Austen, purportedly ordering his bank ("Messrs Demand and Co") to transfer to JA one hundred guineas (£105) in payment for her "Lesley Castle." Henry probably wrote this note at some time after he began his banking career in 1801.

Lesley Castle
an unfinished Novel in Letters.

Letter The first is from
Miss Margaret Lesley to Miss Charlotte Lutterell.
Lesley-Castle Janry. 3d — 1792.

My Brother has just left us. "Matilda (said he at parting) you and Margaret will I am certain take all the care of my dear little one, that she might have received from an indulgent, an affectionate an amiable Mother." Tears rolled down his Cheeks as he spoke these words—the remembrance of her, who had so wantonly disgraced the Maternal character and so openly violated the conjugal Duties, prevented his adding anything farther; he embraced his sweet Child and after saluting Matilda and Me hastily broke from us—and seating himself in his Chaise, pursued the road to Aberdeen.[1] Never was there a better young Man! Ah! how little did he deserve the misfortunes he has experienced in the Marriage State. So good a Husband to so bad a Wife!, for you know my dear Charlotte that the Worthless Louisa left him, her Child and reputation a few weeks ago in company with Danvers and dishonour.[2] Never was there a sweeter face, a finer form, or a less amiable Heart than Louisa owned! Her child already possesses the personal Charms of her unhappy Mother! May she inherit from her Father all his mental ones! Lesley is at present but five and twenty, and has already given himself up to melancholy and Despair; what a difference between him and his Father!, Sir George is 57 and still remains the Beau, the flighty stripling, the gay Lad, and sprightly Youngster, that his Son was really about five years back, and that *he* has affected to appear ever since my remembrance. While our father is fluttering about the Streets of London, gay, dissipated, and Thoughtless at the age of 57, Matilda and I continue secluded from Mankind in our old and Mouldering Castle, which is situated two miles from Perth[3] on a bold projecting Rock, and commands an extensive veiw of the Town and its delightful Environs. But tho' retired from almost all the World, (for we visit no one but the M'Leods, The M'Ken-

---

1 An ancient Scottish city, some 150 miles north of Edinburgh, on the north-east coast.
2 "Rakehelly Dishonor Esqre" (JA's note).
3 An ancient Scottish city in Perthshire, some fifty miles north of Edinburgh and 100 miles south of Aberdeen.

zies, the M'Phersons, the M'Cartneys, the M'donalds, The M'kinnons, the M'lellans, the M'kays, the Macbeths and the Macduffs) we are neither dull nor unhappy; on the contrary there never were two more lively, more agreable or more witty Girls, than we are; not an hour in the Day hangs heavy on our hands. We read, we work, we walk, and when fatigued with these Employments releive our spirits, either by a lively song, a graceful Dance, or by some smart bon-mot, and witty repartée.[1] We are handsome my dear Charlotte, very handsome and the greatest of our Perfections is, that we are entirely insensible of them ourselves. But why do I thus dwell on myself? Let me rather repeat the praise of our dear little Neice the innocent Louisa, who is at present sweetly smiling in a gentle Nap, as she reposes on the Sofa. The dear Creature is just turned of two years old; as handsome as tho' 2 and 20, as sensible as tho' 2 and 30, and as prudent as tho' 2 and 40. To convince you of this, I must inform you that she has a very fine complexion and very pretty features, that she already knows the two first Letters in the Alphabet, and that she never tears her frocks—. If I have not now convinced you of her Beauty, Sense and Prudence, I have nothing more to urge in support of my assertion, and you will therefore have no way of deciding the Affair but by coming to Lesley-castle, and by a personal acquaintance with Louisa, determine for yourself. Ah! my dear Freind, how happy should I be to see you within these venerable Walls! It is now four years since my removal from School has separated me from you; that two such tender Hearts, so closely linked together by the ties of simpathy and Freindship, should be so widely removed from each other, is vastly moving. I live in Perthshire, You in Sussex.[2] We might meet in London, were my Father disposed to carry me there, and were your Mother to be there at the same time. We might meet at Bath, at Tunbridge,[3] or any where else indeed, could we but be at the same place together. We have only to hope that such a period may arrive. My Father does not return to us till Autumn; my Brother will leave Scotland in a few Days; he is impatient to travel. Mistaken Youth!

---

1 French; a clever or witty utterance and a smart reply.

2 Almost at the opposite extremes of Great Britain, since Perthshire is in the east midlands of Scotland and Sussex on the south coast of England: the two counties are some five hundred miles apart.

3 Tunbridge Wells, a spa town in Kent, not far from Charlotte Lutterell's home in Sussex. A lesser rival to Bath, it had reached its peak of popularity in the mid-eighteenth century.

He vainly flatters himself that change of Air will heal the Wounds of a broken Heart! You will join with me I am certain my dear Charlotte, in prayers for the recovery of the unhappy Lesley's peace of Mind, which must ever be essential to that of your sincere freind

M. Lesley.

Letter the second.
From Miss C. Lutterell to Miss M. Lesley in answer
Glenford[1] Febry. 12

I have a thousand excuses to beg for having so long delayed thanking you my dear Peggy for your agreable Letter, which beleive me I should not have deferred doing, had not every moment of my time during the last five weeks been so fully employed in the necessary arrangements for my sisters Wedding, as to allow me no time to devote either to you or myself. And now what provokes me more than any thing else is that the Match is broke off, and all my Labour thrown away. Imagine how great the Dissapointment must be to me, when you consider that after having laboured both by Night and by Day, in order to get the Wedding dinner ready by the time appointed, after having roasted Beef, Broiled Mutton, and Stewed Soup[2] enough to last the new-married Couple through the Honey-moon, I had the mortification of finding that I had been Roasting, Broiling and Stewing both the Meat and Myself to no purpose. Indeed my dear Freind, I never remember suffering any vexation equal to what I experienced on last Monday when my Sister came running to me in the Store-room with her face as White as a Whipt syllabub,[3] and told me that Hervey had been thrown from his Horse, had fractured his Scull and was pronounced by his Surgeon to be in the most emminent Danger.

"Good God! (said I) you dont say so? why what in the name of Heaven will become of all the Victuals! We shall never be able to eat it while it is good. However, we'll call in the Surgeon to help us—. I shall be able to manage the Sir-loin myself; my Mother will eat the Soup, and You and the Doctor must finish the rest." Here I was interrupted, by seeing my poor Sister fall down

---

1 The name of the Lutterells' home in Sussex.
2 Made stock for soup by simmering meat and bones in water.
3 A cold dessert made with milk or cream, sherry, sugar, and lemons, whisked (or "whipt") together.

to appearance Lifeless upon one of the Chests, where we keep our Table linen. I immediately called my Mother and the Maids, and at last we brought her to herself again; as soon as ever she was sensible, she expressed a determination of going instantly to Henry, and was so wildly bent on this Scheme, that we had the greatest Difficulty in the World to prevent her putting it in execution; at last however more by Force than Entreaty we prevailed on her to go into her room; we laid her upon the Bed, and she continued for some Hours in the most dreadful Convulsions. My Mother and I continued in the room with her, and when any intervals of tolerable Composure in Eloisa would allow us, we joined in heartfelt lamentations on the dreadful Waste in our provisions which this Event must occasion, and in concerting some plan for getting rid of them. We agreed that the best thing we could do was to begin eating them immediately, and accordingly we ordered up the cold Ham and Fowls, and instantly began our Devouring Plan on them with great Alacrity. We would have persuaded Eloisa to have taken a Wing of a Chicken, but she would not be persuaded. She was however much quieter than she had been; the Convulsions she had before suffered having given way to an almost perfect Insensibility. We endeavoured to rouse her by every means in our power, but to no purpose. I talked to her of Henry. "Dear Eloisa (said I) there's no occasion for your crying so much about such a trifle. (for I was willing to make light of it in order to comfort her) I beg you would not mind it—. You see it does not vex me in the least; though perhaps *I* may suffer most from it after all; for I shall not only be obliged to eat up all the Victuals I have dressed already, but must if Hervey should recover (which however is not very likely) dress as much for you again; or should he die (as I suppose he will) I shall still have to prepare a Dinner for you whenever you marry any one else. So you see that tho' perhaps for the present it may afflict you to think of Henry's sufferings, Yet I dare say he'll die soon, and then his pain will be over and you will be easy, whereas my Trouble will last much longer for work as hard as I may, I am certain that the pantry cannot be cleared in less than a fortnight." Thus I did all in my power to console her, but without any effect, and at last as I saw that she did not seem to listen to me, I said no more, but leaving her with my Mother I took down the remains of The Ham and Chicken, and sent William to ask how Hervey did. He was not expected to live many Hours; he died the same day. We took all possible Care to break the Melancholy Event to Eloisa in the tenderest manner; yet in spite of every precaution, her Sufferings on hearing it were too violent for her reason, and she continued for many hours in a high Delirium. She is still extremely ill, and her Physicians are greatly afraid of her going into a Decline.[1] We are therefore preparing for Bristol,[2] where we mean to be in the course of the next Week. And now my dear Margaret let me talk a little of your affairs; and in the first place I must inform you that it is confidently reported, your Father is going to be married; I am very unwilling to beleive so unpleasing a report, and at the same time cannot wholly discredit it. I have written to my freind Susan Fitzgerald, for information concerning it, which as she is at present in Town, she will be very able to give me. I know not who is the Lady. I think your Brother is extremely right in the resolution he has taken of travelling, as it will perhaps contribute to obliterate from his remembrance, those disagreable Events, which have lately so much afflicted him—I am happy to find that tho' secluded from all the World, neither You nor Matilda are dull or unhappy—that you may never know what it is to be either is the Wish of your Sincerely Affectionate

C.L.

P.S. I have this instant received an answer from my freind Susan, which I enclose to you, and on which you will make your own reflections.

The enclosed Letter

My dear Charlotte

You could not have applied for information concerning the report of Sir George Lesleys Marriage, to any one better able to give it you than I am. Sir George is certainly married; I was myself present at the Ceremony, which you will not be surprised at when I subscribe myself your

Affectionate Susan Lesley

---

1 A wasting disease, such as tuberculosis. It was a term used when no precise diagnosis was possible.
2 Bristol Hotwells, a spa with a pump-room just outside Bristol, a port and the largest city in the west of England. It was a less fashionable but popular alternative to nearby Bath for pleasure-seekers and for invalids hoping to mend their health.

Letter the third
From Miss Margaret Lesley to Miss C. Lutterell
Lesley Castle February the 16th

I *have* made my own reflections on the letter you enclosed to me, my Dear Charlotte and I will now tell you what those reflections were. I reflected that if by this second Marriage Sir George should have a second family, our fortunes must be considerably diminished—that if his Wife should be of an extravagant turn, she would encourage him to persevere in that Gay and Dissipated way of Life to which little encouragement would be necessary, and which has I fear already proved but too detrimental to his health and fortune—that she would now become Mistress of those Jewels which once adorned our Mother, and which Sir George had always promised us—that if they did not come into Perthshire I should not be able to gratify my curiosity of beholding my Mother-in-law,[1] and that if they did, Matilda would no longer sit at the head of her Father's table[2]—. These my dear Charlotte were the melancholy reflections which crouded into my imagination after perusing Susan's letter to you, and which instantly occurred to Matilda when she had perused it likewise. The same ideas, the same fears, immediately occupied her Mind, and I know not which reflection distressed her most, whether the probable Diminution of our Fortunes, or her own Consequence. We both wish very much to know whether Lady Lesley is handsome and what is your opinion of her; as you honour her with the appellation of your freind, we flatter ourselves that she must be amiable. My Brother is already in Paris. He intends to quit it in a few Days, and to begin his route to Italy.[3] He writes in a most chearfull Manner, says that the air of France has greatly recovered both his Health and Spirits; that he has now entirely ceased to think of Louisa with any degree either of Pity or Affection, that he even feels himself obliged to her for her Elopement, as he

---

1 Stepmother.
2 As the elder sister, Matilda took precedence over Margaret and would sit at the head of the table, with her father at the foot to carve. Susan Lesley, however, as the second wife, would take precedence over both sisters.
3 Journeys to Paris and Italy form part of the classic Grand Tour of an English gentleman. The Tour was usually taken before marriage, as part of a man's education; here, Lesley is taking it as a consolation for the end of his marriage.

thinks it very good fun to be single again. By this, you may perceive that he has entirely regained that chearful Gaiety, and sprightly Wit, for which he was once so remarkable. When he first became acquainted with Louisa which was little more than three years ago, he was one of the most lively, the most agreable young Men of the age—. I beleive you never yet heard the particulars of his first acquaintance with her. It commenced at our cousin Colonel Drummond's; at whose house in Cumberland[1] he spent the Christmas, in which he attained the age of two and twenty. Louisa Burton was the Daughter of a distant Relation of Mrs. Drummond, who dieing a few Months before in extreme poverty, left his only Child then about eighteen to the protection of any of his Relations who would protect her. Mrs. Drummond was the only one who found herself so disposed—Louisa was therefore removed from a miserable Cottage in Yorkshire[2] to an elegant Mansion in Cumberland, and from every pecuniary Distress that Poverty could inflict, to every elegant Enjoyment that Money could purchase—. Louisa was naturally ill-tempered and Cunning; but she had been taught to disguise her real Disposition, under the appearance of insinuating Sweetness, by a father who but too well knew, that to be married, would be the only chance she would have of not being starved, and who flattered himself that with such an extroidinary share of personal beauty, joined to a gentleness of Manners, and an engaging address, she might stand a good chance of pleasing some young Man who might afford to marry a Girl without a Shilling. Louisa perfectly entered into her father's schemes and was determined to forward them with all her care and attention. By dint of Perseverance and Application, she had at length so thoroughly disguised her natural disposition under the mask of Innocence and Softness, as to impose upon every one who had not by a long and constant intimacy with her discovered her real Character. Such was Louisa when the hapless Lesley first beheld her at Drummond-house. His heart which (to use your favourite comparison) was as delicate as sweet and as tender as a Whipt-syllabub, could not resist her attractions. In a very few Days, he was falling in love, shortly after actually fell, and before he had known her a Month, he had married her. My Father was at first highly displeased at so hasty and imprudent a connection; but when he found that they did not mind it, he soon became perfectly reconciled to the match.

---

1 A county in the north-west of England, bordering Scotland.
2 A large county in the north-east of England, east of Cumberland.

The Estate near Aberdeen which my brother possesses by the bounty of his great Uncle independant of Sir George, was entirely sufficient to support him and my Sister in Elegance and Ease.[1] For the first twelvemonth, no one could be happier than Lesley, and no one more amiable to appearance than Louisa, and so plausibly did she act and so cautiously behave that tho' Matilda and I often spent several weeks together with them, yet we neither of us had any suspicion of her real Disposition. After the birth of Louisa however, which one would have thought would have strengthened her regard for Lesley, the mask she had so long supported was by degrees thrown aside, and as probably she then thought herself secure in the affection of her Husband (which did indeed appear if possible augmented by the birth of his Child) she seemed to take no pains to prevent that affection from ever diminishing. Our visits therefore to Dunbeath,[2] were now less frequent and by far less agreable than they used to be. Our absence was however never either mentioned or lamented by Louisa who in the society of young Danvers with whom she became acquainted at Aberdeen (he was at one of the Universities there,) felt infinitely happier than in that of Matilda and your freind, tho' there certainly never were pleasanter Girls than we are. You know the sad end of all Lesleys connubial happiness; I will not repeat it—. Adeiu my dear Charlotte; although I have not yet mentioned any thing of the matter, I hope you will do me the justice to beleive that I *think* and *feel*, a great deal for your Sisters affliction. I do not doubt but that the healthy air of the Bristol-downs[3] will intirely remove it, by erasing from her Mind the remembrance of Henry. I am my dear Charlotte yrs ever

ML—

---

1 Lesley and his wife could live comfortably on the rents paid by the tenants of farms and cottages belonging to the estate. When he took "the road to Aberdeen" at the beginning of the story, he was apparently returning to his estate briefly before he set off for Paris.

2 Probably the name of Lesley's estate near Aberdeen. There is also a fishing village named Dunbeath in the northern Highlands of Scotland, far from Aberdeen. Lesley's estate is presumably named after the village.

3 The hills around the city that, like the hotwells, were considered to have restorative properties. As the hotwells declined in popularity in the late eighteenth century, the downs and the elevated village of Clifton were becoming increasingly fashionable.

Letter the fourth
From Miss C. Lutterell to Miss M. Lesley
Bristol February 27th

My dear Peggy

I have but just received your letter, which being directed to Sussex while I was at Bristol was obliged to be forwarded to me here, and from some unaccountable Delay, has but this instant reached me—. I return you many thanks for the account it contains of Lesley's acquaintance, Love and Marriage with Louisa, which has not the less entertained me for having often been repeated to me before.

I have the satisfaction of informing you that we have every reason to imagine our pantry is by this time nearly cleared, as we left particular orders with the Servants to eat as hard as they possibly could, and to call in a couple of Chairwomen[1] to assist them. We brought a cold Pigeon-pye, a cold turkey, a cold tongue, and half a dozen Jellies[2] with us, which we were lucky enough with the help of our Landlady, her husband, and their three children, to get rid of, in less than two days after our arrival. Poor Eloisa is still so very indifferent both in Health and Spirits, that I very much fear, the air of the Bristol-downs, healthy as it is, has not been able to drive poor Henry from her remembrance—.

You ask me whether your new Mother in law is handsome and amiable—I will now give you an exact description of her bodily and Mental charms. She is short, and extremely well-made; is naturally pale, but rouges a good deal;[3] has fine eyes, and fine teeth, as she will take care to let you know as soon as she sees you, and is altogether very pretty. She is remarkably good-tempered when she has her own way, and very lively when she is not out of humour. She is naturally extravagant and not very affected; she never reads any thing but the letters she receives from me, and never writes anything but her answers to them. She plays, sings and Dances, but has no taste for either, and excells in none, tho' she says she is passionately fond of all. Perhaps you may flatter me so far as to be surprised that one of whom I speak with so

---

1 That is, charwomen; women hired for odd work, or single days.
2 Leftover meats preserved in jelly. All the items mentioned here are the remains, transported to Bristol, of the enormous wedding dinner that Charlotte had prepared for her sister in Sussex.
3 Applies red paint to her cheeks. Since rouge was becoming unfashionable in the 1780s, Susan Lesley is displaying her characteristic bad taste.

little affection should be my particular freind; but to tell you the truth, our freindship arose rather from Caprice on her side, than Esteem on mine. We spent two or three days together with a Lady in Berkshire with whom we both happened to be connected—. During our visit, the Weather being remarkably bad, and our party particularly stupid, she was so good as to conceive a violent partiality for me, which very soon settled in a downright Freindship, and ended in an established correspondence. She is probably by this time as tired of me, as I am of her; but as she is too polite and I am too civil to say so, our letters are still as frequent and affectionate as ever, and our Attachment as firm and Sincere as when it first commenced.—As she has a great taste for the pleasures of London, and of Brighthelmstone,[1] she will I dare say find some difficulty in prevailing on herself ever to satisfy the curiosity I dare say she feels of beholding you, at the expence of quitting those favourite haunts of Dissipation, for the melancholy tho' venerable gloom of the castle you inhabit. Perhaps however if she finds her health impaired by too much amusement, she may acquire fortitude sufficient to undertake a Journey to Scotland in the hope of its proving at least beneficial to her health, if not conducive to her happiness. Your fears I am sorry to say, concerning your father's extravagance, your own fortunes, your Mothers Jewels and your Sister's consequence, I should suppose are but too well founded. My freind herself has four thousand pounds, and will probably spend nearly as much every year in Dress and Public places, if she can get it—she will certainly not endeavour to reclaim Sir George from the manner of living to which he has been so long accustomed, and there is therefore some reason to fear that you will be very well off, if you get any fortune at all. The Jewels I should imagine too will undoubtedly be hers, and there is too much reason to think that she will preside at her Husbands table in preference to his Daughter. But as so melancholy a subject must necessarily extremely distress you, I will no longer dwell on it—.

Eloisa's indisposition has brought us to Bristol at so unfashionable a season of the year,[2] that we have actually seen but one genteel family since we came. Mr and Mrs Marlowe are very agreable people; the ill health of their little boy occasioned their

---

1 Brighton, an increasingly fashionable seaside resort on the Sussex coast that had been patronized by the dissolute Prince of Wales since 1784.

2 While the Bath season was at its height in February, the Bristol season traditionally ran from late March until the end of September.

arrival here; you may imagine that being the only family with whom we can converse, we are of course on a footing of intimacy with them; we see them indeed almost every day, and dined with them yesterday. We spent a very pleasant Day, and had a very good Dinner, tho' to be sure the Veal was terribly underdone, and the Curry had no seasoning. I could not help wishing all dinner-time that I had been at the dressing it—. A brother of Mrs Marlowe, Mr Cleveland is with them at present; he is a good-looking young Man and seems to have a good deal to say for himself. I tell Eloisa that she should set her cap at him,[1] but she does not at all seem to relish the proposal. I should like to see the girl married and Cleveland has a very good estate. Perhaps you may wonder that I do not consider *myself* as well as my Sister in my matrimonial Projects; but to tell you the truth I never wish to act a more principal part at a Wedding than the superintending and directing the Dinner, and therefore while I can get any of my acquaintance to marry for me, I shall never think of doing it myself, as I very much suspect that I should not have so much time for dressing my own Wedding-dinner, as for dressing that of my freinds. Yrs sincerely

CL.

Letter the fifth
Miss Margaret Lesley to Miss Charlotte Luttrell
Lesley-Castle March 18th

On the same day that I received your last kind letter, Matilda received one from Sir George which was dated from Edinburgh, and informed us that he should do himself the pleasure of intro-ducing Lady Lesley to us on the following Evening. This as you may suppose considerably surprised us, particularly as your account of her Ladyship had given us reason to imagine there was little chance of her visiting Scotland at a time that London must be so gay.[2] As it was our business however to be delighted at such a mark of condescension as a visit from Sir George and Lady Lesley, we prepared to return them an answer expressive of the happiness we enjoyed in expectation of such a Blessing, when luckily recollecting that as they were to reach the Castle the next Evening, it would be impossible for my father to receive it before

---

1 That is, attract him as her suitor.
2 The London season ran from late autumn until 4 June, when the King celebrated his official birthday. In March, the season was at its height.

he left Edinburgh, We contented ourselves with leaving them to suppose that we were as happy as we ought to be. At nine in the Evening on the following day, they came, accompanied by one of Lady Lesleys brothers. Her Ladyship perfectly answers the description you sent me of her, except that I do not think her so pretty as you seem to consider her. She has not a bad face, but there is something so extremely unmajestic in her little diminutive figure, as to render her in comparison with the elegant height of Matilda and Myself, an insignificant Dwarf. Her curiosity to see us (which must have been great to bring her more than four hundred miles[1]) being now perfectly gratified, she already begins to mention their return to town, and has desired us to accompany her—. We cannot refuse her request since it is seconded by the commands of our Father, and thirded by the entreaties of Mr Fitzgerald who is certainly one of the most pleasing young Men, I ever beheld. It is not yet determined when we are to go, but when we do we shall certainly take our little Louisa with us. Adeiu my dear Charlotte; Matilda unites in best wishes to You and Eloisa, with yours ever

ML

Letter the sixth
Lady Lesley to Miss Charlotte Luttrell
Lesley-Castle March 20th

We arrived here my sweet Freind about a fortnight ago, and I already heartily repent that I ever left our charming House in Portman-Square[2] for such a dismal old Weather-beaten Castle as this. You can form no idea sufficiently hideous, of its dungeon-like form. It is actually perched upon a Rock to appearance so totally inaccessible, that I expected to have been pulled up by a rope; and sincerely repented having gratified my curiosity to behold my Daughters at the expence of being obliged to enter their prison in so dangerous and ridiculous a Manner. But as soon as I once found myself safely arrived in the inside of this tremendous building, I comforted myself with the hope of having my spirits revived, by the sight of two beautifull Girls, such as the Miss Lesleys had been represented to me, at Edinburgh. But here

---

1 Margaret Lesley's observation is accurate; Perth is some 450 miles northwest of London.

2 A new, large, highly fashionable square on the western outskirts of London, begun in 1764 but not completed until the 1780s.

again, I met with nothing but Disapointment and Surprise. Matilda and Margaret Lesley are two great, tall, out of the way, over-grown, Girls, just of a proper size to inhabit a Castle almost as Large in comparison as themselves. I wish my dear Charlotte that you could but behold these Scotch Giants; I am sure they would frighten you out of your wits. They will do very well as foils to myself, so I have invited them to accompany me to London where I hope to be in the course of a fortnight. Besides these two fair Damsels, I found a little humoured Brat here who I beleive is some relation to them; they told me who she was, and gave me a long rigmerole[1] Story of her father and a Miss *Somebody*[2] which I have entirely forgot. I hate Scandal and detest Children. —. I have been plagued ever since I came here with tiresome visits from a parcel of Scotch wretches, with terrible hard-names; they were so civil, gave me so many invitations, and talked of coming again so soon, that I could not help affronting them. I suppose I shall not see them any more, and yet as a family party we are so stupid, that I do not know what to do with myself. These girls have no Music, but Scotch Airs, no Drawings but Scotch Mountains, and no Books but Scotch Poems—And I hate everything Scotch. In general I can spend half the Day at my toilett[3] with a great deal of pleasure, but why should I dress here, since there is not a creature in the House whom I have any wish to please. —. I have just had a conversation with my Brother in which he has greatly offended me, and which as I have nothing more entertaining to send you I will give you the particulars of. You must know that I have for these 4 or 5 Days past strongly suspected William of entertaining a partiality for my eldest Daughter. I own indeed that had *I* been inclined to fall in love with any woman, I should not have made choice of Matilda Lesley for the object of my passion; for there is nothing I hate so much as a tall Woman: but however there is no accounting for some men's taste and as William is himself nearly six feet high, it is not wonderful that he should be partial to that height. Now as I have very great affection for my Brother and should be extremely sorry to see him unhappy, which I suppose he means to be if he cannot marry Matilda, as moreover I know that his Circumstances will not allow him to marry any one

---

1 That is, rigmarole, an incoherent, long-winded, rambling account.
2 The disgraced Louisa Lesley, who has run away with "Danvers and dishonour."
3 Toilette or dressing table; hence, dressing, applying make-up, arranging hair, etc.

without a fortune, and that Matilda's is entirely dependent on her Father, who will neither have his own inclination nor my permission to give her anything at present, I thought it would be doing a good-natured action by my Brother to let him know as much, in order that he might choose for himself, whether to conquer his passion, or Love and Despair. Accordingly finding myself this Morning alone with him in one of the horrid old rooms of this Castle, I opened the cause to him in the following Manner.

"Well my dear William what do you think of these girls? for my part, I do not find them so plain as I expected: but perhaps you may think me partial to the Daughters of my Husband and perhaps you are right—They are indeed so very like Sir George that it is natural to think...."

"My Dear Susan (cried he in a tone of the greatest amazement) You do not really think they bear the least resemblance to their Father! He is so very plain!—but I beg your pardon—I had entirely forgotten to whom I was speaking—"

"Oh! pray don't mind me; (replied I) every one knows Sir George is horribly ugly, and I assure you I always thought him a fright."

"You surprise me extremely (answered William) by what you say both with respect to Sir George and his Daughters. You cannot think Your Husband so deficient in personal Charms as you speak of, nor can you surely see any resemblance between him and the Miss Lesleys who are in my opinion perfectly unlike him and perfectly Handsome."

"If that is your opinion with regard to the girls it certainly is no proof of their Father's beauty, for if they are perfectly unlike him and very handsome at the same time, it is natural to suppose that he is very plain."

"By no means, (said he) for what may be pretty in a Woman, may be very unpleasing in a Man."

"But, you yourself (replied I) but a few Minutes ago allowed him to be very plain."

"Men are no Judges of Beauty in their own Sex." (said he)

"Neither Men nor Women can think Sir George tolerable."

"Well, well, (said he) we will not dispute about *his* Beauty, but your opinion of his *Daughters* is surely very singular, for if I understood you right, you said you did not find them so plain as you expected to do."!

"Why, do *you* find them plainer then?" (said I)

"I can scarcely beleive you to be serious (returned he) when you speak of their persons in so extroidinary a Manner. Do not you not think the Miss Lesleys are two very handsome Young Women?"

"Lord! No! (cried I) I think them terribly plain!"

"Plain! (replied He) My dear Susan, you cannot really think so! Why what single Feature in the face of either of them, can you possibly find fault with?"

"Oh! trust me for that; (replied I). Come I will begin with the eldest—with Matilda. Shall I, William?" (I looked as cunning as I could when I said it, in order to shame him.)

"They are so much alike (said he) that I should suppose the faults of one, would be the faults of both."

"Well, then, in the first place, they are both so horribly tall!"

"They are *taller* than you are indeed." (said he with a saucy smile.)

"Nay, (said I) I know nothing of that."

"Well, but (he continued) tho' they may be above the common size, their figures are perfectly elegant; and as to their faces, their Eyes are beautifull—."

"I never can think such tremendous, knock-me-down figures in the least degree elegant, and as for their eyes, they are so tall that I never could strain my neck enough to look at them."

"Nay, (replied he) I know not whether you may not be in the right in not attempting it, for perhaps they might dazzle you with their Lustre."

"Oh! Certainly. (said I, with the greatest Complacency, for I assure you my dearest Charlotte I was not in the least offended tho' by what followed, one would suppose that William was conscious of having given me just cause to be so, for coming up to me and taking my hand, he said) "You must not look so grave Susan; you will make me fear I have offended you!"

"Offended me! Dear Brother, how came such a thought in your head! (returned I) No really! I assure you that I am not in the least surprised at your being so warm an advocate for the Beauty of these Girls—"

"Well, but (interrupted William) remember that we have not yet concluded our dispute concerning them. What fault do you find with their complexion?"

"They are so horridly pale."

"They have always a little colour, and after any exercise it is considerably heightened."

"Yes, but if there should ever happen to be any rain in this part of the world, they will never be able to raise more than their common stock—except indeed they amuse themselves with running up and Down these horrid old Galleries and Antichambers[1]—"

"Well, (replied my Brother in a tone of vexation, and glancing an impertinent look at me) if they *have* but little colour, at least, it is all their own."

This was too much my dear Charlotte, for I am certain that he had the impudence by that look, of pretending to suspect the reality of mine. But you I am sure will vindicate my character whenever you may hear it so cruelly aspersed, for you can witness how often I have protested against wearing Rouge, and how much I always told you I disliked it. And I assure you that my opinions are still the same. —. Well, not bearing to be so suspected by my Brother, I left the room immediately, and have been ever since in my own Dressing-room writing to you. What a long Letter have I made of it. But you must not expect to receive such from me when I get to Town; for it is only at Lesley castle, that one has time to write even to a Charlotte Luttrell. —. I was so much vexed by William's Glance, that I could not summon Patience enough, to stay and give him that Advice respecting his Attachment to Matilda which had first induced me from pure Love to him to begin the conversation; and I am now so thoroughly convinced by it, of his violent passion for her, that I am certain he would never hear reason on the Subject, and I shall therefore give myself no more trouble either about him or his favourite. Adeiu my dear Girl—

Yrs affectionately Susan L.

Letter the Seventh
From Miss C. Luttrell to Miss M. Lesley
Bristol the 27th of March

I have received Letters from You and your Mother-in-law within this week which have greatly entertained me, as I find by them that you are both downright jealous of each others Beauty. It is very odd that two pretty Women tho' actually Mother and Daughter cannot be in the same House without falling out about their faces. Do be convinced that you are both perfectly handsome and say no more of the Matter. I suppose this Letter must be directed to Portman Square where probably (great as is your affection for Lesley Castle) you will not be sorry to find yourself.

---

1 Long passages, typically used for hanging paintings (and for exercise in bad weather), and withdrawing chambers, used as reception rooms by the occupants of adjoining bedchambers.

In spite of all that People may say about Green fields and the Country I was always of opinion that London and its Amusements must be very agreable for a while, and should be very happy could my Mother's income allow her to jockey us into its Public-places,[1] during Winter. I always longed particularly to go to Vaux-hall,[2] to see whether the cold Beef there is cut so thin[3] as it is reported, for I have a sly suspicion that few people understand the act of cutting a slice of cold Beef so well as I do: nay it would be hard if I did not know something of the Matter, for it was a part of my Education that I took by far the most pains with. Mama always found me *her* best Scholar, tho' when Papa was alive Eloisa was *his*. Never to be sure were there two more different Dispositions in the World. We both loved Reading. *She* preferred Histories, and *I* Receipts.[4] She loved drawing Pictures, and I drawing Pullets.[5] No one could sing a better Song than She, and no one make a better Pye than I.—And so it has always continued since we have been no longer Children. The only difference is that all disputes on the superior excellence of our Employments *then* so frequent are now no more. We have for many years entered into an agreement always to admire each other's works; I never fail listening to *her* Music, and she is as constant in eating *my* pies. Such at least was the case till Henry Hervey made his appearance in Sussex. Before the arrival of his Aunt in our neighbourhood where she established herself you know about a twelvemonth ago, his visits to her had been at stated times, and of equal and settled Duration; but on her removal to the Hall which is within a walk from our House, they became both more frequent and longer. This as you may suppose could not be pleasing to Mrs Diana who is a professed Enemy to everything which is not directed by Decorum and Formality, or which bears the least resemblance to Ease and Good-breeding. Nay so great was her aversion to her Nephews behaviour that I

---

1 London's numerous cultural pleasures, including theatres, concert halls, dances, artists' studios, picture galleries, museums, exhibitions, and pleasure gardens, as well as churches.

2 Vauxhall Gardens, the oldest of London's pleasure gardens. Its twelve acres, containing shrubbery, walks, statues, and cascades, were located in Lambeth, south of the Thames from Westminster Abbey.

3 The extreme thinness of Vauxhall sliced meat was proverbial and constituted one of the pleasure garden's many attractions.

4 Recipes.

5 Disembowelling young hens preparatory to cooking them.

have often heard her give such hints of it before his face that had not Henry at such times been engaged in conversation with Eloisa, they must have caught his Attention and have very much distressed him. The alteration in my Sister's behaviour which I have before hinted at, now took place. The Agreement we had entered into of admiring each others productions she no longer seemed to regard, and tho' I constantly applauded even every Country-dance, She play'd,[1] yet not even a pidgeon-pye of my making could obtain from her a single word of Approbation. This was certainly enough to put any one in a Passion; however, I was as cool as a Cream-cheese and having formed my plan and concerted a scheme of Revenge, I was determined to let her have her own way and not even to make her a single reproach. My Scheme was to treat her as she treated me, and tho' she might even draw my own Picture or play Malbrook[2] (which is the only tune I ever really liked) not to say so much as "Thank you Eloisa"; tho' I had for many years constantly hollowed whenever she played, *Bravo*, *Bravissimo*, *Encora*, *Da Capro*, *allegretto*, *con espressioné*, and *Poco presto*[3] with many other such outlandish words, all of them as Eloisa told me expressive of my Admiration; and so indeed I suppose they are, as I see some of them in every Page of every Music-book, being the Sentiments I imagine of the Composer.

I executed my Plan with great Punctuality, I can not say success, for Alas! my silence while she played seemed not in the least to displease her; on the contrary she actually said to me one

---

1 Charlotte prides herself on her readiness to applaud even the simple music accompanying a country dance, an English dance of rural origin in which couples stand face to face in two parallel lines.

2 A very popular eighteenth-century French nursery song, "*Malbrouck s'en va-t-en guerre*" (Marlborough is off to battle), that celebrates the military exploits of the Duke of Marlborough as leader of the coalition armies in the War of Spanish Succession (1702-13).

3 A comic mixture of appropriate and inappropriate Italian musical terms. The first three are expressions of admiration: "*Bravo*" and "*Bravissimo*," meaning "excellent" and "outstanding," while "*Encora*" is the traditional demand for more music when an audience is especially pleased. The other terms, however, are all directions for instrumental performers. "*Da capo*" is an indication at the end of a piece to repeat from the beginning; "*allegretto*" calls for the tempo to be somewhat brisk, less brisk than "*allegro*," and "*con espressione*" for particular expression. The final term, "*Poco presto*," is a comic invented phrase: to play "*presto*" is to play very fast, but to play "*Poco presto*" would be to play a little or somewhat very fast.

day "Well Charlotte, I am very glad to find that you have at last left off that ridiculous custom of applauding my Execution[1] on the Harpsichord till you made *my* head ake, and yourself hoarse. I feel very much obliged to you for keeping your Admiration to yourself." I never shall forget the very witty answer I made to this speech.

"Eloisa (said I) I beg you would be quite at your Ease with respect to all such fears in future, for be assured that I shall always keep my Admiration to myself and my own pursuits and never extend it to yours." This was the only very severe thing I ever said in my Life; not but that I have often felt myself extremely satirical but it was the only time I ever made my feelings public.

I suppose there never were two young people who had a greater affection for each other than Henry and Eloisa; no, the Love of your Brother for Miss Burton could not be so strong tho' it might be more violent. You may imagine therefore how provoked my Sister must have been to have him play her such a trick. Poor Girl! She still laments his Death, with undiminished Constancy, notwithstanding he has been dead more than six weeks; but some people mind such things more than others. The ill state of Health into which his Loss has thrown her makes her so weak, and so unable to support the least exertion, that she has been in tears all this morning merely from having taken leave of Mrs Marlowe who with her Husband, Brother and Child are to leave Bristol this Morning. I am sorry to have them go because they are the only family with whom we have here any acquaintance, but I never thought of crying; to be sure Eloisa and Mrs Marlowe have always been more together than with me, and have therefore contracted a kind of affection for each other, which does not make Tears so inexcusable in them as they would be in me. The Marlowes are going to Town, Cleveland accompanies them; as neither Eloisa nor I could catch him I hope You or Matilda may have better Luck. I know not when we shall leave Bristol, Eloisa's Spirits are so low that she is very averse to moving, and yet is certainly by no means mended by her residence here. A week or two will I hope determine our Measures—in the mean time beleive me

etc—etc—Charlotte Luttrell

---

1 Level of performance.

Letter the Eighth
Miss Luttrell to Mrs Marlowe.
Bristol April 4th

I feel myself greatly obliged to you my dear Emma for such a mark of your affection as I flatter myself was conveyed in the proposal you made me of our Corresponding; I assure you that it will be a great releif to me to write to you and as long as my Health and Spirits will allow me, you will find me a very constant Correspondent; I will not say an entertaining one, for you know my situation sufficiently not to be ignorant that in me Mirth would be improper and I know my own Heart too well not to be sensible that it would be unnatural. You must not expect News for we see no one with whom we are in the least acquainted, or in whose proceedings we have any Interest. You must not expect Scandal for by the same rule we are equally debarred either from hearing or inventing it.—You must expect from me nothing but the melancholy effusions of a broken Heart which is ever reverting to the Happiness it once enjoyed and which ill supports its present Wretchedness. The Possibility of being able to write, to speak, to you of my losst Henry will be a Luxury to me, and your Goodness will not I know refuse to read what it will so much releive my Heart to write. I once thought that to have what is in general called a Freind (I mean one of my own Sex to whom I might speak with less reserve than to any other person) independant of my Sister would never be an object of my wishes, but how much was I mistaken! Charlotte is too much engrossed by two confidential Correspondents of that sort, to supply the place of one to me, and I hope you will not think me girlishly romantic, when I say that to have some kind and compassionate Freind who might listen to my Sorrows without endeavouring to console me was what I had for some time wished for, when our acquaintance with you, the intimacy which followed it and the particular affectionate Attention you paid me almost from the first, caused me to entertain the flattering Idea of those attentions being improved on a closer acquaintance into a Freindship which, if you were what my wishes formed you would be the greatest Happiness I could be capable of enjoying. To find that such Hopes are realized is a satisfaction indeed, a satisfaction which is now almost the only one I can ever experience.—I feel myself so languid that I am sure were you with me you would oblige me to leave off writing, and I can not give you a greater proof of my Affection for you than by acting, as I know you would wish me to do, whether Absent or Present. I am my dear Emmas sincere freind

E.L.

Letter the Ninth
Mrs Marlowe to Miss Lutterell
Grosvenor[1] Street, April 10th

Need I say my dear Eloisa how wellcome your Letter was to me? I cannot give a greater proof of the pleasure I received from it, or of the Desire I feel that our Correspondence may be regular and frequent than by setting you so good an example as I now do in answering it before the end of the week—. But do not imagine that I claim any merit in being so punctual; on the contrary I assure you, that it is a far greater Gratification to me to write to you, than to spend the Evening either at a Concert or a Ball. Mr Marlowe is so desirous of my appearing at some of the Public places every evening that I do not like to refuse him, but at the same time so much wish to remain at Home, that independant of the Pleasure I experience in devoting any portion of my Time to my Dear Eloisa, yet the Liberty I claim from having a Letter to write of spending an Evening at home with my little Boy, You know me well enough to be sensible, will of itself be a sufficient Inducement (if one is necessary) to my maintaining with Pleasure a Correspondence with you. As to the Subjects of your Letters to me, whether Grave or Merry, if they concern you they must be equally interesting to me; Not but that I think the Melancholy Indulgence of your own Sorrows by repeating them and dwelling on them to me, will only encourage and increase them, and that it will be more prudent in you to avoid so sad a subject; but yet knowing as I do what a soothing and Melancholy Pleasure it must afford you, I cannot prevail on myself to deny you so great an Indulgence, and will only insist on your not expecting me to encourage you in it, by my own Letters; on the contrary I intend to fill them with such lively Wit and entertaining Humour as shall even provoke a Smile in the sweet but Sorrowfull Countenance of my Eloisa.

In the first place you are to learn that I have met your Sisters three freinds Lady Lesley and her Daughters, twice in Public since

---

1 Among the most prestigious addresses in London, with many notable residents.

I have been here. I know you will be impatient to hear my opinion of the Beauty of three Ladies of whom You have heard so much. Now, as you are too ill and too unhappy to be vain, I think I may venture to inform you that I like none of their faces so well as I do your own. Yet they are all handsome—Lady Lesley indeed I have seen before; her Daughters I beleive would in general be said to have a finer face than her Ladyship, and Yet what with the charms of a Blooming Complexion,[1] a little Affectation and a great deal of Small-talk, (in each of which She is superior to the Young Ladies) she will I dare say gain herself as many Admirers as the more regular features of Matilda, and Margaret. I am sure you will agree with me in saying that they can none of them be of a proper size for real Beauty, when you know that two of them are taller and the other shorter than ourselves. In spite of this Defect (or rather by reason of it) there is something very noble and majestic in the figures of the Miss Lesleys, and something agreably Lively in the Appearance of their pretty little Mother-in-law. But tho' one may be majestic and the other Lively, yet the faces of neither possess that Bewitching Sweetness of my Eloisas, which her present Languor is so far from diminishing. What would my Husband and Brother say of us, if they knew all the fine things I have been saying to you in this Letter. It is very hard that a pretty Woman is never to be told she is so by any one of her own Sex, without that person's being suspected to be either her determined Enemy, or her professed Toad-eater.[2] How much more amiable are women in that particular! one Man may say forty civil things to another without our supposing that he is ever paid for it, and provided he does his Duty by our Sex, we care not how Polite he is to his own.

Mrs Luttrell will be so good as to accept my Compliments, Charlotte, my Love, and Eloisa the best wishes for the recovery of her Health and Spirits that can be offered by her Affectionate Freind E. Marlowe.

I am afraid this Letter will be but a poor Specimen of my Powers in the Witty Way; and your opinion of them will not be greatly increased when I assure you that I have been as entertaining as I possibly could—.

---

1 Apparently a euphemism, since Lady Lesley owes her "bloom" to rouge.
2 A "toady," or sycophant. The term derives from the practice, among mountebanks' assistants, of pretending to swallow a toad; the mountebank would then pretend to expel the poisons supposedly ingested.

Letter the Tenth
From Miss Margaret Lesley to Miss Charlotte Luttrell
Portman Square April 13th

My dear Charlotte

We left Lesley-Castle on the 28th of Last Month, and arrived safely in London after a Journey of seven Days; I had the pleasure of finding your Letter here waiting my Arrival, for which you have my grateful Thanks. Ah! my dear Freind I every day more regret the serene and tranquil Pleasures of the Castle we have left, in exchange for the uncertain and unequal Amusements of this vaunted City. Not that I will pretend to assert that these uncertain and unequal Amusements are in the least Degree unpleasing to me; on the contrary I enjoy them extremely and should enjoy them even more, were I not certain that every appearance I make in Public but rivetts the Chains of those unhappy Beings whose Passion it is impossible not to pity, tho' it is out of my power to return. In short my Dear Charlotte it is my sensibility for the sufferings of so many amiable Young Men, my Dislike of the extreme Admiration I meet with, and my Aversion to being so celebrated both in Public, in Private, in Papers, and in Printshops,[1] that are the reasons why I cannot more fully enjoy, the Amusements so various and pleasing of London. How often have I wished that I possessed as little personal Beauty as you do; that my figure were as inelegant; my face as unlovely; and my Appearance as unpleasing as yours! But Ah! what little chance is there of so desirable an Event; I have had the Small-pox,[2] and must therefore submit to my unhappy fate.

I am now going to intrust you my dear Charlotte with a secret which has long disturbed the tranquility of my days, and which is of a kind to require the most inviolable Secrecy from you. Last Monday se'night[3] Matilda and I accompanied Lady Lesley to a Rout[4] at the Honourable Mrs Kickabout's; we were escorted by Mr Fitzgerald who is a very amiable Young Man in the main, tho' perhaps a little Singular in his Taste—He is in love with Matilda—. We had scarcely paid our Compliments to the Lady of the House

1 In newspapers and in prints bought in print-sellers' shops.
2 Since Margaret Lesley has already had smallpox, she has no chance of contracting it again and thus no further chance of being disfigured by the scarring that often attended the disease.
3 Seven nights ago; a week last Monday.
4 A fashionable gathering, reception, or evening party.

and curtseyed to half a Score different people when my Attention was attracted by the appearance of a Young Man the most lovely of his Sex, who at that Moment entered the Room with another Gentleman and Lady. From the first moment I beheld him, I was certain that on him depended the future Happiness of my Life. Imagine my surprise when he was introduced to me by the name of Cleveland— I instantly recognized him as the Brother of Mrs Marlowe, and the acquaintance of my Charlotte at Bristol. Mr and Mrs M. were the Gentleman and Lady who accompanied him. (You do not think Mrs Marlowe handsome?) The elegant address of Mr Cleveland, his polished Manners and Delightful Bow, at once confirmed my attachment. He did not speak; but I can imagine every thing he would have said, had he opened his Mouth. I can picture to myself the cultivated Understanding, the Noble Sentiments, and elegant Language which would have shone so conspicuous in the conversation of Mr Cleveland. The approach of Sir James Gower (one of my too numerous Admirers) prevented the Discovery of any such Powers, by putting an end to a Conversation we had never commenced, and by attracting my attention to himself. But Oh! how inferior are the accomplishments of Sir James to those of his so greatly envied Rival! Sir James is one of the most frequent of our Visitors, and is almost always of our Parties. We have since often met Mr and Mrs Marlowe but no Cleveland—he is always engaged some where else. Mrs Marlowe fatigues me to Death every time I see her by her tiresome Conversations about You and Eloisa. She is so Stupid! I live in the hope of seeing her irrisistable Brother to night, as we are going to Lady Flambeau's, who is I know intimate with the Marlowes. Our party will be Lady Lesley, Matilda, Fitzgerald, Sir James Gower, and myself. We see little of Sir George, who is almost always at the Gaming-table. Ah! my poor Fortune where art thou by this time? We see more of Lady L. who always makes her appearance (highly rouged) at Dinner-time. Alas! what Delightful Jewels will she be decked in this evening at Lady Flambeau's! Yet I wonder how she can herself delight in wearing them; surely she must be sensible of the ridiculous impropriety of loading her little diminutive figure with such superfluous ornaments; is it possible that she can not know how greatly superior an elegant simplicity is to the most studied apparel? Would she but present them to Matilda and me, how greatly should we be obliged to her. How becoming would Diamonds be on our fine majestic figures! And how surprising it is that such an Idea should never have occurred to *her*. I am sure if I have reflected in this Manner once, I have fifty times. Whenever I see Lady Lesley dressed in them such reflections immediately come across me. My own Mother's Jewels too! But I will say no more on so melancholy a Subject—Let me entertain you with something more pleasing—Matilda had a letter this Morning from Lesley, by which we have the pleasure of finding that he is at Naples has turned Roman-catholic, obtained one of the Pope's Bulls[1] for annulling his 1st Marriage and has since actually married a Neapolitan Lady of great Rank and Fortune. He tells us moreover that much the same sort of affair has befallen his first Wife the worthless Louisa who is likewise at Naples has turned Roman-catholic, and is soon to be married[2] to a Neapolitan Nobleman of great and Distinguished Merit. He says, that they are at present very good Freinds, have quite forgiven all past errors and intend in future to be very good Neighbours. He invites Matilda and me to pay him a visit in Italy and to bring him his little Louisa whom both her Mother, Step-Mother, and himself are equally desirous of beholding. As to our accepting his invitation, it is at present very uncertain; Lady Lesley advises us to go without loss of time; Fitzgerald offers to escort us there, but Matilda has some doubts of the Propriety of such a Scheme—She owns it would be very agreable. I am certain she likes the Fellow. My Father desires us not to be in a hurry, as perhaps if we wait a few months both he and Lady Lesley will do themselves the pleasure of attending us. Lady Lesley says no, that nothing will ever tempt her to forego the Amusements of Brighthelmstone for a Journey to Italy merely to see our Brother. "No (says the disagreable Woman) I have once in my Life been fool enough to travel I dont know how many hundred Miles to see two of the Family, and I found it did not answer, so Deuce take me, if ever I am so foolish again." So says her Ladyship, but Sir George still perseveres in saying that perhaps in a Month or two, they may accompany us.

Adeiu my Dear Charlotte—

Yr faithful Margaret Lesley

---

1 Papal edicts. Since Lesley has "turned Roman-catholic" and since his Protestant wife has committed adultery, he can obtain a papal affirmation that his marriage is no longer valid. He can thus marry again in Italy, but not in England, where the papal edict has no authority.

2 Like Lesley, Louisa can marry again in Italy, as her first marriage has been annulled.

The first Act of a Comedy—

Characters

Popgun
Charles
Postilion
Chorus of ploughboys
and
Strephon[1]

Maria
Pistoletta
Hostess
Cook
and
Chloe

Scene—an Inn—
Enter Hostess, Charles, Maria, and Cook.

Hostss. to Maria) If the gentry in the Lion[2] should want beds,
  shew them number 9.—
Maria) Yes Mistress.   exit Maria—
Hostss. to Cook) If their Honours[3] in the Moon ask for the bill
  of fare,[4] give it to them.
Cook) —I wull,[5] I wull.   exit Cook.
Hostss. to Charles) If their Ladyships[6] in the Sun ring their
  Bell—answer it.
Charles) Yes Ma'am.—   Exeunt Severally—

---

1 A traditional name for a lover in pastoral poetry; his beloved is traditionally named Chloe.
2 The public rooms in the inn all have names: the Lion, the Moon, and
   the Sun. The bedrooms, however, have numbers, as they would today.
3 A title of respect, somewhat more deferential than "the gentry."
4 Menu.
5 Dialect for "will."
6 Still more deferential than "their Honours," implying that the occupants
   are titled.

Scene changes to the Moon, and discovers
Popgun and Pistoletta.

Pistoltta.) Pray papa how far is it to London?

Popgun) My Girl, my Darling, my favourite of all my Children,
who art the picture of thy poor Mother who died two
months ago, with whom I am going to Town to marry to
Strephon, and to whom I mean to bequeath my whole
Estate, it wants seven Miles.[1]

Scene changes to the Sun—
Enter Chloe and a chorus of ploughboys.

Chloe) Where am I? At Hounslow.[2]—Where go I? To London—
What to do? To be married—. Unto whom? Unto Strephon.
Who is he? A Youth. Then I will sing a Song.

Song

I go to Town
And when I come down,
I shall be married to Stree-phon
And that to me will be fun.

Chorus) Be fun, be fun, be fun,
And that to me will be fun,

Enter Cook

Cook) Here is the bill of fare.

Chloe reads) 2 Ducks, a leg of beef, a stinking partridge,[3] and a
tart.—I will have the leg of beef and the partridge.

exit Cook.

And now I will sing another Song.

Song—

I am going to have my dinner,
After which I shan't be thinner,
I wish I had here Strephon
For he would carve the partridge if it should be
a tough one

---

1 There are seven miles left to travel.

2 A town about fourteen miles west of London, not seven, as Popgun
imagines.

3 Presumably stinking because it has been hung for a long time, to give it
additional flavour. The usual term for birds hung for the correct period
of time is "high"; "stinking" suggests that the process has been carried
too far.

Chorus) Tough one, tough one, tough one,
          For he would carve the partridge if it should be
          a tough one.
               Exit Chloe and Chorus—.
          Scene changes to the inside of the Lion.
               Enter Strephon and Postilion

Streph.) You drove me from Staines[1] to this place, from whence
    I mean to go to Town to marry Chloe. How much is your
    due?
Post.) Eighteen pence.
Streph.) Alas, my freind, I have but a bad guinea[2] with which I
    mean to support myself in Town. But I will pawn to you an
    undirected Letter[3] that I received from Chloe.
Post.) Sir, I accept your offer.

                    End of the first Act.—

---

1 A town about five miles west of Hounslow.
2 A forgery of the gold coin worth twenty-one shillings. Forging coins was
   punishable by death; Strephon's plan to use his guinea in London is a
   dangerous one.
3 A letter with no address.

Volume the Third

Evelyn

To Miss Mary Lloyd,[1]
The following Novel is by permission
Dedicated,
by her Obedt. humble Servt.
The Author

Evelyn

In a retired part of the County of Sussex there is a village (for what I know to the Contrary) called Evelyn,[2] perhaps one of the most beautiful Spots in the south of England. A Gentleman passing through it on horseback about twenty years ago,[3] was so entirely of my opinion in this respect, that he put up at the little Alehouse[4] in it and enquired with great earnestness whether there were any house to be lett in the Parish.[5] The Landlady,[6] who as well as every one else in Evelyn was remarkably amiable, shook her head at this question, but seemed unwilling to give him any answer. He could not bear this uncertainty—yet knew not how to obtain the information he desired. To repeat a question which had already appear'd to make the good woman uneasy was impossible—. He turned from her in visible agitation. "What a situation am I in!" said he to himself as he walked to the window and threw up the sash.[7] He found himself revived by the Air, which he felt to a much greater degree when he had opened the window than he had done before. Yet it was but for a moment—.

---

1 Mary Lloyd (1771-1843), a friend and neighbour of JA, and the younger sister of Martha Lloyd, to whom "Frederic and Elfrida" is dedicated. Martha and Mary, with another sister, Eliza, and their newly widowed mother, had rented Deane Parsonage since the spring of 1789, but were forced to leave it before James Austen became curate at Deane in 1792, after his marriage in March of that year.

2 An imaginary village.

3 This sets the action in about 1772, some three years before JA's birth in 1775.

4 A public house, "distinguished from a tavern, where they sell wine" (Johnson).

5 A subdivision of an English county, with its own church.

6 The hostess of the alehouse.

7 A sash window, which could be raised and lowered. Sash windows became popular in the late eighteenth century, letting in more light and air than the leaded casement windows they replaced.

The agonizing pain of Doubt and Suspence again weighed down his Spirits. The good woman who had watched in eager silence every turn of his Countenance with that benevolence which characterizes the inhabitants of Evelyn, intreated him to tell her the cause of his uneasiness. "Is there anything Sir in my power to do that may releive Your Greifs—Tell me in what Manner I can sooth them, and beleive me that the freindly balm of Comfort and Assistance shall not be wanting; for indeed Sir I have a simpathetic Soul."

"Amiable Woman (said Mr Gower, affected almost to tears by this generous offer) This Greatness of mind in one to whom I am almost a Stranger, serves but to make me the more warmly wish for a house in this sweet village—. What would I not give to be your Neighbour, to be blessed with your Acquaintance, and with the farther knowledge of your virtues! Oh! with what pleasure would I form myself by such an example! Tell me then, best of Women,[1] is there no possibility?—I cannot speak—you know my meaning—"

"Alas! Sir, replied Mrs Willis, there is *none*. Every house in this village, from the sweetness of the Situation, and the purity of the Air, in which neither Misery, Illhealth, or Vice are ever wafted, is inhabited. And yet, (after a short pause) there is a Family, who tho' warmly attached to the spot, yet from a peculiar Generosity of Disposition would perhaps be willing to oblige you with their house." He eagerly caught at this idea, and having gained a direction to the place, he set off immediately on his walk to it. As he approached the House, he was delighted with its situation. It was in the exact center of a small circular paddock,[2] which was enclosed by a regular paling,[3] and bordered with a plantation of Lombardy poplars,[4] and Spruce firs alternately placed in three

---

1 An allusion to "the best of men," the phrase repeatedly applied to the superlatively generous and proficient hero of Richardson's *Sir Charles Grandison*.

2 "A small inclosure for deer or other animals" (Johnson). Circularity was associated with the landscape gardening of Lancelot ("Capability") Brown (1715-83), who would surround the park of a country house with a border of trees and provide a walk around the estate.

3 A fence made of pales, pointed lengths of wood driven into the ground.

4 A tall, narrow, columnar variety of poplar, originating in Lombardy in northern Italy and brought to Britain in the eighteenth century. While not an indigenous tree, it was used by Brown and other landscape gardeners to delineate property limits.

rows.[1] A gravel walk ran through this beautiful Shrubbery,[2] and as the remainder of the paddock was unincumbered with any other Timber, the surface of it perfectly even and smooth, and grazed by four white Cows which were disposed at equal distances from each other, the whole appearance of the place as Mr Gower entered the Paddock was uncommonly striking. A beautifully-rounded, gravel road without any turn or interruption led immediately to the house. Mr Gower rang—the Door was soon opened. "Are Mr and Mrs Webb at home?" "My Good Sir they are—" replied the Servant; And leading the way, conducted Mr Gower up stairs into a very elegant Dressing room, where a Lady rising from her seat, welcomed him with all the Generosity which Mrs Willis had attributed to the Family.

"Welcome best of Men[3]—Welcome to this House, and to every thing it contains. William, tell your Master of the happiness I enjoy—invite him to partake of it—. Bring up some Chocolate[4] immediately; Spread a Cloth in the dining Parlour, and carry in the venison pasty[5]—. In the mean time let the Gentleman have some sandwiches, and bring in a Basket of Fruit—Send up some Ices and a bason of Soup, and do not forget some Jellies and Cakes." Then turning to Mr Gower, and taking out her purse, "Accept this my good Sir,—. Beleive me you are welcome to everything that is in my power to bestow.—I wish my purse were weightier, but Mr Webb must make up my deficiences—. I know he has cash in the house to the amount of an hundred pounds, which he shall bring you immediately." Mr Gower felt overpowered by her generosity as he put the purse in his pocket, and from the excess of his Gratitude, could scarcely express himself intelligibly when he accepted her offer of the hundred pounds. Mr Webb soon entered the room, and repeated every protestation of Freindship and Cordiality which his Lady had already made—. The Chocolate, The Sandwiches, the Jellies, the Cakes, the Ice,

---

1 An allusion to Grandison Hall in Richardson's *Sir Charles Grandison*. There the orchard is bordered "with three rows of trees, at proper distances from each other; one of pines; one of cedars; one of Scotch firs, in the like semicircular order" (Vol. 7, Letter 5).
2 A plantation of shrubs, with paths for walking and admiring views.
3 See p. 156, note 1.
4 A drink of hot chocolate, a luxury item. It was made by dissolving cocoa—a paste or cake of ground and roasted cacao seeds—into milk, and sweetening it with vanilla and other substances.
5 A pie made from the flesh of deer, another luxury dish.

and the Soup soon made their appearance, and Mr Gower having tasted something of all, and pocketted the rest, was conducted into the dining parlour, where he eat a most excellent Dinner and partook of the most exquisite Wines, while Mr and Mrs Webb stood by him still pressing him to eat and drink a little more. "And now my good Sir, said Mr Webb, when Mr Gower's repast was concluded, what else can we do to contribute to your happiness and express the Affection we bear you. Tell us what you wish more to receive, and depend upon our gratitude for the communication of your wishes." "Give me then your house and Grounds; I ask for nothing else." "It is yours, exclaimed both at once; from this moment it is yours." This Agreement concluded on and the present accepted by Mr Gower, Mr Webb rang to have the Carriage ordered, telling William at the same time to call the Young Ladies.

"Best of Men, said Mrs Webb, we will not long intrude upon your Time."

"Make no Apologies dear Madam, replied Mr Gower, You are welcome to stay this half hour if you like it."

They both burst forth into raptures of Admiration at his politeness, which they agreed served only to make their Conduct appear more inexcusable in trespassing on his time.

The Young Ladies soon entered the room. The eldest of them was about seventeen, the other, several years younger. Mr Gower had no sooner fixed his Eyes on Miss Webb than he felt that something more was necessary to his happiness than the house he had just received—Mrs Webb introduced him to her daughter. "Our dear freind Mr Gower my Love—He has been so good as to accept of this house, small as it is, and to promise to keep it for ever." "Give me leave to assure you Sir, said Miss Webb, that I am highly sensible of your kindness in this respect, which from the shortness of my Father's and Mother's acquaintance with You, is more than usually flattering." Mr Gower bowed—"You are too obliging Ma'am—I assure you that I like the house extremely— and if they would complete their generosity by giving me their elder daughter in marriage with a handsome portion,[1] I should have nothing more to wish for." This compliment brought a blush into the cheeks of the lovely Miss Webb, who seemed however to refer herself to her father and Mother. *They* looked delighted at each other—At length Mrs Webb breaking silence, said—"We bend under a weight of obligations to you which we can never

1 A large dowry.

repay. Take our girl, take our Maria, and on her must the difficult task fall, of endeavouring to make some return to so much Benefiscence." Mr Webb added, "Her fortune is but ten thousand pounds, which is almost too small a sum to be offered." This objection however being instantly removed by the generosity of Mr Gower, who declared himself satisfied with the sum mentioned, Mr and Mrs Webb, with their youngest daughter took their leave, and on the next day, the nuptials of their eldest with Mr Gower were celebrated.—This amiable Man now found himself perfectly happy; united to a very lovely and deserving young woman, with an handsome fortune, an elegant house, settled in the village of Evelyn, and by that means enabled to cultivate his acquaintance with Mrs Willis, could he have a wish ungratified?—For some months he found that he could *not*, till one day as he was walking in the Shrubbery with Maria leaning on his arm, they observed a rose full-blown lying on the gravel; it had fallen from a rose tree which with three others had been planted by Mr Webb to give a pleasing variety to the walk. These four Rose trees served also to mark the quarters of the Shrubbery, by which means the Traveller might always know how far in his progress round the Paddock he was got—. Maria stooped to pick up the beautiful flower, and with all her Family Generosity presented it to her Husband. "My dear Frederic, said she, pray take this charming rose." "Rose! exclaimed Mr Gower—. Oh! Maria, of what does not that remind me! Alas my poor Sister, how have I neglected you!" The truth was that Mr Gower was the only son of a very large Family, of which Miss Rose Gower was the thirteenth daughter. This Young Lady whose merits deserved a better fate than she met with, was the darling of her relations— From the clearness of her skin and the Brilliancy of her Eyes, she was fully entitled to all their partial affection. Another circumstance contributed to the general Love they bore her, and that was one of the finest heads of hair in the world. A few Months before her Brother's marriage, her heart had been engaged by the attentions and charms of a young Man whose high rank and expectations seemed to foretell objections from his Family to a match which would be highly desirable to theirs. Proposals were made on the young Man's part, and proper objections on his Father's—He was desired to return from Carlisle[1] where he was with his beloved Rose, to the family seat in Sussex. He was

---

1   A city in Cumberland in the northwest of England, near the Scottish border, some 350 miles from Sussex.

obliged to comply, and the angry father then finding from his Conversation how determined he was to marry no other woman, sent him for a fortnight to the Isle of Wight under the care of the Family Chaplain, with the hope of overcoming his Constancy by Time and Absence in a foreign Country.[1] They accordingly prepared to bid a long adeiu to England—The young Nobleman was not allowed to see his Rosa. They set sail—A storm arose which baffled the arts of the Seamen. The Vessel was wrecked on the coast of Calshot[2] and every Soul on board perished. This sad Event soon reached Carlisle, and the beautiful Rose was affected by it, beyond the power of Expression. It was to soften her affliction by obtaining a picture of her unfortunate Lover that her brother undertook a Journey into Sussex, where he hoped that his petition would not be rejected, by the severe yet afflicted Father. When he reached Evelyn he was not many miles from ——— Castle, but the pleasing events which befell him in that place had for a while made him totally forget the object of his Journey and his unhappy Sister. The little incident of the rose however brought everything concerning her to his recollection again, and he bitterly repented his neglect. He returned to the house immediately and agitated by Greif, Apprehension and Shame wrote the following Letter to Rosa.

July 14th ———. Evelyn

My dearest Sister

As it is now four months since I left Carlisle, during which period I have not once written to you, You will perhaps unjustly accuse me of Neglect and Forgetfulness. Alas! I blush when I own the truth of your accusation.—Yet if you are still alive, do not think too harshly of me, or suppose that I could for a moment forget the situation of my Rose. Beleive me I will forget you no longer, but will hasten as soon as possible to ——— Castle if I find by your answer that you are still alive. Maria joins me in every dutiful and affectionate wish, and I am yours sincerely

Fr. Gower.

---

1 The Isle of Wight is not, of course, a foreign country, but a small island off the coast of Hampshire, separated from the mainland by the Solent Estuary and visible from Portsmouth.

2 The channel between the mainland and the Isle of Wight is very narrow, and not known for storms of any kind. Calshot Castle, overlooking the Solent, was built by Henry VIII in 1539 as part of a chain of coastal defences against the French and Spanish.

He waited in the most anxious expectation for an answer to his Letter, which arrived as soon as the great distance from Carlisle would admit of.—But alas, it came not from Rosa.

Carlisle July 17th ——

Dear Brother

My Mother has taken the liberty of opening your Letter to poor Rose, as she has been dead these six weeks. Your long absence and continued Silence gave us all great uneasiness and hastened her to her Grave. Your Journey to —— Castle therefore may be spared. You do not tell us where you have been since the time of your quitting Carlisle, nor in any way account for your tedious absence, which gives us some surprise. We all unite in Compts. to Maria, and beg to know who she is—.

Your affecte. Sister

M. Gower.

This Letter, by which Mr Gower was obliged to attribute to his own conduct, his Sister's death, was so violent a shock to his feelings, that in spite of his living at Evelyn where Illness was scarcely ever heard of, he was attacked by a fit of the gout, which confining him to his own room afforded an opportunity to Maria of shining in that favourite character of Sir Charles Grandison's, a nurse.[1] No woman could ever appear more amiable than Maria did under such circumstances, and at last by her unremitting attentions had the pleasure of seeing him gradually recover the use of his feet. It was a blessing by no means lost on him, for he was no sooner in a condition to leave the house, than he mounted his horse, and rode to —— Castle, wishing to find whether his Lordship softened by his Son's death, might have been brought to consent to the match, had both *he* and Rosa been alive. His amiable Maria followed him with her Eyes till she could see him no longer, and then sinking into her chair overwhelmed with Greif, found that in his absence she could enjoy no comfort.

Mr Gower arrived late in the evening at the castle, which was situated on a woody Eminence commanding a beautiful prospect

---

1 Another allusion to the hero of *Sir Charles Grandison*, among whose numerous accomplishments is expertise in tending the injured and sick. His patients include the badly wounded Jeronymo della Porretta and, near the end of the novel, his own newly-wed wife, the former Harriet Byron, who exclaims: "Every cordial, every medicine, did he administer to me with his own hands" (Vol. 7, Letter 48).

of the Sea. Mr Gower did not dislike the situation, tho' it was certainly greatly inferior to that of his own house. There was an irregularity in the fall of the ground, and a profusion of old Timber which appeared to him illsuited to the stile of the Castle, for it being a building of a very ancient date, he thought it required the Paddock of Evelyn lodge to form a Contrast, and enliven the structure. The gloomy appearance of the old Castle frowning on him as he followed its' winding approach, struck him with terror. Nor did he think himself safe, till he was introduced into the Drawing room where the Family were assembled to tea. Mr Gower was a perfect stranger to every one in the Circle but tho' he was always timid in the Dark and easily terrified when alone, he did not want that more necessary and more noble courage which enabled him without a Blush to enter a large party of superior Rank, whom he had never seen before, and to take his Seat amongst them with perfect Indifference. The name of Gower was not unknown to Lord ———. He felt distressed and astonished; yet rose and received him with all the politeness of a well-bred Man. Lady ——— who felt a deeper sorrow at the loss of her son, than his Lordships harder heart was capable of, could hardly keep her Seat when she found that he was the Brother of her lamented Henry's Rosa. "My Lord said Mr Gower as soon as he was seated, You are perhaps surprised at receiving a visit from a Man whom you could not have the least expectation of seeing here. But my Sister my unfortunate Sister is the real cause of my thus troubling you: That luckless Girl is now no more—and tho' *she* can receive no pleasure from the intelligence, yet for the satisfaction of her Family I wish to know whether the Death of this unhappy Pair has made an impression on your heart sufficiently strong to obtain that consent to their Marriage which in happier circumstances you would not be persuaded to give supposing that they now were both alive." His Lordship seemed lossed in astonishment. Lady ——— could not support the mention of her Son, and left the room in tears; the rest of the Family remained attentively listening, almost persuaded that Mr Gower was distracted. "Mr Gower, replied his Lordship This is a very odd question—It appears to me that you are supposing an impossibility— No one can more sincerely regret the death of my Son than I have always done, and it gives me great concern to know that Miss Gower's was hastened by his—. Yet to suppose them alive is destroying at once the Motive for a change in my sentiments concerning the affair." "My Lord, replied Mr Gower in anger, I see that you are a most inflexible Man, and that not even the death of your Son can make you wish his future Life happy. I will no longer detain your Lordship. I see, I plainly see that you are a very vile Man—And now I have the honour of wishing all your Lordships, and Ladyships a good Night." He immediately left the room, forgetting in the heat of his Anger the lateness of the hour, which at any other time would have made him tremble, and leaving the whole Company unanimous in their opinion of his being Mad. When however he had mounted his horse and the great Gates of the Castle had shut him out, he felt an universal tremor through out his whole frame.[1] If we consider his Situation indeed, alone, on horseback, as late in the year as August, and in the day, as nine o'clock, with no light to direct him but that of the Moon almost full, and the Stars which alarmed him by their twinkling, who can refrain from pitying him?—No house within a quarter of a mile, and a Gloomy Castle blackened by the deep shade of Walnuts and Pines, behind him.—He felt indeed almost distracted with his fears, and shutting his Eyes till he arrived at the Village to prevent his seeing either Gipsies or Ghosts, he rode on a full gallop all the way.

---

1 The trembling of his entire body.

Catharine, or the Bower

To Miss Austen[1]

Madam

Encouraged by your warm patronage of The beautiful Cassandra, and The History of England, which through your generous support, have obtained a place in every library in the Kingdom, and run through threescore Editions,[2] I take the liberty of begging the same Exertions in favour of the following Novel, which I humbly flatter myself, possesses Merit beyond any already published, or any that will ever in future appear, except such as may proceed from the pen of Your Most Grateful Humble Servt.

The Author

Steventon August 1792—

Catharine[3] had the misfortune, as many heroines have had before her, of losing her Parents when she was very young, and of being brought up under the care of a Maiden Aunt, who while she tenderly loved her, watched over her conduct with so scrutinizing a severity, as to make it very doubtful to many people, and to Catharine amongst the rest, whether she loved her or not. She had frequently been deprived of a real pleasure through this jealous Caution, had been sometimes obliged to relinquish a Ball because an Officer was to be there, or to dance with a Partner of her Aunt's introduction in preference to one of her own Choice. But her Spirits were naturally good, and not easily depressed, and she possessed such a fund of vivacity and good humour as could only be damped by some very serious vexation.—Besides these antidotes against every disappointment, and consolations under them, she had another, which afforded her constant relief in all

---

1 JA's elder sister, Cassandra.
2 Even the most popular works of fiction, such as Daniel Defoe's *Robinson Crusoe* or Samuel Richardson's *Pamela*, went through many fewer than sixty editions in the eighteenth century. "The History of England," another of JA's juvenilia dedicated to Cassandra, is not included in this Broadview volume.
3 Originally "Kitty." JA changed her name to "Catharine" in most but not all instances, and occasionally used the spelling "Catherine."

her misfortunes, and that was a fine shady Bower,[1] the work of her own infantine Labours assisted by those of two young Companions who had resided in the same village—. To this Bower, which terminated a very pleasant and retired walk in her Aunt's Garden, she always wandered whenever anything disturbed her, and it possessed such a charm over her senses, as constantly to tranquillize her mind and quiet her spirits—Solitude and reflection might perhaps have had the same effect in her Bed Chamber, yet Habit had so strengthened the idea which Fancy had first suggested, that such a thought never occurred to Kitty who was firmly persuaded that her Bower alone could restore her to herself. Her imagination was warm, and in her Freindships, as well as in the whole tenure[2] of her Mind, she was enthousiastic.[3] This beloved Bower had been the united work of herself and two amiable Girls, for whom since her earliest Years, she had felt the tenderest regard. They were the daughters of the Clergyman of the Parish with whose Family, while it had continued there, her Aunt had been on the most intimate terms, and the little Girls tho' separated for the greatest part of the Year by the different Modes of their Education, were constantly together during the holidays of the Miss Wynnes. In those days of happy Childhood, now so often regretted by Kitty this arbour had been formed, and separated perhaps for ever from these dear freinds, it encouraged more than any other place the tender and Melancholly recollections, of hours rendered pleasant by *them*, at once so sorrowful, yet so soothing! It was now two years since the death of Mr Wynne, and the consequent dispersion of his Family who had been left by it in great distress. They had been reduced to a state of absolute dependance on some relations, who though very opulent, and very nearly connected with them, had with difficulty been prevailed on to contribute anything towards their Support. Mrs Wynne was fortunately spared the knowledge and participation of their distress, by her release from a painful illness a few months before the death of her husband. —. The eldest daughter had been obliged to accept the offer of one of her cousins to

---

1 "An arbour; a sheltered place covered with green trees, twined and bent" (Johnson).

2 That is, tenor.

3 By the 1790s, the term "enthusiastic" was being used more positively than earlier in the century, when it was associated primarily with excessive religious zeal.

equip her for the East Indies,[1] and tho' infinitely against her inclinations had been necessitated to embrace the only possibility that was offered to her, of a Maintenance; Yet it was *one*, so opposite to all her ideas of Propriety, so contrary to her Wishes, so repugnant to her feelings, that she would almost have preferred Servitude to it, had Choice been allowed her—. Her personal Attractions had gained her a husband as soon as she had arrived at Bengal[2] and she had now been married nearly a twelvemonth. Splendidly, yet unhappily married. United to a Man of double her own age, whose disposition was not amiable, and whose Manners were unpleasing, though his Character was respectable. Kitty had heard twice from her freind since her marriage, but her Letters were always unsatisfactory, and though she did not openly avow her feelings, yet every line proved her to be Unhappy. She spoke with pleasure of nothing, but of those Amusements which they had shared together and which could return no more, and seemed to have no happiness in veiw but that of returning to England again. Her sister had been taken by another relation the Dowager[3] Lady Halifax as a companion to her Daughters, and had accompanied her family into Scotland about the same time of Cecilia's leaving England. From Mary therefore Kitty had the power of hearing more frequently, but her Letters were scarcely more comfortable—. There was not indeed that hopelessness of sorrow in her situation as in her sisters; she was not married, and could yet look forward to a change in her circumstances; but situated for the present without any immediate hope of it, in a family where, tho' all were her relations she had no freind, she wrote usually in depressed Spirits, which her separation from her Sister and her Sister's Marriage had greatly contributed to make so.—Divided thus from the two she loved best on Earth, while Cecilia and Mary were still more endeared to her by their loss, everything that brought a remembrance of them was doubly cherished, and the Shrubs they had planted, and the keepsakes they had given were rendered sacred—. The

---

1   Young women had excellent prospects of finding husbands in India,
    where numerous single Englishmen were employed by the East India
    Company. Equipment for the voyage included light clothing for the hot
    climate, linen, medicine, etc.
2   A province in northeast India, where the East India Company was
    based.
3   A widow in possession of a title or property inherited from her late
    husband.

living of Chetwynde was now in the possession of a Mr Dudley, whose Family unlike the Wynnes, were productive only of vexation and trouble to Mrs Percival,[1] and her Neice. Mr Dudley, who was the younger Son of a very noble Family, of a Family more famed for their Pride than their opulence, tenacious of his Dignity, and jealous of his rights, was forever quarrelling, if not with Mrs P herself, with her Steward and Tenants concerning tythes,[2] and with the principal Neighbours themselves concerning the respect and parade, he exacted. His Wife, an ill-educated, untaught Woman of ancient family, was proud of that family almost without knowing why, and like him too was haughty and quarrelsome, without considering for what. Their only daughter, who inherited the ignorance, the insolence, and pride of her parents, was from that Beauty of which she was unreasonably vain, considered by them as an irresistable Creature, and looked up to as the future restorer, by a Splendid Marriage, of the dignity which their reduced Situation and Mr Dudley's being obliged to take orders for a Country Living had so much lessened. They at once despised the Percivals as people of mean family, and envied them as people of fortune. They were jealous of their being more respected than themselves and while they affected to consider them as of no Consequence, were continually seeking to lessen them in the opinion of the Neighbourhood by Scandalous and Malicious reports. Such a family as this, was ill calculated to console Kitty for the loss of the Wynnes, or to fill up by their society, those occasionally irksome hours which in so retired a Situation would sometimes occur for want of a Companion. Her aunt was most excessively fond of her, and miserable if she saw her for a moment out of spirits; Yet she lived in such constant apprehension of her marrying imprudently if she were allowed the opportunity of Choosing, and was so dissatisfied with her behaviour when she saw her with Young Men, for it was, from her natural disposition remarkably open and unreserved, that though she frequently wished for her Neice's sake, that the Neighbourhood were larger, and that She had used herself to mix

---

1   Despite being a "Maiden Aunt," Mrs. Percival is so titled as a sign of respect for her age. In the manuscript, JA changed her name from "Peterson" to "Percival," although not consistently.

2   That is, tithes (tenths), taxes amounting to one tenth of a farm's annual production, supposed to be paid by landowners to the rector of a parish. In practice, however, rather than paying the rector in kind, landowners would make fixed payments.

more with it, yet the recollection of there being young Men in almost every Family in it, always conquered the Wish. The same fears that prevented Mrs Peterson's joining much in the Society of her Neighbours, led her equally to avoid inviting her relations to spend any time in her House—She had therefore constantly repelled the Annual attempt of a distant relation to visit her at Chetwynde, as there was a young Man in the Family of whom she had heard many traits that alarmed her. This Son was however now on his travels,[1] and the repeated solicitations of Kitty, joined to a consciousness of having declined with too little Ceremony the frequent overtures, of her Freinds to be admitted, and a real wish to see them herself, easily prevailed on her to press with great Earnestness the pleasure of a visit from them during the Summer. Mr and Mrs Stanley were accordingly to come, and Catharine, in having an object to look forward to, a something to expect that must inevitably releive the dullness of a constant tete-a tete with her Aunt, was so delighted, and her spirits so elevated, that for the three or four days immediately preceding their Arrival, she could scarcely fix herself to any employment. In this point Mrs Percival always thought her defective, and frequently complained of a want of Steadiness and perseverance in her occupations, which were by no means congenial to the eagerness of Kitty's Disposition, and perhaps not often met with in any young person. The tediousness too of her Aunt's conversation and the want of agreable Companions greatly encreased this desire of Change in her Employments, for Kitty found herself much sooner tired of Reading, Working,[2] or Drawing, in Mrs Peterson's parlour than in her own Arbour, where Mrs Peterson for fear of its being damp never accompanied her.

As her Aunt prided herself on the exact propriety and Neatness with which everything in her Family was conducted, and had no higher Satisfaction than that of knowing her house to be always in complete Order, as her fortune was good, and her Establishment[3] Ample, few were the preparations Necessary for the reception of her Visitors. The day of their arrival so long expected, at length came, and the Noise of the Coach and 4 as it

---

1 Taking the Grand Tour of France and, normally, of other countries in Europe.
2 Undertaking needlework, such as embroidery: a genteel occupation for a young lady.
3 The domestic staff, responsible for running household affairs and providing for the reception of visitors.

drove round the sweep,[1] was to Catherine a more interesting sound, than the Music of an Italian Opera, which to most Heroines is the hight of Enjoyment. Mr and Mrs Stanley were people of Large Fortune and high Fashion. He was a Member of the house of Commons, and they were therefore most agreably necessitated to reside half the Year in Town;[2] where Miss Stanley had been attended by the most capital Masters from the time of her being six years old to the last Spring, which comprehending a period of twelve Years had been dedicated to the acquirement of Accomplishments which were now to be displayed and in a few Years entirely neglected. She was elegant in her appearance, rather handsome, and naturally not deficient in Abilities; but those Years which ought to have been spent in the attainment of useful knowledge and Mental Improvement, had been all bestowed in learning Drawing, Italian and Music, more especially the latter, and she now united to these Accomplishments, an Understanding unimproved by reading and a Mind totally devoid either of Taste or Judgement. Her temper was by Nature good, but unassisted by reflection, she had neither patience under Disappointment, nor could sacrifice her own inclinations to promote the happiness of others. All her Ideas were towards the Elegance of her appearance, the fashion of her dress, and the Admiration she wished them to excite. She professed a love of Books without Reading, was Lively without Wit, and generally Good humoured without Merit. Such was Camilla Stanley; and Catherine, who was prejudiced by her appearance, and who from her solitary Situation was ready to like anyone, tho' her Understanding and Judgement would not otherwise have been easily satisfied, felt almost convinced when she saw her, that Miss Stanley would be the very companion She wanted, and in some degree make amends for the loss of Cecilia and Mary Wynne. She therefore attached herself to Camilla from the first day of her arrival, and from being the only young People in the house, they were by inclination constant Companions. Kitty was herself a great reader, tho' perhaps not a very deep one, and felt therefore highly delighted to find that Miss Stanley was equally fond of it.

---

1 A curved carriage drive, leading to a house.
2 A Member of Parliament would remain in London during the winter season, from the New Year until 4 June, when the King's official birthday was celebrated. He would spend the remainder of the year at his country seat.

Eager to know that their sentiments as to Books were similar, she very soon began questioning her new Acquaintance on the subject; but though She was well read in Modern history herself, she Chose rather to speak first of Books of a lighter kind, of Books universally read and Admired.

"You have read Mrs Smith's Novels,[1] I suppose?" said she to her Companion—. "Oh! Yes, replied the other, and I am quite delighted with them—They are the sweetest things in the world—" "And which do you prefer of them?" "Oh! dear, I think there is no comparison between them—Emmeline is *so much* better than any of the others—"

"Many people think so, I know; but there does not appear so great a disproportion in their Merits to *me*; do you think it is better written?"

"Oh! I do not know anything about *that*—but it is better in *everything*—Besides, Ethelinde is so long[2]—" "That is a very common Objection I beleive, said Kitty, but for my own part, if a book is well written, I always find it too short."

"So do I, only I get tired of it before it is finished." "But did not you find the story of Ethelinde very interesting? And the Descriptions of Grasmere,[3] are not they Beautiful?" "Oh! I missed them all, because I was in such a hurry to know the end of it—Then from an easy transition she added, We are going to the Lakes[4] this Autumn, and I am quite Mad with Joy; Sir Henry Devereux has promised to go with us, and that will make it so pleasant, you know—"

"I dare say it will; but I think it is a pity that Sir Henry's powers of pleasing were not reserved for an occasion where they might be more wanted.—However I quite envy you the pleasure

---

1 Charlotte Smith (1749-1806) had published four novels by August 1792, the date of "Catharine," according to its dedication. These were *Emmeline, the Orphan of the Castle* (1788), *Ethelinde, or the Recluse of the Lake* (1789), *Celestina* (1791), and *Desmond* (1792).

2 *Ethelinde* was published in five volumes; *Emmeline* and *Celestina* were four-volume novels; *Desmond*, the shortest of the four, was published in three. None of JA's own novels occupied more than three volumes.

3 A small, picturesque lake in the Lake District, in the northwest of England, a favourite destination for tourists. The opening chapters of *Ethelinde* are set on the shores of Grasmere, which Smith depicts in idyllic fashion.

4 The Lake District is also the intended destination of Elizabeth Bennet and the Gardiners for their "tour of pleasure" (*Pride and Prejudice*, Vol. 2, ch. 4).

of such a Scheme." "Oh! I am quite delighted with the thoughts of it; I can think of nothing else. I assure you I have done nothing for this last Month but plan what Cloathes I should take with me, and I have at last determined to take very few indeed besides my travelling Dress, and so I advise you to do, when ever you go; for I intend in case we should fall in with any races,[1] or stop at Matlock[2] or Scarborough,[3] to have some Things made for the occasion."

"You intend then to go into Yorkshire?"

"I beleive not—indeed I know nothing of the Route, for I never trouble myself about such things—. I only know that we are to go from Derbyshire to Matlock and Scarborough, but to which of them first, I neither know nor care[4]—I am in hopes of meeting some particular freinds of mine at Scarborough—Augusta told me in her last Letter that Sir Peter talked of going; but then you know that is so uncertain. I cannot bear Sir Peter, he is such a horrid Creature—"

"He *is*, is he?" said Kitty, not knowing what else to say. "Oh! he is quite Shocking." Here the Conversation was interrupted, and Kitty was left in a painful Uncertainty, as to the particulars of Sir Peter's Character; She knew only that he was Horrid and Shocking, but why, and in what, yet remained to be discovered. She could scarcely resolve what to think of her new Acquaintance; She appeared to be shamefully ignorant as to the Geography of England, if she had understood her right, and equally devoid of Taste and Information. Kitty was however unwilling to decide hastily; she was at once desirous of doing Miss Stanley justice, and of having her own Wishes in her answered; she determined therefore to suspend all Judgement for some time. After Supper, the Conversation turning on the State of Affairs in the political World, Mrs P, who was firmly of opinion that the whole race of Mankind were degenerating, said that for her part, Everything she beleived

---

1 Horse races, a popular site for matchmaking. Spectators, male and female, would wear their finest clothes; Camilla here intends to buy elaborate outfits for special occasions, such as race meetings.

2 A town in the Peak District of Derbyshire, also visited by Elizabeth and the Gardiners (*Pride and Prejudice*, Vol. 2, ch. 19).

3 A seaside resort in Yorkshire, on the east coast. Stopping at Matlock en route to the Lake District was practicable, but going via Scarborough would entail a lengthy detour.

4 Camilla is doubly confused: she is unaware that Matlock is in the county of Derbyshire, or that Scarborough is in Yorkshire.

was going to rack and ruin, all order was destroyed over the face of the World, The house of Commons she heard did not break up sometimes till five in the Morning,[1] and Depravity never was so general before; concluding with a wish that she might live to see the Manners of the People in Queen Elizabeth's reign, restored again. "Well Ma'am, said her Neice, but I hope you do not mean with the times to restore Queen Elizth. herself."

"Queen Elizth., said Mrs Stanley who never hazarded a remark on History that was not well founded, lived to a good old Age, and was a very Clever Woman."[2]

"True Ma'am, said Kitty; but I do not consider either of those Circumstances as meritorious in herself, and they are very far from making me wish her return, for if she were to come again with the same Abilities and the same good Constitution She might do as much Mischeif and last as long as she did before— then turning to Camilla who had been sitting very silent for some time, she added What do *you* think of Elizabeth Miss Stanley? I hope you will not defend her."

"Oh! dear, said Miss Stanley, I know nothing of Politics, and cannot bear to hear them mentioned." Kitty started at this repulse, but made no answer; that Miss Stanley must be ignorant of what she could not distinguish from Politics, she felt perfectly convinced.—She retired to her own room, perplexed in her opinion about her new Acquaintance, and fearful of her being very unlike Cecilia and Mary. She arose the next morning to experience a fuller conviction of this, and every future day encreased it—. She found no variety in her conversation; She received no information from her but in fashions, and no Amusement but in her performance on the Harpsichord; and after repeated endeavours to find her what she wished, she was obliged to give up the attempt and to consider it as fruitless. There had occasionally appeared a something like humour in Camilla which had inspired her with hopes, that she might at least have a natural Genius, tho' not an improved one, but these Sparklings of Wit happened so seldom, and were so ill-supported that she was at last convinced of their being merely accidental. All her stock of knowledge was exhausted in a very few Days, and when Kitty had learnt from her, how large their house in Town was, when the fashionable Amusements began, who were the celebrated Beau-

---

1 An allusion to the early stages of reaction in England against the threat of sedition inspired by the French Revolution.
2 Queen Elizabeth (1533-1603) died at the age of sixty-nine.

ties and who the best Millener, Camilla had nothing further to teach, except the Characters of any of her Acquaintance as they occurred in Conversation, which was done with equal Ease and Brevity, by saying that the person was either the sweetest Creature in the world, and one of whom she was doatingly fond, or horrid, Shocking and not fit to be seen.

As Catherine was very desirous of gaining every possible information as to the Characters of the Halifax Family, and concluded that Miss Stanley must be acquainted with them, as she seemed to be so with every one of any Consequence, she took an opportunity as Camilla was one day enumerating all the people of rank that her Mother visited, of asking her whether Lady Halifax were among the number.

"Oh! Thank you for reminding me of her, She is the sweetest Woman in the world, and one of our most intimate Acquaintance; I do not suppose there is a day passes during the six Months that we are in Town, but what we see each other in the course of it—. And I correspond with all the Girls."

"They *are* then a very pleasant Family? said Kitty. They ought to be so indeed, to allow of such frequent Meetings, or all Conversation must be at an end."

"Oh! dear, not at all, said Miss Stanley, for sometimes we do not speak to each other for a month together. We meet perhaps only in Public, and then you know we are often not able to get near enough; but in that case we always nod and smile."

"Which does just as well—. But I was going to ask you whether you have ever seen a Miss Wynne with them?"

"I know who you mean perfectly—she wears a blue hat—. I have frequently seen her in Brook Street, when I have been at Lady Halifax's Balls—She gives one every Month during the Winter—. But only think how good it is in her to take care of Miss Wynne, for she is a very distant relation, and so poor that, as Miss Halifax told me, her Mother was obliged to find her in Cloathes.[1] Is not it shameful?"

"That she should be so poor;? it is indeed, with such wealthy connexions as the Family have."

"Oh! no; I mean, was not it shameful in Mr Wynne to leave his Children so distressed, when he had actually the Living of Chetwynde and two or three Curacies,[2] and only four Children

---

1 Supply clothes for her.
2 In addition to his living at Chetwynde, Mr. Wynne had other livings, or curacies, at which he employed curates to take over his clerical duties.

to provide for—. What would he have done if he had had ten, as many people have?"

"He would have given them all a good Education and have left them all equally poor."

"Well I do think there never was so lucky a Family. Sir George Fitzgibbon you know sent the eldest Girl to India entirely at his own Expence, where they say she is most nobly married and the happiest Creature in the World—Lady Halifax you see has taken care of the youngest and treats her as if she were her Daughter; She does not go out into Public with her to be sure; but then she is always present when her Ladyship gives her Balls, and nothing can be kinder to her than Lady Halifax is; she would have taken her to Cheltenham[1] last year, if there had been room enough at the Lodgings, and therefore I dont think that *she* can have anything to complain of. Then there are the two Sons; one of them the Bishop of M—— has got into the Army as a Leiutenant I suppose; and the other is extremely well off I know, for I have a notion that somebody puts him to School somewhere in Wales.[2] Perhaps you knew them when they lived here?"

"Very well, We met as often as your Family and the Halifaxes do in Town, but as we seldom had any difficulty in getting near enough to speak, we seldom parted with merely a Nod and a Smile. They were indeed a most charming Family, and I beleive have scarcely their Equals in the World; The Neighbours we now have at the Parsonage, appear to more disadvantage in coming after them."

"Oh! horrid Wretches! I wonder You can endure them."

"Why, what would you have one do?"

"Oh! Lord, If I were in your place, I should abuse them all day long."

"So I do, but it does no good."

"Well, I declare it is quite a pity that they should be suffered to live. I wish my Father would propose knocking all their Brains out, some day or other when he is in the House. So abominably proud of their Family! And I dare say after all, that there is nothing particular in it."

---

1 A fashionable spa resort in Gloucestershire.

2 Attending a Welsh boarding school was a dubious privilege. Welsh schools were cheaper and less well equipped than their English counterparts. Their remoteness, however, could be useful for patrons who wished their charges to remain at a distance.

"Why Yes, I beleive they *have* reason to value themselves on it, if any body has; for you know he is Lord Amyatt's Brother."

"Oh! I know all that very well, but it is no reason for their being so horrid. I remember I met Miss Dudley last Spring with Lady Amyatt at Ranelagh,[1] and she had such a frightful Cap on, that I have never been able to bear any of them since.—And so you used to think the Wynnes very pleasant?"

"You speak as if their being so were doubtful! Pleasant! Oh! they were every thing that could interest and Attach. It is not in my power to do Justice to their Merits, tho' not to feel them, I think must be impossible. They have unfitted me for any Society but their own!"

"Well, That is just what I think of the Miss Halifaxes; by the bye, I must write to Caroline tomorrow, and I do not know what to say to her. The Barlows too are just such other sweet Girls; but I wish Augusta's hair was not so dark. I cannot bear Sir Peter— Horrid Wretch! He is *always* laid up with the Gout, which is exceedingly disagreable to the Family."

"And perhaps not very pleasant to *himself*—. But as to the Wynnes; do you really think them very fortunate?"

"Do I? Why, does not every body? Miss Halifax and Caroline and Maria all say that they are the luckiest Creatures in the World. So does Sir George Fitzgibbon and so do Everybody."

"That is, Every body who have themselves conferred an obligation on them. But do you call it lucky, for a Girl of Genius and Feeling to be sent in quest of a Husband to Bengal, to be married there to a Man of whose Disposition she has no opportunity of judging till her Judgement is of no use to her, who may be a Tyrant, or a Fool or both for what she knows to the Contrary. Do you call *that* fortunate?"

"I know nothing of all that; I only know that it was extremely good in Sir George to fit her out and pay for her Passage, and that she would not have found Many who would have done the same."

"I wish she had not found *one*, said Kitty with great Eagerness, she might then have remained in England and been happy."

"Well, I cannot conceive the hardship of going out in a very agreable Manner with two or three sweet Girls for Companions,

---

1 Ranelagh Gardens, a pleasure garden in Chelsea, on the edge of London, with a large rotunda at the centre that contained an orchestra and boxes for taking refreshments. Paintings, sculptures, lighting effects, and fireworks were among its attractions.

having a delightful voyage to Bengal or Barbadoes[1] or wherever it is, and being married soon after one's arrival to a very charming Man immensely rich—. I see no hardship in all that."

"Your representation of the Affair, said Kitty laughing, certainly gives a very different idea of it from Mine. But supposing all this to be true, still, as it was by no means certain that she would be so fortunate either in her voyage, her Companions, or her husband; in being obliged to run the risk of their proving very different, she undoubtedly experienced a great hardship—. Besides, to a Girl of any Delicacy, the voyage in itself, since the object of it is so universally known, is a punishment that needs no other to make it very severe."

"I do not see that at all. She is not the first Girl who has gone to the East Indies for a Husband, and I declare I should think it very good fun if I were as poor."

"I beleive you would think very differently *then*. But at least you will not defend her Sister's situation? Dependant even for her Cloathes on the bounty of others, who of course do not pity her, as by your own account, they consider her as very fortunate."

"You are extremely nice[2] upon my word; Lady Halifax is a delightful Woman, and one of the sweetest tempered Creatures in the World; I am sure I have every reason to speak well of her, for we are under most amazing Obligations to her. She has frequently chaperoned me when my Mother has been indisposed, and last Spring she lent me her own horse three times, which was a prodigious favour, for it is the most beautiful Creature that ever was seen, and I am the only person she ever lent it to.

"And then, continued she, the Miss Halifaxes are quite delightful—. Maria is one of the cleverest Girls that ever were known—Draws in Oils,[3] and plays anything by sight. She promised me one of her Drawings before I left Town, but I entirely forgot to ask her for it—. I would give any thing to have one."

"But was not it very odd, said Kitty, that the Bishop should send Charles Wynne to sea, when he must have had a much better chance of providing for him in the Church, which was the profession that Charles liked best, and the one for which his

---

1 Both British colonies, but Barbados, a sugar-producing island in the West Indies, is very distant from Bengal in the East Indies, where Miss Wynne has been sent.

2 Fastidious, squeamish.

3 Paints or sketches in oils, considered a higher achievement than working with watercolour or crayon.

Father had intended him? The Bishop I know had often promised Mr Wynne a living, and as he never gave him one, I think it was incumbant on him to transfer the promise to his Son."

"I beleive you think he ought to have resigned his Bishopric to him; you seem determined to be dissatisfied with every thing that has been done for them."

"Well, said Kitty, this is a subject on which we shall never agree, and therefore it will be useless to continue it farther, or to mention it again—" She then left the room, and running out of the House was soon in her dear Bower where she could indulge in peace all her affectionate Anger against the relations of the Wynnes, which was greatly heightened by finding from Camilla that they were in general considered as having acted particularly well by them—. She amused herself for some time in Abusing, and Hating them all, with great Spirit, and when this tribute to her regard for the Wynnes, was paid, and the Bower began to have its usual influence over her Spirits, she contributed towards settling them, by taking out a book, for she had always one about her, and reading—. She had been so employed for nearly an hour, when Camilla came running towards her with great Eagerness, and apparently great Pleasure—. "Oh! my Dear Catherine, said she, half out of Breath—I have such delightful News for You—But you shall guess what it is—We are all the happiest Creatures in the World; would you beleive it, the Dudleys have sent us an invitation to a Ball at their own House—. What Charming People they are! I had no idea of there being so much Sense in the whole Family—I declare I quite doat upon them—. And it happens so fortunately too, for I expect a new Cap from Town tomorrow which will just do for a Ball—Gold Net.[1]—It will be a most angelic thing—Every Body will be longing for the pattern[2]—" The expectation of a Ball was indeed very agreable intelligence to Kitty, who fond of Dancing and seldom able to enjoy it, had reason to feel even greater pleasure in it than her Freind; for to *her*, it was now no novelty—. Camilla's delight however was by no means inferior to Kitty's, and she rather expressed the most of the two. The Cap came and every other preparation was soon completed; while these were in agitation the Days passed gaily away, but when Directions were no longer necessary, Taste could no longer be displayed, and Difficulties no longer overcome, the short period that intervened before the day of the Ball hung

---

1 A cap with a hairnet made of golden thread, fashionable in the 1790s.
2 Commercially printed patterns were scarce and much sought after.

heavily on their hands, and every hour was too long. The very few Times that Kitty had ever enjoyed the Amusement of Dancing was an excuse for *her* impatience, and an apology for the Idleness it occasioned to a Mind naturally very Active; but her Freind without such a plea was infinitely worse than herself. She could do nothing but wander from the house to the Garden, and from the Garden to the avenue, wondering when Thursday would come, which she might easily have ascertained, and counting the hours as they passed which served only to lengthen them. —. They retired to their rooms in high Spirits on Wednesday night, but Kitty awoke the next Morning with a violent Toothake. It was in vain that she endeavoured at first to deceive herself; her feelings were witnesses too acute of it's reality; with as little success did she try to sleep it off, for the pain she suffered prevented her closing her Eyes—. She then summoned her Maid and with the Assistance of the Housekeeper, every remedy that the receipt book[1] or the head of the latter contained, was tried, but ineffectually; for though for a short time releived by them, the pain still returned. She was now obliged to give up the endeavour, and to reconcile herself not only to the pain of a Toothake, but to the loss of a Ball; and though she had with so much eagerness looked forward to the day of its arrival, had received such pleasure in the necessary preparations, and promised herself so much delight in it, Yet she was not so totally void of philosophy as many Girls of her age, might have been in her situation. She considered that there were Misfortunes of a much greater magnitude than the loss of a Ball, experienced every day by somepart of Mortality, and that the time might come when She would herself look back with Wonder and perhaps with Envy on her having known no greater vexation. By such reflections as these, she soon reasoned herself into as much Resignation and Patience as the pain she suffered, would allow of, which after all was the greatest Misfortune of the two, and told the sad Story when she entered the Breakfast room, with tolerable Composure. Mrs Percival more greived for her toothake than her Disappointment, as she feared that it would not be possible to prevent her Dancing with a *Man* if she went, was eager to try everything that had already been applied to alleviate the pain, while at the same time She declared it was impossible for her to leave the House. Miss Stanley who joined to her concern for her Freind, felt a mixture of Dread lest

---

1 A printed or manuscript collection of home remedies and prescriptions for ailments, including toothache.

her Mother's proposal that they should all remain at home, might be accepted, was very violent in her sorrow on the occasion, and though her apprehensions on the subject were soon quieted by Kitty's protesting that sooner than allow any one to stay with her, she would herself go, she continued to lament it with such unceasing vehemence as at last drove Kitty to her own room. Her Fears for herself being now entirely dissipated left her more than ever at leisure to pity and persecute her Freind who tho' safe when in her own room, was frequently removing from it to some other in hopes of being more free from pain, and then had no opportunity of escaping her—.

"To be sure, there never was anything so shocking, said Camilla; To come on such a day too! For one would not have minded it you know had it been at *any other* time. But it always is so. I never was at a Ball in my Life, but what something happened to prevent somebody from going! I wish there were no such things as Teeth in the World; they are nothing but plagues to one, and I dare say that People might easily invent something to eat with instead of them; Poor Thing! what pain you are in! I declare it is quite Shocking to look at you. But you w'ont have it out, will you? For Heaven's sake do'nt; for there is nothing I dread so much. I declare I had rather undergo the greatest Tortures in the World than have a tooth drawn.[1] Well! how patiently you do bear it! how can you be so quiet? Lord, if I were in your place I should make such a fuss, there would be no bearing me. I should torment you to Death."

"So you do, as it is." thought Kitty.

"For my own part, Catherine said Mrs Percival I have not a doubt but that you caught this toothake by sitting so much in that Arbour, for it is always damp. I know it has ruined your Constitution entirely; and indeed I do not beleive it has been of much service to mine; I sate down in it last May to rest myself, and I have never been quite well since—. I shall order John to pull it all down I assure you."

"I know you will not do that Ma'am, said Kitty, as you must be convinced how unhappy it would make me."

"You talk very ridiculously Child; it is all whim and Nonsense. Why cannot you fancy this room an Arbour?"

"Had this room been built by Cecilia and Mary, I should have valued it equally Ma'am, for it is not merely the name of an Arbour, which charms me."

---

1 Since extraction would take place without anaesthetic, Camilla's fears are understandable. See p. 345, note 2.

"Why indeed Mrs Percival, said Mrs Stanley, I must think that Catherine's affection for her Bower is the effect of a Sensibility that does her Credit. I love to see a Freindship between young Persons and always consider it as a sure mark of an amiable affectionate disposition. I have from Camilla's infancy taught her to think the same, and have taken great pains to introduce her to young people of her own age who were likely to be worthy of her regard. nothing forms the taste more than sensible and Elegant Letters—. Lady Halifax thinks just like me—. Camilla corresponds with her Daughters, and I believe I may venture to say that they are none of them *the worse* for it." These ideas were too modern to suit Mrs Percival who considered a correspondence between Girls as productive of no good, and as the frequent origin of imprudence and Error by the effect of pernicious advice and bad Example. She could not therefore refrain from saying that for her part, she had lived fifty Years in the world without having ever had a correspondent, and did not find herself at all the less respectable for it—. Mrs Stanley could say nothing in answer to this, but her Daughter who was less governed by Propriety said in her thoughtless way, "But who knows what you might have been Ma'am, if you *had* had a Correspondent; perhaps it would have made you quite a different Creature. I declare I would not be without those I have for all the World. It is the greatest delight of my Life, and you cannot think how much their Letters have formed my taste as Mama says, for I hear from them generally every week."

"You received a Letter from Augusta Barlow to day, did not you my Love? said her Mother—. She writes remarkably well I know."

"Oh! Yes Ma'am, the most delightful Letter you ever heard of. She sends me a long account of the new Regency walking dress[1] Lady Susan has given her, and it is so beautiful that I am quite dieing with envy for it."

"Well, I am prodigiously happy to hear such pleasing news of my young freind; I have a high regard for Augusta, and most sincerely partake in the general Joy on the occasion. But does she say nothing else? it seemed to be a long Letter—Are they to be at Scarborough?"

---

1 A late insertion that must have been made after February 1811, when the Regency Act proclaimed that the Prince of Wales would reign in place of his incapacitated father, George III. The Regency lasted until the death of George III in 1820, three years after Austen's death in July 1817.

"Oh! Lord, she never once mentions it, now I recollect it; and I entirely forgot to ask her when I wrote last. She says nothing indeed except about the Regency." "She *must* write well thought Kitty, to make a long Letter upon a Bonnet and Pelisse."[1] She then left the room tired of listening to a conversation which tho' it might have diverted her had she been well, served only to fatigue and depress her, while in pain. Happy was it for *her*, when the hour of dressing came, for Camilla satisfied with being surrounded by her Mother and half the Maids in the House did not want her assistance, and was too agreably employed to want her Society. She remained therefore alone in the parlour, till joined by Mr Stanley and her Aunt, who however after a few enquiries, allowed her to continue undisturbed and began their usual conversation on Politics. This was a Subject on which they could never agree, for Mr Stanley who considered himself as perfectly qualified by his Seat in the House, to decide on it without hesitation, resolutely maintained that the Kingdom had not for ages been in so flourishing and prosperous a state,[2] and Mrs Percival with equal warmth, tho' perhaps less argument, as vehemently asserted that the whole Nation would speedily be ruined, and everything as she expressed herself be at sixes and sevens. It was not however unamusing to Kitty to listen to the Dispute, especially as she began then to be more free from pain, and without taking any share in it herself, she found it very entertaining to observe the eagerness with which they both defended their opinions, and could not help thinking that Mr Stanley would not feel more disappointed if her Aunt's expectations were fulfilled, than her Aunt would be mortified by their failure. After waiting a considerable time Mrs Stanley and her daughter appeared, and Camilla in high Spirits, and perfect good humour with her own looks, was more violent than ever in her lamentations over her Freind as she practised her scotch Steps[3] about the room—. At length they departed, and Kitty better able to amuse herself than she had been the whole Day before, wrote a long account of her Misfortunes to Mary Wynne. When her Letter was concluded she

---

1 A long cloak of satin or velvet, the usual outerwear of the time.

2 Stanley is a member of the Whig government of William Pitt the Younger, who had been Prime Minister since 1783. Pitt was far more popular than his predecessor, Lord North, who was Prime Minister during the War of American Independence (1775-83).

3 Scottish steps were incorporated into English country dances, but Scottish reels were considered too lively for dancing in public places.

had an opportunity of witnessing the truth of that assertion which says that Sorrows are lightened by Communication, for her toothake was then so much relieved that she began to entertain an idea of following her Freinds to Mr Dudley's. They had been gone an hour, and as every thing relative to her Dress was in complete readiness, She considered that in another hour since there was so little a way to go, She might be there—. They were gone in Mr Stanley's Carriage and therefore She might follow in her Aunt's. As the plan seemed so very easy to be executed, and promising so much pleasure, it was after a few Minutes deliberation finally adopted, and running up stairs, She rang in great haste for her Maid. The Bustle and Hurry which then ensued for nearly an hour was at last happily concluded by her finding herself very well-dressed and in high Beauty. Anne was then dispatched in the same haste to order the Carriage, while her Mistress was putting on her gloves, and arranging the folds of her dress. In a few Minutes she heard the Carriage drive up to the Door, and tho' at first surprised at the expedition with which it had been got ready, she concluded after a little reflection that the Men had received some hint of her intentions beforehand, and was hastening out of the room, when Anne came running into it in the greatest hurry and agitation, exclaiming "Lord Ma'am! Here's a Gentleman in a Chaise and four[1] come, and I cannot for my Life conceive who it is! I happened to be crossing the hall when the Carriage drove up, and I knew nobody would be in the way to let him in but Tom, and he looks so awkward you know Ma'am, now his hair is just done up,[2] that I was not willing the gentleman should see him, and so I went to the door myself. And he is one of the handsomest young Men you would wish to see; I was almost ashamed of being seen in my Apron[3] Ma'am, but however he is vastly handsome and did not seem to mind it at all.—And he asked me whether the Family were at home; and so I said everybody was gone out but you Ma'am, for I would not deny you because I was sure you would like to see him. And then he asked me whether Mr and Mrs Stanley were not here, and so I said Yes, and then—

---

1 A light carriage drawn by four horses, and thus an exceptionally dashing form of transport.
2 Tom the footman has had his hair elaborately arranged, as was customary in a fashionable household; the footman would wear a splendid uniform and was expected to make a fine appearance.
3 A working apron, made of coarse linen, not a decorative lady's apron.

"Good Heavens! said Kitty, what can all this mean! And who can it possibly be! Did you never see him before? And Did not he tell you his Name?"

"No Ma'am, he never said anything about it—So then I asked him to walk into the parlour, and he was prodigious agreable, and—"

"Whoever he is, said her Mistress, he has made a great impression upon you Nanny—But where did he come from? and what does he want here?"

"Oh! Ma'am, I was going to tell you, that I fancy his business is with You; for he asked me whether you were at leisure to see anybody, and desired I would give his Compliments to you, and say he should be very happy to wait on you—However I thought he had better not come up into your Dressing room, especially as everything is in such a litter,[1] so I told him if he would be so obliging as to stay in the parlour, I would run up Stairs and tell you he was come, and I dared to say that you would wait upon *him*. Lord Ma'am, I'd lay anything that he is come to ask you to dance with him tonight, and has got his Chaise ready to take you to Mr Dudley's."

Kitty could not help laughing at this idea, and only wished it might be true, as it was very likely that she would be too late for any other partner—"But what in the name of wonder, can he have to say to me? Perhaps he is come to rob the house—. he comes in stile at least; and it will be some consolation for our losses to be robbed by a Gentleman in a Chaise and 4—. What Livery[2] has his Servants?"

"Why that is the most wonderful thing about him Ma'am, for he has not a single servant with him, and came with hack horses;[3] But he is as handsome as a Prince for all that, and has quite the look of one—. Do dear Ma'am, go down, for I am sure you will be delighted with him—"

"Well, I beleive I must go; but it is very odd! What can he have to say to me." Then giving one look at herself in the Glass, she walked with great impatience, tho' trembling all the while from not knowing what to expect, down Stairs, and after pausing a

---

1 Untidiness associated with feminine disorder.
2 The uniform worn by a servant; its quality would signify the wealth and importance of the servant's employer.
3 Hackney horses, hired from a stable. Lacking servants and horses of his own, the visitor is of questionable social status. He has apparently hired four horses in an attempt to enhance his appearance.

moment at the door to gather Courage for opening it, she resolutely entered the room.

The Stranger, whose appearance did not disgrace the account she had received of it from her Maid, rose up on her entrance, and laying aside the Newspaper he had been reading, advanced towards her with an air of the most perfect Ease and Vivacity, and said to her, "It is certainly a very awkward circumstance to be thus obliged to introduce myself, but I trust that the necessity of the case will plead my Excuse, and prevent your being prejudiced by it against me—. *Your* name, I need not ask Ma'am—. Miss Percival is too well known to me by description to need any information of that." Kitty, who had been expecting him to tell his own name, instead of hers, and who from having been little in company, and never before in such a situation, felt herself unable to ask it, tho' she had been planning her speech all the way down stairs, was so confused and distressed by this unexpected address that she could only return a slight curtesy to it and accepted the chair he reached her, without knowing what she did. The gentleman then continued. "You are, I dare say, surprised to see me returned from France so soon, and nothing indeed but business would have brought me to England; a very Melancholy affair has now occasioned it, and I was unwilling to leave it without paying my respects to the Family in Devonshire[1] whom I have so long wished to be acquainted with—."

Kitty, who felt much more surprised at his supposing her *to be so*, than at seeing a person in England, whose having ever left it was perfectly unknown to her, still continued silent from Wonder and Perplexity, and her visitor still continued to talk. "You will suppose Madam that I was not the *less* desirous of waiting on you, from your having Mr and Mrs Stanley with You—. I hope they are well? And Mrs Percival how does *she* do?" Then without waiting for an answer he gaily added, "But my dear Miss Percival you are going out I am sure; and I am detaining you from your appointment. How can I ever expect to be forgiven for such injustice! Yet how can I, so circumstanced, forbear to offend! You seem dressed for a Ball? But this is the Land of gaiety I know; I have for many years been desirous of visiting it. You have Dances I suppose at least every week—But where are the rest of your party gone, and what kind Angel in compassion to me, has excluded *you* from it?"

"Perhaps Sir, said Kitty extremely confused by his manner of speaking to her, and highly displeased with the freedom of his

---

1 A county in the southwest of England.

Conversation towards one who had never seen him before and did not *now* know his name, perhaps Sir, you are acquainted with Mr and Mrs Stanley; and your business may be with *them?*"

"You do me too much honour Ma'am, replied he laughing, in supposing me to be acquainted with Mr and Mrs Stanley; I merely know them by sight; very distant relations; only my Father and Mother; Nothing more. I assure you."

"Gracious Heaven! said Kitty, are *you* Mr Stanley then?—I beg a thousand pardons—Though really upon recollection I do not know for what—for you never told me your name—"

"I beg your pardon—I made a very fine Speech when you entered the room, all about introducing myself; I assure you it was very great for *me.*"

"The speech had certainly great Merit, said Kitty smiling; I thought so at the time; but since you never mentioned your name in it, as an *introductory one* it might have been better."

There was such an air of good humour and Gaiety in Stanley, that Kitty, tho' perhaps not authorized to address him with so much familiarity on so short an acquaintance, could not forbear indulging the natural Unreserve and Vivacity of her own Disposition, in speaking to him, as he spoke to her. She was intimately acquainted too with his Family who were her relations, and she chose to consider herself entitled by the connexion to forget how little a while they had known each other. "Mr and Mrs Stanley and your Sister are extremely well, said She, and will I dare say be very much surprised to see you—But I am sorry to hear that your return to England has been occasioned by any unpleasant circumstance."

"Oh! Do'nt talk of it, said he, it is a most confounded shocking affair, and makes me miserable to think of it; But where are my Father and Mother, and your Aunt gone? Oh! Do you know that I met the prettiest little waiting maid in the World, when I came here; she let me into the house; I took her for you at first."

"You did me a great deal of honour, and give me more credit for good nature than I deserve, for I *never* go to the door when any one comes."

"Nay do not be angry; I mean no offence. But tell me, where are you going to so smart? Your carriage is just coming round."

"I am going to a Dance at a Neighbour's, where your Family and my Aunt are already gone."

"Gone, without you! what's the meaning of *that?* But I suppose you are like myself, rather long in dressing."

"I must have been so indeed, if that were the case for they have been gone nearly these two hours; The reason however was not what you suppose—I was prevented going by a pain—"

"By a pain! interrupted Stanley, Oh! heavens, that is dreadful indeed! No Matter where the pain was. But my dear Miss Percival, what do you say to my accompanying you? And suppose you were to dance with me too? *I* think it would be very pleasant."

"I can have no objection to either I am sure, said Kitty laughing to find how near the truth her Maid's conjecture had been; on the contrary I shall be highly honoured by both, and I can answer for Your being extremely welcome to the Family who give the Ball."

"Oh! hang them; who cares for that; they cannot turn me out of the house. But I am afraid I shall cut a sad figure among all your Devonshire Beaux in this dusty, travelling apparel,[1] and I have not wherewithal to change it. You can procure me some powder[2] perhaps, and I must get a pair of Shoes from one of the Men, for I was in such a devil of a hurry to leave Lyons[3] that I had not time to have anything pack'd up but some linen."[4] Kitty very readily undertook to procure for him everything he wanted, and telling the footman to shew him into Mr Stanley's dressing room,[5] gave Nanny orders to send in some powder and pomatum, which orders Nanny chose to execute in person. As Stanley's preparations in dressing were confined to such very trifling articles, Kitty of course expected him in about ten minutes; but she found that it had not been merely a boast of vanity in saying that he was dilatory in that respect, as he kept her waiting for him above half an hour, so that the Clock had struck ten before he entered the room and the rest of the party had gone by eight.

"Well, said he as he came in, have not I been very quick? I never hurried so much in my Life before."

---

1 Probably a riding outfit, including boots and overcoat; most inappropriate for a ball, at which both men and women would wear their finest clothes.

2 Hair powder, usually white or grey, was still used by men of fashion in the early 1790s.

3 A large city in central eastern France, Lyons was a popular destination on the Grand Tour.

4 Shirts, made of linen.

5 The Stanleys have been given a large visitor's apartment, with a bedroom and two dressing rooms. The arrangement, like the footman's attire, suggests the size and importance of Mrs. Percival's house.

"In that case you certainly have, replied Kitty, for all Merit you know is comparative."

"Oh! I knew you would be delighted with me for making so much haste—. But come, the Carriage is ready; so, do not keep me waiting." And so saying he took her by the hand, and led her out of the room. "Why, my dear Cousin, said he when they were seated, this will be a most agreable surprize to every body to see you enter the room with such a smart Young Fellow as I am—I hope your Aunt w'ont be alarmed."

"To tell you the truth, replied Kitty, I think the best way to prevent it, will be to send for her, or your Mother before we go into the room, especially as you are a perfect stranger, and must of course be introduced to Mr and Mrs Dudley—"

"Oh! Nonsense, said he; I did not expect *you* to stand upon such Ceremony; Our acquaintance with each other renders all such Prudery, ridiculous; Besides, if we go in together, we shall be the whole talk of the Country—"

"To *me* replied Kitty, that would certainly be a most powerful inducement; but I scarcely know whether my Aunt would consider it as such—. Women at her time of life, have odd ideas of propriety you know."

"Which is the very thing that you ought to break them of; and why should you object to entering a room with me where all our relations are, when you have done me the honour to admit me without any chaprone into your Carriage? Do not you think your Aunt will be as much offended with you for one, as for the other of these mighty crimes."

"Why really said Catherine, I do not know but that she may; however, it is no reason that I should offend against Decorum a second time, because I have already done it once."

"On the contrary, that is the very reason which makes it impossible for you to prevent it, since you cannot offend for the *first time* again."

"You are very ridiculous, said she laughing, but I am afraid your arguments divert me too much to convince me."

"At least they will convince you that I am very agreable, which after all, is the happiest conviction for me, and as to the affair of Propriety we will let that rest till we arrive at our Journey's end—. This is a monthly Ball[1] I suppose. Nothing but Dancing here—."

---

1 A public ball, with an entrance fee, as opposed to the private ball given by Mr. Dudley.

"I thought I had told you that it was given by a Mr Dudley—"

"Oh! aye so you did; but why should not Mr Dudley give one every month? By the bye who *is that* Man? Every body gives Balls now I think; I beleive I must give one myself soon—. Well, but how do you like my Father and Mother? And poor little Camilla too, has not she plagued you to death with the Halifaxes?" Here the Carriage fortunately stopped at Mr Dudley's, and Stanley was too much engaged in handing her out of it, to wait for an answer, or to remember that what he had said required one. They entered the small vestibule which Mr Dudley had raised to the Dignity of a Hall, and Kitty immediately desired the footman who was leading the way upstairs, to inform either Mrs Peterson, or Mrs Stanley of her arrival, and beg them to come to her, but Stanley unused to any contradiction and impatient to be amongst them, would neither allow her to wait, or listen to what she said, and forcibly seizing her arm within his, overpowered her voice with the rapidity of his own, and Kitty half angry, and half laughing was obliged to go with him up stairs, and could even with difficulty prevail on him to relinquish her hand before they entered the room. Mrs Percival was at that very moment engaged in conversation with a Lady at the upper end of the room,[1] to whom she had been giving a long account of her Neice's unlucky disappointment, and the dreadful pain that she had with so much fortitude, endured the whole Day—"I left her however, said She, thank heaven!, a little better, and I hope she has been able to amuse herself with a book, poor thing! for she must otherwise be very dull. She is probably in bed by this time, which while she is so poorly, is the best place for her you know Ma'am." The Lady was going to give her assent to this opinion, when the Noise of voices on the stairs, and the footman's opening the door as if for the entrance of Company, attracted the attention of every body in the room; and as it was in one of those Intervals between the Dances when every one seemed glad to sit down, Mrs Peterson had a most unfortunate opportunity of seeing her Neice whom she had supposed in bed, or amusing herself as the height of gaity with a book, enter the room most elegantly dressed, with a smile on her Countenance, and a glow of mingled Chearfulness and Confusion on her Cheeks, attended by a young Man uncommonly handsome, and who without any of her Confusion, appeared to have all

---

1 The musicians were placed at the end of the room opposite to the door through which guests entered.

her vivacity. Mrs Percival, colouring with anger and Astonishment, rose from her Seat, and Kitty walked eagerly towards her, impatient to account for what she saw appeared wonderful to every body, and extremely offensive to *her*, while Camilla on seeing her Brother ran instantly towards him, and very soon explained who he was by her words and her actions. Mr Stanley, who so fondly doated on his Son, that the pleasure of seeing him again after an absence of three Months prevented his feeling for the time any anger against him for returning to England without his knowledge, received him with equal surprise and delight; and soon comprehending the cause of his Journey, forbore any further conversation with him, as he was eager to see his Mother, and it was necessary that he should be introduced to Mr Dudley's family. This introduction to any one but Stanley would have been highly unpleasant, for they considered their dignity injured by his coming uninvited to their house, and received him with more than their usual haughtiness; But Stanley who with a vivacity of temper seldom subdued, and a contempt of censure not to be overcome, possessed an opinion of his own Consequence, and a perseverance in his own schemes which were not to be damped by the conduct of others, appeared not to perceive it. The Civilities therefore which they coldly offered, he received with a gaiety and ease peculiar to himself, and then attended by his Father and Sister walked into another room where his Mother was playing at Cards,[1] to experience another Meeting, and undergo a repetition of pleasure, Surprise, and Explanations. While these were passing, Camilla eager to communicate all she felt to some one who would attend to her, returned to Catherine, and seating herself by her, immediately began—"Well, did you ever know anything so delightful as this? But it always is so; I never go to a Ball in my Life but what something or other happens unexpectedly that is quite charming!"

"A Ball replied Kitty, seems to be a most eventful thing to You—".

"Oh! Lord, it is indeed—But only think of my brother's returning so suddenly—And how shocking a thing it is that has brought him over! I never heard anything so dreadful—!"

---

1 A room with card tables was a standard feature of a ball, providing entertainment for those, such as Mrs. Stanley, who did not dance, or for those resting from dancing.

"What is it pray that has occasioned his leaving France? I am sorry to find that it is a melancholy event."

"Oh! it is beyond anything you can conceive! His favourite Hunter[1] who was turned out in the park on his going abroad, somehow or other fell ill—No, I beleive it was an accident, but however it was something or other, or else it was something else, and so they sent an Express[2] immediately to Lyons where my Brother was, for they knew that he valued this Mare more than anything else in the World besides; and so my Brother set off directly for England, and without packing up another Coat; I am quite angry with him about it; it was so shocking you know to come away without a change of Cloathes—"

"Why indeed said Kitty, it seems to have been a very shocking affair from beginning to end."

"Oh! it is beyond anything You can conceive! I would rather have had *anything* happen than that he should have lossed that mare."

"Except his coming away without an other coat."

"Oh! yes, that has vexed me more than you can imagine—. Well, and so Edward got to Brampton[3] just as the poor Thing was dead,—but as he could not bear to remain there *then*, he came off directly to Chetwynde on purpose to see us—. I hope he may not go abroad again."

"Do you think he will not?"

"Oh! dear, to be sure he must, but I wish he may not with all my heart—. You cannot think how fond I am of him! By the bye are not you in love with him yourself?"

"To be sure I am replied Kitty laughing, I am in love with every handsome Man I see."

"That is just like me—*I* am always in love with every handsome Man in the World."

"There you outdo me replied Catherine for I am only in love with those I *do* see." Mrs Percival who was sitting on the other side of her, and who began now to distinguish the words, *Love* and *handsome Man*, turned hastily towards them, and said "What are you talking of Catherine?" To which Catherine immediately answered with the simple artifice of a Child, "Nothing Ma'am."

---

1 A horse used for hunting. They were often thoroughbreds and thus expensive.
2 A messenger sent to deliver news as rapidly as possible.
3 The name of the Stanleys' country seat, where they spend their summers when Parliament is not sitting.

She had already received a very severe lecture from her Aunt on the imprudence of her behaviour during the whole evening; She blamed her for coming to the Ball, for coming in the same Carriage with Edward Stanley, and still more for entering the room with him. For the last-mentioned offence Catherine knew not what apology to give, and tho' she longed in answer to the second to say that she had not thought it would be civil to make Mr Stanley *walk*, she dared not so to trifle with her aunt, who would have been but the more offended by it. The first accusation however she considered as very unreasonable, as she thought herself perfectly justified in coming. This conversation continued till Edward Stanley entering the room came instantly towards her, and telling her that every one waited for *her* to begin the next Dance led her to the top of the room,[1] for Kitty impatient to escape from so unpleasant a Companion, without the least hesitation, or one civil scruple at being so distinguished, immediately gave him her hand, and joyfully left her Seat. This Conduct however was highly resented by several young Ladies present, and among the rest by Miss Stanley whose regard for her brother tho' *excessive*, and whose affection for Kitty tho' *prodigious*, were not proof against such an injury to her importance and her peace. Edward had however only consulted his own inclinations in desiring Miss Peterson to begin the Dance, nor had he any reason to know that it was either wished or expected by anyone else in the Party. As an heiress she was certainly of consequence, but her Birth gave her no other claim to it, for her Father had been a Merchant. It was this very circumstance which rendered this unfortunate affair so offensive to Camilla, for tho' she would sometimes boast in the pride of her heart, and her eagerness to be admired that she did not know who her grandfather had been, and was as ignorant of everything relative to Genealogy as to Astronomy, (and she might have added, Geography) yet she was really proud of her family and Connexions, and easily offended if they were treated with Neglect. "I should not have minded it, said she to her Mother, if she had been *anybody* else's daughter; but to see her pretend to be above *me*, when her Father was only a tradesman,[2]

---

1 Dancers at the top of the room lead the way in the dance, and therefore occupy the place of honour. That Stanley takes this place with Catharine is a double breach of propriety: neither he nor his partner has the rank or social standing to justify the move.

2 Catharine's father is, in fact, a merchant, an important distinction, since tradesmen were considerably lower on the social scale.

is too bad! It is such an affront to our whole Family! I declare I think Papa ought to interfere in it, but he never cares about anything but Politics. If I were Mr Pitt or the Lord Chancellor,[1] he would take care I should not be insulted, but he never thinks about *me*; And it is so provoking that *Edward* should let her stand there. I wish with all my heart that he had never come to England! I hope she may fall down and break her neck, or sprain her Ancle." Mrs Stanley perfectly agreed with her daughter concerning the affair, and tho' with less violence, expressed almost equal resentment at the indignity. Kitty in the meantime remained insensible of having given any one Offence, and therefore unable either to offer an apology, or make a reparation; her whole attention was occupied by the happiness she enjoyed in dancing with the most elegant young Man in the room, and every one else was equally unregarded. The Evening indeed to *her*, passed off delightfully; he was her partner during the greatest part of it,[2] and the united attractions that he possessed of Person, Address and vivacity, had easily gained that preference from Kitty which they seldom fail of obtaining from every one. She was too happy to care either for her Aunt's illhumour which she could not help remarking, or for the Alteration in Camilla's behaviour which forced itself at last on her observation. Her Spirits were elevated above the influence of Displeasure in any one, and she was equally indifferent as to the Cause of Camilla's, or the continuance of her Aunt's. Though Mr Stanley could never be really offended by any imprudence or folly in his Son that had given him the pleasure of seeing him, he was yet perfectly convinced that Edward ought not to remain in England, and was resolved to hasten his leaving it as soon as possible; but when he talked to Edward about it, he found him much less disposed towards returning to France, than to accompany them in their projected tour, which he assured his Father would be infinitely more pleasant to him, and that as to the affair of travelling he considered it of no importance, and what might be pursued at any little odd time, when he had nothing better to do.

---

1 Two of the most powerful men in Britain after the monarch, George III. William Pitt the Younger (1759-1806) was Prime Minister in 1783-1801 and 1804-06. The Lord Chancellor's responsibilities include presiding over the House of Lords and the judiciary. The office was filled by the overbearing Edward, Lord Thurlow (1731-1806) from 1778 until his dismissal by Pitt in June 1792.
2 A breach of etiquette; dancing with the same partner for more than two consecutive dances was considered impolite.

He advanced these objections in a manner which plainly shewed that he had scarcely a doubt of their being complied with, and appeared to consider his father's arguments in opposition to them, as merely given with a veiw to keep up his authority, and such as he should find little difficulty in combating. He concluded at last by saying, as the chaise in which they returned together from Mr Dudley's reached Mrs Percivals, "Well Sir, we will settle this point some other time, and fortunately it is of so little consequence, that an immediate discussion of it is unnecessary." He then got out of the chaise and entered the house without waiting for his Father's reply. It was not till their return that Kitty could account for that coldness in Camilla's behaviour to her, which had been so pointed as to render it impossible to be entirely unnoticed. When however they were seated in the Coach with the two other Ladies, Miss Stanley's indignation was no longer to be suppressed from breaking out into words, and found the following vent.

"Well, I must say *this*, that I never was at a stupider Ball in my Life! But it always is so; I am always disappointed in them for some reason or other. I wish there were no such things."

"I am sorry Miss Stanley, said Mrs Percival drawing herself up, that you have not been amused; every thing was meant for the best I am sure, and it is a poor encouragement for your Mama to take you to another if you are so hard to be satisfied."

"I do not know what you mean Ma'am about Mama's *taking* me to another. You know I am come out."

"Oh! dear Mrs Percival, said Mrs Stanley, you must not beleive every thing that my lively Camilla says, for her Spirits are prodigiously high sometimes, and she frequently speaks without thinking. I am sure it is impossible for *any one* to have been at a more elegant or agreable dance, and so she wishes to express herself I am certain."

"To be sure I do, said Camilla very sulkily, only I must say that it is not very pleasant to have any body behave so rude to one as to be quite shocking! I am sure I am not at all offended, and should not care if all the World were to stand above me, but still it is extremely abominable, and what I cannot put up with. It is not that I mind it in the least, for I had just as soon stand at the bottom as at the top all night long, if it was not so very disagreeable—. But to have a person come in the middle of the Evening and take everybody's place is what I am not used to, and tho' I do not care a pin about it myself, I assure you I shall not easily forgive or forget it."

This speech which perfectly explained the whole affair to Kitty, was shortly followed on her side by a very submissive apology, for she had too much good Sense to be proud of her family, and too much good Nature to live at variance with any one. The Excuses she made, were delivered with so much real concern for the Offence, and such unaffected Sweetness, that it was almost impossible for Camilla to retain that anger which had occasioned them; She felt indeed most highly gratified to find that no insult had been intended and that Catherine was very far from forgetting the difference in their birth for which she could *now* only pity her, and her good humour being restored with the same Ease in which it had been affected, she spoke with the highest delight of the Evening, and declared that she had never before been at so pleasant a Ball. The same endeavours that had procured the forgiveness of Miss Stanley ensured to her the cordiality of her Mother, and nothing was wanting but Mrs P's good humour to render the happiness of the others complete; but She, offended with Camilla for her affected Superiority, Still more so with her brother for coming to Chetwynde, and dissatisfied with the whole Evening, continued silent and Gloomy and was a restraint on the vivacity of her Companions. She eagerly seized the very first opportunity which the next Morning offered to her of speaking to Mr Stanley on the subject of his Son's return, and after having expressed her opinion of its being a very silly affair that he came at all, concluded with desiring him to inform Mr Edward Stanley that it was a rule with her never to admit a young Man into her house as a visitor for any length of time.

"I do not speak Sir, she continued, out of any disrespect to You, but I could not answer it to myself to allow of his stay; there is no knowing what might be the consequence of it, if he were to continue here, for girls nowadays will always give a handsome young Man the preference before any other, tho' for why, I never could discover, for what after all is Youth and Beauty?—It is but a poor substitute for real worth and Merit; Beleive me Cousin that, what ever people may say to the contrary, there is certainly nothing like Virtue for making us what we ought to be, and as to a young Man's, being Young and handsome and having an agreable person, it is nothing at all to the purpose for he had much better be respectable. I always *did* think so, and I always *shall*, and therefore you will oblige me very much by desiring your Son to leave Chetwynde, or I cannot be answerable for what may happen between him and my Neice. You will be surprised to hear *me* say it, she continued, lowering her voice, but truth will out, and I must own that Kitty is one of the most impudent Girls that ever existed. I assure you Sir, that I have seen her sit and laugh and whisper with a young Man whom she has not seen above half a dozen times. Her behaviour indeed is scandalous, and therefore I beg you will send your Son away immediately, or everything will be at sixes and sevens." Mr Stanley who from one part of her Speech had scarcely known to what length her insinuations of Kitty's impudence were meant to extend, now endeavoured to quiet her fears on the occasion, by assuring her, that on every account he meant to allow only of his Son's continuing that day with them, and that she might depend on his being more earnest in the affair from a wish of obliging her. He added also that he knew Edward to be very desirous himself of returning to France, as he wisely considered all time lost that did not forward the plans in which he was at present engaged, tho' he was but too well convinced of the contrary himself. His assurance in some degree quieted Mrs P, and left her tolerably relieved of her Cares and Alarms, and better disposed to behave with civility towards his Son during the short remainder of his Stay at Chetwynde. Mr Stanley went immediately to Edward, to whom he repeated the Conversation that had passed between Mrs P and himself, and strongly pointed out the necessity of his leaving Chetwynde the next day, since his word was already engaged for it. His son however appeared struck only by the ridiculous apprehensions of Mrs Peterson; and highly delighted at having occasioned them himself, seemed engrossed alone in thinking how he might encrease them, without attending to any other part of his Father's Conversation. Mr Stanley could get no determinate Answer from him, and tho' he still hoped for the best, they parted almost in anger on his side.

His Son though by no means disposed to marry, or any otherwise attached to Miss Percival than as a good-natured lively Girl who seemed pleased with him, took infinite pleasure in alarming the jealous fears of her Aunt by his attentions to her, without considering what effect they might have on the Lady herself. He would always sit by her when she was in the room, appeared dissatisfied if she left it, and was the first to enquire whether she meant soon to return. He was delighted with her Drawings, and enchanted with her performance on the Harpsichord; Everything that she said, appeared to interest him; his Conversation was addressed to her alone, and she seemed to be the sole object of his attention. That such efforts should succeed with one so tremblingly alive[1] to every alarm of the kind as Mrs Percival, is by no means unnatural, and that they should have equal influence with her Neice whose imagination was lively, and whose Disposition romantic, who was already extremely pleased with him, and of course desirous that he might be so with her, is as little to be wondered at. Every moment as it added to the conviction of his liking her, made him still more pleasing, and strengthened in her Mind a wish of knowing him better. As for Mrs Percival, she was in tortures the whole Day; Nothing that she had ever felt before on a similar occasion was to be compared to the sensations which then distracted her; her fears had never been so strongly, or indeed so reasonably excited.—Her dislike of Stanly, her anger at her Neice, her impatience to have them separated conquered every idea of propriety and Goodbreeding, and though he had never mentioned any intention of leaving them the next day, she could not help asking him after Dinner, in her eagerness to have him gone, at what time he meant to set out.

"Oh! Ma'am, replied he, if I am off by twelve at night, you may think yourself lucky; and if I am not, you can only blame yourself for having left so much as the *hour* of my departure to my own disposal." Mrs Percival coloured very highly at this speech, and without addressing herself to any one in particular, immediately began a long harangue on the shocking behaviour of modern Young Men, and the wonderful Alteration that had taken place in them, since her time, which she illustrated with many instructive anecdotes of the Decorum and Modesty which had marked the Characters of those whom she had known, when she had been young. This however did not prevent his walking in the Garden with her Neice, without any other companion for nearly an hour in the course of the Evening. They had left the room for that purpose with Camilla at a time when Mrs Peterson had been out of it, nor was it for some time after her return to it, that she could discover where they were. Camilla had taken two or three turns with them in the walk which led to the Arbour, but soon growing tired of listening to a Conversation in which she was seldom invited to join, and from its turning occasionally on Books, very little able to do it, she left them together in the arbour, to wander alone to some other part of the Garden, to eat the fruit, and examine Mrs Peterson's Greenhouse. Her absence was so far from being regretted, that it was scarcely noticed by them, and they continued conversing together on almost every subject, for

1 See p. 95, note 2.

Stanley seldom dwelt long on any, and had something to say on all, till they were interrupted by her Aunt.

Kitty was by this time perfectly convinced that both in Natural Abilities, and acquired information, Edward Stanley was infinitely superior to his Sister. Her desire of knowing that he was so, had induced her to take every opportunity of turning the Conversation on History and they were very soon engaged in an historical dispute, for which no one was more calculated than Stanley who was so far from being really of any party, that he had scarcely a fixed opinion on the Subject. He could therefore always take either side, and always argue with temper. In his indifference on all such topics he was very unlike his Companion, whose judgement being guided by her feelings which were eager and warm, was easily decided, and though it was not always infallible, she defended it with a Spirit and Enthouisasm which marked her own reliance on it. They had continued therefore for sometime conversing in this manner on the character of Richard the 3d, which he was warmly defending when he suddenly seized hold of her hand, and exclaiming with great emotion, "Upon my honour you are entirely mistaken," pressed it passionately to his lips, and ran out of the arbour. Astonished at this behaviour, for which she was wholly unable to account, she continued for a few Moments motionless on the Seat where he had left her, and was then on the point of following him up the narrow walk through which he had passed, when on looking up the one that lay immediately before the arbour, she saw her Aunt walking towards her with more than her usual quickness. This explained at once the reason of his leaving her, but his leaving her in such Manner was rendered still more inexplicable by it. She felt a considerable degree of confusion at having been seen by her in such a place with Edward, and at having that part of his conduct, for which she could not herself account, witnessed by one to whom all gallantry was odious. She remained therefore confused distressed and irresolute, and suffered her Aunt to approach her, without leaving the Arbour. Mrs Percival's looks were by no means calculated to animate the spirits of her Neice, who in silence awaited her accusation, and in silence meditated her Defence. After a few Moments suspence, for Mrs Peterson was too much fatigued to speak immediately, she began with great Anger and Asperity, the following harangue. "Well; *this* is beyond anything I could have supposed. *Profligate* as I *knew* you to be, I was not prepared for such a sight. This is beyond any thing you ever did *before*; beyond any thing I ever heard of in my Life! Such Impudence, I never witnessed before in such a Girl! And this is the reward for all the cares I have taken in your Education; for all my troubles and Anxieties, and Heaven knows how many they have been! All I wished for, was to breed you up virtuously; I never wanted you to play upon the Harpsichord, or draw better than any one else; but I had hoped to see you respectable and good; to see you able and willing to give an example of Modesty and Virtue to the Young people here abouts. I bought you Blair's Sermons,[1] and Coelebs in Search of a Wife,[2] I gave you the key to my own Library, and borrowed a great many good books of my Neighbours for you, all to this purpose. But I might have spared myself the trouble—Oh! Catherine, you are an abandoned Creature, and I do not know what will become of you. I am glad however, she continued softening into some degree of Mildness, to see that you have some shame for what you have done, and if you are really sorry for it, and your future life is a life of penitence and reformation perhaps you may be forgiven. But I plainly see that every thing is going to sixes and sevens and all order will soon be at an end throughout the Kingdom."

"Not however Ma'am the sooner, I hope, from any conduct of mine, said Catherine in a tone of great humility, for upon my honour I have done nothing this evening that can contribute to overthrow the establishment of the kingdom."

"You are mistaken Child, replied she; the welfare of every Nation depends upon the virtue of it's individuals, and any one who offends in so gross a manner against decorum and propriety, is certainly hastening it's ruin. You have been giving a bad example to the World, and the World is but too well disposed to receive such."

"Pardon me Madam, said her Neice; but I *can* have given an Example only to *You*, for You alone have seen the offence. Upon my word however, there is no danger to fear from what I have done; Mr Stanley's behaviour has given me as much surprise, as it has done to You, and I can only suppose that it was the effect of his high spirits, authorized in his opinion by our relationship. But do you consider Madam that it is growing very late? Indeed

---

1 The Reverend Hugh Blair (1718-1800), Professor of Rhetoric at Edinburgh University, published his much admired sermons in five volumes between 1777 and 1801.

2 A didactic novel of 1809 by Hannah More. Austen originally wrote "Seccar's explanation of the catechism," alluding to *Lectures on the Catechism of the Church of England* (1769) by Archbishop Thomas Secker.

You had better return to the house." This speech as she well knew, would be unanswerable with her Aunt, who instantly rose, and hurried away under so many apprehensions for her health, as banished for the time all anxiety about her Neice, who walked quietly by her side, revolving within her own Mind the occurrence that had given her Aunt so much alarm. "I am astonished at my own imprudence, said Mrs Percival; How could I be so forgetful as to sit down out of doors at such a time of night? I shall certainly have a return of my rheumatism after it—I begin to feel very chill already. I must have caught a dreadful cold by this time—I am sure of being lain-up all the winter after it—" Then reckoning with her fingers, "Let me see; This is July; the cold Weather will soon be coming in—August—September—October—November—December—January—February—March—April—Very likely I may not be tolerable again before May. I must and will have that arbour pulled down—it will be the death of me; who knows *now*, but what I may never recover—Such things *have* happened—My particular freind Miss Sarah Hutchinson's death was occasioned by nothing more—She staid out late one Evening in April, and got wet through for it rained very hard, and never changed her Cloathes when she came home—It is unknown how many people have died in consequence of catching Cold! I do not beleive there is a disorder in the World except the Smallpox which does not spring from it." It was in vain that Kitty endeavoured to convince her that her fears on the occasion were groundless; that it was not yet late enough to catch cold, and that even if it were, she might hope to escape any other complaint, and to recover in less than ten Months. Mrs Percival only replied that she hoped she knew more of Ill health than to be convinced in such a point by a Girl who had always been perfectly well, and hurried up stairs leaving Kitty to make her apologies to Mr and Mrs Stanley for going to bed—. Tho' Mrs Percival seemed perfectly satisfied with the goodness of the Apology herself, Yet Kitty felt somewhat embarrassed to find that the only one she could offer to their Visitors was that her Aunt had *perhaps* caught cold, for Mrs Peterson charged her to make light of it, for fear of alarming them. Mr and Mrs Stanley however who well knew that their Cousin was easily terrified on that Score, received the account of it with very little surprise, and all proper concern. Edward and his Sister soon came in, and Kitty had no difficulty in gaining an explanation of his Conduct from him, for he was too warm on the subject himself, and too eager to learn its success, to refrain from making immediate Enquiries about it; and She could not help feeling both surprised and offended at the ease and Indifference with which he owned that all his intentions had been to frighten her Aunt by pretending an affection for *her*; a design so very incompatible with that partiality which she had at one time been almost convinced of his feeling for her. It is true that she had not yet seen enough of him to be actually in love with him, yet she felt greatly disappointed that so handsome, so elegant, so lively a young Man should be so perfectly free from any such Sentiment as to make it his principal Sport. There was a Novelty in his character which to *her* was extremely pleasing; his person was uncommonly fine, his Spirits and Vivacity suited to her own, and his Manners at once so animated and insinuating, that she thought it must be impossible for him to be otherwise than amiable, and was ready to give him Credit for being perfectly so. He knew the powers of them himself; to them he had often been endebted for his father's forgiveness of faults which had he been awkward and inelegant would have appeared very serious; to them, even more than to his person or his fortune, he owed the regard which almost every one was disposed to feel for him, and which Young Women in particular were inclined to entertain. Their influence was acknowledged on the present occasion by Kitty, whose Anger they entirely dispelled, and whose Chearfulness they had power not only to restore, but to raise—. The Evening passed off as agreably as the one that had preceded it; they continued talking to each other, during the cheif part of it, And such was the power of his Address, and the Brilliancy of his Eyes, that when they parted for the Night, tho' Catherine had but a few hours before totally given up the idea, yet she felt almost convinced again that he was really in love with her. She reflected on their past Conversation, and tho' it had been on various and indifferent subjects, and she could not exactly recollect any Speech on his side expressive of such a partiality, she was still however nearly certain of it's being so; But fearful of being vain enough to suppose such a thing without sufficient reason, she resolved to suspend her final determination on it, till the next day, and more especially till their parting which she thought would infallibly explain his regard if any he had—. The more she had seen of him, the more inclined was she to like him, and the more desirous that he should like *her*. She was convinced of his being naturally very clever and very well disposed, and that his thoughtlessness and negligence, which tho' they appeared to *her* as very becoming in *him*, she was aware would by many people be considered as defects in his Character, merely proceeded from a vivacity always pleasing in Young Men, and were far from testifying a weak or vacant Understanding. Having settled this point within herself, and being perfectly convinced by her own arguments of it's truth, she went to bed in high Spirits, determined to study his Character, and watch his Behaviour still more the next day. She got up with the same good resolutions and would probably have put them in execution, had not Anne informed her as soon as she entered the room that Mr Edward Stanley was already gone. At first she refused to credit the information, but when her Maid assured her that he had ordered a Carriage the evening before to be there at seven o'clock in the Morning and that she herself had actually seen him depart in it a little after eight, she could no longer deny her beleif to it. "And this, thought she to herself blushing with anger at her own folly, this is the affection for me of which I was so certain. Oh! what a silly Thing is Woman! How vain, how unreasonable! To suppose that a young Man would be seriously attached in the course of four and twenty hours, to a Girl who has nothing to recommend her but a good pair of eyes! And he is really gone! Gone perhaps without bestowing a thought on me! Oh! why was not I up by eight o'clock? But it is a proper punishment for my Lazyness and Folly, and I am heartily glad of it. I deserve it all, and ten times more for such insufferable vanity. It will at least be of service to me in that respect; it will teach me in future *not* to think Every Body is in love with me. Yet I *should* like to have seen him before he went, for perhaps it may be many Years before we meet again. By his Manner of leaving us however, he seems to have been perfectly indifferent about it. How very odd, that he should go without giving us notice of it, or taking leave of any one! But it is just like a Young Man, governed by the whim of the Moment, or actuated merely by the love of doing anything oddly! Unaccountable Beings indeed! And Young Women are equally ridiculous! I shall soon begin to think like my Aunt that everything is going to Sixes and Sevens, and that the whole race of Mankind are degenerating." She was just dressed, and on the point of leaving her room to make her personal enquiries after Mrs Peterson, when Miss Stanley knocked at her door, and on her being admitted began in her Usual Strain a long harangue upon her Father's being so shocking as to make Edward go at all, and upon Edward's being so horrid as to leave them at such an hour in the Morning. "You have no idea, said she, how surprised I was, when he came into my Room to bid me good bye—"

"Have you seen him then, this Morning?" said Kitty.

"Oh Yes! And I was so sleepy that I could not open my eyes. And so he said, Camilla, goodbye to you for I am going away—. I have not time to take leave of any body else, and I dare not trust myself to see Kitty, for then you know I should never get away—"

"Nonsense, said Kitty; he did not say that, or he was in joke if he did."

"Oh! no I assure You he was as much in earnest as he ever was in his life; he was too much out of Spirits to joke *then*. And he desired me when we all met at Breakfast to give his Compts.[1] to your Aunt, and his Love to You, for you was a nice Girl he said, and he only wished it were in his power to be more with You. You were just the Girl to suit him, because you were so lively and good-natured, and he wished with all his heart that you might not be married before he came back, for there was nothing he liked better than being here. Oh! You have no idea what fine things he said about You, till at last I fell a sleep and he went away. But he certainly is in love with you—I am sure he is—I have thought so a great while I assure You."

"How can You be so ridiculous? said Kitty smiling with pleasure; I do not beleive him to be so easily affected. But he *did* desire his Love to me then? And wished I might not be married before his return? And said I was a nice Girl, did he?"

"Oh! dear, Yes, And I assure You it is the greatest praise in his opinion, that he can bestow on any body; I can hardly ever persuade him to call *me* one, tho' I beg him sometimes for an hour together."

"And do You really think that he was sorry to go?"

"Oh! You can have no idea how wretched it made him. He would not have gone this Month, if my Father had not insisted on it; Edward told me so himself yesterday. He said that he wished with all his heart he had never promised to go abroad, for that he repented it more and more every day; that it interfered with all his other schemes, and that since Papa had spoke to him about it, he was more unwilling to leave Chetwynde than ever."

"Did he really say all this? And why would your father insist upon his going? 'His leaving England interfered with all his other plans, and his Conversation with Mr Stanley had made him still more averse to it.' What can this Mean?"

"Why that he is excessively in love with You to be sure; what other plans can he have? And I suppose my father said that if he

---

1 I.e., compliments.

had not been going abroad, he should have wished him to marry you immediately.—But I must go and see your Aunt's plants—There is one of them that I quite doat on—and two or three more besides—"

"Can Camilla's explanation be true? said Catherine to herself, when her freind had left the room. And after all my doubts and Uncertainties, can Stanley really be averse to leaving England for *my sake* only? 'His plans interrupted.' And what indeed can his plans be, but towards Marriage? Yet *so soon* to be in love with me!—But it is the effect perhaps only of a warmth of heart which to *me* is the highest recommendation in any one. A Heart disposed to love—And such under the appearance of so much Gaity and Inattention, is Stanley's! Oh! how much does it endear him to me! But he is gone—Gone perhaps for Years—Obliged to tear himself from what he most loves, his happiness is sacrificed to the vanity of his Father! In what anguish he must have left the house! Unable to see me, or to bid me adeiu, while I, senseless wretch, was daring to sleep. This, then explains his leaving us at such a time of day—. He could not trust himself to see me—. Charming Young Man! How much must you have suffered! I *knew* that it was impossible for one so elegant, and so well bred, to leave any Family in such a Manner, but for a Motive like this unanswerable." Satisfied, beyond the power of Change, of this, She went in high spirits to her Aunt's apartment, without giving a Moment's recollection on the vanity of Young Women, or the unaccountable conduct of Young Men. ———

Lady Susan[1]

1 There is no reference to the narrative by this or any other title in documents surviving from JA's lifetime. The manuscript, inherited by family members and now held in the Morgan Library, New York, was bound in the late nineteenth century with the title "Lady Susan" on the front cover. JA's nieces and nephew Anna Lefroy, Caroline Austen, and James Edward Austen Leigh all refer to the manuscript by the name of "Lady Susan" in their correspondence over plans for the first publication of the text in the second edition of the *Memoir* (1871).

Letter 1.
Lady Susan Vernon[1] to Mr. Vernon.—

Langford, Decr.—

My dear Brother[2]

I can no longer refuse myself the pleasure of profitting by your kind invitation when we last parted, of spending some weeks with you at Churchill, and therefore if quite convenient to you and Mrs. Vernon to receive me at present, I shall hope within a few days to be introduced to a sister,[3] whom I have so long desired to be acquainted with.—My kind friends here are most affectionately urgent with me to prolong my stay, but their hospitable and chearful dispositions lead them too much into society for my present situation and state of mind;[4] and I impatiently look forward to the hour when I shall be admitted into your delightful retirement.[5] I long to be made known to your dear little Children, in whose hearts I shall be very eager to secure an interest.— I shall soon have occasion for all my fortitude, as I am on the point of separation from my own daughter.—The long illness of her dear Father prevented my paying her that attention which Duty and affection equally dictated, and I have but too much reason to fear that the Governess to whose care I consigned her, was unequal to the charge.—I have therefore resolved on placing her at one of the best Private Schools in Town,[6] where I shall have an opportunity of leaving her myself, in my way to you. I am deter-

---

1 Lady Susan's title, in particular the use of her first name, indicates that she is the daughter of a Duke, Marquess, or Earl, the senior ranks of the British aristocracy. As such, she continues to carry the title "Lady," even when she marries.

2 Brother-in-law; Lady Susan's deceased husband's brother. A common usage of the time.

3 Sister-in-law, the wife of Lady Susan's brother-in-law.

4 A widow would spend a year of deep or full mourning wearing black and leading a quiet life; in the next year of half- or second-mourning, some public appearances would be permissible and the dress code would be relaxed.

5 Secluded home, far from the bustle of urban life.

6 Girls were often educated at home, but some were sent to school, either for the educational and social benefits of a school education or because they were not wanted at home. A private school was usually small, and owned by the senior teacher; the curriculum would offer girls a range of dancing, drawing, deportment, and French, all skills for domestic and social use. The social elite referred to London familiarly as "Town."

mined you see, not to be denied admittance at Churchill.—It would indeed give me most painful sensations to know that it were not in your power to receive me.—Yr. most obliged and affec: Sister

S. Vernon.[1]—

Letter 2ᵈ·
Lady Susan to Mrs. Johnson.

Langford

You were mistaken my dear Alicia, in supposing me fixed at this place for the rest of the winter. It greives me to say how greatly you were mistaken, for I have seldom spent three months more agreably than those which have just flown away.—At present nothing goes smoothly.—The Females of the Family are united against me.—You foretold how it would be, when I first came to Langford; and Manwaring is so uncommonly pleasing that I was not without apprehensions myself. I remember saying to myself as I drove to the House, "I like this Man; pray Heaven no harm come of it!"—But I was determined to be discreet, to bear in mind my being only four months a widow, and to be as quiet as possible,—and I have been so;—my dear Creature, I have admitted no one's attentions but Manwaring's, I have avoided all general flirtation whatever, I have distinguished no Creature besides of all the Numbers resorting hither, except Sir James Martin, on whom I bestowed a little notice in order to detach him from Miss Manwaring. But if the World could know my motive *there*, they would honour me.—I have been called an unkind Mother, but it was the sacred impulse of maternal affection, it was the advantage of my Daughter that led me on; and if that Daughter were not the greatest simpleton on Earth, I might have been rewarded for my Exertions as I ought.—Sir James did make proposals to me for Frederica[2]—but Frederica, who was born to be the torment of my life, chose to set herself so violently against the match, that I thought it better to lay aside the scheme for the present.—I have more than once repented that I did not marry him myself, and were he but one degree less contemptibly weak

---

1 A formal signature was conventional, even between close friends and relatives. Jane Austen frequently signed her letters to close relatives "JA." Even to her sister Cassandra, she sometimes signed "J. Austen."

2 Sir James has made a formal offer of marriage, with related financial settlements, to Lady Susan for her daughter, Frederica.

I certainly should, but I must own myself rather romantic[1] in that respect, and that Riches only, will not satisfy me. The event of all this is very provoking.—Sir James is gone, Maria highly incensed, and Mrs. Manwaring insupportably jealous;—so jealous in short, and so enraged against me, that in the fury of her temper I should not be surprised at her appealing to her Guardian if she had the liberty of addressing him—but there your Husband stands my friend, and the kindest, most amiable action of his Life was his throwing her off[2] forever on her Marriage.—Keep up his resentment therefore I charge you.—We are now in a sad state; no house was ever more altered; the whole family are at war, and Manwaring scarcely dares speak to me. It is time for me to be gone; I have therefore determined on leaving them, and shall spend I hope a comfortable day with you in Town within this week.—If I am as little in favour with Mr. Johnson as ever, you must come to me at No. 10 Wigmore St.[3]—but I hope this may not be the case, for as Mr. Johnson with all his faults is a Man to whom that great word "Respectable" is always given, and I am known to be so intimate with his wife, his slighting me has an awkward Look.—I take Town in my way to that insupportable spot, a Country Village, for I am really going to Churchill.—Forgive me my dear friend, it is my last resource. Were there another place in England open to me, I would prefer it.—Charles Vernon is my aversion, and I am afraid of his wife.—At Churchill however I must remain till I have something better in veiw. My young Lady accompanies me to Town, where I shall deposit her under the care of Miss Summers in Wigmore Street, till she becomes a little more reasonable. She will make good connections there, as the Girls are all of the best Families.—The price is immense, and much beyond what I can ever attempt to pay.—Adeiu. I will send you a line, as soon as I arrive in Town.—Yours Ever,

S. Vernon.

1　The word "romantic" was shifting to its modern meaning at this time; Lady Susan's usage seems to acknowledge the older sense of "fanciful" or "foolish."

2　I.e., disowning her, having nothing more to do with her. In *Pride and Prejudice*, Mr. Collins, hearing of Lydia's elopement with Wickham, advises Mr. Bennet "to throw off your unworthy child from your affection for ever, and leave her to reap the fruits of her own heinous offence" (Vol. 3, ch. 6).

3　All of the London addresses in *Lady Susan* are located in the smart, newly-built streets on Portman estate land just north of Oxford Street.

Letter 3.
Mrs. Vernon to Lady De Courcy.

Churchill

My dear Mother

I am very sorry to tell you that it will not be in our power to keep our promise of spending the Christmas with you;[1] and we are prevented that happiness by a circumstance which is not likely to make us any amends.—Lady Susan in a letter to her Brother, has declared her intention of visiting us almost immediately—and as such a visit is in all probability merely an affair of convenience, it is impossible to conjecture it's length. I was by no means prepared for such an event, nor can I now account for her Ladyship's conduct.—Langford appeared so exactly the place for her in every respect, as well from the elegant and expensive stile of Living there, as from her particular attachment to Mrs. Manwaring, that I was very far from expecting so speedy a distinction, tho' I always imagined from her increasing friendship for us since her Husband's death, that we should at some future period be obliged to receive her.—Mr. Vernon I think was a great deal too kind to her, when he was in Staffordshire.[2] Her behaviour to him, independant of her general Character, has been so inexcusably artful and ungenerous since our marriage was first in agitation, that no one less amiable and mild than himself could have overlooked it at all; and tho' as his Brother's widow and in narrow circumstances it was proper to render her pecuniary assistance, I cannot help thinking his pressing invitation to her to visit us at Churchill perfectly unnecessary.—Disposed however as he always is to think the best of every one, her display of Greif, and professions of regret, and general resolutions of prudence were sufficient to soften his heart, and make him really confide in her sincerity. But as for myself, I am still unconvinced; and plausibly as her Ladyship has now written, I cannot make up my mind, till I better understand her real meaning in coming to us.—You may guess therefore my dear Madam with what feelings I look forward to her arrival. She will have occasion for all those attractive Powers for which she is celebrated, to gain any share of my regard; and I shall certainly endeavour to guard myself against their

---

1 Traditionally, Christmas had not been a major focus of social festivity, but by about 1800, it had begun to be regarded as a festival that families might celebrate together.

2 A part-rural, part-industrial county in the English Midlands, 150 miles northwest of London.

influence, if not accompanied by something more substantial.—
She expresses a most eager desire of being acquainted with me,
and makes very gracious mention of my children, but I am not
quite weak enough to suppose a woman who has behaved with
inattention if not unkindness to her own child, should be
attached to any of mine. Miss Vernon is to be placed at a school
in Town before her Mother comes to us, which I am glad of, for
her sake and my own. It must be to her advantage to be separated
from her Mother; and a girl of sixteen who has received so
wretched an education would not be a very desirable companion
here.—Reginald has long wished I know to see this captivating
Lady Susan, and we shall depend on his joining our party soon.—
I am glad to hear that my Father continues so well, and am, with
best Love &c, Cath Vernon.—

Letter 4.
Mr. De Courcy to Mrs. Vernon.

Parklands

My dear Sister
    I congratulate you and Mr. Vernon on being about to receive
into your family, the most accomplished coquette[1] in England.
—As a very distinguished Flirt, I have been always taught to consider her; but it has lately fallen in my way to hear some particulars of her conduct at Langford, which prove that she does not
confine herself to that sort of honest flirtation which satisfies
most people, but aspires to the more delicious gratification of
making a whole family miserable.—By her behaviour to Mr.
Manwaring, she gave jealousy and wretchedness to his wife, and
by her attentions to a young Man previously attached to Mr.
Manwaring's sister, deprived an amiable girl of her Lover.—I
learnt all this from a Mr. Smith now in this neighbourhood—(I
have dined with him at Hurst and Wilford)—who is just come
from Langford, where he was a fortnight in the house with her
Ladyship, and who is therefore well qualified to make the communication.—What a Woman she must be!—I long to see her,
and shall certainly accept your kind invitation, that I may form
some idea of those bewitching powers which can do so much—
engaging at the same time and in the same house the affections
of two Men who were neither of them at liberty to bestow them—

---

1   Calculated flirt. Flirtatious behaviour was much frowned on throughout
    the eighteenth century and any literary coquette, unless a comic or
    repentant figure, would be subject to condemnation.

and all this, without the charm of youth.—I am glad to find that Miss Vernon does not come with her Mother to Churchill, as she has not even manners to recommend her, and according to Mr. Smith's account, is equally dull and proud. Where Pride and Stupidity unite, there can be no dissimulation worthy notice, and Miss Vernon shall be consigned to unrelenting contempt; but by all that I can gather, Lady Susan possesses a degree of captivating Deceit which it must be pleasing to witness and detect. I shall be with you very soon, and am your affec. Brother

R De Courcy.—

Letter 5.
Lady Susan to Mrs. Johnson

Churchill

I received your note my dear Alicia, just before I left Town, and rejoice to be assured that Mr. Johnson suspected nothing of your engagement the evening before; it is undoubtedly better to deceive him entirely;—since he will be stubborn, he must be tricked.—I arrived here in safety, and have no reason to complain of my reception from Mr. Vernon; but I confess myself not equally satisfied with the behaviour of his Lady.—She is perfectly well bred indeed, and has the air of a woman of fashion, but her manners are not such as can persuade me of her being prepossessed in my favour.—I wanted her to be delighted at seeing me—I was as amiable as possible on the occasion—but all in vain—she does not like me.—To be sure, when we consider that I *did* take some pains to prevent my Brother-in-law's marrying her, this want of cordiality is not very surprising—and yet it shews an illiberal and vindictive spirit to resent a project which influenced me six years ago, and which never succeeded at last.—I am sometimes half disposed to repent that I did not let Charles buy Vernon Castle when we were obliged to sell it, but it was a trying circumstance, especially as the sale took place exactly at the time of his marriage—and everybody ought to respect the delicacy of those feelings, which could not endure that my Husband's Dignity should be lessened by his younger brother's having possession of the Family Estate.[1]—Could Matters have been

---

1 Family properties and estates were expected to be maintained by the holder to pass, on his death, to his eldest son, thus maintaining a family's wealth and prosperity. Having to sell estates indicates financial mismanagement or the holder living beyond his means. Selling to a younger brother would keep the estate in the family, though it might well create embarrassment for the seller.

so arranged as to prevent the necessity of our leaving the Castle, could we have lived with Charles and kept him single, I should have been very far from persuading my husband to dispose of it elsewhere;—but Charles was then on the point of marrying Miss De Courcy, and the event has justified me. Here are Children in abundance, and what benefit could have accrued to me from his purchasing Vernon?—My having prevented it, may perhaps have given his wife an unfavourable impression—but where there is a disposition to dislike a motive will never be wanting; and as to money-matters, it has not with-held him from being very useful to me. I really have a regard for him, he is so easily imposed on!

The house is a good one, the Furniture fashionable, and everything announces plenty and elegance.—Charles is very rich I am sure; when a Man has once got his name in a Banking House he rolls in money.[1] But they do not know what to do with their fortune, keep very little company, and never go to Town but on business.—We shall be as stupid as possible.—I mean to win my Sister in law's heart through her Children; I know all their names already, and am going to attach myself with the greatest sensibility[2] to one in particular, a young Frederic, whom I take on my lap and sigh over for his dear Uncle's sake.—

Poor Manwaring!—I need not tell you how much I miss him—how perpetually he is in my Thoughts.—I found a dismal Letter from him on my arrival here, full of complaints of his wife and sister, and lamentations on the cruelty of his fate. I passed off the letter as his wife's, to the Vernons, and when I write to him, it must be under cover to you.[3]—

Yours Ever, S V.—

---

1 A younger son with no prospect of inheriting the family estate, Charles has taken on a profession, as a partner in a bank. Most banks of the time were privately owned and relatively small; partners could make their fortunes, but they also had unlimited liability, so the risks were high. In 1801, JA's brothers, Henry and Frank, became named partners in the banking house of Austen, Maunde, and Austen; Henry's bank business failed in 1816, and he was declared bankrupt.

2 Refined and cultivated awareness of one's own feelings, a quality much prized in the late eighteenth century, though its excesses were much-satirized.

3 Within a letter addressed to Mrs. Johnson. Envelopes were not yet used: the letter itself would be folded, sealed, and addressed on the outside.

Letter 6.

Mrs. Vernon to Mr. De Courcy

Churchill

Well my dear Reginald, I have seen this dangerous creature, and must give you some description of her, tho' I hope you will soon be able to form your own judgement. She is really excessively pretty.—However you may chuse to question the allurements of a Lady no longer young, I must for my own part declare that I have seldom seen so lovely a woman as Lady Susan.—She is delicately fair, with fine grey eyes and dark eyelashes; and from her appearance one would not suppose her more than five and twenty, tho' she must in fact be ten years older.—I was certainly not disposed to admire her, tho' always hearing she was beautiful; but I cannot help feeling that she possesses an uncommon union of Symmetry, Brilliancy and Grace.[1]—Her address[2] to me was so gentle, frank and even affectionate, that if I had not known how much she has always disliked me for marrying Mr. Vernon, and that we had never met before, I should have imagined her an attached friend.—One is apt I beleive to connect assurance of manner with coquetry, and to expect that an impudent address will necessarily attend an impudent mind;—at least I was myself prepared for an improper degree of confidence in Lady Susan; but her countenance is absolutely sweet, and her voice and manner winningly mild.—I am sorry it is so, for what is this but Deceit?—Unfortunately one knows her too well.—She is clever and agreable, has all that knowledge of the world which makes conversation easy, and talks very well, with a happy command of Language, which is too often used I beleive to make Black appear White.—She has already almost persuaded me of her being warmly attached to her daughter, tho' I have so long been convinced of the contrary. She speaks of her with so much tenderness and anxiety, lamenting so bitterly the neglect of her education, which she represents however as wholly unavoidable, that I

---

1 What Sir Joshua Reynolds called "the lore of symmetry and grace" (Sir Joshua Reynolds, "The Art of Painting," in *Works* [2 vols, 1797], Vol. 2, p. 192, line 592) was widely regarded as a standard of beauty. According to Thomas Reid, "The last and noblest part of beauty is grace ... [which] consists of those motions, either of the whole body, or of a part or feature, which express the most perfect propriety of conduct and sentiment in an amiable character" (Thomas Reid, *Essays on the Intellectual Powers of Man* [1785], Essay 8, "On Beauty," pp. 762-63).

2 Manner of speaking; bearing in conversation.

am forced to recollect how many successive Springs her Ladyship spent in Town,[1] while her daughter was left in Staffordshire to the care of servants or a Governess very little better,[2] to prevent my beleiving whatever she says.

If her manners have so great an influence on my resentful heart, you may guess how much more strongly they operate on Mr. Vernon's generous temper.—I wish I could be as well satisfied as he is, that it was really her choice to leave Langford for Churchill; and if she had not staid three months there before she discovered that her friends' manner of Living did not suit her situation or feelings, I might have beleived that concern for the loss of such a Husband as Mr. Vernon, to whom her own behaviour was far from unexceptionable, might for a time make her wish for retirement. But I cannot forget the length of her visit to the Manwarings, and when I reflect on the different mode of Life which she led with them, from that to which she must now submit, I can only suppose that the wish of establishing her reputation by following, tho' late, the path of propriety, occasioned her removal from a family where she must in reality have been particularly happy. Your friend Mr. Smith's story however cannot be quite true, as she corresponds regularly with Mrs. Manwaring; at any rate it must be exaggerated;—it is scarcely possible that two men should be so grossly deceived by her at once.—Yrs &c Cath Vernon.

Letter 7.
Lady Susan to Mrs. Johnson

Churchill

My dear Alicia

You are very good in taking notice of Frederica, and I am grateful for it as a mark of your friendship; but as I cannot have a doubt of the warmth of that friendship, I am far from exacting so heavy a sacrifice. She is a stupid girl, and has nothing to rec-

---

1 The main London social season for the aristocracy and gentry took place in the early months of the year, coinciding with the sitting of Parliament and ending when the warm weather of early summer encouraged people to return to their country estates; in the late eighteenth century, George III's birthday, on 4 June, formally marked the end of the season.

2 The pernicious effects of leaving children in the care of servants (who were almost certainly uneducated) were frequently mentioned in the eighteenth century. See Appendix D.

ommend her.—I would not therefore on any account have you encumber one moment of your precious time by sending for her to Edward St.,[1] especially as every visit is so many hours deducted from the grand affair of Education, which I really wish to be attended to, while she remains with Miss Summers.—I want her to play and sing with some portion of Taste, and a good deal of assurance, as she has *my* hand and arm, and a tolerable voice. *I* was so much indulged in my infant years that I was never obliged to attend to anything, and consequently am without those accomplishments which are now necessary to finish a pretty Woman. Not that I am an advocate for the prevailing fashion of acquiring a perfect knowledge in all the Languages Arts and Sciences;[2]—it is throwing time away;—to be Mistress of French, Italian, German, Music, Singing, Drawing &c will gain a Woman some applause, but will not add one Lover to her list. Grace and Manner after all are of the greatest importance. I do not mean therefore that Frederica's acquirements should be more than superficial, and I flatter myself that she will not remain long enough at school to understand anything thoroughly.[3]—I hope to see her the wife of Sir James within a twelvemonth.—You know on what I ground my hope, and it is certainly a good foundation, for School must be very humiliating to a girl of Freder-

---

1 The former name of the part of Wigmore Street lying between Marylebone Lane and Duke Street, therefore effectively in the same street as Frederica's school.

2 As the rest of the paragraph makes clear, this does not mean the equivalent of a modern academic subject-based education, but even so, Lady Susan is exaggerating. The acknowledged purpose of women's education was to enable them to be good wives; unofficially, it was to give them the accomplishments that would enable them to get husbands. The curriculum would be similar to that recommended in Mrs. Chapone's popular *Letters on the Improvement of the Mind*: domestic economy to enable them to manage a home after marriage, accomplishments such as "Dancing and the knowledge of the French tongue ...To write a free and legible hand, and to understand common arithmetic," and, for girls with aptitude, music and drawing (Hester Chapone, *Letters on the Improvement of the Mind, Addressed to a Young Lady* [2 vols, 1773], pp. 48-49, 115-20).

3 Mary Wollstonecraft was highly critical of the education a girl was likely to receive in a boarding school however long she remained: "Few things are learnt thoroughly, but many follies contracted, and an immoderate fondness for dress among the rest" (*Thoughts on the Education of Daughters* [1787], p. 58).

ica's age;[1] and by the bye, you had better not invite her any more on that account, as I wish her to find her situation as unpleasant as possible.—I am sure of Sir James at any time, and could make him renew his application by a Line.—I shall trouble you meanwhile to prevent his forming any other attachment when he comes to Town;—ask him to your House occasionally, and talk to him about Frederica that he may not forget her.—

Upon the whole I commend my own conduct in this affair extremely, and regard it as a very happy mixture of circumspection and tenderness. Some Mothers would have insisted on their daughter's accepting so great an offer on the first overture, but I could not answer it to myself to force Frederica into a marriage from which her heart revolted; and instead of adopting so harsh a measure, merely propose to make it her own choice by rendering her thoroughly uncomfortable till she does accept him. But enough of this tiresome girl.—

You may well wonder how I contrive to pass my time here—and for the first week, it was most insufferably dull.—Now however, we begin to mend;—our party is enlarged by Mrs. Vernon's brother, a handsome young Man, who promises me some amusement. There is something about him that rather interests me, a sort of sauciness, of familiarity which I shall teach him to correct. He is lively and seems clever, and when I have inspired him with greater respect for me than his sister's kind offices have implanted, he may be an agreable Flirt.—There is exquisite pleasure in subduing an insolent spirit, in making a person predetermined to dislike, acknowledge one's superiority.—I have disconcerted him already by my calm reserve; and it shall be my endeavour to humble the Pride of these self-important De Courcies still lower, to convince Mrs. Vernon that her sisterly cautions have been bestowed in vain, and to persuade Reginald that she has scandalously belied[2] me. This project will serve at least to amuse me, and prevent my feeling so acutely this dreadful separation from You and all whom I love. Adeiu.

Yours Ever

S. Vernon.

---

1 Frederica is sixteen, an age at which many girls would have finished their education and be taking a full part in adult social life.

2 Calumniated by false statements.

Letter 8.

Mrs. Vernon to Lady De Courcy.

Churchill

My dear Mother

You must not expect Reginald back again for some time. He desires me to tell you that the present open weather induces him to accept Mr. Vernon's invitation to prolong his stay in Sussex that they may have some hunting together.[1]—He means to send for his Horses immediately,[2] and it is impossible to say when you may see him in Kent.[3] I will not disguise my sentiments on this change from you my dear Madam, tho' I think you had better not communicate them to my Father, whose excessive anxiety about Reginald would subject him to an alarm which might seriously affect his health and spirits. Lady Susan has certainly contrived in the space of a fortnight to make my Brother like her.—In short, I am persuaded that his continuing here beyond the time originally fixed for his return, is occasioned as much by a degree of fascination towards her, as by the wish of hunting with Mr. Vernon, and of course I cannot receive that pleasure from the length of his visit which my Brother's company would otherwise give me.—I am indeed provoked at the artifice of this unprincipled Woman. What stronger proof of her dangerous abilities can be given, than this perversion of Reginald's judgement, which when he entered the house was so decidedly against her?—In his last letter he actually gave me some particulars of her behaviour at Langford, such as he received from a Gentleman who knew her perfectly well, which if true must raise abhorrence against her, and which Reginald himself was entirely disposed to credit.—His opinion of her I am sure, was as low as of any Woman in England, and when he first came it was evident that he considered her as one entitled neither to

---

1 The hunting season lasted through the winter to the end of March, and open weather—that is, mild weather, free of frost and fog—created ideal conditions for it. Sussex is a rural county on the south coast of England.

2 A gentleman keen on hunting would bring his own horses with him when making an extensive stay away from home during the hunting season.

3 A rural county adjoining Sussex to the East, with a long coastline. Parts of Kent were well known to JA because the Knight family, who adopted her brother Edward, had extensive estates there, most of which Edward inherited; one of her earliest extant letters, dated September 1796, was sent from Rowling in East Kent (*Letters*, p. 5).

Delicacy[1] nor respect, and that he felt she would be delighted with the attentions of any Man inclined to flirt with her.

Her behaviour I confess has been calculated to do away such an idea, I have not detected the smallest impropriety in it,—nothing of vanity, of pretension, of Levity—and she is altogether so attractive, that I should not wonder at his being delighted with her, had he known nothing of her previous to this personal acquaintance;—but against reason, against conviction, to be so well pleased with her as I am sure he is, does really astonish me.—His admiration was at first very strong, but no more than was natural; and I did not wonder at his being struck by the gentleness and delicacy of her Manners;—but when he has mentioned her of late, it has been in terms of more extraordinary praise, and yesterday he actually said, that he could not be surprised at any effect produced on the heart of Man by such Loveliness and such Abilities; and when I lamented in reply the badness of her disposition, he observed that whatever might have been her errors, they were to be imputed to her neglected Education and early Marriage, and that she was altogether a wonderful Woman.—

This tendency to excuse her conduct, or to forget it in the warmth of admiration vexes me; and if I did not know that Reginald is too much at home at Churchill to need an invitation for lengthening his visit, I should regret Mr. Vernon's giving him any.—

Lady Susan's intentions are of course those of absolute coquetry, or a desire of universal admiration. I cannot for a moment imagine that she has anything more serious in veiw, but it mortifies me to see a young Man of Reginald's sense duped by her at all.—I am &c.

Cath Vernon.—

Letter 9.
Mrs. Johnson to Lady Susan

Edward St.—
My dearest Friend

I congratulate you on Mr. De Courcy's arrival, and advise you by all means to marry him; his Father's Estate is we know considerable, and I beleive certainly entailed.[2]—Sir Reginald is very infirm, and not likely to stand in your way long.—I hear the

---

1 Delicate regard for her feelings.
2 Legally bound to be inherited by the eldest son.

young Man well spoken of, and tho' no one can really deserve you my dearest Susan, Mr. De Courcy may be worth having.—Manwaring will storm of course, but you may easily pacify him. Besides, the most scrupulous point of honour could not require you to wait for *his* emancipation.[1]—I have seen Sir James,—he came to Town for a few days last week, and called several times in Edward Street. I talked to him about you and your daughter, and he is so far from having forgotten you, that I am sure he would marry either of you with pleasure.—I gave him hopes of Frederica's relenting, and told him a great deal of her improvements.—I scolded him for making Love to Maria Manwaring; he protested that he had been only in joke, and we both laughed heartily at her disappointment, and in short were very agreable.—He is as silly as ever.—Yours faithfully

Alicia.—

Letter 10.
Lady Susan to Mrs. Johnson

Churchill

I am much obliged to you my dear Friend, for your advice respecting Mr. De Courcy, which I know was given with the fullest conviction of it's expediency, tho' I am not quite determined on following it.—I cannot easily resolve on anything so serious as Marriage, especially as I am not at present in want of money, and might perhaps till the old Gentleman's death, be very little benefited by the match. It is true that I am vain enough to beleive it within my reach.—I have made him sensible of my power, and can now enjoy the pleasure of triumphing over a Mind prepared to dislike me, and prejudiced against all my past actions. His sister too, is I hope convinced how little the ungenerous representations of any one to the disadvantage of another will avail, when opposed to the immediate influence of Intellect and Manner.—I see plainly that she is uneasy at my progress in the good opinion of her Brother, and conclude that nothing will be wanting on her part to counteract me;—but having once made him doubt the justice of her opinion of me, I think I may defy her.—

It has been delightful to me to watch his advances towards intimacy, especially to observe his altered manner in consequence of my repressing by the calm dignity of my deportment, his insolent approach to direct familiarity.—My conduct has been

---

1 Given the rarity and difficulty of divorce at the time, this effectively means the death of Manwaring's wife.

equally guarded from the first, and I never behaved less like a Coquette in the whole course of my Life, tho' perhaps my desire of dominion was never more decided. I have subdued him entirely by sentiment and serious conversation, and made him I may venture to say at least *half* in Love with me, without the semblance of the most common-place flirtation. Mrs. Vernon's consciousness of deserving every sort of revenge that it can be in my power to inflict, for her ill-offices, could alone enable her to perceive that I am actuated by any design in behaviour so gentle and unpretending.—Let her think and act as she chuses however; I have never yet found that the advice of a Sister could prevent a young Man's being in love if he chose it.—We are advancing now towards some kind of confidence, and in short are likely to be engaged in a kind of platonic friendship.[1]—On *my* side, you may be sure of its' never being more, for if I were not already as much attached to another person as I can be to any one, I should make a point of not bestowing my affection on a Man who had dared to think so meanly of me.—

Reginald has a good figure, and is not unworthy the praise you have heard given him, but is still greatly inferior to our friend at Langford.—He is less polished, less insinuating than Manwaring, and is comparatively deficient in the power of saying those delightful things which put one in good humour with oneself and all the world. He is quite agreable enough however, to afford me amusement, and to make many of those hours pass very pleasantly which would be otherwise spent in endeavouring to overcome my sister in law's reserve, and listening to her Husband's insipid talk.—

Your account of Sir James is most satisfactory, and I mean to give Miss Frederica a hint of my intentions very soon.—Yours &c

S. Vernon.

Letter 11.
Mrs. Vernon to Lady De Courcy.

I really grow quite uneasy my dearest Mother about Reginald, from witnessing the very rapid increase of Lady Susan's influence. They are now on terms of the most particular friendship, fre-

---

1 A relationship intimate and affectionate, but not sexual, following the example of Plato. The phrase was often used in the fiction of the late eighteenth century, usually with scepticism: Jane West, for example, talks of "the specious affectation of Platonic affection" (*A Tale of the Times* [3 vols, 1799], Vol. 3, p. 146).

quently engaged in long conversations together, and she has contrived by the most artful coquetry to subdue his Judgement to her own purposes.—It is impossible to see the intimacy between them, so very soon established, without some alarm, tho' I can hardly suppose that Lady Susan's veiws extend to marriage.—I wish you could get Reginald home again, under any plausible pretence. He is not at all disposed to leave us, and I have given him as many hints of my Father's precarious state of health, as common decency will allow me to do in my own house.—Her power over him must now be boundless, as she has entirely effaced all his former ill-opinion, and persuaded him not merely to forget, but to justify her conduct.—Mr. Smith's account of her proceedings at Langford, where he accused her of having made Mr. Manwaring and a young Man engaged to Miss Manwaring distractedly in love with her, which Reginald firmly beleived when he came to Churchill, is now he is persuaded only a scandalous invention. He has told me so in a warmth of manner which spoke his regret at having ever beleived the contrary himself.—

How sincerely do I greive that she ever entered this house!—I always looked forward to her coming with uneasiness—but very far was it, from originating in anxiety for Reginald.—I expected a most disagreable companion to myself, but could not imagine that my Brother would be in the smallest danger of being captivated by a Woman, with whose principles he was so well acquainted, and whose Character he so heartily despised. If you can get him away, it will be a good thing.

Yrs. affec:ly,

Cath Vernon.

Letter 12.
Sir Reginald De Courcy to his Son

Parklands

I know that young Men in general do not admit of any enquiry, even from their nearest relations, into affairs of the heart; but I hope my dear Reginald that you will be superior to such as allow nothing for a Father's anxiety, and think themselves privileged to refuse him their confidence and slight his advice.— You must be sensible that as an only son and the representative of an ancient Family, your conduct in Life is most interesting to your connections.[1]—In the very important concern of Marriage

---

1 Because of his status as heir to family fortune and estates, Reginald's relatives have a legitimate interest in his conduct.

especially, there is everything at stake; your own happiness, that of your Parents, and the credit of your name.—I do not suppose that you would deliberately form an absolute engagement[1] of that nature without acquainting your Mother and myself, or at least without being convinced that we should approve your choice; but I cannot help fearing that you may be drawn in by the Lady who has lately attached you, to a Marriage, which the whole of your Family, far and near, must highly reprobate.

Lady Susan's age is itself a material objection, but her want of character is one so much more serious, that the difference of even twelve years becomes in comparison of small account.— Were you not blinded by a sort of fascination, it would be ridiculous in me to repeat the instances of great misconduct on her side, so very generally known.—Her neglect of her husband, her encouragement of other Men, her extravagance and dissipation were so gross and notorious, that no one could be ignorant of them at the time, nor can now have forgotten them.—To our Family, she has always been represented in softened colours by the benevolence of Mr. Charles Vernon; and yet inspite of his generous endeavours to excuse her, we know that she did, from the most selfish motives, take all possible pains to prevent his marrying Catherine.—

My Years and increasing Infirmities make me very desirous my dear Reginald, of seeing you settled in the world.—To the Fortune of your wife, the goodness of my own, will make me indifferent; but her family and character must be equally unexceptionable. When your choice is so fixed as that no objection can be made to either, I can promise you a ready and chearful consent; but it is my Duty to oppose a Match, which deep Art only could render probable, and must in the end make wretched.

It is possible that her behaviour may arise only from Vanity, or a wish of gaining the admiration of a Man whom she must imagine to be particularly prejudiced against her; but it is more likely that she should aim at something farther.—She is poor, and may naturally seek an alliance which must be advantageous to herself.—You know your own rights, and that it is out of my power to prevent your inheriting the family Estate.[2] My Ability of dis-

---

1 Firm commitment to marriage (which Reginald could only break at the cost of a public scandal and the loss of his reputation).

2 I.e., because the estate is entailed. The same legal arrangement binds Mr. Bennet in *Pride and Prejudice*, so that he cannot prevent Mr. Collins inheriting the Longbourn estate.

tressing you during my Life,[1] would be a species of revenge to which I should hardly stoop under any circumstances.—I honestly tell you my Sentiments and Intentions. I do not wish to work on your Fears, but on your Sense and Affection.—It would destroy every comfort of my Life, to know that you were married to Lady Susan Vernon. It would be the death of that honest Pride with which I have hitherto considered my son, I should blush to see him, to hear of him, to think of him.—

I may perhaps do no good, but that of releiving my own mind, by this Letter; but I felt it my Duty to tell you that your partiality for Lady Susan is no secret to your friends, and to warn you against her.—I should be glad to hear your reasons for disbeleiving Mr. Smith's intelligence;[2]—you had no doubt of it's authenticity a month ago.—

If you can give me your assurance of having no design beyond enjoying the conversation of a clever woman for a short period, and of yeilding admiration only to her Beauty and Abilities without being blinded by them to her faults, you will restore me to happiness; but if you cannot do this, explain to me at least what has occasioned so great an alteration in your opinion of her.

I am &c

Regd. De Courcy.

Letter 13.
Lady De Courcy to Mrs. Vernon—

Parklands

My dear Catherine,

Unluckily I was confined to my room when your last letter came, by a cold which affected my eyes so much as to prevent my reading it myself, so I could not refuse your Father when he offered to read it to me, by which means he became acquainted to my great vexation with all your fears about your Brother. I had intended to write to Reginald myself, as soon as my eyes would let me; to point out as well as I could the danger of an intimate acquaintance with so artful a woman as Lady Susan, to a young Man of his age and high expectations. I meant moreover to have reminded him of our being quite alone now, and very much in need of him to keep up our spirits these long winter evenings. Whether it would have done any good, can never be settled now;

---

1 By withholding the allowance that will form Reginald's income until his father dies.
2 Information.

but I am excessively vexed that Sir Reginald should know anything of a matter which we foresaw would make him so uneasy.—He caught all your fears the moment he had read your Letter, and I am sure has not had the business out of his head since;—he wrote by the same post to Reginald, a long letter full of it all, and particularly asking an explanation of what he may have heard from Lady Susan to contradict the late[1] shocking reports. His answer came this morning, which I shall enclose to you, as I think you will like to see it; I wish it was more satisfactory, but it seems written with such a determination to think well of Lady Susan, that his assurances as to Marriage &c, do not set my heart at ease.—I say all I can however to satisfy your Father, and he is certainly less uneasy since Reginald's letter. How provoking it is my dear Catherine, that this unwelcome Guest of yours, should not only prevent our meeting this Christmas, but be the occasion of so much vexation and trouble.—Kiss the dear Children for me.—Your affect: Mother

C. De Courcy.—

Letter 14.
Mr. De Courcy to Sir Reginald—

Churchill

My dear Sir

I have this moment received your Letter, which has given me more astonishment than I ever felt before. I am to thank my Sister I suppose, for having represented me in such a light as to injure me in your opinion, and give you all this alarm.—I know not why she should chuse to make herself and her family uneasy by apprehending an Event, which no one but herself I can affirm, would ever have thought possible. To impute such a design to Lady Susan would be taking from her every claim to that excellent understanding which her bitterest Enemies have never denied her; and equally low must sink my pretensions to common sense, if I am suspected of matrimonial veiws in my behaviour to her.—Our difference of age must be an insuperable objection, and I entreat you my dear Sir to quiet your mind, and no longer harbour a suspicion which cannot be more injurious to your own peace, than to our Understandings.

I can have no veiw in remaining with Lady Susan than to enjoy for a short time (as you have yourself expressed it) the conversation of a Woman of high mental powers. If Mrs. Vernon would allow something to my affection for herself and her husband in

---

1 Recently made.

the length of my visit, she would do more justice to us all;—but my Sister is unhappily prejudiced beyond the hope of conviction against Lady Susan.—From an attachment to her husband which in itself does honour to both, she cannot forgive those endeavours at preventing their union, which have been attributed to selfishness in Lady Susan. But in this case, as well as in many others, the World has most grossly injured that Lady, by supposing the worst, where the motives of her conduct have been doubtful.—

Lady Susan had heard something so materially to the disadvantage of my Sister, as to persuade her that the happiness of Mr. Vernon, to whom she was always much attached, would be absolutely destroyed by the Marriage. And this circumstance while it explains the true motive of Lady Susan's conduct, and removes all the blame which has been so lavished on her, may also convince us how little the general report of any one ought to be credited, since no character however upright, can escape the malevolence of slander. If my sister in the security of retirement, with as little opportunity as inclination to do Evil, could not avoid Censure, we must not rashly condemn those who living in the World and surrounded with temptation, should be accused of Errors which they are known to have the power of committing.—

I blame myself severely for having so easily beleived the scandalous tales invented by Charles Smith to the prejudice of Lady Susan, as I am now convinced how greatly they have traduced her. As to Mrs. Manwaring's jealousy, it was totally his own invention; and his account of her attaching Miss Manwaring's Lover was scarcely better founded. Sir James Martin had been drawn-in by that young Lady to pay her some attention, and as he is a Man of fortune, it was easy to see that *her* veiws extended to Marriage.—It is well-known that Miss Manwaring is absolutely on the catch for a husband, and no one therefore can pity her, for losing by the superior attractions of another woman, the chance of being able to make a worthy Man completely miserable.—Lady Susan was far from intending such a conquest, and on finding how warmly Miss Manwaring resented her Lover's defection, determined, inspite of Mr. and Mrs. Manwaring's most earnest entreaties, to leave the family.—I have reason to imagine that she did receive serious Proposals from Sir James, but her removing from Langford immediately on the discovery of his attachment, must acquit her on that article, with every Mind of common candour.[1]—You will, I am sure my dear Sir, feel the

---

1 Openness, freedom from malice or prejudice.

truth of this reasoning, and will hereby learn to do justice to the character of a very injured woman.—

I know that Lady Susan in coming to Churchill was governed only by the most honourable and amiable intentions.—Her prudence and economy[1] are exemplary, her regard for Mr. Vernon equal even to *his* deserts, and her wish of obtaining my sister's good opinion merits a better return than it has received.—As a Mother she is unexceptionable. Her solid affection for her Child is shewn by placing her in hands, where her Education will be properly attended to; but because she has not the blind and weak partiality of most Mothers, she is accused of wanting Maternal Tenderness.—Every person of Sense however will know how to value and commend her well directed affection, and will join me in wishing that Frederica Vernon may prove more worthy than she has yet done, of her Mother's tender cares.

I have now my dear Sir, written my real sentiments of Lady Susan; you will know from this Letter, how highly I admire her Abilities, and esteem her Character; but if you are not equally convinced by my full and solemn assurance that your fears have been most idly created, you will deeply mortify and distress me.—I am &c

R De Courcy.—

Letter 15.
Mrs. Vernon to Lady De Courcy.

Churchill
My dear Mother

I return you Reginald's letter, and rejoice with all my heart that my Father is made easy by it. Tell him so, with my congratulations;—but between ourselves, I must own it has only convinced *me* of my Brother's having no *present* intention of marrying Lady Susan—not that he is in no danger of doing so three months hence.—He gives a very plausible account of her behaviour at Langford, I wish it may be true, but his intelligence must come from herself, and I am less disposed to beleive it, than to lament the degree of intimacy subsisting between them, implied by the discussion of such a subject.

I am sorry to have incurred his displeasure, but can expect nothing better while he is so very eager in Lady Susan's justification.—He is very severe against me indeed, and yet I hope I have not been hasty in my judgement of her.—Poor Woman! tho' I

---

1 Management of expenses, or of her way of living more generally.

have reasons enough for my dislike, I can not help pitying her at present as she is in real distress, and with too much cause.—She had this morning a letter from the Lady with whom she has placed her daughter, to request that Miss Vernon might be immediately removed, as she had been detected in an attempt to run away. Why, or whither she intended to go, does not appear; but as her situation seems to have been unexceptionable, it is a sad thing and of course highly afflicting to Lady Susan.—

Frederica must be as much as sixteen, and ought to know better, but from what her Mother insinuates I am afraid she is a perverse girl. She has been sadly neglected however, and her Mother ought to remember it.—

Mr. Vernon set off for Town as soon as she had determined what should be done. He is if possible to prevail on Miss Summers to let Frederica continue with her, and if he cannot succeed, to bring her to Churchill for the present, till some other situation can be found for her.—Her Ladyship is comforting herself meanwhile by strolling along the Shrubbery[1] with Reginald, calling forth all his tender feelings I suppose on this distressing occasion. She has been talking a great deal about it to me, she talks vastly well, I am afraid of being ungenerous or I should say she talks *too* well to feel so very deeply. But I will not look for Faults. She may be Reginald's Wife—Heaven forbid it!—but why should I be quicker sighted than any body else?—Mr. Vernon declares that he never saw deeper distress than hers, on the receipt of the Letter— and is his Judgement inferior to mine?—

She was very unwilling that Frederica should be allowed to come to Churchill, and justly enough, as it seems a sort of reward to Behaviour deserving very differently. But it was impossible to take her any where else, and she is not to remain here long.—

"It will be absolutely necessary, said she, as you my dear sister must be sensible, to treat my daughter with some severity while she is here;—a most painful necessity, but I will *endeavour* to submit to it.—I am afraid I have been often too indulgent, but my poor Frederica's temper could never bear opposition well. You must support and encourage me—You must urge the necessity of reproof, if you see me too lenient."

All this sounds very reasonably.—Reginald is so incensed against the poor silly Girl!—Surely it is not to Lady Susan's credit

---

1 The gardens of most country estates included a shrubbery, a private area close to the house, with paths spread with gravel for ease of walking and intersecting beds planted with ornamental trees and shrubs.

that he should be so bitter against her daughter; his idea of her must be drawn from the Mother's description.—

Well, whatever may be his fate, we have the comfort of knowing that we have done our utmost to save him. We must commit the event to an Higher Power.—Yours Ever &c

Cath Vernon.

Letter 16.
Lady Susan to Mrs. Johnson

Churchill

Never my dearest Alicia, was I so provoked in my life as by a Letter this morning from Miss Summers. That horrid girl of mine has been trying to run away.—I had not a notion of her being such a little Devil before;—she seemed to have all the Vernon Milkiness;[1] but on receiving the letter in which I declared my intentions about Sir James, she actually attempted to elope;[2] at least, I cannot otherwise account for her doing it.—She meant I suppose to go to the Clarkes in Staffordshire, for she has no other acquaintance. But she *shall* be punished, she *shall* have him. I have sent Charles to Town to make matters up if he can, for I do not by any means want her here. If Miss Summers will not keep her, you must find me out another school, unless we can get her married immediately.—Miss S. writes word that she could not get the young Lady to assign any cause for her extraordinary conduct, which confirms me in my own private explanation of it.—

Frederica is too shy I think, and too much in awe of me, to tell tales; but if the mildness of her Uncle *should* get anything from her, I am not afraid. I trust I shall be able to make my story as good as her's.—If I am vain of any thing, it is of my eloquence. Consideration and Esteem as surely follow command of Language, as Admiration waits on Beauty. And here I have opportunity enough for the exercise of my Talent, as the cheif of my time is spent in Conversation. Reginald is never easy unless we are by ourselves, and when the weather is tolerable we pace the shrubbery for hours together.—I like him on the whole very well, he is clever and has a good deal to say, but he is sometimes impertinent[3] and trouble-

---

1 Mildness: softness: gentleness: a usage now rare. Lady Susan may also be alluding to Lady Macbeth's well-known reference to "th'milk of human kindness" (*Macbeth*, Act 1, Sc. 4).

2 Run away (though without the modern implication of fleeing with a lover for the purposes of marriage).

3 Meddling with another person's private affairs; intrusive, but not necessarily presumptuous or insolent.

some.—There is a sort of ridiculous delicacy about him which requires the fullest explanation of whatever he may have heard to my disadvantage, and is never satisfied till he thinks he has ascertained the beginning and end of everything.—

This is *one* sort of Love—but I confess it does not particularly recommend itself to me.—I infinitely prefer the tender and liberal spirit of Manwaring, which impressed with the deepest conviction of my merit, is satisfied that whatever I do must be right; and look with a degree of Contempt on the inquisitive and doubting Fancies of that Heart which seems always debating on the reasonableness of it's Emotions. Manwaring is indeed beyond compare superior to Reginald—superior in every thing but the power of being with me.—Poor fellow! he is quite distracted by Jealousy, which I am not sorry for, as I know no better support of Love.—He has been teizing[1] me to allow of his coming into this country, and lodging somewhere near me *incog*[2]—but I forbid every thing of the kind.—Those women are inexcusable who forget what is due to themselves and the opinion of the World.—

S. Vernon—

Letter 17.
Mrs. Vernon to Lady De Courcy.

Churchill

My dear Mother

Mr. Vernon returned on Thursday night, bringing his neice with him. Lady Susan had received a line from him by that day's post informing her that Miss Summers had absolutely refused to allow of Miss Vernon's continuance in her Academy.[3] We were therefore prepared for her arrival, and expected them impatiently the whole evening.—They came while we were at Tea,[4] and I

---

1 Pestering: irritating through persistence.

2 Slang abbreviation of the latin "incognito," meaning in a state of concealment or hidden identity.

3 The word derives from the name of the garden in which Plato taught his pupils. It was later taken up by learned bodies, including the Royal Academy, founded in 1768 for the purpose of cultivating and improving the arts of painting, sculpture, and architecture. It was more widely used to denote a superior kind of school.

4 Tea was drunk at the end of dinner, the main meal of the day, which in the country was usually eaten in the mid-late afternoon. The separate meal of "afternoon tea" was not introduced until later in the nineteenth century.

never saw any creature look so frightened in my life as Frederica when she entered the room.—

Lady Susan who had been shedding tears before and shewing great agitation at the idea of the meeting, received her with perfect self-command, and without betraying the least tenderness of spirit.—She hardly spoke to her, and on Frederica's bursting into tears as soon as we were seated, took her out of the room and did not return for some time; when she did, her eyes looked very red, and she was as much agitated as before.—We saw no more of her daughter.—

Poor Reginald was beyond measure concerned to see his fair friend in such distress, and watched her with so much tender solicitude that I, who occasionally caught her observing his countenance with exultation, was quite out of patience.—This pathetic[1] representation lasted the whole evening, and so ostentatious and artful a display has entirely convinced me that she did in fact feel nothing.—

I am more angry with her than ever since I have seen her daughter.—The poor girl looks so unhappy that my heart aches for her.—Lady Susan is surely too severe, because Frederica does not seem to have the sort of temper to make severity necessary.— She looks perfectly timid, dejected and penitent.—

She is very pretty, tho' not so handsome as her Mother, nor at all like her. Her complexion is delicate, but neither so fair, nor so blooming as Lady Susan's[2]—and she has quite the Vernon cast of countenance, the oval face and mild dark eyes, and there is peculiar sweetness in her look when she speaks either to her Uncle or me, for as we behave kindly to her, we have of course engaged her gratitude.—Her Mother has insinuated that her temper is untractable, but I never saw a face less indicative of any evil disposition than her's; and from what I now see of the behaviour of each to the other, the invariable severity of Lady Susan, and the silent dejection of Frederica, I am led to beleive as heretofore that the former has no real Love for her daughter and has never done her justice, or treated her affectionately.

---

1 Full of pathos (here, of course, used ironically).
2 The concept of "bloom," which denoted women's highest moment of health and beauty, is significant throughout JA's writings. "A few years before, Anne Elliot had been a very pretty girl, but her bloom had vanished early," writes JA at the beginning of *Persuasion* (Vol. 1, ch. 1), and the novel records the way in which Anne recovers her "bloom" and her former lover, Wentworth.

I have not yet been able to have any conversation with my neice; she is shy, and I think I can see that some pains are taken to prevent her being much with me.—Nothing satisfactory transpires as to her reason for running away.—Her kind hearted Uncle you may be sure, was too fearful of distressing her, to ask many questions as they travelled.—I wish it had been possible for me to fetch her instead of him;—I think I should have discovered the truth in the course of a Thirty miles Journey.[1]—

The small Pianoforté[2] has been removed within these few days at Lady Susan's request, into her Dressing room, and Frederica spends great part of the day there;—*practising* it is called, but I seldom hear any noise when I pass that way.—What she does with herself there I do not know, there are plenty of books in the room, but it is not every girl who has been running wild the first fifteen years of her life, that can or will read.—Poor Creature! the prospect from her window is not very instructive, for that room overlooks the Lawn you know with the shrubbery on one side, where she may see her Mother walking for an hour together, in earnest conversation with Reginald.—A girl of Frederica's age must be childish indeed, if such things do not strike her.—Is it not inexcusable to give such an example to a daughter?—Yet Reginald still thinks Lady Susan the best of Mothers—still condemns Frederica as a worthless girl!—He is convinced that her attempt to run away, proceeded from no justifiable cause, and had no provocation. I am sure I cannot say that it *had*, but while Miss Summers declares that Miss Vernon shewed no sign of Obstinacy or Perverseness during her whole stay in Wigmore Street till she was detected in this scheme, I cannot so readily credit what Lady Susan has made him and wants to make me beleive, that it was merely an impatience of restraint, and a desire of escaping from the tuition of Masters which brought on the plan of an elopement.—Oh! Reginald, how is your judgement enslaved!—He scarcely dares even allow her to be handsome, and when I speak of her beauty, replies only that her eyes have no Brilliancy.

Sometimes he is sure that she is deficient in Understanding, and at others that her temper only is in fault. In short when a person is always to deceive, it is impossible to be consistent. Lady Susan finds it necessary for her own justification that Frederica

---

1   At a normal travelling rate for a carriage, somewhere around six miles an hour, this would take about five hours.

2   Pianofortes had been introduced into England in the middle of the eighteenth century, and by the 1790s were common in genteel homes.

should be to blame, and probably has sometimes judged it expedient to accuse her of ill-nature and sometimes to lament her want of sense. Reginald is only repeating after her Ladyship.—

I am &c

Cath Vernon

Letter 18.
From the same to the same.—

Churchill

My dear Madam

I am very glad to find that my description of Frederica Vernon has interested you, for I do beleive her truly deserving of our regard, and when I have communicated a notion that has recently struck me, your kind impression in her favour will I am sure be heightened. I cannot help fancying that she is growing partial to my brother, I so very often see her eyes fixed on his face with a remarkable expression of pensive admiration!—He is certainly very handsome—and yet more—there is an openness in his manner that must be highly prepossessing, and I am sure she feels it so.—Thoughtful and pensive in general her countenance always brightens with a smile when Reginald says anything amusing; and let the subject be ever so serious that he may be conversing on, I am much mistaken if a syllable of his uttering, escape her.—

I want to make *him* sensible of all this, for we know the power of gratitude on such a heart as his; and could Frederica's artless affection detach him from her Mother, we might bless the day which brought her to Churchill. I think my dear Madam, you would not disapprove of her as a Daughter. She is extremely young to be sure, has had a wretched Education and a dreadful example of Levity in her Mother; but yet I can pronounce her disposition to be excellent, and her natural abilities very good.—

Tho' totally without accomplishment, she is by no means so ignorant as one might expect to find her, being fond of books and spending the cheif of her time in reading. Her Mother leaves her more to herself now than she *did*, and I have her with me as much as possible, and have taken great pains to overcome her timidity. We are very good friends, and tho' she never opens her lips before her Mother, she talks enough when alone with me, to make it clear that if properly treated by Lady Susan she would always appear to much greater advantage. There cannot be a more gentle, affectionate heart, or more obliging manners, when acting without restraint. Her little Cousins are all very fond of her.—Yrs. affect:ly

Cath Vernon

Letter 19.
Lady Susan to Mrs. Johnson

Churchill

You will be eager I know to hear something farther of Frederica, and perhaps may think me negligent for not writing before.— She arrived with her Uncle last Thursday fortnight, when of course I lost no time in demanding the reason of her behaviour, and soon found myself to have been perfectly right in attributing it to my own letter.—The purport of it frightened her so thoroughly that with a mixture of true girlish perverseness and folly, without considering that she could not escape from my authority by running away from Wigmore Street, she resolved on getting out of the house, and proceeding directly by the stage[1] to her friends the Clarkes, and had really got as far as the length of two streets in her journey, when she was fortunately miss'd, pursued, and overtaken.—

Such was the first distinguished exploit of Miss Frederica Susanna Vernon, and if we consider that it was atchieved at the tender age of sixteen we shall have room for the most flattering prognostics of her future renown.—I am excessively provoked however at the parade of propriety which prevented Miss Summers from keeping the girl; and it seems so extraordinary a peice of nicety, considering what are my daughter's family connections, that I can only suppose the Lady to be governed by the fear of never getting her money.—Be that as it may however, Frederica is returned on my hands, and having now nothing else to employ her, is busy in pursueing the plan of Romance begun at Langford.—She is actually falling in love with Reginald De Courcy.— To disobey her Mother by refusing an unexceptionable offer is not enough; her affections must likewise be given without her Mother's approbation.—I never saw a girl of her age, bid fairer to be the sport of Mankind. Her feelings are tolerably lively, and she is so charmingly artless in their display, as to afford the most reasonable hope of her being ridiculed and despised by every Man who sees her.—

---

1   Stage-coaches offered a form of public transport; coaches travelled "from different parts of London to all parts of the kingdom, almost every day." It cost 3 1/2d per mile to sit inside the coach, but it was cheaper to sit outside with the coach driver (John Trusler, *The London Advertiser and Guide: Containing Every Instruction and Information useful and necessary to Persons living in London, and coming to reside there* [1786], p. 87). Respectable ladies would not travel alone by stage-coach.

Artlessness will never do in Love matters, and that girl is born a simpleton who has it either by nature or affectation.—I am not yet certain that Reginald sees what she is about; nor is it of much consequence;—she is now an object of indifference to him, she would be one of contempt were he to understand her Emotions.—Her beauty is much admired by the Vernons, but it has no effect on *him*. She is in high favour with her Aunt altogether—because she is so little like myself of course. She is exactly the companion for Mrs. Vernon, who dearly loves to be first, and to have all the sense and all the wit of the Conversation to herself;—Frederica will never eclipse her.—When she first came, I was at some pains to prevent her seeing much of her Aunt, but I have since relaxed, as I beleive I may depend on her observing the rules I have laid down for their discourse.—

But do not imagine that with all this Lenity, I have for a moment given up my plan of her marriage;—No, I am unalterably fixed on that point, tho' I have not yet quite resolved on the manner of bringing it about.—I should not chuse to have the business brought forward here, and canvassed by the wise heads of Mr. and Mrs. Vernon; and I cannot just now afford to go to Town.—Miss Frederica therefore must wait a little.—

Yours Ever
S. Vernon.—

Letter 20.
Mrs. Vernon to Lady De Courcy.

Churchill

We have a very unexpected Guest with us at present, my dear Mother.—He arrived yesterday.—I heard a carriage at the door as I was sitting with my Children while they dined, and supposing I should be wanted left the Nursery soon afterwards and was half way down stairs, when Frederica as pale as ashes came running up, and rushed by me into her own room.—I instantly followed, and asked her what was the matter.—"Oh! cried she, he is come, Sir James is come—and what am I to do?"—This was no explanation; I begged her to tell me what she meant. At that moment we were interrupted by a knock at the door;—it was Reginald, who came by Lady Susan's direction to call Frederica down.—"It is Mr. De Courcy, said she, colouring violently, Mama has sent for me, and I must go."—

We all three went down together, and I saw my Brother examining the terrified face of Frederica with surprise.—In the breakfast room we found Lady Susan and a young Man of genteel appearance, whom she introduced to me by the name of Sir James Martin, the very person, as you may remember, whom it was said she had been at pains to detach from Miss Manwaring.—But the conquest it seems was not designed for herself, or she has since transferred it to her daughter, for Sir James is now desperately in love with Frederica, and with full encouragement from Mama.—The poor girl however I am sure dislikes him; and tho' his person and address are very well, he appears both to Mr. Vernon and me a very weak young Man.—

Frederica looked so shy, so confused, when we entered the room, that I felt for her exceedingly. Lady Susan behaved with great attention to her Visitor, and yet I thought I could perceive that she had no particular pleasure in seeing him.—Sir James talked a good deal, and made many civil excuses to me for the liberty he had taken in coming to Churchill, mixing more frequent laughter with his discourse than the subject required;—said many things over and over again, and told Lady Susan three times that he had seen Mrs. Johnson a few Evenings before.—He now and then addressed Frederica, but more frequently her Mother.—The poor girl sat all this time without opening her lips;—her eyes cast down, and her colour varying every instant, while Reginald observed all that passed, in perfect silence.—

At length Lady Susan, weary I beleive of her situation, proposed walking, and we left the two Gentlemen together to put on our Pelisses.[1]—

As we went upstairs Lady Susan begged permission to attend me for a few moments in my Dressing room, as she was anxious to speak with me in private.—I led her thither accordingly, and as soon as the door was closed she said, "I was never more surprised in my life than by Sir James's arrival, and the suddenness of it requires some apology to *You* my dear Sister, tho' to *me* as a Mother, it is highly flattering.—He is so warmly attached to my daughter that he could exist no longer without seeing her.—Sir James is a young Man of an amiable[2] disposition, and excellent character;—a little too much of the *Rattle*[3] perhaps, but a year or two will rectify *that*, and he is in other respects so very eligible a

---

1 A long cloak, with armhole slits and a shoulder cape or hood, often made of a rich fabric; it was normal outerwear for early nineteenth-century gentlewomen.

2 With pleasing qualities; a friendly disposition.

3 A constant chatterer. A well-known social type in the life and literature of JA's time.

Match for Frederica that I have always observed his attachment with the greatest pleasure, and am persuaded that you and my Brother will give the alliance your hearty approbation.—I have never before mentioned the likelihood of it's taking place to any one, because I thought that while Frederica continued at school, it had better not be known to exist;—but now, as I am convinced that Frederica is too old ever to submit to school confinement, and have therefore begun to consider her union with Sir James as not very distant, I had intended within a few days to acquaint yourself and Mr. Vernon with the whole business.—I am sure my dear Sister, you will excuse my remaining silent on it so long, and agree with me that such circumstances, while they continue from any cause in suspense, cannot be too cautiously concealed.— When you have the happiness of bestowing your sweet little Catherine some years hence on a Man, who in connection and character is alike unexceptionable, you will know what I feel now;—tho' Thank Heaven! you cannot have all my reasons for rejoicing in such an Event.—Catherine will be amply provided for, and not like my Frederica endebted to a fortunate Establishment[1] for the comforts of Life."—

She concluded by demanding my congratulations.—I gave them somewhat awkwardly I beleive;—for in fact, the sudden disclosure of so important a matter took from me the power of speaking with any clearness.—She thanked me however most affectionately for my kind concern in the welfare of herself and her daughter, and then said,

"I am not apt to deal in professions, my dear Mrs. Vernon, and I never had the convenient talent of affecting sensations foreign to my heart; and therefore I trust you will beleive me when I declare that much as I had heard in your praise before I knew you, I had no idea that I should ever love you as I now do;—and I must farther say that your friendship towards me is more particularly gratifying, because I have reason to beleive that some attempts were made to prejudice you against me.—I only wish that They—whoever they are—to whom I am endebted for such kind intentions, could see the terms on which we now are together, and understand the real affection we feel for each other!—But I will not detain you any longer.—God bless you, for your goodness to me and my girl, and continue to you all your present happiness."

---

1 Material situation on marriage.

What can one say of such a woman, my dear Mother?—such earnestness, such solemnity of expression!—And yet I cannot help suspecting the truth of everything she said.—

As for Reginald, I beleive he does not know what to make of the matter.—When Sir James first came, he appeared all astonishment and perplexity. The folly of the young Man, and the confusion of Frederica entirely engrossed him; and tho' a little private discourse with Lady Susan has since had it's effect, he is still hurt I am sure at her allowing of such a Man's attentions to her daughter.—

Sir James invited himself with great composure to remain here a few days;—hoped we would not think it odd, was aware of it's being very impertinent, but he took the liberty of a relation,[1] and concluded by wishing with a laugh, that he might be really one soon.—Even Lady Susan seemed a little disconcerted by this forwardness;—in her heart I am persuaded, she sincerely wishes him gone.—

But something must be done for this poor Girl, if her feelings are such as both her Uncle and I beleive them to be. She must not be sacrificed to Policy or Ambition, she must not be even left to suffer from the dread of it.—The Girl, whose heart can distinguish[2] Reginald De Courcy, deserves, however he may slight her, a better fate than to be Sir James Martin's wife.—As soon as I can get her alone, I will discover the real Truth, but she seems to wish to avoid me.—I hope this does not proceed from any thing wrong, and that I shall not find out I have thought too well of her.—Her behaviour before Sir James certainly speaks the greatest consciousness and Embarrassment; but I see nothing in it more like Encouragement.—

Adeiu my dear Madam,
Yrs &c. Cath Vernon.—

Letter 21.
Miss Vernon to Mr. De Courcy—.
Sir,

I hope you will excuse this liberty, I am forced upon it by the greatest distress, or I should be ashamed to trouble you.—I am very miserable about Sir James Martin, and have no other way in the world of helping myself but by writing to you, for I am for-

---

1 Sir James's inviting himself to stay with the Vernons, whom he has never met before, is an act of gross social impoliteness.
2 Recognise the (good) qualities of.

bidden ever speaking to my Uncle or Aunt on the subject; and this being the case, I am afraid my applying to you will appear no better than equivocation, and as if I attended only to the letter and not the spirit of Mama's commands, but if *you* do not take my part, and persuade her to break it off, I shall be half-distracted, for I can not bear him.—No human Being but *you* could have any chance of prevailing with her.—If you will therefore have the unspeakable great kindness[1] of taking my part with her, and persuading her to send Sir James away, I shall be more obliged to you than it is possible for me to express.—I always disliked him from the first, it is not a sudden fancy I assure you Sir, I always thought him silly and impertinent and disagreable, and now he is grown worse than ever.—I would rather work for my bread than marry him.[2]—I do not know how to apologise enough for this Letter, I know it is taking so great a liberty, I am aware how dreadfully angry it will make Mama, but I must run the risk.—I am Sir, Your most Humble Servt.

F. S. V.—

Letter 22.
Lady Susan to Mrs. Johnson

Churchill

This is insufferable!—My dearest friend, I was never so enraged before, and must releive myself by writing to you, who I know will enter into all my feelings.—Who should come on Tuesday but Sir James Martin?—Guess my astonishment and vexation—for as you well know, I never wished him to be seen at Churchill. What a pity that you should not have known his intentions!—Not content with coming, he actually invited himself to remain here a few days. I could have poisoned him;—I made the best of it however, and told my story with great success to Mrs. Vernon who, whatever might be her real sentiments, said nothing in opposition to mine. I made a point also of Frederica's behaving civilly to Sir James, and gave her to understand that I was absolutely determined on her marrying him.—She said something of her misery, but that was all.—I have for some time been more particularly resolved on the Match, from seeing the rapid increase of her affection for Reginald, and from not feeling perfectly secure that a knowledge of *that* affection might not in the

---

1 An acceptable grammatical construction in the early nineteenth century.
2 The sentiment was a conventional one in fiction, but was not usually tested. See p. 274, note 2.

end awaken a return.—Contemptible as a regard founded only on compassion, must make them both, in my eyes, I felt by no means assured that such might not be the consequence.—It is true that Reginald had not in any degree grown cool towards me;—but yet he had lately mentioned Frederica spontaneously and unnecessarily, and once had said something in praise of her person.—

He was all astonishment at the appearance of my visitor; and at first observed Sir James with an attention which I was pleased to see not unmixed with jealousy;—but unluckily it was impossible for me really to torment him, as Sir James tho' extremely gallant to me, very soon made the whole party understand that his heart was devoted to my daughter.—

I had no great difficulty in convincing De Courcy when we were alone, that I was perfectly justified, all things considered, in desiring the match; and the whole business seemed most comfortably arranged.—They could none of them help perceiving that Sir James was no Solomon,[1] but I had positively forbidden Frederica's complaining to Charles Vernon or his wife, and they had therefore no pretence for Interference, tho' my impertinent Sister I beleive wanted only opportunity for doing so.—

Everything however was going on calmly and quietly; and tho' I counted the hours of Sir James's stay, my mind was entirely satisfied with the posture of affairs.—Guess then what I must feel at the sudden disturbance of all my schemes, and that too from a quarter, whence I had least reason to apprehend it.—Reginald came this morning into my Dressing room, with a very unusual solemnity of countenance, and after some preface informed me in so many words, that he wished to reason with me on the Impropriety and Unkindness of allowing Sir James Martin to address my Daughter, contrary to *her* inclination.—I was all amazement.—When I found that he was not to be laughed out of his design, I calmly required an explanation, and begged to know by what he was impelled and by whom commissioned to reprimand me.

He then told me, mixing in his speech a few insolent compliments and ill timed expressions of Tenderness to which I listened with perfect indifference, that my daughter had acquainted him with some circumstances concerning herself, Sir James, and me, which gave him great uneasiness.—

---

1 The Old Testament king, Solomon, was proverbial for his wisdom.

In short, I found that she had in the first place actually written to him, to request his interference, and that on receiving her Letter he had conversed with her on the subject of it, in order to understand the particulars and assure himself of her real wishes!—

I have not a doubt but that the girl took this opportunity of making down right Love to him; I am convinced of it, from the manner in which he spoke of her. Much good, may such Love do him!—I shall ever despise the Man who can be gratified by the Passion, which he never wished to inspire, nor solicited the avowal of.—I shall always detest them both.—He can have no true regard for me, or he would not have listened to her;—And she, with her little rebellious heart and indelicate feelings to throw herself into the protection of a young Man with whom she had scarcely ever exchanged two words before. I am equally confounded at *her* Impudence and *his* Credulity.—How dared he beleive what she told him in my disfavour!—Ought he not to have felt assured that I must have unanswerable Motives for all that I had done!—Where was his reliance on my Sense or Goodness then; where the resentment which true Love would have dictated against the person defaming me, that person too, a Chit, a Child, without Talent or Education, whom he had been always taught to despise?—

I was calm for some time, but the greatest degree of Forbearance may be overcome; and I hope I was afterwards sufficiently keen.[1]—He endeavoured, long endeavoured to soften my resentment, but that woman is a fool indeed who while insulted by accusation, can be worked on by compliments.—At length he left me as deeply provoked as myself, and he shewed his anger *more.*—I was quite cool, but he gave way to the most violent indignation.—I may therefore expect it will the sooner subside; and perhaps his may be vanished for ever, while mine will be found still fresh and implacable.

He is now shut up in his apartment, whither I heard him go, on leaving mine.—How unpleasant, one would think, must his reflections be!—But some people's feelings are incomprehensible.—I have not yet tranquillized myself enough to see Frederica. *She* shall not soon forget the occurrences of this day.—She shall find that she has poured forth her tender Tale of Love in vain, and exposed herself forever to the contempt of the whole world, and the severest Resentment of her injured Mother.—Yrs. affect:ly

S. Vernon

---

1 Operating like a sharp instrument, piercing, and causing pain.

Letter 23.

Mrs. Vernon to Lady De Courcy

Churchill

Let me congratulate you, my dearest Mother. The affair which has given us so much anxiety is drawing to a happy conclusion. Our prospect is most delightful;—and since matters have now taken so favourable a turn, I am quite sorry that I ever imparted my apprehensions to you; for the pleasure of learning that the Danger is over, is perhaps dearly purchased by all that you have previously suffered.—

I am so much agitated by Delight that I can scarcely hold a pen, but am determined to send you a few lines by James, that you may have some explanation of what must so greatly astonish you, as that Reginald should be returning to Parklands.—

I was sitting about half an hour ago with Sir James in the Breakfast parlour, when my Brother called me out of the room.— I instantly saw that something was the matter;—his complexion was raised, and he spoke with great emotion.—You know his eager manner, my dear Madam, when his mind is interested.—

"Catherine, said he, I am going home today. I am sorry to leave you, but I must go.—It is a great while since I have seen my Father and Mother.—I am going to send James forward with my Hunters immediately, if you have any Letter therefore he can take it.[1]—I shall not be at home myself till Wednesday or Thursday, as I shall go through London, where I have business.—But before I leave you, he continued, speaking in a lower voice and with still greater energy, I must warn you of one thing.—Do not let Frederica Vernon be made unhappy by that Martin.—He wants to marry her—her Mother promotes the Match—but *she* cannot endure the idea of it.—Be assured that I speak from the fullest conviction of the Truth of what I say.—I *know* that Frederica is made wretched by Sir James' continuing here.—She is a sweet girl, and deserves a better fate.—Send him away immediately. *He* is only a fool—but what her Mother can mean, Heaven only knows!—Good bye, he added shaking my hand with earnestness—I do not know when you will see me again. But remember

---

1 At a time when the post was expensive, letters were paid for by the recipient at a rate per sheet of paper (unless a frank, a signature of a person who was entitled to send mail without charge, such as a Member of Parliament, was superscribed on the letter), and people regularly took the opportunity of having mail carried by their family, friends, neighbours, or servants.

what I tell you of Frederica;—you *must* make it your business to
see justice done her.—She is an amiable girl, and has a very superior Mind to what we have ever given her credit for.—"

He then left me and ran upstairs.—I would not try to stop
him, for I knew what his feelings must be; the nature of mine as
I listened to him, I need not attempt to describe.—For a minute
or two I remained in the same spot, overpowered by wonder—of
a most agreable sort indeed; yet it required some consideration to
be tranquilly happy.—

In about ten minutes after my return to the parlour, Lady
Susan entered the room.—I concluded of course that she and
Reginald had been quarrelling, and looked with anxious curios-
ity for a confirmation of my beleif in her face.—Mistress of
Deceit however she appeared perfectly unconcerned, and after
chatting on indifferent subjects for a short time, said to me,

"I find from Wilson that we are going to lose Mr. De Courcy.
—Is it true that he leaves Churchill this morning?"—

I replied that it was.—

"He told us nothing of all this last night, said she laughing, or
even this morning at Breakfast. But perhaps he did not know it
himself.—Young Men are often hasty in their resolutions—and
not more sudden in forming, than unsteady in keeping them.—I
should not be surprised if he were to change his mind at last, and
not go."—

She soon afterwards left the room.—I trust however my dear
Mother, that we have no reason to fear an alteration of his present plan; things have gone too far.—They must have quarrelled,
and about Frederica too.—Her calmness astonishes me.—What
delight will be yours in seeing him again, in seeing him still worthy your Esteem, still capable of forming your Happiness!

When I next write, I shall be able I hope to tell you that Sir
James is gone, Lady Susan vanquished, and Frederica at peace.—
We have much to do, but it shall be done.—I am all impatience
to know how this astonishing change was effected.—I finish as I
began, with the warmest congratulations.—Yrs. Ever,

Cath Vernon.

Letter 24.
From the same to the same.

Churchill

Little did I imagine my dear Mother, when I sent off my last
letter, that the delightful perturbation of spirits I was then in,
would undergo so speedy, so melancholy a reverse!—I never can

sufficiently regret that I wrote to you at all.—Yet who could have foreseen what has happened? My dear Mother, every hope which but two hours ago made me so happy, is vanished. The quarrel between Lady Susan and Reginald is made up, and we are all as we were before. One point only is gained; Sir James Martin is dismissed.—What are we now to look forward to?—I am indeed disappointed. Reginald was all but gone; his horse was ordered, and almost brought to the door!—Who would not have felt safe?—

For half an hour I was in momentary expectation of his departure.—After I had sent off my Letter to you, I went to Mr. Vernon and sat with him in his room, talking over the whole matter.—I then determined to look for Frederica, whom I had not seen since breakfast.—I met her on the stairs and saw that she was crying.

"My dear Aunt, said she, he is going, Mr. De Courcy is going, and it is all my fault. I am afraid you will be angry, but indeed I had no idea it would end so."—

"My Love, replied I, do not think it necessary to apologize to me on that account.—I shall feel myself under an obligation to any one who is the means of sending my brother home;—because, (recollecting myself) I know my Father wants very much to see him. But what is it that *you* have done to occasion all this?"—

She blushed deeply as she answered, "I was so unhappy about Sir James that I could not help—I have done something very wrong I know—but you have not an idea of the misery I have been in, and Mama had ordered me never to speak to you or my Uncle about it,—and"—

"You therefore spoke to my Brother, to engage *his* interference";—said I, wishing to save her the explanation.—

"No—but I wrote to him.—I did indeed.—I got up this morning before it was light—I was two hours about it—and when my Letter was done, I thought I never should have courage to give it.—After breakfast however, as I was going to my own room I met him in the passage, and then as I knew that everything must depend on that moment, I forced myself to give it.—He was so good as to take it immediately;—I dared not look at him—and ran away directly.—I was in such a fright that I could hardly breathe.—My dear Aunt, you do not know how miserable I have been."

"Frederica, said I, you ought to have told *me* all your distresses.—You would have found in me a friend always ready to assist you.—Do you think that your Uncle and I should not have espoused your cause as warmly as my Brother?"—

"Indeed I did not doubt your goodness, said she colouring again, but I thought that Mr. De Courcy could do anything with my Mother;—but I was mistaken;—they have had a dreadful quarrel about it, and he is going.—Mama will never forgive me, and I shall be worse off than ever."—

"No, you shall not, replied I.—In such a point as this, your Mother's prohibition ought not to have prevented your speaking to me on the subject. She has no right to make you unhappy, and she shall *not* do it.—Your applying however to Reginald can be productive only of Good to all parties. I beleive it is best as it is.—Depend upon it that you shall not be made unhappy any longer."

At that moment, how great was my astonishment at seeing Reginald come out of Lady Susan's Dressing room. My heart misgave me instantly. His confusion on seeing me was very evident.—Frederica immediately disappeared.

"Are you going?—said I. You will find Mr. Vernon in his own room."—

"No Catherine, replied he.—I am *not* going.—Will you let me speak to you a moment?"

We went into my room. "I find, continued he, his confusion increasing as he spoke, that I have been acting with my usual foolish Impetuosity.—I have entirely misunderstood Lady Susan, and was on the point of leaving the house under a false impression of her conduct.—There has been some very great mistake—we have been all mistaken I fancy.—Frederica does not know her Mother—Lady Susan means nothing but her Good—but Frederica will not make a friend of her.—Lady Susan therefore does not always know what will make her daughter happy.—Besides *I* could have no right to interfere—Miss Vernon was mistaken in applying to me.—In short Catherine, everything has gone wrong—but it is now all happily settled.—Lady Susan I beleive wishes to speak to you about it, if you are at leisure."—

"Certainly;" replied I, deeply sighing at the recital of so lame a story.—I made no remarks however, for words would have been vain. Reginald was glad to get away, and I went to Lady Susan; curious indeed to hear her account of it.—

"Did not I tell you, said she with a smile, that your Brother would not leave us after all?"

"You did indeed, replied I very gravely, but I flattered myself that you would be mistaken."

"I should not have hazarded such an opinion, returned she, if it had not at that moment occurred to me, that his resolution of going might be occasioned by a Conversation in which we had been this morning engaged, and which had ended very much to his Dissatisfaction from our not rightly understanding each other's meaning.—This idea struck me at the moment, and I instantly determined that an accidental dispute in which I might probably be as much to blame as himself, should not deprive you of your Brother.—If you remember, I left the room almost immediately.—I was resolved to lose no time in clearing up these mistakes as far as I could.—The case was this.—Frederica had set herself violently against marrying Sir James"—

—"And can your Ladyship wonder that she should? cried I with some warmth.—Frederica has an excellent Understanding, and Sir James has none."

"I am at least very far from regretting it, my dear Sister, said she; on the contrary, I am grateful for so favourable a sign of my Daughter's sense. Sir James is certainly under par[1]—(his boyish manners make him appear the worse)—and had Frederica possessed the penetration, the abilities, which I could have wished in my daughter, or had I even known her to possess so much as she does, I should not have been anxious for the match."

"It is odd that you alone should be ignorant of your Daughter's sense."

"Frederica never does justice to herself;—her manners are shy and childish.—She is besides afraid of me; she scarcely loves me.—During her poor Father's life she was a spoilt child; the severity which it has since been necessary for me to shew, has entirely alienated her affection;—neither has she any of that Brilliancy of Intellect, that Genius,[2] or vigour of Mind which will force itself forward."

"Say rather that she has been unfortunate in her Education."

"Heaven knows my dearest Mrs. Vernon, how fully I am aware of *that*; but I would wish to forget every circumstance that might throw blame on the memory of one, whose name is sacred with me."

Here she pretended to cry.—I was out of patience with her.—"But what, said I, was your Ladyship going to tell me about your disagreement with my Brother?"—

"It originated in an action of my Daughter's, which equally marks her want of Judgement, and the unfortunate Dread of me I have been mentioning.—She wrote to Mr. De Courcy."—

---

1 Beneath the normal, expected standard or condition.
2 Natural aptitude.

"I know she did.—You had forbidden her speaking to Mr. Vernon or to me on the cause of her distress:—what could she do therefore but apply to my Brother?"

"Good God!—she exclaimed, what an opinion must you have of me!—Can you possibly suppose that I was aware of her unhappiness? that it was my object to make my own child miserable, and that I had forbidden her speaking to you on the subject, from a fear of your interrupting the Diabolical scheme?—Do you think me destitute of every honest, every natural feeling?—Am I capable of consigning *her* to everlasting Misery, whose welfare it is my first Earthly Duty to promote?"—

"The idea is horrible.—What then was your intention when you insisted on her silence?"—

"Of what use my dear Sister, could be any application to you, however the affair might stand? Why should I subject you to entreaties, which I refused to attend to myself?—Neither for your sake, for hers, nor for my own, could such a thing be desireable.—Where my own resolution was taken, I could not wish for the interference, however friendly, of another person.—I was mistaken, it is true, but I beleived myself to be right."—

"But what was this mistake, to which your Ladyship so often alludes? From whence arose so astonishing a misapprehension of your Daughter's feelings?—Did not you know that she disliked Sir James?—"

"I knew that he was not absolutely the Man whom she would have chosen.—But I was persuaded that her objections to him did not arise from any perception of his Deficiency.—You must not question me however my dear Sister, too minutely on this point—continued she, taking me affectionately by the hand.—I honestly own that there is something to conceal.—Frederica makes me very unhappy.—Her applying to Mr. De Courcy hurt me particularly."

"What is it that you mean to infer said I, by this appearance of mystery?—If you think your daughter at all attached to Reginald, her objecting to Sir James could not less deserve to be attended to, than if the cause of her objecting had been a consciousness of his folly.—And why should your Ladyship at any rate quarrel with my brother for an interference which you must know, it was not in his nature to refuse, when urged in such a manner?"

"His disposition you know is warm,[1] and he came to expostulate with me, his compassion all alive for this ill-used Girl, this

---

1 Ardent; excitable; prone to becoming heated.

Heroine in distress!—We misunderstood each other. He believed me more to blame than I really was; I considered his interference as less excusable than I now find it. I have a real regard for him, and was beyond expression mortified to find it as I thought so ill bestowed. We were both warm, and of course both to blame.—His resolution of leaving Churchill is consistent with his general eagerness;—when I understood his intention however, and at the same time began to think that we had perhaps been equally mistaken in each other's meaning, I resolved to have an explanation before it were too late.—For any Member of your Family I must always feel a degree of affection, and I own it would have sensibly[1] hurt me, if my acquaintance with Mr. De Courcy had ended so gloomily. I have now only to say farther, that as I am convinced of Frederica's having a reasonable dislike to Sir James, I shall instantly inform him that he must give up all hope of her.—I reproach myself for having ever, tho' so innocently, made her unhappy on that score.—She shall have all the retribution[2] in my power to make;—if she value her own happiness as much as I do, if she judge wisely and command herself as she ought, she may now be easy.—Excuse me, my dearest Sister, for thus trespassing on your time, but I owed it to my own Character; and after this explanation I trust I am in no danger of sinking in your opinion."

I could have said "Not much indeed;"—but I left her almost in silence.—It was the greatest stretch of Forbearance I could practise. I could not have stopped myself, had I begun.—Her assurance, her Deceit—but I will not allow myself to dwell on them;—they will strike you sufficiently. My heart sickens within me.—

As soon as I was tolerably composed, I returned to the Parlour. Sir James's carriage was at the door, and he, merry as usual, soon afterwards took his leave.—How easily does her Ladyship encourage, or dismiss a Lover!—

In spite of this release, Frederica still looks unhappy, still fearful perhaps of her Mother's anger, and tho' dreading my Brother's departure jealous, it may be, of his staying.—I see how closely she observes him and Lady Susan.—Poor Girl, I have now no hope for her. There is not a chance of her affection being returned.—He thinks very differently of her, from what he used

---

1 Acutely, intensely.
2 Restitution, without any of the modern implication of punishment for evil done.

to do, he does her some justice, but his reconciliation with her Mother precludes every dearer hope.—

Prepare my dear Madam, for the worst.—The probability of their marrying is surely heightened. He is more securely her's than ever.—When that wretched Event takes place, Frederica must belong wholly to us.—

I am thankful that my last Letter will precede this by so little, as every moment that you can be saved from feeling a Joy which leads only to disappointment is of consequence.—

Yrs. Ever, Cath Vernon.

Letter 25.
Lady Susan to Mrs. Johnson

Churchill

I call on you dear Alicia, for congratulations. I am again myself;—gay and triumphant.—When I wrote to you the other day, I was in truth in high irritation, and with ample cause.—Nay, I know not whether I ought to be quite tranquil now, for I have had more trouble in restoring peace than I ever intended to submit to.—This Reginald has a proud spirit of his own!—a spirit too, resulting from a fancied sense of superior Integrity which is peculiarly insolent.—I shall not easily forgive him I assure you. He was actually on the point of leaving Churchill!—I had scarcely concluded my last, when Wilson brought me word of it.—I found therefore that something must be done, for I did not chuse to have my character at the mercy of a Man whose passions were so violent and resentful.—It would have been trifling with my reputation, to allow of his departing with such an impression in my disfavour;—in this light, condescension[1] was necessary.—

I sent Wilson to say that I desired to speak with him before he went.—He came immediately. The angry emotions which had marked every feature when we last parted, were partially subdued. He seemed astonished at the summons, and looked as if half wishing and half fearing to be softened by what I might say.—

If my Countenance expressed what I aimed at, it was composed and dignified—and yet with a degree of pensiveness which might convince him that I was not quite happy.—

"I beg your pardon Sir, for the liberty I have taken in sending to you, said I; but as I have just learnt your intention of leaving this place to day, I feel it my duty to entreat that you will not on

---

1 Gracious deference or submissiveness to an inferior.

my account shorten your visit here, even an hour.—I am perfectly aware that after what has passed between us, it would ill suit the feelings of either to remain longer in the same house.—

So very great, so total a change from the intimacy of Friendship, must render any future intercourse the severest punishment;—and your resolution of quitting Churchill is undoubtedly in unison with our situation and with those lively feelings which I know you to possess.—But at the same time, it is not for me to suffer such a sacrifice, as it must be, to leave Relations to whom you are so much attached and are so dear. My remaining here cannot give that pleasure to Mr. and Mrs. Vernon which your society must;—and my visit has already perhaps been too long. My removal therefore, which must at any rate take place soon, may with perfect convenience be hastened;—and I make it my particular request that I may not in any way be instrumental in separating a family so affectionately attached to each other.— Where *I* go, is of no consequence to anyone; of very little to myself; but *you* are of importance to all your connections."

Here I concluded, and I hope you will be satisfied with my speech.—It's effect on Reginald justifies some portion of vanity, for it was no less favourable than instantaneous.—Oh! how delightful it was, to watch the variations of his Countenance while I spoke, to see the struggle between returning Tenderness and the remains of Displeasure.—There is something agreable in feelings so easily worked on. Not that I envy him their possession, nor would for the world have such myself, but they are very convenient when one wishes to influence the passions of another. And yet this Reginald, whom a very few words from me softened at once into the utmost submission, and rendered more tractable, more attached, more devoted than ever, would have left me in the first angry swelling of his proud heart, without deigning to seek an explanation!—

Humbled as he now is, I cannot forgive him such an instance of Pride; and am doubtful whether I ought not to punish him, by dismissing him at once after this our reconciliation, or by marrying and teizing him for ever.—But these measures are each too violent to be adopted without some deliberation. At present my Thoughts are fluctuating between various schemes.—I have many things to compass.—I must punish Frederica, and pretty severely too, for her application to Reginald;—I must punish him for receiving it so favourably, and for the rest of his conduct. I must torment my Sister-in-law for the insolent triumph of her Look and Manner since Sir James has been dismissed—for in reconciling Reginald to me, I was not able to save that ill-fated young Man;—and I must make myself amends for the humiliations to which I have stooped within these few days.—To effect all this I have various plans.—I have also an idea of being soon in Town, and whatever may be my determination as to the rest, I shall probably put *that* project in execution—for London will be always the fairest field of action, however my veiws may be directed, and at any rate, I shall there be rewarded by your society and a little Dissipation for a ten weeks penance at Churchill.—

I beleive I owe it to my own Character, to complete the match between my daughter and Sir James, after having so long intended it.—Let me know your opinion on this point.—Flexibility of Mind, a Disposition easily biassed by others, is an attribute which you know I am not very desirous of obtaining;—nor has Frederica any claim to the indulgence of her whims, at the expence of her Mother's inclination.—Her idle Love for Reginald too;—it is surely my duty to discourage such romantic nonsense.—All things considered therefore, it seems encumbent on me to take her to Town, and marry her immediately to Sir James.

When my own will is effected, contrary to his, I shall have some credit in being on good terms with Reginald, which at present in fact I have not, for tho' he is still in my power, I have given up the very article by which our Quarrel was produced, and at best, the honour of victory is doubtful.—

Send me your opinion on all these matters, my dear Alicia, and let me know whether you can get Lodgings to suit me within a short distance of you.—Yr. most attached

S. Vernon.

Letter 26.
Mrs. Johnson to Lady Susan.

Edward St.—

I am gratified by your reference, and this is my advice; that you come to Town yourself without loss of time, but that you leave Frederica behind. It would surely be much more to the purpose to get yourself well established by marrying Mr. De Courcy, than to irritate him and the rest of his family, by making her marry Sir James.—You should think more of yourself, and less of your Daughter.—She is not of a disposition to do you credit in the World, and seems precisely in her proper place, at Churchill with the Vernons;—but *You* are fitted for society, and it is shameful to have you exiled from it.—Leave Frederica therefore to punish herself for the plague she has given you, by indulging that romantic tender-heartedness which will always ensure her misery enough; and come yourself to Town, as soon as you can.—

I have another reason for urging this.—Manwaring came to Town last week, and has contrived, inspite of Mr. Johnson, to make opportunities of seeing me.—He is absolutely miserable about you, and jealous to such a degree of De Courcy, that it would be highly unadvisable for them to meet at present;[1] and yet if you do not allow him to see you here, I cannot answer for his not committing some great imprudence—such as going to Churchill for instance, which would be dreadful.—Besides, if you take my advice, and resolve to marry De Courcy, it will be indispensably necessary for you to get Manwaring out of the way, and you only can have influence enough to send him back to his wife.—

I have still another motive for your coming. Mr. Johnson leaves London next Tuesday. He is going for his health to Bath, where if the waters are favourable to his constitution and my wishes, he will be laid up with the gout many weeks.[2]—During his absence we shall be able to chuse our own society, and have true enjoyment.—I would ask you to Edward St. but that he once forced from me a kind of promise never to invite you to my house. Nothing but my being in the utmost distress for Money, could have extorted it from me.—I can get you however a very nice Drawing room-apartment in Upper Seymour St.,[3] and we may be always together, there or here, for I consider my promise to Mr. Johnson as comprehending only (at least in his absence) your not sleeping in the House.—

Poor Manwaring gives me such histories of his wife's jealousy!—Silly woman, to expect constancy from so charming a Man!—But she was always silly; intolerably so, in marrying him

---

1 The implication here is that they might quarrel publicly or even fight a duel, either of which would cause a public scandal. Duelling was illegal in the early nineteenth century, but duels were fought occasionally in fact, and more often in fiction.

2 The natural mineral water from the springs of the spa town of Bath were seen as particularly effective for gout. Gout, a very painful inflammation of the joints, was often thought to be caused by overeating and overdrinking.

3 A drawing-room apartment is a suite of rooms, possibly quite extensive, including a reception room for visitors; the term is still in use, particularly in Edinburgh, in describing apartments in Georgian buildings.

at all. She, the Heiress of a large Fortune, he without a shilling!—
One Title I know she might have had, besides Baronets.[1]—Her
folly in forming the connection was so great, that tho' Mr. Johnson was her Guardian and I do not in general share his feelings,
I never can forgive her.—

Adeiu. Yours, *Alicia.*—

Letter 27.
Mrs. Vernon to Lady De Courcy.

Churchill
This Letter my dear Mother, will be brought you by Reginald.
His long visit is about to be concluded at last, but I fear the separation takes place too late to do us any good.—*She* is going to
Town, to see her particular friend, Mrs. Johnson. It was at first
her intention that Frederica should accompany her for the benefit of Masters,[2] but we over-ruled her there. Frederica was
wretched in the idea of going, and I could not bear to have her at
the mercy of her Mother. Not all the Masters in London could
compensate for the ruin of her comfort. I should have feared too
for her health, and for everything in short but her Principles; *there*
I beleive she is not to be injured, even by her Mother, or all her
Mother's friends;—but with those friends (a very bad set I doubt
not) she must have mixed, or have been left in total solitude, and
I can hardly tell which would have been worse for her.—If she is
with her Mother moreover, she must alas! in all probability, be
with Reginald—and that would be the greatest evil of all.—

Here, we shall in time be at peace.—Our regular employments, our Books and conversation, with Exercise, the Children,
and every domestic pleasure in my power to procure her, will, I
trust, gradually overcome this youthful attachment. I should not
have a doubt of it, were she slighted for any other woman in the
world, than her own Mother.—

How long Lady Susan will be in Town, or whether she returns
here again, I know not.—I could not be cordial in my invitation;
but if she chuses to come, no want of cordiality on my part will
keep her away.—

---

1 Baronet was a hereditary title ranking above a knight, but baronets were
technically regarded as commoners and did not sit in the House of
Lords; only the more senior titles—Duke, Marquess, Earl, Viscount, and
Baron—were regarded as aristocracy.

2 To study with professional teachers of arts such as drawing and music.

I could not help asking Reginald if he intended being in Town this winter,[1] as soon as I found that her Ladyship's steps would be bent thither; and tho' he professed himself quite undetermined, there was a something in his Look and voice as he spoke, which contradicted his words.—I have done with Lamentation.—I look upon the Event as so far decided, that I resign myself to it in despair. If he leaves you soon for London, every thing will be concluded.—Yours affect:ly

Cath Vernon.

Letter 28.
Mrs. Johnson to Lady Susan

Edward St.—

My dearest Friend,

I write in the greatest distress; the most unfortunate event has just taken place. Mr. Johnson has hit on the most effectual manner of plaguing us all.—He had heard I imagine by some means or other, that you were soon to be in London, and immediately contrived to have such an attack of the Gout, as must at least delay his journey to Bath, if not wholly prevent it.—I am persuaded the Gout is brought on, or kept off at pleasure;—it was the same, when I wanted to join the Hamiltons to the Lakes;[2] and three years ago when *I* had a fancy for Bath, nothing could induce him to have a gouty symptom.

I have received yours, and have engaged the Lodgings in consequence.—I am pleased to find that my Letter had so much effect on you, and that De Courcy is certainly your own.—Let me hear from you as soon as you arrive, and in particular tell me what you mean to do with Manwaring.—It is impossible to say

---

1 For the social season which began after Christmas (see p. 215, note 1).

2 The Lake District in the north west of England became a popular tourist destination in the late eighteenth century as interest grew in sublime and picturesque locations. Interest was focused by William Gilpin's *Observations Relative Chiefly to Picturesque Beauty, Made in the Year 1772, on Several Parts of England; particularly the Mountains, and Lakes of Cumberland and Westmoreland* (2 vols), first published in 1786 and frequently reprinted. Going to the Lake District was a substantial expedition for travellers from London, who would have to travel more than 200 miles to get there.

when I shall be able to see you. My confinement must be great. It is such an abominable trick, to be ill here, instead of at Bath, that I can scarcely command myself at all.—At Bath, his old Aunts would have nursed him, but here it all falls upon me—and he bears pain with such patience that I have not the common excuse for losing my temper.

Yrs. Ever, Alicia.

Letter 29.
Lady Susan to Mrs. Johnson

Upper Seymour St.

My dear Alicia

There needed not this last fit of the Gout to make me detest Mr. Johnson; but now the extent of my aversion is not to be estimated.—To have you confined, a Nurse, in his apartment!— My dear Alicia, of what a mistake were you guilty in marrying a Man of his age!—just old enough to be formal, ungovernable and to have the Gout—too old to be agreable, and too young to die.

I arrived last night about five, and had scarcely swallowed my dinner when Manwaring made his appearance.—I will not dissemble what real pleasure his sight afforded me, nor how strongly I felt the contrast between his person and manners, and those of Reginald, to the infinite disadvantage of the latter.—For an hour or two, I was even stagger'd in my resolution of marrying him— and tho' this was too idle and nonsensical an idea to remain long on my mind, I do not feel very eager for the conclusion of my marriage, or look forward with much impatience to the time when Reginald according to our agreement is to be in Town.—I shall probably put off his arrival, under some pretence or other. He must not come till Manwaring is gone.

I am still doubtful at times, as to Marriage.—If the old Man would die, I might not hesitate; but a state of dependance on the caprice of Sir Reginald, will not suit the freedom of my spirit;— and if I resolve to wait for that event, I shall have excuse enough at present, in having been scarcely ten months a Widow.

I have not given Manwaring any hint of my intention—or allowed him to consider my acquaintance with Reginald as more than the commonest flirtation;—and he is tolerably appeased.— Adeiu till we meet.—I am enchanted with my Lodgings. Yrs. Ever,

S. Vernon.—

Letter 30.
Lady Susan to Mr. De Courcy.[1]—

Upper Seymour St.

I have received your Letter; and tho' I do not attempt to conceal that I am gratified by your impatience for the hour of meeting, I yet feel myself under the necessity of delaying that hour beyond the time originally fixed.—Do not think me unkind for such an exercise of my power, or accuse me of Instability, without first hearing my reasons.—In the course of my journey from Churchill, I had ample leisure for reflection on the present state of our affairs, and every reveiw has served to convince me that they require a delicacy and cautiousness of conduct, to which we have hitherto been too little attentive.—We have been hurried on by our feelings to a degree of Precipitance which ill accords with the claims of our Friends, or the opinion of the world.—We have been unguarded in forming this hasty Engagement; but we must not complete the imprudence by ratifying it, while there is so much reason to fear the Connection would be opposed by those Friends on whom you depend.

It is not for us to blame any expectation on your Father's side of your marrying to advantage; where possessions are so extensive as those of your Family, the wish of increasing them, if not strictly reasonable, is too common to excite surprise or resentment.—He has a right to require a woman of fortune in his daughter in law; and I am sometimes quarreling with myself for suffering you to form a connection so imprudent.—But the influence of reason is often acknowledged too late by those who feel like me.—

I have now been but a few months a widow; and however little endebted to my Husband's memory for any happiness derived from him during an Union of some years, I cannot forget that the indelicacy of so early a second marriage, must subject me to the censure of the World, and incur what would be still more insupportable, the displeasure of Mr. Vernon.—I might perhaps harden myself in time against the injustice of general reproach; but the loss of *his* valued Esteem, I am as you well know, ill fitted to endure;—and when to this, may be added the consciousness of having injured you with your Family, how am I to support myself.—With feelings so poignant as mine, the conviction of

---

1 By the conventions of the time, an unrelated man and woman should only begin to correspond by letter once they were formally engaged to each other.

having divided the son from his Parents, would make me, even with *you*, the most miserable of Beings.—

It will surely therefore be advisable to delay our Union, to delay it till appearances are more promising, till affairs have taken a more favourable turn.—To assist us in such a resolution, I feel that absence will be necessary. We must not meet.—Cruel as this sentence may appear, the necessity of pronouncing it, which can alone reconcile it to myself, will be evident to you when you have considered our situation in the light in which I have found myself imperiously[1] obliged to place it.—You may be, you must be well assured that nothing but the strongest conviction of Duty, could induce me to wound my own feelings by urging a lengthened separation; and of Insensibility to yours, you will hardly suspect me.—Again therefore I say that we ought not, we must not yet meet.—By a removal for some Months from each other, we shall tranquillize the sisterly fears of Mrs. Vernon, who, accustomed herself to the enjoyment of riches, considers Fortune as necessary every where, and whose sensibilities are not of a nature to comprehend ours.—

Let me hear from you soon, very soon. Tell me that you submit to my Arguments, and do not reproach me for using such.— I cannot bear reproaches. My spirits are not so high as to need being repressed.—I must endeavour to seek amusement abroad,[2] and fortunately many of my Friends are in Town—among them, the Manwarings.—You know how sincerely I regard both Husband and Wife.—I am ever, Faithfully Yours

S. Vernon—

Letter 31.
Lady Susan to Mrs. Johnson

Upper Seymour St.

My dear Friend,

That tormenting creature Reginald is here. My Letter which was intended to keep him longer in the Country, has hastened him to Town. Much as I wish him away however, I cannot help being pleased with such a proof of attachment. He is devoted to me, heart and soul.—He will carry this note himself, which is to serve as an Introduction to you, with whom he longs to be acquainted. Allow him to spend the Evening with you, that I may be in no danger of his returning here.—I have told him that I am

---

1 By overmastering necessity; urgently.
2 In company, out of the home.

not quite well, and must be alone—and should he call again there might be confusion, for it is impossible to be sure of servants.—Keep him therefore I entreat you in Edward St.—You will not find him a heavy companion, and I allow you to flirt with him as much as you like. At the same time do not forget my real interest;—say all that you can to convince him that I shall be quite wretched if he remain here;—you know my reasons—Propriety and so forth.—I would urge them more myself, but that I am impatient to be rid of him, as Manwaring comes within half an hour.

Adeiu. S V.—

Letter 32.
Mrs. Johnson to Lady Susan—

Edward St.

My dear Creature,

I am in agonies, and know not what to do, nor what *you* can do.—Mr. De Courcy arrived, just when he should not. Mrs. Manwaring had that instant entered the House, and forced herself into her Guardian's presence, tho' I did not know a syllable of it till afterwards, for I was out when both she and Reginald came, or I would have sent him away at all events; but *she* was shut up with Mr. Johnson, while *he* waited in the Drawing room for me.—

She arrived yesterday in pursuit of her Husband;—but perhaps you know this already from himself.—She came to this house to entreat my Husband's interference, and before I could be aware of it, everything that you could wish to be concealed, was known to him; and unluckily she had wormed out of Manwaring's servant that he had visited you every day since your being in Town, and had just watched him to your door herself!—What could I do?—Facts are such horrid things!—All is by this time known to De Courcy, who is now alone with Mr. Johnson.—Do not accuse me;—indeed, it was impossible to prevent it.—Mr. Johnson has for some time suspected De Courcy of intending to marry you, and would speak with him alone, as soon as he knew him to be in the House.—

That detestable Mrs. Manwaring, who for your comfort, has fretted herself thinner and uglier than ever, is still here, and they have been all closeted together. What can be done?—If Manwaring is now with you, he had better be gone.—At any rate I hope he will plague his wife more than ever.—With anxious wishes, Yrs. faithfully

Alicia.

Letter 33.
Lady Susan to Mrs. Johnson.

Upper Seymour St.

This Eclaircissement[1] is rather provoking.—How unlucky that you should have been from home!—I thought myself sure of you at 7.[2]—I am undismayed however. Do not torment yourself with fears on my account.—Depend upon it, I can make my own story good with Reginald. Manwaring is just gone; he brought me the news of his wife's arrival. Silly Woman! what does she expect by such manouvres?[3]—yet, I wish she had staid quietly at Langford.—

Reginald will be a little enraged at first, but by Tomorrow's Dinner, every thing will be well again.—Adeiu. *S V.*

Letter 34.
Mr. De Courcy to Lady Susan.

Hotel

I write only to bid you Farewell.—The spell is removed. I see you as you are.—Since we parted yesterday, I have received from indisputable authority, such an history of you, as must bring the most mortifying conviction of the Imposition I have been under, and the absolute necessity of an immediate and eternal separation from you.—You cannot doubt to what I allude;—Langford—Langford—that word will be sufficient.—I received *my* information in Mr. Johnson's house, from Mrs. Manwaring herself.—

You know how I have loved you, you can intimately judge of my present feelings; but I am not so weak as to find indulgence in describing them to a woman who will glory in having excited their anguish, but whose affection they have never been able to gain.

R De Courcy.

---

1 Clearing up of obscure matters; originally a French theatrical term to denote a dramatic revelation.

2 After the social events of the day, and before the likely late dinner hour and subsequent evening entertainments, in fashionable London.

3 Imported from the French in the middle of the eighteenth century, the term "manoeuvre" soon expanded from its original meaning of a strategic military movement. By the 1790s, it was often used to describe calculated and adroit social positioning.

Letter 35.
Lady Susan to Mr. De Courcy.

Upper Seymour St.

I will not attempt to describe my astonishment on reading the note, this moment received from you. I am bewilder'd in my endeavours to form some rational conjecture of what Mrs. Manwaring can have told you, to occasion so extraordinary a change in your sentiments.—Have I not explained everything to you with respect to myself which could bear a doubtful meaning, and which the illnature of the world had interpreted to my Discredit?—What can you *now* have heard to stagger your Esteem for me?—Have I ever had a concealment from you?—Reginald, you agitate me beyond expression.—I cannot suppose that the old story of Mrs. Manwaring's jealousy can be revived again, or at least, be *listened* to again.—Come to me immediately, and explain what is at present absolutely incomprehensible.—Beleive me, the single word of *Langford* is not of such potent intelligence, as to supersede the necessity of more.—If we *are* to part, it will at least be handsome to take your personal Leave.—But I have little heart to jest; in truth, I am serious enough—for to be sunk, tho' but an hour, in your opinion, is an humiliation to which I know not how to submit. I shall count every moment till your arrival.

S. V.

Letter 36.
Mr. De Courcy to Lady Susan

Hotel

Why would you write to me?—Why do you require particulars?—But since it must be so, I am obliged to declare that all the accounts of your misconduct during the life and since the death of Mr. Vernon which had reached me in common with the World in general, and gained my entire beleif before I saw you, but which you by the exertion of your perverted Abilities had made me resolve to disallow, have been unanswerably proved to me.—Nay, more, I am assured that a Connection, of which I had never before entertained a thought, has for some time existed, and still continues to exist between you and the Man, whose family you robbed of it's Peace, in return for the hospitality with which you were received into it!—That you have corresponded with him ever since your leaving Langford—not with his wife—but with him—and that he now visits you every day.—Can you, dare you deny it?—And all this at the time when I was an encouraged, an accepted Lover!—From what have I not escaped!—I have only to be grateful.—Far from me be all Complaint, and every sigh of regret. My own Folly had endangered me, my Preservation I owe to the kindness, the Integrity of another.—But the unfortunate Mrs. Manwaring, whose agonies while she related the past, seem'd to threaten her reason—how is *she* to be consoled?

After such a discovery as this, you will scarcely affect farther wonder at my meaning in bidding you Adeiu.—My Understanding is at length restored, and teaches me no less to abhor the Artifices which had subdued me, than to despise myself for the weakness, on which their strength was founded.—

R. De Courcy.—

Letter 37.
Lady Susan to Mr. De Courcy

Upper Seymour St.

I am satisfied—and will trouble you no more when these few Lines are dismissed.[1]—The Engagement which you were eager to form a fortnight ago, is no longer compatible with your veiws, and I rejoice to find that the prudent advice of your Parents has not been given in vain.—Your restoration to Peace will, I doubt not, speedily follow this act of filial Obedience, and I flatter myself with the hope of surviving *my* share in this disappointment.

SV.

Letter 38.
Mrs. Johnson to Lady Susan

Edward St.

I am greived, tho' I cannot be astonished at your rupture with Mr. De Courcy;—he has just informed Mr. Johnson of it by letter. He leaves London he says to day.—Be assured that I partake in all your feelings, and do not be angry if I say that our intercourse even by letter must soon be given up.—It makes me miserable—but Mr. Johnson vows that if I persist in the connection, he will settle in the country for the rest of his life—and you know it is impossible to submit to such an extremity[2] while any other alternative remains.—

---

1 Sent; disposed of.

2 For a woman who finds her enjoyments in the busy social round of London, the threat of living permanently on her husband's country estate, which might well be at some distance from any social centre, is a powerful one.

You have heard of course that the Manwarings are to part;[1] I am afraid Mrs. M. will come home to us again. But she is still so fond of her Husband and frets so much about him that perhaps she may not live long.—

Miss Manwaring is just come to Town to be with her Aunt, and they say, that she declares she will have Sir James Martin before she leaves London again.—If I were you, I would certainly get him myself.—I had almost forgot to give you my opinion of De Courcy, I am really delighted with him, he is full as handsome I think as Manwaring, and with such an open, good humoured Countenance that one cannot help loving him at first sight.—Mr. Johnson and he are the greatest friends in the World. Adeiu, my dearest Susan.—I wish matters did not go so perversely. That unlucky visit to Langford!—But I dare say you did all for the best, and there is no defying Destiny.[2]—

Yr. sincerely attached
Alicia.

Letter 39.
Lady Susan to Mrs. Johnson

Upper Seymour St.

My dear Alicia

I yeild to the necessity which parts us. Under such circumstances you could not act otherwise. Our friendship cannot be impaired by it; and in happier times, when your situation is as independant as mine, it will unite us again in the same Intimacy as ever.—For this, I shall impatiently wait; and meanwhile can safely assure you that I never was more at ease, or better satisfied with myself and every thing about me, than at the present hour.—Your Husband I abhor—Reginald I despise—and I am secure of never seeing either again. Have I not reason to rejoice?—Manwaring is more devoted to me than ever; and were he at liberty, I doubt if I could resist even Matrimony offered by *him.* This Event, if his wife live with you, it may be in your power to hasten.

---

1 A very significant step, at a period when divorce could only be obtained by an Act of Parliament. Even if the woman was not at fault, she would suffer far more than the man in any formal separation or divorce. Her social position would be affected and, her property or income having usually passed by law to her husband, she would be entirely reliant upon others for her maintenance.

2 An ironic allusion to the usual novelistic reliance upon Providence to produce a happy ending to the heroine's vicissitudes.

The violence of her feelings, which must wear her out, may be easily kept in irritation.—I rely on your friendship for this.—I am now satisfied that I never could have brought myself to marry Reginald; and am equally determined that Frederica never *shall*. Tomorrow I shall fetch her from Churchill, and let Maria Manwaring tremble for the consequence. Frederica shall be Sir James's wife before she quits my house. *She* may whimper and the Vernons may storm;—I regard them not. I am tired of submitting my will to the Caprices of others—of resigning my own Judgement in deference to those, to whom I owe no Duty, and for whom I feel no respect.—I have given up too much—have been too easily worked on; but Frederica shall now find the difference.—Adeiu, dearest of Friends. May the next Gouty Attack be more favourable—and may you always regard me as unalterably Yours

S. Vernon.—

Letter 40.
Lady De Courcy to Mrs. Vernon

Parklands

My dear Catherine

I have charming news for you, and if I had not sent off my Letter this morning, you might have been spared the vexation of knowing of Reginald's being gone to Town, for he is returned, Reginald is returned, not to ask our consent to his marrying Lady Susan, but to tell us that they are parted forever!—He has been only an hour in the House, and I have not been able to learn particulars, for he is so very low, that I have not the heart to ask questions; but I hope we shall soon know all.—This is the most joyful hour he has ever given us, since the day of his birth. Nothing is wanting but to have you here, and it is our particular wish and entreaty that you would come to us as soon as you can. You have owed us a visit many long weeks.—I hope nothing will make it inconvenient to Mr. Vernon, and pray bring all my Grand Children, and your dear Neice is included of course; I long to see her.—It has been a sad heavy winter hitherto, without Reginald, and seeing nobody from Churchill; I never found the season so dreary before, but this happy meeting will make us young again.—Frederica runs much in my thoughts, and when Reginald has recovered his usual good spirits, (as I trust he soon will) we will try to rob him of his heart once more, and I am full of hopes of seeing their hands joined at no great distance.

Yr. affect: Mother
C. De Courcy.

Letter 41.

Mrs. Vernon to Lady De Courcy.

Churchill

My dear Madam

Your Letter has surprised me beyond measure. Can it be true that they are really separated—and for ever?—I should be over-joyed if I dared depend on it, but after all that I have seen, how can one be secure?—And Reginald really with you!—My sur-prise is the greater, because on wednesday, the very day of his coming to Parklands, we had a most unexpected and unwel-come visit from Lady Susan, looking all chearfulness and good humour, and seeming more as if she were to marry him when she got back to Town, than as if parted from him for ever.—She staid nearly two hours, was as affectionate and agreable as ever, and not a syllable, not a hint was dropped of any Disagreement or Coolness between them. I asked her whether she had seen my Brother since his arrival in Town—not as you may suppose with any doubt of the fact—but merely to see how she looked.—She immediately answered without any embarrassment that he had been kind enough to call on her on Monday, but she beleived he had already returned home—which I was very far from crediting.—

Your kind invitation is accepted by us with pleasure, and on Thursday next, we and our little ones will be with you.—Pray Heaven! Reginald may not be in Town again by that time!—

I wish we could bring dear Frederica too, but I am sorry to add that her Mother's errand hither was to fetch her away; and miserable as it made the poor Girl, it was impossible to detain her. I was thoroughly unwilling to let her go, and so was her Uncle; and all that could be urged, we *did* urge. But Lady Susan declared that as she was now about to fix herself in Town for several months she could not be easy if her Daughter were not with her, for Masters, &c.—Her Manner, to be sure, was very kind and proper—and Mr. Vernon *beleives* that Frederi-ca will now be treated with affection. I wish I could think so too!—

The poor girl's heart was almost broke at taking leave of us. I charged her to write to me very often, and to remember that if she were in any distress, we should be always her friends.—I took care to see her alone, that I might say all this, and I hope made her a little more comfortable.—But I shall not be easy till I can go to Town and judge of her situation myself.—

I wish there were a better prospect than now appears, of the Match, which the conclusion of your Letter declares your expectation of.—At present it is not very likely.—

Yrs. &c

Cath Vernon.

Conclusion

This Correspondence, by a meeting between some of the Parties and a separation between the others, could not, to the great detriment of the Post office Revenue,[1] be continued longer.—Very little assistance to the State[2] could be derived from the Epistolary Intercourse of Mrs. Vernon and her Neice, for the former soon perceived by the stile of Frederica's Letters, that they were written under her Mother's inspection, and therefore deferring all particular enquiry till she could make it personally in Town, ceased writing minutely or often.—

Having learnt enough in the meanwhile from her openhearted Brother, of what had passed between him and Lady Susan to sink the latter lower than ever in her opinion, she was proportionably more anxious to get Frederica removed from such a Mother, and placed under her own care; and tho' with little hope of success, was resolved to leave nothing unattempted that might offer a chance of obtaining her sister in law's consent to it.—Her anxiety on the subject made her press for an early visit to London; and Mr. Vernon who, as it must have already appeared, lived only to do whatever he was desired, soon found some accomodating Business to call him thither.—With a heart full of the Matter, Mrs. Vernon waited on Lady Susan, shortly after her arrival in Town; and was met with such an easy and chearful affection as made her almost turn from her with horror.—No remembrance of Reginald, no consciousness of Guilt, gave one look of embarrassment.—She was in excellent spirits, and seemed eager to shew at once, by every possible attention to

---

1   The cost of mail was paid by the recipient. Within London, until 1801, it cost one penny to receive a letter of a single sheet; outside London, the charge was 3d for a single sheet travelling up to fifteen miles, with higher rates for multiple sheets and longer distances.

2   The postal service was operated through private enterprise, but fees were paid to the state.

her Brother and Sister, her sense of their kindness, and her pleasure in their society.—

Frederica was no more altered than Lady Susan;—the same restrained Manners, the same timid Look in the presence of her Mother as heretofore, assured her Aunt of her Situation's being uncomfortable, and confirmed her in the plan of altering it.—No unkindness however on the part of Lady Susan appeared. Persecution on the subject of Sir James was entirely at an end—his name merely mentioned to say that he was not in London; and in all her conversation she was solicitous only for the welfare and improvement of her Daughter, acknowledging in terms of grateful delight that Frederica was now growing every day more and more what a Parent could desire.—

Mrs. Vernon surprised and incredulous, knew not what to suspect, and without any change in her own veiws, only feared greater difficulty in accomplishing them. The first hope of any thing better was derived from Lady Susan's asking her whether she thought Frederica looked quite as well as she had done at Churchill, as she must confess herself to have sometimes an anxious doubt of London's perfectly agreeing with her.—

Mrs. Vernon encouraging the doubt, directly proposed her Neice's returning with them into the country. Lady Susan was unable to express her sense of such kindness; yet knew not from a variety of reasons how to part with her Daughter; and as, tho' her own plans were not yet wholly fixed, she trusted it would ere long be in her power to take Frederica into the country herself, concluded by declining entirely to profit by such unexampled attention.—Mrs. Vernon however persevered in the offer of it; and tho' Lady Susan continued to resist, her resistance in the course of a few days seemed somewhat less formidable.

The lucky alarm of an Influenza,[1] decided what might not have been decided quite so soon.—Lady Susan's maternal fears were then too much awakened for her to think of any thing but Frederica's removal from the risk of infection. Above all Disorders in the World, she most dreaded the Influenza for her daughter's constitution. Frederica returned to Churchill with her Uncle and Aunt, and three weeks afterwards Lady Susan announced her being married to Sir James Martin.—

---

1   Influenza was, then as now, a highly infectious disease that could kill, and epidemics were much feared. There were major epidemics in England in 1782, 1785, and 1794.

Mrs. Vernon was then convinced of what she had only suspected before, that she might have spared herself all the trouble of urging a removal, which Lady Susan had doubtless resolved on from the first.—Frederica's visit was nominally for six weeks;—but her Mother, tho' inviting her to return in one or two affectionate Letters, was very ready to oblige the whole Party by consenting to a prolongation of her stay, and in the course of two months ceased to write of her absence, and in the course of two more, to write to her at all.

Frederica was therefore fixed in the family of her Uncle and Aunt, till such time as Reginald De Courcy could be talked, flattered and finessed[1] into an affection for her—which, allowing leisure for the conquest of his attachment to her Mother, for his abjuring all future attachments and detesting the Sex, might be reasonably looked for in the course of a Twelvemonth. Three Months might have done it in general, but Reginald's feelings were no less lasting than lively.—

Whether Lady Susan was, or was not happy in her second Choice—I do not see how it can ever be ascertained—for who would take her assurance of it, on either side of the question?—The World must judge from Probability.—She had nothing against her, but her Husband and her Conscience.

Sir James may seem to have drawn an harder Lot than mere Folly merited.—I leave him therefore to all the Pity that any body can give him. For myself, I confess that *I* can pity only Miss Manwaring, who coming to Town and putting herself to an expence in Cloathes, which impoverished her for two years, on purpose to secure him, was defrauded of her due by a Woman ten years older than herself.

Finis.

---

1 Brought or modified by finesse or delicate handling. The *OED* (2012) gives JA's phrase here as the first example of the use of the verb "finesse" in this sense (though it erroneously cites the sentence as from "The Watsons" and from 1814).

The Watsons[1]

---

1 The manuscript is untitled. JA's nephew, James Edward Austen Leigh, chose "The Watsons" when the work was published for the first time in the second edition of the *Memoir* (1871) "for the sake of having a title by which to designate it" (*Later Manuscripts*, p. 295).

The first winter assembly[1] in the Town of D.— in Surry[2] was to be held on Tuesday October the 13th,[3] and it was generally expected to be a very good one; a long list of Country Families[4] was confidently run over as sure of attending, and sanguine hopes were entertained that the Osbornes themselves would be there.— The Edwardes' invitation to the Watsons followed of course. The Edward's were people of fortune who lived in the Town and kept their Coach;[5] the Watsons inhabited a village about three miles distant, were poor and had no close carriage; and ever since there had been Balls in the place, the former were accustomed to invite the Latter to dress dine and sleep at their House, on every monthly return throughout the winter.—On the present occasion, as only two of Mr. Watson's children were at home, and one was always necessary as companion to himself, for he was sickly and had lost his wife, one only could profit by the kindness of their friends; Miss Emma Watson who was very recently returned to her family from the care of an Aunt who had brought her up,[6]

---

1 Most provincial towns had a formal social season over the autumn and winter months, including a series of evening assemblies, funded by subscriptions from those who planned to attend or who wished to patronise the event, and held at local inns or assembly rooms. JA's early letters make frequent reference to her attendance at the assemblies at Basingstoke, the nearest substantial town to her home in Steventon.

2 "D." is generally assumed to be Dorking, a market town twenty-seven miles south of London and the only substantial town in the county of Surrey of which the name begins with a D. JA was still undecided about the setting when she began "The Watsons"; "D." is written after the deletion of "L.," which might possibly stand for Leatherhead, a smaller town in Surrey about ten miles north of Dorking, but "D." is the first choice a few lines later.

3 Mid-October was the usual time for winter assemblies to begin, but the precision of this date is unusual in JA's writing. In the years nearest the assumed date of composition, 13 October fell on a Tuesday in 1795, 1801, and 1807.

4 The families of the gentry who would live on their estates outside the town.

5 Owning one's own coach or carriage was a visible marker of substantial wealth. The cost of the carriage and its fittings would be substantial, and the vehicle would require horses to pull it and one or more servants to maintain and drive it.

6 In an age of large families, high mortality, and emphasis on inheritance, it was common for wealthy childless couples to bring up a child of poorer relatives, or relatives with large families of their own, and adopt him or her as their heir. JA's brother Edward was brought up by the wealthy Knight family, who were distant relatives, and became their heir.

was to make her first public appearance in the Neighbourhood;—and her eldest sister, whose delight in a Ball was not lessened by a ten years Enjoyment, had some merit in chearfully undertaking to drive her and all her finery in the old Chair[1] to D. on the important morning.—As they splashed along the dirty Lane Miss Watson thus instructed and cautioned her inexperienced Sister.—"I dare say it will be a very good Ball, and among so many officers, you will hardly want partners. You will find Mrs. Edwards' maid very willing to help you, and I would advise you to ask Mary Edwards's opinion if you are at all at a loss for she has a very good Taste.—If Mr. Edwards does not lose his money at Cards, you will stay as late as you can wish for; if he does, he will hurry you home perhaps—but you are sure of some comfortable Soup.[2]—I hope you will be in good looks—. I should not be surprised if you were to be thought one of the prettiest girls in the room, there is a great deal in Novelty. Perhaps Tom Musgrave may take notice of you—but I would advise you by all means not to give him any encouragement. He generally pays attention to every new girl, but he is a great flirt and never means anything serious."

"I think I have heard you speak of him before, said Emma. Who is he?" "A young Man of very good fortune, quite independant,[3] and remarkably agreable, an universal favourite wherever he goes. Most of the girls hereabouts are in love with him, or have been. I beleive I am the only one among them that have escaped with a whole heart, and yet I was the first he paid attention to, when he came into this Country,[4] six years ago; and very great attention indeed did he pay me. Some people say that he has never seemed to like any girl so well Since, tho' he is always behaving in a particular way to one or another."—"And how came *your* heart to be the only cold one?—" said Emma smiling. "There was a reason for that—replied Miss Watson changing colour.—I have not been very well used Emma among them, I hope you will have better luck."—"Dear Sister, I beg your par-

---

1 A rib chair, or Yarmouth cart, was a very modest open carriage without springs or lining, usually with two wheels, and drawn by a single horse.
2 At public assemblies, only light refreshments would be provided, so participants would eat before they went and after they came home.
3 Tom Musgrave is in control of enough income to be self-supporting, rather than living on an allowance until he inherited property and funds on the death of his father.
4 Neighbourhood.

don, if I have unthinkingly given you pain."—"When first we knew Tom Musgrave, continued Miss Watson without seeming to hear her, I was very much attached to a young Man—of the name of Purvis—a particular friend of Robert's, who used to be with us a great deal. Every body thought it would have been a Match." A sigh accompanied these words, which Emma respected in silence—; but her Sister after a short pause went on—. "You will naturally ask why it did not take place, and why he is married to another Woman, while I am still single.—But you must ask him—not me—you must ask Penelope.—Yes Emma, Penelope was at the bottom of it all.—She thinks everything fair for a Husband; I trusted her, she set him against me, with a veiw of gaining him herself and it ended in his discontinuing his visits and soon after marrying somebody else.—Penelope makes light of her conduct, but *I* think such Treachery very bad. It has been the ruin of my happiness. I shall never love any Man as I loved Purvis. I do not think Tom Musgrave should be named with him in the same day.—" "You quite shock me by what you say of Penelope—said Emma. Could a sister do such a thing?—Rivalry, Treachery between Sisters!—I shall be afraid of being acquainted with her—but I hope it was not so. Appearances were against her—" "You do not know Penelope.—There is nothing she would not do to get married—she would as good as tell you so herself.—Do not trust her with any secrets of your own, take warning by me, do not trust her; she has her good qualities, but she has no Faith, no Honour, no Scruples, if she can promote her own advantage.—I wish with all my heart she was well married. I declare I had rather have her well-married than myself."—"Than yourself!—yes I can suppose so. A heart, wounded like yours can have little inclination for Matrimony."—"Not much indeed—but you know we must marry.—I could do very well single for my own part—A little Company, and a pleasant Ball now and then, would be enough for me, if one could be young for ever, but my Father cannot provide for us,[1] and it is very bad to grow old and be poor and laughed at.[2]—I have lost Purvis it is true, but very few people

---

1 Mr. Watson's income as a clergyman will die with him.

2 The plight of single, genteel women with no fortune was unenviable: at best they might find a home with richer relatives, and at worst they lived in outright poverty. In *Emma*, Emma Woodhouse, heiress to £30,000, might declare she will never marry, but her neighbour, Miss Bates, shows the financial and social vulnerability of a genteel woman with a very small income.

marry their first Loves. I should not refuse a man because he was not Purvis—. Not that I can ever quite forgive Penelope."— Emma shook her head in acquiescence.—"Penelope however has had her Troubles—continued Miss Watson.—She was sadly disappointed in Tom Musgrave, who afterwards transferred his attentions from me to her, and whom she was very fond of;—but he never means anything serious, and when he had trifled with her long enough, he began to slight her for Margaret, and poor Penelope was very wretched—. And since then, she has been trying to make some match at Chichester;[1] she wont tell us with whom, but I beleive it is a rich old Dr. Harding, Uncle to the friend she goes to see;—and she has taken a vast deal of trouble about him and given up a great deal of Time to no purpose as yet.—When she went away the other day, she said it should be the last time.—I suppose you did not know what her particular Business was at Chichester nor guess at the object that could take her away, from Stanton just as you were coming home after so many years absence."—"No indeed, I had not the smallest suspicion of it. I considered her engagement to Mrs. Shaw just at that time as very unfortunate for me. I had hoped to find all my Sisters at home; to be able to make an immediate friend of each."—"I suspect the Doctor to have had an attack of the Asthma,—and that she was hurried away on that account—the Shaws are quite on her side.—At least I believe so—but she tells me nothing. She professes to keep her own counsel; she says, and truly enough, that "Too many Cooks spoil the Broth."—"I am sorry for her anxieties, said Emma,—but I do not like her plans or her opinions. I shall be afraid of her.—She must have too masculine and bold a temper.—To be so bent on Marriage—to pursue a Man merely for the sake of Situation—is a sort of thing that shocks me; I cannot understand it. Poverty is a great Evil, but to a woman of Education and feeling it ought not, it cannot be the greatest.—I would rather be Teacher at a school (and I can think of nothing worse)[2] than marry a Man I did not like.—" "I would

---

1 A small market town near the south coast, about fifty miles from Dorking.
2 Schoolteaching was one of the few occupations open to educated women at the time, but it was hard work for little income, and would involve even more loss of status than becoming a governess in a private house. Mary Wollstonecraft, who had worked as a teacher, wrote in *Thoughts on the Education of Daughters* (1787) that a "teacher at a school is only a kind of upper servant, who has more work than the menial ones" (see Appendix D).

rather do any thing than be Teacher at a school—said her Sister. *I* have been at school, Emma, and know what a Life they lead; *you* never have.—I should not like marrying a disagreable Man any more than yourself,—but I do not think there *are* many very disagreable Men;—I think I could like any goodhumoured Man with a comfortable Income.—I suppose my Aunt brought you up to be rather refined." "Indeed I do not know.—My Conduct must tell you how I have been brought up. I am no judge of it myself. I cannot compare my aunt's method with any other persons, because I know no other."—"But I can see in a great many things that you are very refined. I have observed it ever since you came home, and I am afraid it will not be for your happiness. Penelope will laugh at you very much." "*That* will not be for my happiness I am sure.—If my opinions are wrong, I must correct them—if they are above my Situation, I must endeavour to conceal them.—But I doubt whether Ridicule,—Has Penelope much wit?"—"Yes—she has great spirits, and never cares what she says."—"Margaret is more gentle I imagine?"—"Yes—especially in company; she is all gentleness and mildness when anybody is by.—But she is a little fretful and perverse among ourselves.— Poor Creature!—she is possessed with the notion of Tom Musgrave's being more seriously in love with her, than he ever was with any body else, and is always expecting him to come to the point. This is the second time within this twelvemonth that she has gone to spend a month with Robert and Jane on purpose to egg him on, by her absence—but I am sure she is mistaken, and that he will no more follow her to Croydon[1] now than he did last March.—He will never marry unless he can marry somebody very great; Miss Osborne perhaps, or something in that stile.—" "Your account of this Tom Musgrave, Elizabeth, gives me very little inclination for his acquaintance." "You are afraid of him, I do not wonder at you."—"No indeed—I dislike and despise him."— "Dislike and Despise Tom Musgrave! No, *that* you never can. I defy you not to be delighted with him if he takes notice of you.— I hope he will dance with you—and I dare say he will, unless the Osbornes come with a large party, and then he will not speak to any body else."—"He seems to have most engaging manners!— said Emma.—Well, we shall see how irresistable Mr. Tom Musgrave and I find each other.—I suppose I shall know him as soon as I enter the Ball-room;—he *must* carry some of his Charms in

---

1   A small market town about twenty miles north east of Dorking, and
    about ten miles south of central London.

his face."—"You will not find him in the Ball room I can tell you, you will go early that Mrs. Edwards may get a good place by the fire, and he never comes till late; and if the Osbornes are coming, he will wait in the Passage, and come in with them.—I should like to look in upon you Emma. If it was but a good day with my Father, I would wrap myself up, and James should drive me over, as soon as I had made Tea for him, and I should be with you by the time the Dancing began." "What! would you come late at night in this Chair?"—"To be sure I would.—There, I said you were very refined;—and *that's* an instance of it."—Emma for a moment made no answer—at last she said—"I wish Elizabeth, you had not made a point of my going to this Ball, I wish you were going instead of me. Your pleasure would be greater than mine. I am a stranger here, and know nobody but the Edwards-es,—my Enjoyment therefore must be very doubtful. Yours among all your acquaintance would be certain.—It is not too late to change. Very little apology could be requisite to the Edwardes, who must be more glad of your company than of mine, and I should most readily return to my Father; and should not be at all afraid to drive this quiet old Creature, home. Your Cloathes I would undertake to find means of sending to you."—"My dearest Emma cried Elizabeth warmly—do you think I would do such a thing?—Not for the Universe—but I shall never forget your goodnature in proposing it. You must have a sweet temper indeed!—I never met with any thing like it!—And would you really give up the Ball, that I might be able to go to it!—Beleive me Emma, I am not so selfish as that comes to. No, tho' I am nine years older than you are, I would not be the means of keeping you from being seen.—You are very pretty, and it would be very hard that you should not have as fair a chance as we have all had, to make your fortune.—No Emma, whoever stays at home this winter, it sha'nt be you. I am sure I should never have forgiven the person who kept me from a Ball at nineteen." Emma expressed her gratitude, and for a few minutes they jogged on in silence.—Elizabeth first spoke.—"You will take notice who Mary Edwards dances with."—"I will remember her partners if I can—but you know they will be all strangers to me." "Only observe whether she dances with Captain Hunter, more than once;[1] I have my fears in that quarter. Not that her Father

---

1 By the etiquette of the time, dancing with the same partner more than
   once in an evening would be a mark of special favour. In *Pride and
   Prejudice*, Mrs. Bennet is delighted that Mr. Bingley dances twice with

or Mother like officers,[1] but if she does you know, it is all over with poor Sam.—And I have promised to write him word who she dances with."

"Is Sam attached to Miss Edwardes?"—"Did not you know *that?*"—"How should I know it?—How should I know in Shropshire,[2] what is passing of that nature in Surry?—It is not likely that circumstances of such delicacy should make any part of the scanty communication which passed between you and me for the last fourteen years."

"I wonder I never mentioned it when I wrote. Since you have been at home, I have been so busy with my poor Father and our great wash[3] that I have had no leisure to tell you anything—but indeed I concluded you knew it all.—He has been very much in love with her these two years, and it is a great disappointment to him that he cannot always get away to our Balls—but Mr. Curtis wo'nt often spare him, and just now it is a sickly time at Guilford"—[4] "Do you suppose Miss Edwardes inclined to like him—?" "I am afraid not: You know she is an only Child, and will have at least ten thousand pounds."[5]—"But still she may like our Brother." "Oh! no—. The Edwardes look much higher. Her Father and Mother would never consent to it. Sam is only a Sur-

---

Jane: "Only think of *that*, my dear; he actually danced with her twice," she tells Mr. Bennet (Vol. 1, ch. 3).

1 A career in the army was regarded as a genteel occupation for younger, often impecunious, sons of the gentry. In the late 1790s and early 1800s, since England was at war with France, regiments were billeted in or near communities in the South of England for short periods of time before moving on, and were inevitably seen as a disruptive element for eligible young women of the area.

2 A rural county on the border of Wales, more than 150 miles to the north west of Surrey.

3 Not the normal wash, but the much larger-scale enterprise that would take place in households in autumn and spring, and would cause considerable upheaval for several days.

4 A small market town about fifteen miles west of Dorking and about thirty miles south west of London, more usually spelt Guildford.

5 A woman with this asset, which would normally become the property of her husband on marriage, could expect to attract a wealthy man. Emma Woodhouse accepts that Mr. Elton "had not thrown himself away" in marrying a woman with a fortune "of so many thousands as would always be called ten" (*Emma*, Vol. 2, ch. 4).

geon[1] you know.—Sometimes I think she does like him. But Mary Edwardes is rather prim and reserved; I do not always know what she would be at."—"Unless Sam feels on sure grounds with the Lady herself, it seems a pity to me that he should be encouraged to think of her at all."—"A young Man must think of somebody, said Elizabeth—and why should not he be as lucky as Robert, who has got a good wife and six thousand pounds?"

"We must not all expect to be individually lucky replied Emma. The Luck of one member of a Family is Luck to all.—" "Mine is all to come I am sure—said Elizabeth giving another sigh to the remembrance of Purvis.—I have been unlucky enough, and I cannot say much for you, as my Aunt married again so foolishly.—Well—you will have a good Ball I dare say. The next turning will bring us to the Turnpike.[2] You may see the Church Tower over the hedge, and the White Hart[3] is close by it.—I shall long to know what you think of Tom Musgrave." Such were the last audible sounds of Miss Watson's voice, before they passed thro' the Turnpike gate and entered on the pitching[4] of the Town—the jumbling and noise of which made farther Conversation most thoroughly undesirable.—The old Mare trotted heavily on, wanting no direction of the reins to take the right Turning, and making only one Blunder, in proposing to stop at the Milleners,[5] before she drew up towards Mr. Edward's door.—Mr.

---

1   The profession of surgeon had begun in a very humble way, only splitting from the occupation of barber in 1745. By the late century, surgeons were professionally qualified and recognised as superior to apothecaries; the establishment of the Royal College of Surgeons in 1800 gave them added professional status. However, they were not high on the social scale. "I have ... scratched out the Introduction between Lord P. & his Brother, & Mr. Griffin," JA wrote to her niece Anna, who had asked advice on a draft of a novel she was writing in 1814; "A Country Surgeon ... would not be introduced to Men of their rank" (see Appendix A).

2   A toll-gate in the form of a barrier placed across the road, which would be lifted when a toll was paid. Turnpike roads, the precursor of the modern toll roads, were common in the late eighteenth and early nineteenth centuries.

3   There is a public house called the White Hart in Dorking, but JA may have had in mind the White Horse, a substantial coaching inn in the High Street.

4   A road surface made of cobblestones.

5   More commonly spelt "milliners," the shop would sell a range of goods including hats, ribbons, and lace.

Edwards lived in the best house in the Street, and the best in the place, if Mr. Tomlinson the Banker might be indulged in calling his newly erected House at the end of the Town with a Shrubbery and sweep[1] in the Country.—Mr. Edwards's House was higher than most of its neighbours with windows on each side the door, the windows guarded by posts and chain, the door approached by a flight of stone steps.—"Here we are—said Elizabeth—as the Carriage ceased moving—safely arrived;—and by the Market Clock, we have been only five and thirty minutes coming.—which *I* think is doing pretty well, tho' it would be nothing for Penelope.—Is not it a nice Town?—The Edwards' have a noble house you see, and They live quite in stile. The door will be opened by a Man in Livery with a powder'd head,[2] I can tell you."

Emma had seen the Edwardses only one morning at Stanton, they were therefore all but Strangers to her, and tho' her spirits were by no means insensible to the expected joys of the Evening, she felt a little uncomfortable in the thought of all that was to precede them. Her conversation with Elizabeth too giving her some very unpleasant feelings with respect to her own family, had made her more open to disagreable impressions from any other cause, and increased her sense of the awkwardness of rushing into Intimacy on so slight an acquaintance.—There was nothing in the manners of Mrs. or Miss Edwardes to give immediate change to these Ideas;—the Mother tho' a very friendly woman, had a reserved air, and a great deal of formal Civility—and the daughter, a genteel looking girl of twenty-two, with her hair in papers,[3] seemed very naturally to have caught something of the Stile of the Mother who had brought her up.—Emma was soon left to know what they could be, by Elizabeth's being obliged to

---

1 A shrubbery is a small private garden near the house, with walks lined by shrubs and trees; a sweep is a driveway between the boundary of the grounds and the house itself, shaped in a half-circle to allow room for carriages to turn.

2 The servants of the wealthy would wear a uniform, and their hair would be sprinkled with a scented powder made of fine flour or starch. Powdered hair was a fashion popular for all classes earlier in the eighteenth century, but by 1800, it was retained largely for servants and for provincial professional men such as the lawyer Robert Watson. See pp. 186, 308.

3 To introduce fashionable curls, the hair was twisted round pieces of soft paper, usually overnight.

hurry away—and some very, very languid remarks on the probable Brilliancy of the Ball, were all that broke at intervals a silence of half an hour before they were joined by the Master of the house.—Mr. Edwards had a much easier, and more communicative air than the Ladies of the Family; he was fresh from the Street, and he came ready to tell whatever might interest.—After a cordial reception of Emma, he turned to his daughter with "Well Mary, I bring you good news.—The Osbornes will certainly be at the Ball to night.—Horses for two Carriages are ordered from the White Hart, to be at Osborne Castle by nine."—"I am glad of it—observed Mrs. Edwards, because their coming gives a credit to our Assemblies. The Osbornes being known to have been at the first Ball, will dispose a great many people to attend the second.—It is more than they deserve, for in fact they add nothing to the pleasure of the Evening, they come so late, and go so early;—but Great People have always their charm."—Mr. Edwards proceeded to relate every other little article of news which his morning's lounge[1] had supplied him with, and they chatted with greater briskness, till Mrs. Edwards's moment for dressing arrived, and the young Ladies were carefully recommended to lose no time.—Emma was shewn to a very comfortable apartment, and as soon as Mrs. Edwards's civilities could leave her to herself, the happy occupation, the first Bliss of a Ball began.—The girls, dressing in some measure together, grew unavoidably better acquainted; Emma found in Miss Edwards the shew of good sense, a modest unpretending mind, and a great wish of obliging—and when they returned to the parlour where Mrs. Edwards was sitting respectably attired in one of the two Sattin gowns which went thro' the winter, and a new Cap from the Milliners, they entered it with much easier feelings and more natural smiles than they had taken away.—Their dress was now to be examined; Mrs. Edwards acknowledged herself too old-fashioned to approve of every modern extravagance however sanctioned—and tho' complacently veiwing her daughter's good looks, would give but a qualified admiration; and Mr. Edwards not less satisfied with Mary, paid some Compliments of good humoured Gallantry to Emma at her expence.—The discussion led to more intimate remarks, and Miss Edwardes gently asked Emma if she were not often reckoned very like her youngest brother.—Emma thought she could perceive a faint blush accompany the question, and there seemed something still more suspi-

1 Stroll; leisurely walk.

cious in the manner in which Mr. Edwards took up the subject. "—You are paying Miss Emma no great compliment I think Mary, said he hastily—. Mr. Samuel Watson is a very good sort of young man, and I dare say a very clever Surgeon, but his complexion has been rather too much exposed to all weathers,[1] to make a likeness to him very flattering." Mary apologized in some confusion. "She had not thought a strong Likeness at all incompatible with very different degrees of Beauty.—There might be resemblance in Countenance; and the complexion, and even the features be very unlike."—"I know nothing of my Brother's Beauty, said Emma, for I have not seen him since he was seven years old—but my father reckons us alike." "Mr. Watson!—cried Mr. Edwardes, Well, you astonish me.—There is not the least likeness in the world; Your brother's eyes are grey, yours are brown, He has a long face, and a wide mouth.—My dear, do *you* perceive the least resemblance?"—"Not the least.—Miss Emma Watson puts me very much in mind of her eldest Sister, and sometimes I see a look of Miss Penelope—and once or twice there has been a glance of Mr. Robert—but I cannot perceive any likeness to Mr. Samuel." "I see the likeness between her and Miss Watson,[2] replied Mr. Edwards, very strongly—but I am not sensible of the others.—I do not much think she is like any of the Family *but* Miss Watson; but I am very sure there is no resemblance between her and Sam."—This matter was settled, and they went to Dinner.—"Your Father, Miss Emma, is one of my oldest friends—said Mr. Edwardes, as he helped her to wine, when they were drawn round the fire to enjoy their Desert,[3]—We must drink to his better health.—It is a great concern to me I assure you that he should be such an Invalid.—I know nobody who likes a game of cards in a social way, better than he does;— and very few people that play a fairer rubber.[4]—It is a thousand pities that he should be so deprived of the pleasure. For now we have a quiet little Whist club that meets three times a week at the

<hr />

1 A country surgeon would spend much of his time travelling to and from patients in villages, usually on horseback and therefore exposed to the weather.
2 Elizabeth, as the eldest sister, would be referred to as "Miss Watson" by those outside the family; the younger sisters would be referred to as "Miss Penelope," "Miss Margaret," and "Miss Emma."
3 Dessert would probably consist of dried fruit or sweets, often eaten away from the table.
4 Usually a set of three games of whist.

White Hart, and if he could but have his health, how much he would enjoy it." "I dare say he would Sir—and I wish with all my heart he were equal to it." "Your Club would be better fitted for an Invalid, said Mrs. Edwards if you did not keep it up so late."— This was an old greivance.—"So late, my dear, what are you talking of? cried the Husband with sturdy pleasantry—. We are always at home before midnight. They would laugh at Osborne Castle to hear you call *that* late; they are but just rising from dinner at midnight."[1]—"That is nothing to the purpose,—retorted the Lady calmly. The Osbornes are to be no rule for us. You had better meet every night, and break up two hours sooner." So far, the subject was very often carried;—but Mr. and Mrs. Edwards were so wise as never to pass that point; and Mr. Edwards now turned to something else.—He had lived long enough in the Idleness of a Town to become a little of a Gossip, and having some curiosity to know more of the Circumstances of his young Guest, than had yet reached him, he began with, "I think Miss Emma, I remember your Aunt very well about thirty years ago; I am pretty sure I danced with her in the old rooms at Bath,[2] the year before I married—. She was a very fine woman then—but like other people I suppose she is grown somewhat older since that time.— I hope she is likely to be happy in her second choice."

"I hope so, I beleive so, Sir"—said Emma in some agitation.— "Mr. Turner had not been dead a great while I think?"—"About two years Sir." "I forget what her name is now?"—"O'brien." "Irish![3] Ah! I remember—and she is gone to settle in Ireland.—I do not wonder that you should not wish to go with her into *that* Country Miss Emma—but it must be a great deprivation to her, poor Lady!—After bringing you up like a Child of her own."—"I was not so ungrateful Sir, said Emma warmly, as to wish to be

---

1   Mr. Edwards is exaggerating, but the timing of dinner was closely
     related to the status, and its length the capacity for leisure, of its partici-
     pants. The Watsons dine at 3:00 p.m.; see p. 300. Dinner among genteel
     country families might take place at 4:30 or 5:00 p.m.

2   The old or Lower Assembly Rooms were built in 1708, in the centre of
     the town near the river. As Bath expanded, the new or Upper Assembly
     Rooms were opened in 1771 in the higher, more modern part of the city
     to the north.

3   The Irish fortune-hunter was a stock figure in the literature of the
     period. Mrs. Turner would.be a very attractive marriage proposition; on
     marriage, all her property would belong to her husband, unless there
     was a legal agreement adjusting the arrangement.

any where but with her.—It did not suit them, it did not suit Captain O'brien that I should be of the party."—"Captain!—repeated Mrs. Edwards, the Gentleman is in the army then?" "Yes Ma'am."—"Aye—there is nothing like your officers for captivating the Ladies, Young or old.—There is no resisting a Cockade[1] my dear."—"I hope there is."—said Mrs. Edwards gravely, with a quick glance at her daughter;—and Emma had just recovered from her own perturbation in time to see a blush on Miss Edwards's cheek, and in remembering what Elizabeth had said of Captain Hunter, to wonder and waver between his influence and her brother's.—"Elderly Ladies should be careful how they make a second choice," observed Mr. Edwardes.—"Carefulness—Discretion—should not be confined to Elderly Ladies, or to a second choice, added his wife. It is quite as necessary to young Ladies in their first."—"Rather more so, my dear, replied he—because young Ladies are likely to feel the effects of it longer. When an old Lady plays the fool, it is not in the course of nature that she should suffer from it many years." Emma drew her hand across her eyes—and Mrs. Edwards on perceiving it, changed the subject to one of less anxiety to all.—With nothing to do but to expect the hour of setting off, the afternoon was long to the two young Ladies; and tho' Miss Edwards was rather discomposed at the very early hour which her mother always fixed for going, that early hour itself was watched for with some eagerness.—The entrance of the Tea things[2] at seven o'clock was some releif—and luckily Mr. and Mrs. Edwards always drank a dish extraordinary,[3] and ate an additional muffin[4] when they were going to sit up late, which lengthened the ceremony almost to the wished for moment. At a little before eight, the Tomlinsons carriage was heard to go by, which was the constant signal for Mrs. Edwards

1 A ribbon, knot of ribbons, or rosette worn by a soldier as a badge of office, and so, by extension, the soldier himself.
2 Tea was made where it was to be drunk. Teapot, tea, kettles or urn, cream jug, sugar bowl, cups and saucers, crockery, and cutlery for any accompanying food were all brought into the room on a "tea-board" by servants. The whole process constituted quite a "ceremony."
3 An additional cupful of tea. Tea was then served in a very wide cup without a handle, and was often referred to as a "dish"; it was permissible to pour the tea out into the saucer and drink from that, presumably because the liquid would cool down more quickly that way.
4 Small flat cake made from yeast batter, often split and toasted, with butter and/or jam.

to order hers to the door; and in a very few minutes, the party were transported from the quiet warmth of a snug parlour, to the bustle, noise and draughts of air of the broad Entrance-passage of an Inn.—Mrs. Edwards carefully guarding her own dress, while she attended with yet greater solicitude to the proper security of her young Charges' shoulders and Throats, led the way up the wide staircase, while no sound of a Ball but the first Scrape of one violin, blessed the ears of her followers, and Miss Edwards on hazarding the anxious enquiry of whether there were many people come yet was told, by the Waiter as she knew she should, that "Mr. Tomlinson's family were in the room." In passing along a short gallery to the Assembly-room, brilliant in lights before them, They were accosted by a young Man in a morning dress and Boots,[1] who was standing in the doorway of a Bedchamber, apparently on purpose to see them go by.—"Ah! Mrs. Edwards— how do you do?—How do you do Miss Edwards?—he cried, with an easy air;—You are determined to be in good time I see, as usual.—The Candles are but this moment lit—" "I like to get a good seat by the fire you know, Mr. Musgrave," replied Mrs. Edwards. "I am this moment going to dress, said he—I am waiting for my stupid fellow.—We shall have a famous Ball, The Osbornes are certainly coming; you may depend upon *that* for I was with Lord Osborne this morning—" The party passed on— Mrs. Edwards's sattin gown swept along the clean floor of the Ball-room, to the fire place at the upper end, where one party only were formally seated, while three or four Officers were lounging together, passing in and out from the adjoining card-room.—A very stiff meeting between these near neighbours ensued—and as soon as they were all duely placed again, Emma in the low whisper which became the solemn scene, said to Miss Edwardes, "The gentleman we passed in the passage, was Mr. Musgrave, then.—He is reckoned remarkably agreable I understand.—"Miss Edwards answered hesitatingly—"Yes—he is very much liked by many people.—But *we* are not very intimate."— "He is rich, is not he?"—"He has about eight or nine hundred pounds a year[2] I beleive.—He came into possession of it, when he was very young, and my Father and Mother think it has given him rather an unsettled turn.—He is no favourite with them."—

---

1 I.e., his outdoor clothes as worn during the day, rather than the more formal dress that would be expected for the assembly.

2 A very comfortable income for a single man, and enough to maintain a family in a modestly genteel way.

The cold and empty appearance of the Room and the demure air of the small cluster of Females at one end of it began soon to give way; the inspiriting sound of other Carriages was heard, and continual accessions of portly Chaperons, and strings of smartly-dressed girls were received, with now and then a fresh, Gentleman Straggler, who if not enough in Love to station himself near any fair Creature seemed glad to escape into the Card-room.— Among the increasing numbers of Military Men, one now made his way to Miss Edwards, with an air of Empressément,[1] which decidedly said to her Companion "I am Captain Hunter."—And Emma, who could not but watch her at such a moment, saw her looking rather distressed, but by no means displeased, and heard an engagement formed for the two first dances,[2] which made her think her Brother Sam's a hopeless case.—Emma in the mean while was not unobserved, or unadmired herself.—A new face and a very pretty one, could not be slighted—her name was whispered from one party to another, and no sooner had the signal been given, by the Orchestra's striking up a favourite air, which seemed to call the young men to their duty, and people the centre of the room, than she found herself engaged to dance with a Brother officer, introduced by Captain Hunter.—Emma Watson was not more than of the middle height—well made and plump, with an air of healthy vigour.—Her skin was very brown, but clear, smooth and glowing[3]—; which with a lively Eye, a sweet smile, and an open Countenance, gave beauty to attract, and expression to make that beauty improve on acquaintance.—Having no reason to be dissatisfied with her partner, the Evening began very pleasantly to her; and her feelings perfectly coincided with the re-iterated observation of others, that it was an excellent Ball.—The two first dances were not quite over, when the return-

---

1 Animated display of cordiality; both the word itself, and the use of the French term in connection with Captain Hunter, suggest an element of artificiality and self-regard in his "display." In *Cecilia* (1782), Burney's Captain Aresby shows his foolish self-importance by using French terms: "I should be so unhappy as to commit any *faux pas* by too much *empressement*" (Book 7, ch. 9).

2 By convention, dances were arranged and performed in pairs. Each pair was regarded as a single dance for the purposes of choosing partners.

3 Pale skin was often regarded as desirable, since a brown skin was associated with manual labour outside the home. Attitudes were changing, however, in the light of the growing trend for wealthy people to make tourist expeditions.

ing sound of Carriages after a long interruption, called general notice, and "the Osbornes are coming, the Osbornes are coming"—was repeated round the room.—After some minutes of extraordinary bustle without, and watchful curiosity within, the important Party, preceded by the attentive Master of the Inn to open a door which was never shut, made their appearance. They consisted of Lady Osborne, her son Lord Osborne, her daughter Miss Osborne; Miss Carr, her daughter's friend, Mr. Howard formerly Tutor to Lord Osborne, now Clergyman of the Parish in which the Castle stood,[1] Mrs. Blake, a widow-sister who lived with him, her son a fine boy of ten years old, and Mr. Tom Musgrave; who probably imprisoned within his own room, had been listening in bitter impatience to the sound of the Music, for the last half hour. In their progress up the room, they paused almost immediately behind Emma, to receive the Compliments of some acquaintance, and she heard Lady Osborne observe that they had made a point of coming early for the gratification of Mrs. Blake's little boy, who was uncommonly fond of dancing.—Emma looked at them all as they passed—but chiefly and with most interest on Tom Musgrave, who was certainly a genteel, good looking young man.—Of the females, Lady Osborne had by much the finest person;—tho' nearly fifty, she was very handsome, and had all the Dignity of Rank.—Lord Osborne was a very fine young man; but there was an air of Coldness, of Carelessness, even of Awkwardness about him, which seemed to speak him out of his Element in a Ball room. He came in fact only because it was judged expedient for him to please the Borough[2]—he was not fond of Women's company, and he never danced.—Mr. Howard was an agreable-looking Man, a little more than Thirty.—At the conclusion of the two Dances, Emma found herself, she knew not how, seated amongst the Osborne

---

1 The sons of aristocratic families were usually educated at home, at least in their early years, by a clergyman responsible for their moral as well as their academic training. Since such families would probably have the right to appoint ministers of parishes on their estates, it was also common for the clergyman concerned to be rewarded with such an appointment.

2 The senior group of (male) citizens who, in an era of very limited franchise, would control the election of a member of Parliament for the town. Lord Osborne would, by right of his title, be a member of the House of Lords; clearly, however, there would be political advantage in being on good terms with the local electorate.

Set; and she was immediately struck with the fine Countenance and animated gestures of the little boy, as he was standing before his Mother, wondering when they should begin.—"You will not be surprised at Charles's impatience, said Mrs. Blake, a lively pleasant-looking little Woman of five or six and thirty, to a Lady who was standing near her, when you know what a partner he is to have. Miss Osborne has been so very kind as to promise to dance the two first dances with him."—"Oh! yes—we have been engaged this week, cried the boy, and we are to dance down every couple."—On the other side of Emma, Miss Osborne, Miss Carr, and a party of young Men were standing engaged in very lively consultation—and soon afterwards she saw the smartest officer of the Sett, walking off to the Orchestra to order the dance,[1] while Miss Osborne passing before her, to her little expecting Partner hastily said—"Charles, I beg your pardon for not keeping my engagement,[2] but I am going to dance these two dances with Colonel Beresford. I know you will excuse me, and I will certainly dance with you after Tea."[3] And without staying for an answer, she turned again to Miss Carr, and in another minute was led by Colonel Beresford to begin the Set.[4] If the poor little boy's face had in it's happiness been interesting to Emma, it was infinitely more so under this sudden reverse;—he stood the picture of dis-appointment, with crimson'd cheeks, quivering lips, and eyes bent on the floor. His mother, stifling her own mortification, tried to sooth his, with the prospect of Miss Osborne's second prom-ise; but tho' he contrived to utter with an effort of Boyish Brav-ery "Oh! I do not mind it"—it was very evident by the unceasing

1 The first dance would usually be led off by the highest ranking lady present and her partner. There were conventions concerning the order of dances and, within these, the lady at the top of the set would "call" (i.e., determine which tune and which dance figures were to be offered) and her partner would convey these instructions to the musicians. For subsequent dances, the duty of "calling" passed to the second and third ranked ladies and so on, in turn.

2 Miss Osborne is insulting Charles by treating her agreement to dance with him as expendable in a way that would have been socially unforgiv-able had he been an adult.

3 At assemblies, there would be an interval in the dancing at which light refreshments were served.

4 The set would be the line of couples who would perform the dance as a group. In small gatherings, there might only be one set; in larger gather-ings, the dancers would divide into several sets in order to provide man-ageable units.

agitation of his features that he minded it as much as ever.—
Emma did not think, or reflect;—she felt and acted—."I shall be
very happy to dance with you Sir, if you like it," said she, holding
out her hand with the most unaffected goodhumour.—The Boy
in one moment restored to all his first delight looked joyfully at
his Mother; And stepping forward with an honest and Simple
Thank you Ma'am was instantly ready to attend his new acquaintance.—The Thankfulness of Mrs. Blake was more diffuse;—with
a look, most expressive of unexpected pleasure, and lively Gratitude, she turned to her neighbour with repeated and fervent
acknowledgements of so great and condescending[1] a kindness to
her boy.—Emma with perfect truth could assure her that she
could not be giving greater pleasure than she felt herself—and
Charles being provided with his gloves and charged to keep them
on,[2] they joined the Set which was now rapidly forming, with
nearly equal complacency.[3]—It was a Partnership which could
not be noticed without surprise. It gained her a broad stare from
Miss Osborne and Miss Carr as they passed her in the dance.
"Upon my word Charles you are in luck, (said the former as she
turned him,) you have got a better partner than me—" to which
the happy Charles answered "Yes."—Tom Musgrave who was
dancing with Miss Carr, gave her many inquisitive glances; and
after a time Lord Osborne himself came and under pretence of
talking to Charles, stood to look at his partner.—Tho' rather distressed by such observation, Emma could not repent what she
had done, so happy had it made both the boy and his Mother; the
latter of whom was continually making opportunity of addressing
her with the warmest civility.—Her little partner she found, tho'
bent cheifly on dancing, was not unwilling to speak, when her
questions or remarks gave him any thing to say; and she learnt,
by a sort of inevitable enquiry that he had two brothers and a sister, that they and their Mama all lived with his Uncle at Wickstead,[4] that his Uncle taught him Latin,[5] that he was very fond of

---

1 Stooping graciously from a position of dignity.
2 Men's ball attire included white gloves, which they were expected to
  wear through the dancing.
3 Pleasure, with an active sense of delight and enjoyment.
4 Presumably fictional; there is no village or substantial estate of that
  name recorded in Surrey.
5 Competence in Latin, and also in Greek, was still seen as an essential
  part of education for the sons of the aristocracy and gentry. They

riding, and had a horse of his own given him by Lord Osborne; and that he had been out once already with Lord Osborne's Hounds.—At the end of these Dances Emma found they were to drink tea;—Miss Edwards gave her a caution to be at hand, in a manner which convinced her of Mrs. Edwards's holding it very important to have them both close to her when she moved into the Tearoom; and Emma was accordingly on the alert to gain her proper station. It was always the pleasure of the company to have a little bustle and croud when they thus adjourned for refreshment;—The Tea room was a small room within the Card room, and in passing thro' the latter, where the passage was straightened[1] by Tables, Mrs. Edwards and her party were for a few moments hemmed in. It happened close by Lady Osborne's Cassino Table;[2] Mr. Howard who belonged to it spoke to his Nephew; and Emma on perceiving herself the object of attention both to Lady Osborne and him, had just turned away her eyes in time, to avoid seeming to hear her young companion delightedly whisper aloud—"Oh! Uncle, do look at my partner. She is so pretty!" As they were immediately in motion again however, Charles was hurried off without being able to receive his Uncle's suffrage.[3]—On entering the Tea room, in which two long Tables were prepared, Lord Osborne was to be seen quite alone at the end of one, as if retreating as far as he could from the Ball, to enjoy his own thoughts, and gape without restraint.—Charles instantly pointed him out to Emma—"There's Lord Osborne—Let you and I go and sit by him."—"No, no, said Emma laughing you must sit with my friends." Charles was now free enough to hazard a few questions in his turn. "What o'clock was it?—" "Eleven."—"Eleven!—And I am not at all sleepy. Mama said I should be asleep before ten.—Do you think Miss Osborne will keep her word with me, when Tea is over?" "Oh! yes.—I suppose so"—tho' she felt that she had no better reason to give than that

---

learned principles of grammar, oratory, and rhetoric, together with a detailed understanding of the moral and philosophical issues discussed by classical thinkers and a literary appreciation of poetry and prose.

1 Straitened; made narrow.

2 Casino is a card game that can be played by two people, or by four in pairs, as here. There are particular values to certain cards or combinations of cards; the object of the game is to collect points, and it requires a good memory and capacity for deduction. The table would be "Lady Osborne's" because she would be the senior person in rank.

3 Approval; agreement.

Miss Osborne had *not* kept it before.—"When shall you come to Osborne Castle?"—"Never, probably.—I am not acquainted with the family." "But you may come to Wickstead and see Mama, and she can take you to the Castle.—There is a monstrous curious stuffed Fox there, and a Badger—any body would think they were alive. It is a pity you should not see them."—

On rising from Tea, there was again a scramble for the pleasure of being first out of the room, which happened to be increased by one or two of the Card parties having just broken up and the players being disposed to move exactly the different way. Among these was Mr. Howard—his Sister leaning on his arm—and no sooner were they within reach of Emma, than Mrs. Blake calling her notice by a friendly touch, said "Your goodness to Charles, my dear Miss Watson, brings all his family upon you. Give me leave to introduce my Brother—Mr. Howard." Emma curtsied, the gentleman bowed—made a hasty request for the honour of her hand in the two next dances, to which as hasty an affirmative was given, and they were immediately impelled in opposite directions.—Emma was very well pleased with the circumstance;—there was a quietly-chearful, gentlemanlike air in Mr. Howard which suited her—and in a few minutes afterwards, the value of her Engagement increased when as she was sitting in the Card room somewhat screened by a door, she heard Lord Osborne, who was lounging on a vacant Table near her, call Tom Musgrave towards him and say, "Why do not you dance with that beautiful Emma Watson?—I want you to dance with her—and I will come and stand by you."—"I was determining on it this very moment my Lord; I'll be introduced and dance with her directly.—" "Aye do—and if you find she does not want much Talking to, you may introduce me by and bye."—"Very well my Lord—. If she is like her Sisters, she will only want to be listened to.—I will go this moment. I shall find her in the Tea room. That stiff old Mrs. Edwards has never done tea."—Away he went—Lord Osborne after him—and Emma lost no time in hurrying from her corner, exactly the other way, forgetting in her haste that she left Mrs. Edwardes behind.—"We had quite lost you—said Mrs. Edwards—who followed her with Mary, in less than five minutes.—If you prefer this room to the other, there is no reason why you should not be here, but we had better all be together." Emma was saved the Trouble of apologizing, by their being joined at the moment by Tom Musgrave, who requesting Mrs. Edwards aloud to do him the honour of presenting him to Miss Emma Watson, left that good Lady without any choice in the business, but that of testifying by the coldness of her manner that she did it unwillingly. The honour of dancing with her, was solicited without loss of time—and Emma, however she might like to be thought a beautiful girl by Lord or Commoner, was so little disposed to favour Tom Musgrave himself, that she had considerable satisfaction in avowing her prior Engagement.—He was evidently surprised and discomposed.—The stile of her last partner had probably led him to beleive her not overpowered with applications.—"My little friend Charles Blake, he cried, must not expect to engross you the whole evening. We can never suffer this—It is against the rules of the Assembly[1]—and I am sure it will never be patronised[2] by our good friend here Mrs. Edwards; she is by much too nice[3] a judge of Decorum to give her license to such a dangerous Particularity."[4]—"I am not going to dance with Master Blake Sir." The Gentleman a little disconcerted, could only hope he might be more fortunate another time—and seeming unwilling to leave her, tho' his friend Lord Osborne was waiting in the Doorway for the result, as Emma with some amusement perceived—he began to make civil enquiries after her family.—"How comes it, that we have not the pleasure of seeing your Sisters here this Evening?—Our Assemblies have been used to be so well treated by them, that we do not know how to take this neglect."—"My eldest Sister is the only one at home—and she could not leave my Father—" "Miss Watson the only one at home!—You astonish me!—It seems but the day before yesterday that I saw them all three in this Town. But I am afraid I have been a very sad neighbour of late. I hear dreadful complaints of my negligence wherever I go,—and I confess it is a shameful length of time since I was at Stanton.—But I shall *now* endeavour to make myself amends for the past."—Emma's calm curtsey in

---

1 Following the example of the major social centres such as Bath, the Assembly may have written rules of conduct and behaviour, but it is more likely that Tom is referring generally to social conventions. In fact, it was questionable whether a couple should dance successive pairs of dances together: when Isabella Thorpe tells James Morland that "it would make us the talk of the place [the Upper Rooms in Bath], if we were not to change partners," he replies that "in these public assemblies it is as often done as not" (*Northanger Abbey*, Vol. 1, ch. 8). The conventions, however, might well be stricter at local assemblies.
2 Supported; encouraged.
3 Precise or particular.
4 Either particular distinction, or exception to the rule.

reply must have struck him as very unlike the encouraging warmth he had been used to receive from her Sisters, and gave him probably the novel sensation of doubting his own influence, and of wishing for more attention than she bestowed.—The dancing now recommenced; Miss Carr being impatient to *call*, everybody was required to stand up—and Tom Musgrave's curiosity was appeased, on seeing—Mr. Howard come forward and claim Emma's hand.—"That will do as well for *me*"—was Lord Osborne's remark, when his friend carried him the news—and he was continually at Howard's Elbow during the two dances.—The frequency of his appearance there, was the only unpleasant part of her engagement, the only objection she could make to Mr. Howard.—In himself, she thought him as agreable as he looked; tho' chatting on the commonest topics he had a sensible, unaffected, way of expressing himself, which made them all worth hearing, and she only regretted that he had not been able to make his pupil's Manners as unexceptionable as his own.—The two dances seemed very short, and she had her partner's authority for considering them so.—At their conclusion the Osbornes and their Train were all on the move. "We are off at last, said his Lordship to Tom—How much longer do *you* stay in this Heavenly place?—till Sunrise?"—"No. faith! my Lord, I have had quite enough of it I assure you—I shall not shew myself here again when I have had the honour of attending Lady Osborne to her Carriage. I shall retreat in as much secrecy as possible to the most remote corner of the House, where I shall order a Barrel of Oysters,[1] and be famously snug." "Let us see you soon at the Castle; and bring me word, how she looks by daylight."—Emma and Mrs. Blake parted as old acquaintance, and Charles shook her by the hand and wished her "good bye" at least a dozen times. From Miss Osborne and Miss Carr she received something like a jirking curtsey as they passed her;[2] even Lady Osborne gave her a look of complacency—and his Lordship actually came back after the others were out of the room, to "beg her pardon", and look in the window seat behind her for the gloves which were visibly compressed in his hand.—As Tom Musgrave

---

1 Oysters were farmed off the south east coast of England—Whitstable oysters, from the North Kent coast, were seen as particularly good—and were widely eaten; they were by no means a delicacy.

2 A significant acknowledgement of acquaintance, however reluctant. Presumably JA means "jerking."

was seen no more, we may suppose his plan to have succeeded, and imagine him mortifying with his Barrel of Oysters, in dreary solitude—or gladly assisting the Landlady in her Bar to make fresh Negus[1] for the happy Dancers above. Emma could not help missing the party, by whom she had been, tho' in some respects unpleasantly, distinguished, and the two Dances which followed and concluded the Ball, were rather flat, in comparison with the others.—Mr. Edwards having play'd with good luck, they were some of the last in the room—"Here we are, back again I declare—said Emma sorrowfully, as she walked into the Dining room, where the Table was prepared, and the neat Upper maid was lighting the Candles—"My dear Miss Edwards—how soon it is at an end!—I wish it could all come over again!—" A great deal of kind pleasure was expressed in her having enjoyed the Evening so much—and Mr. Edwards was as warm as herself, in praise of the fullness, brilliancy and spirit of the Meeting tho' as he had been fixed the whole time at the same Table in the same Room, with only one change of Chairs, it might have seemed a matter scarcely perceived.—But he had won four rubbers out of five, and every thing went well. His daughter felt the advantage of this gratified state of mind, in the course of the remarks and retrospections which now ensued, over the welcome Soup.—"How came you not to dance with either of the Mr. Tomlinsons, Mary?—said her Mother. "I was always engaged when they asked me." "I thought you were to have stood up with Mr. James, the two last dances; Mrs. Tomlinson told me he was gone to ask you—and I had heard you say two minutes before that you were *not* engaged.—" "Yes—but—there was a mistake—I had misunderstood—I did not know I was engaged,—I thought it had been for the two Dances after, if we staid so long—but Captain Hunter assured me it was for those very Two.—"—"So, you ended with Captain Hunter Mary, did you? said her Father. And who did you begin with?" "Captain Hunter," was repeated, in a very humble tone—"Hum!—That is being constant however. But who else did you dance with?" "Mr. Norton, and Mr. Styles." "And who are they?" "Mr. Norton is a Cousin of Captain Hunter's."—And who is Mr. Styles?" "One of his particular friends."—"All in the same Regiment added Mrs. Edwards.—Mary was surrounded by Red

---

1 A drink usually made from fortified wine mixed with hot water, sweetened with sugar, and sometimes flavoured with spices; it was often served at balls as refreshment.

coats[1] the whole Evening. I should have been better pleased to see her dancing with some of our old Neighbours I confess.—" "Yes, yes, we must not neglect our old Neighbours—. But if these Soldiers are quicker than other people in a Ball room, what are young Ladies to do?" "I think there is no occasion for their engaging themselves so many Dances before hand, Mr. Edwards."—"No—perhaps not—but I remember my dear when you and I did the same."—Mrs. Edwards said no more, and Mary breathed again.—A great deal of goodhumoured pleasantry followed—and Emma went to bed in charming Spirits, her head full of Osbornes, Blakes and Howards.—

The next morning brought a great many visitors. It was the way of the place always to call on Mrs. Edwards on the morning after a Ball, and this neighbourly inclination was increased in the present instance by a general spirit of curiosity on Emma's account, as Everybody wanted to look again at the girl who had been admired the night before by Lord Osborne—. Many were the eyes, and various the degrees of approbation with which she was examined. Some saw no fault, and some no Beauty—. With some her brown skin was the annihilation of every grace, and others could never be persuaded that she were half so handsome as Elizabeth Watson had been ten years ago.—The morning passed quietly away in discussing the merits of the Ball with all this succession of Company—and Emma was at once astonished by finding it Two o'clock, and considering that she had heard nothing of her Father's Chair. After this discovery she had walked twice to the window to examine the Street, and was on the point of asking leave to ring the bell and make enquiries, when the light sound of a Carriage driving up to the door set her heart at ease. She stepd again to the window—but instead of the convenient tho' very un-smart Family Equipage perceived a neat Curricle.[2]—Mr. Musgrave was shortly afterwards announced;—and Mrs. Edwards put on her very stiffest look at the sound.—Not at all dismayed however by her chilling air, he paid his Compliments to each of the Ladies with no unbecoming Ease, and continuing to address Emma, presented her a note, which he had

---

1 Part of the distinctive uniform of the army, and generally recognised as a dangerous attraction to young ladies. Lydia Bennet's excited dreams of Brighton include the soldiers' camp, "crowded with the young and the gay, and dazzling with scarlet" (*Pride and Prejudice*, Vol. 2, ch. 18).

2 A light two-wheeled carriage drawn by two horses abreast, generally considered fashionable for a young man to drive.

"the honour of bringing from her Sister; But to which he must observe that a verbal postscript from himself would be requisite."—The note, which Emma was beginning to read rather *before* Mrs. Edwards had entreated her to use no ceremony, contained a few lines from Elizabeth importing that their Father in consequence of being unusually well had taken the sudden resolution of attending the visitation[1] that day, and that as his Road lay quite wide from R.,[2] it was impossible for her to come home till the following morning, unless the Edwardses would send her which was hardly to be expected, or she could meet with any chance conveyance, or did not mind walking so far.—She had scarcely run her eye thro' the whole, before she found herself obliged to listen to Tom Musgrave's farther account. "I received that note from the fair hands of Miss Watson only ten minutes ago, said he—I met her in the village of Stanton, whither my good Stars prompted me to turn my Horses heads—she was at that moment in quest of a person to employ on the Errand, and I was fortunate enough to convince her that she could not find a more willing or speedy Messenger than myself—. Remember, I say nothing of my Disinterestedness.—My reward is to be the indulgence of conveying you to Stanton in my Curricle.—Tho' they are not written down, I bring your Sister's Orders for the same.—"
Emma felt distressed; she did not like the proposal—she did not wish to be on terms of intimacy with the Proposer—and yet fearful of encroaching on the Edwardes', as well as wishing to go home herself, she was at a loss how entirely to decline what he offered—. Mrs. Edwards continued silent, either not understanding the case, or waiting to see how the young Lady's inclination lay. Emma thanked him—but professed herself very unwilling to give him so much trouble. "The Trouble was of course, Honour, Pleasure, Delight. What had he or his Horses to do?"—Still she hesitated. "She beleived she must beg leave to decline his assistance—She was rather afraid of the sort of carriage—. The distance was not beyond a walk.—"—Mrs. Edwards was silent no longer. She enquired into the particulars—and then said "We shall be extremely happy Miss Emma, if you can give us the pleasure of your company till tomorrow—but if you can not con-

---

1 A meeting or gathering connected to a regular visit by a bishop or archdeacon to examine into the affairs of the parish. JA, as the daughter, sister, and cousin of clergymen, must have been very familiar with such events.

2 Presumably this should be "D.," as above. See p. 271, note 2.

veniently do so, our Carriage is quite at your Service, and Mary
will be pleased with the opportunity of seeing your Sister."—This
was precisely what Emma had longed for, and she accepted the
offer most thankfully; acknowledging that as Elizabeth was
entirely alone, it was her wish to return home to dinner.—The
plan was warmly opposed by their visitor. "I cannot suffer it
indeed. I must not be deprived of the happiness of escorting you.
I assure you there is not a possibility of fear with my Horses. You
might guide them yourself. *Your Sisters* all know how quiet they
are; They have none of them the smallest scruple in trusting themselves with me, even on a Race-Course.—Beleive me—added he
lowering his voice—*You* are quite safe, the danger is only *mine*."—
Emma was not more disposed to oblige him for all this.—"And as
to Mrs. Edwardes' carriage being used the day after a Ball, it is a
thing quite out of rule I assure you—never heard of before—the
old Coachman will look as black as his Horses—. Won't he Miss
Edwards?"—No notice was taken. The Ladies were silently firm,
and the gentleman found himself obliged to submit.—"What a
famous Ball we had last night!—he cried, after a short pause. How
long did you keep it up, after the Osbornes and I went away?"—
"We had two dances more."—"It is making it too much of a
fatigue I think, to stay so late.—I suppose your Set was not a very
full one."—"Yes, quite as full as ever, except the Osbornes. There
seemed no vacancy anywhere—and everybody danced with
uncommon spirit to the very last."—Emma said this—tho' against
her conscience.—"Indeed! perhaps I might have looked in upon
you again, if I had been aware of as much;—for I am rather fond
of dancing than not.—Miss Osborne is a charming girl, is not
she?" "I do not think her handsome," replied Emma, to whom all
this was cheifly addressed. "Perhaps she is not critically[1] handsome, but her Manners are delightful. And Fanny Carr is a most
interesting little creature. You can imagine nothing more *naive* or
piquante; and what do you think of *Lord Osborne* Miss Watson?"
"That he would be handsome even, tho' he were *not* a Lord—and
perhaps—better bred; more desirous of pleasing, and shewing
himself pleased in a right place.—" "Upon my word, you are
severe upon my friend!—I assure you Lord Osborne is a very good
fellow."—"I do not dispute his virtues—but I do not like his careless air."—"If it were not a breach of confidence, replied Tom with
an important look, perhaps I might be able to win a more
favourable opinion of poor Osborne.—" Emma gave him no

---

1 Precisely; by the standards of critical judgement.

Encouragement, and he was obliged to keep his friend's secret.—
He was also obliged to put an end to his visit—for Mrs. Edwards'
having ordered her Carriage, there was no time to be lost on
Emma's side in preparing for it.—Miss Edwards accompanied her
home, but as it was Dinner hour at Stanton, staid with them only
a few minutes.—"Now my dear Emma, said Miss Watson, as soon
as they were alone, you must talk to me all the rest of the day, without stopping, or I shall not be satisfied. But first of all Nanny shall
bring in the dinner. Poor thing!—You will not dine as you did yesterday, for we have nothing but some fried beef.—How nice Mary
Edwards looks in her new pelisse![1]—And now tell me how you like
them all, and what I am to say to Sam. I have begun my Letter,
Jack Stokes is to call for it tomorrow, for his Uncle is going within
a mile of Guilford the next day.[2]—" Nanny brought in the dinner;—"We will wait upon ourselves, continued Elizabeth, and then
we shall lose no time.—And so, you would not come home with
Tom Musgrave?"—"No. You had said so much against him that I
could not wish either for the obligation, or the Intimacy which the
use of his Carriage must have created—. I should not even have
liked the appearance of it."—"You did very right; tho' I wonder at
your forbearance, and I do not think I could have done it myself.—
He seemed so eager to fetch you, that I could not say no, tho' it
rather went against me to be throwing you together, so well as I
knew his Tricks;—but I did long to see you, and it was a clever way
of getting you home; Besides—it wont do to be too nice.—Nobody
could have thought of the Edwards' letting you have their
Coach,—after the Horses being out so late.—But what am I to say
to Sam?"—"If you are guided by me, you will not encourage him
to think of Miss Edwards.—The Father is decidedly against him,
the Mother shews him no favour, and I doubt his having any interest with Mary. She danced twice with Captain Hunter, and I think
shews him in general as much Encouragement as is consistent
with her disposition, and the circumstances she is placed in.—She
once mentioned Sam, and certainly with a little confusion—but
that was perhaps merely oweing to the consciousness of his liking
her, which may very probably have come to her knowledge."—

---

1 A long cloak, with slits for armholes, and a shoulder-cape or hood, an
essential item of clothing for genteel women of the period.

2 Charges for mail sent through the formal system depended on the distance involved and the weight of the letter (double rates were payable on
two-sheet letters, and so on), and were paid by the recipient, so it was
very common to send letters informally by travellers, as here.

"Oh! dear! yes—she has heard enough of that from us all. Poor Sam!—He is out of luck as well as other people.—For the life of me Emma, I cannot help feeling for those that are cross'd in Love.—Well—now begin, and give me an account of every thing as it happened.—" Emma obeyed her—and Elizabeth listened with very little interruption till she heard of Mr. Howard as a partner.—"Dance with Mr. Howard.—Good Heavens! You don't say so!—Why—He is quite one of the great and Grand ones;—Did not you find him very high?[1]—" "His manners are of a kind to give *me* much more Ease and confidence than Tom Musgraves." "Well—go on. I should have been frightened out of my wits, to have had anything to do with the Osborne's set."—Emma concluded her narration.—"And so, you really did not dance with Tom Musgrave at all?—But you must have liked him, you must have been struck with him altogether."—"I do *not* like him, Elizabeth—. I allow his person and air to be good—and that his manners to a certain point—his address[2] rather—is pleasing.—But I see nothing else to admire in him.—On the contrary, he seems very vain, very conceited, absurdly anxious for Distinction, and absolutely contemptible in some of the measures he takes for becoming so.—There is a ridiculousness about him that entertains me—but his company gives me no other agreable Emotion."— "My dearest Emma!—You are like nobody else in the World.—It is well Margaret is not by.—You do not offend *me*, tho' I hardly know how to beleive you. But Margaret would never forgive such words." "I wish Margaret could have heard him profess his ignorance of her being out of the Country;[3]—he declared it seemed only two days since he had seen her.—" "Aye—that is just like him, and yet this is the Man, she *will* fancy so desperately in love with her.—He is no favourite of mine, as you well know, Emma;—but you must think him agreable. Can you lay your hand on your heart, and say you do not?"—"Indeed I can. Both Hands; and spread to their widest extent.—" "I should like to know the Man you *do* think agreable." "His name is Howard." "Howard! Dear me. I cannot think of *him*, but as playing cards with Lady Osborne, and looking proud.—I must own however that it *is* a releif to me, to find you can speak as you do, of Tom Musgrave; my heart did misgive me that you would like him too well. You talked so stoutly beforehand, that I was sadly afraid your

---

1 Lofty; arrogant.
2 Manner of speaking and behaving.
3 Away from the neighbourhood.

Brag would be punished.—I only hope it will last;—and that he will not come on to pay you much attention; it is a hard thing for a woman to stand against the flattering ways of a Man, when he is bent upon pleasing her.—" As their quietly-sociable little meal concluded, Miss Watson could not help observing how comfortably it had passed. "It is so delightful to me, said she, to have Things going on in peace and goodhumour. Nobody can tell how much I hate quarrelling. Now, tho' we have had nothing but fried beef, how good it has all seemed.—I wish everybody were as easily satisfied as you—but poor Margaret is very snappish, and Penelope owns she had rather have Quarrelling going on, than nothing at all."—Mr. Watson returned in the Evening, not the worse for the exertion of the day, and consequently pleased with what he had done, and glad to talk of it, over his own Fireside.— Emma had not foreseen any interest to herself in the occurrences of a Visitation—but when she heard Mr. Howard spoken of as the Preacher, and as having given them an excellent Sermon, she could not help listening with a quicker Ear.—"I do not know when I have heard a Discourse more to my mind—continued Mr. Watson—or one better delivered.—He reads extremely well, with great propriety and in a very impressive manner; and at the same time without any Theatrical grimace or violence.—I own, I do not like much action in the pulpit—I do not like the studied air and artificial inflexions of voice, which your very popular and most admired Preachers generally have.—A simple delivery is much better calculated to inspire Devotion, and shews a much better Taste.[1]—Mr. Howard read like a Scholar and a gentleman."—"And what had you for dinner Sir?"—said his eldest

---

1 Churchgoing was the norm in early nineteenth-century England, and fashionable or popular preachers commanded a wide audience; evangelicals were particularly known for their fiery and dramatic oratory. The way in which sermons were delivered was a matter of study and debate, and JA here seems to support traditional arguments against new ideas. Hugh Blair's influential *Lectures on Rhetoric and Belles Lettres* (2 vols, 1783) included a lecture on "Eloquence in the Pulpit" that acknowledged the difficulty of getting the tone right—"The Grave, when it is predominant, is apt to run into a dull uniform solemnity. The Warm, when it wants gravity, borders on the theatrical"—and warns against simply following the fashions set by popular preachers. Blair insists that the purpose of preaching is "to give ... at once, clear views, and persuasive impressions of religious truth." He did not, however, approve of sermons being read rather than given from memory or expanded from notes (Vol. 2, pp. 107, 105, 118).

Daughter.—He related the Dishes and told what he had ate himself.[1] "Upon the whole, he added, I have had a very comfortable day; my old friends were quite surprised to see me amongst them—and I must say that everybody paid me great attention, and seemed to feel for me as an Invalid.—They would make me sit near the fire, and as the partridges were pretty high,[2] Dr. Richards would have them sent away to the other end of the Table, that they might not offend Mr. Watson—which I thought very kind of him.—But what pleased me as much as anything was Mr. Howard's attention;—There is a pretty steep flight of steps up to the room we dine in—which do not quite agree with my gouty foot[3]—and Mr. Howard walked by me from the bottom to the top, and would make me take his arm.—It struck me as very becoming in so young a Man, but I am sure I had no claim to expect it; for I never saw him before in my Life.—By the bye, he enquired after one of my Daughters, but I do not know which. I suppose you know among yourselves."—

———

On the third day after the Ball, as Nanny at five minutes before three, was beginning to bustle into the parlour with the Tray and the Knife-case, she was suddenly called to the front door, by the sound of as smart a rap as the end of a riding-whip could give—and tho' charged by Miss Watson to let nobody in, returned in half a minute, with a look of awkward dismay, to hold the parlour door open for Lord Osborne and Tom Musgrave.—The Surprise of the young Ladies may be imagined. No visitors would have been welcome at such a moment; but such visitors as these—such a one as Lord Osborne at least, a nobleman and a stranger, was really distressing.—He looked a little embarrassed himself,—as,

---

1 A formal public dinner would include a large number of dishes, but there might be two courses at most, each offering an array of sweet and savoury dishes. The host would supervise the initial serving of soup and would carve the large joints of meat, after which diners would help themselves to the dishes they wished to eat; they were not expected to taste everything.

2 Game birds were generally hung for several days after being killed in order for the meat to develop a stronger, richer flavour. As a result they could smell strongly.

3 Gout, now recognised as a form of arthritis, was a very common ailment, particularly among elderly and sedentary men.

on being introduced by his easy, voluble friend, he muttered something of doing himself the honour of waiting on Mr. Watson.[1]—Tho' Emma could not but take the compliment of the visit to herself, she was very far from enjoying it. She felt all the inconsistency of such an acquaintance with the very humble stile in which they were obliged to live; and having in her Aunt's family been used to many of the Elegancies of Life, was fully sensible of all that must be open to the ridicule of Richer people in her present home.—Of the pain of such feelings, Elizabeth knew very little;—her simpler Mind, or juster reason saved her from such mortification—and tho' shrinking under a general sense of Inferiority, she felt no particular Shame.—Mr. Watson, as the Gentlemen had already heard from Nanny, was not well enough to be down stairs;—With much concern they took their seats—Lord Osborne near Emma, and the convenient Mr. Musgrave in high spirits at his own importance, on the other side of the fireplace with Elizabeth.—*He* was at no loss for words;—but when Lord Osborne had hoped that Emma had not caught cold at the Ball, he had nothing more to say for some time, and could only gratify his Eye by occasional glances at his fair neighbour.—Emma was not inclined to give herself much trouble for his Entertainment—and after hard labour of mind, he produced the remark of it's being a very fine day, and followed it up with the question of, "Have you been walking this morning?" "No, my Lord. We thought it too dirty." "You should wear half-boots."[2]—After another pause, "Nothing sets off a neat ancle more than a half-boot; nankin galoshed with black[3] looks very well.—Do not you like Half-boots?" "Yes—but unless they are so stout as to injure their beauty, they are not fit for country walking.—" "Ladies should ride in dirty weather.—Do you ride?" "No my Lord." "I wonder every Lady does not.—A woman never looks better than on horseback.—" "But every woman may not have the inclina-

---

1 It was usual for a gentleman to call on his partner after a ball, but Lord Osborne had not danced with Emma Watson, and his statement that he is "waiting on," or making a formal visit to, Mr. Watson creates social awkwardness, since the two have been neighbours for more than a decade without being on such terms.

2 High shoes reaching well above the ankle and fastened by laces at the front were popular.

3 Nankin is a yellowish cotton cloth originating in Nanking, China. A galosh is a piece of leather running round the lower part of the boot above the sole. The boots would be fashionable, but not very practical.

tion, or the means." "If they knew how much it became them, they would all have the inclination—and I fancy Miss Watson—when once they had the inclination, the means would soon follow."—"Your Lordship thinks we always have our own way.— *That* is a point on which Ladies and Gentlemen have long disagreed—But without pretending to decide it, I may say that there are some circumstances which even *Women* cannot controul.—Female Economy will do a great deal my Lord, but it cannot turn a small income into a large one."—Lord Osborne was silenced. Her manner had been neither sententious nor sarcastic, but there was a something in its' mild seriousness, as well as in the words themselves which made his Lordship think;—and when he addressed her again, it was with a degree of considerate propriety, totally unlike the half-awkward, half-fearless stile of his former remarks.—It was a new thing with him to wish to please a woman; it was the first time that he had ever felt what was due to a woman, in Emma's situation.—But as he wanted neither Sense nor a good disposition, he did not feel it without effect.— "You have not been long in this Country I understand, said he in the tone of a Gentleman. I hope you are pleased with it."—He was rewarded by a gracious answer, and a more liberal full veiw of her face than she had yet bestowed. Unused to exert himself, and happy in contemplating her, he then sat in silence for some minutes longer, while Tom Musgrave was chattering to Elizabeth, till they were interrupted by Nanny's approach, who half opening the door and putting in her head, said "Please Ma'am, Master wants to know why he be'nt to have his dinner."—The Gentlemen, who had hitherto disregarded every symptom, however positive, of the nearness of that Meal, now jumped up with apologies, while Elizabeth called briskly after Nanny "to tell Betty to take up the Fowls."—"I am sorry it happens so—she added, turning goodhumouredly towards Musgrave—but you know what early hours we keep.—" Tom had nothing to say for himself, he knew it very well, and such honest simplicity, such shameless Truth rather bewildered him.—Lord Osborne's parting Compliments took some time, his inclination for speech seeming to increase with the shortness of the term for indulgence.—He recommended Exercise in defiance of dirt—spoke again in praise of Half-boots—begged that his Sister might be allow'd to send Emma the name of her Shoemaker—and concluded with saying, "My Hounds will be hunting this Country next week—I beleive they will throw off at Stanton Wood on Wednesday at nine o'clock.[1]—I mention this, in hopes of your being drawn out to see what's going on.—If the morning's tolerable, pray do us the honour of giving us your good wishes in person."[2]—The Sisters looked on each other with astonishment, when their Visitors had withdrawn. "Here's an unaccountable Honour! cried Elizabeth at last. Who would have thought of Lord Osborne's coming to Stanton.—He is very handsome;—but Tom Musgrave looks all to nothing, the smartest and most fashionable man of the two. I am glad he did not say anything to me; I would not have had to talk to such a great man for the world. Tom was very agreable, was not he?—But did you hear him ask where Miss Penelope and Miss Margaret were, when he first came in?—It put me out of patience.—I am glad Nanny had not laid the Cloth however, it would have looked so awkward;—just the Tray did not signify.—"

To say that Emma was not flattered by Lord Osborne's visit, would be to assert a very unlikely thing, and describe a very odd young Lady; but the gratification was by no means unalloyed. His coming was a sort of notice which might please her vanity, but did not suit her pride, and she would rather have known that he wished the visit without presuming to make it, than have seen him at Stanton.—Among other unsatisfactory feelings it once occurred to her to wonder why Mr. Howard had not taken the same privilege of coming, and accompanied his Lordship—but she was willing to suppose that he had either known nothing about it, or had declined any share in a measure which carried quite as much Impertinence in it's form as Good breeding.[3]— Mr. Watson was very far from being delighted, when he heard what had passed;—a little peevish under immediate pain, and illdisposed to be pleased, he only replied—"Phoo! Phoo!—What occasion could there be for Lord Osborne's coming. I have lived

---

1 To "throw off" was to free the hounds from their leashes, and so begin the hunt. In the early nineteenth century, 9:00 a.m. was the usual time to begin the hunt.

2 The hunt would usually begin outside at an inn or other landmark, and it was customary for local people to gather to see the colourful and lively spectacle of horsemen, horses, and hounds.

3 The Osbornes and the Watsons, despite living near each other for years, have not been on visiting terms. This would have been the choice of the Osbornes, who, as the socially superior family, would have had to make the first visit. The Watsons should now, by protocol, return the visit, but this is awkward, as the purpose of Lord Osborne's visit is unclear.

here fourteen years without being noticed by any of the family. It is some foolery of that idle fellow Tom Musgrave. I cannot return the visit.—I would not if I could." And when Tom Musgrave was met with again, he was commissioned with a message of excuse to Osborne Castle, on the too-sufficient plea of Mr. Watson's infirm state of health.—A week or ten days rolled quietly away after this visit, before any new bustle arose to interrupt even for half a day, the tranquil and affectionate intercourse of the two Sisters, whose mutual regard was increasing with the intimate knowledge of each other which such intercourse produced.—The first circumstance to break in on this serenity, was the receipt of a letter from Croydon to announce the speedy return of Margaret, and a visit of two or three days from Mr. and Mrs. Robert Watson who undertook to bring her home and wished to see their Sister Emma.—It was an expectation to fill the thoughts of the Sisters at Stanton, and to busy the hours of one of them at least— for as Jane had been a woman of fortune, the preparations for her entertainment were considerable, and as Elizabeth had at all times more good will than method in her guidance of the house, she could make no change without a Bustle.—An absence of fourteen years had made all her Brothers and Sisters Strangers to Emma, but in her expectation of Margaret there was more than the awkwardness of such an alienation; she had heard things which made her dread her return; and the day which brought the party to Stanton seemed to her the probable conclusion of almost all that had been comfortable in the house.—Robert Watson was an Attorney at Croydon, in a good way of Business; very well satisfied with himself for the same, and for having married the only daughter of the attorney to whom he had been Clerk, with a fortune of six thousand pounds.[1]—Mrs. Robert was not less pleased with herself for having had that six thousand pounds, and for being now in possession of a very smart house in Croydon, where she gave genteel parties, and wore fine Cloathes.—In her person there was nothing remarkable; her manners were pert and conceited.—Margaret was not without beauty; she had a slight,

---

1 An attorney, or solicitor, was a dignified profession in local urban circles, though modest in terms of the social standards of the gentry. In *Pride and Prejudice*, Mrs. Bennet's father, an attorney in the local town of Meryton, had left her £4,000; her sister had married Mr. Phillips, "who had been a clerk to their father, and succeeded him in the business" (Vol. 1, ch. 7), a connection that the Bingley sisters describe as "low" (Vol. 1, ch. 8).

pretty figure, and rather wanted Countenance[1] than good features;—but the sharp and anxious expression of her face, made her beauty in general little felt.—On meeting her long-absent Sister, as on every occasion of shew, her manner was all affection and her voice all gentleness; continual smiles and a very slow articulation being her constant resource when determined on pleasing.—

She was now so "delighted to see dear, dear Emma" that she could hardly speak a word in a minute.—"I am sure we shall be great friends"—she observed, with much sentiment, as they were sitting together.—Emma scarcely knew how to answer such a proposition—and the manner in which it was spoken, she could not attempt to equal. Mrs. Robert Watson eyed her with much familiar curiosity and Triumphant Compassion;—the loss of the Aunt's fortune was uppermost in her mind, at the moment of meeting;—and she could not but feel how much better it was to be the daughter of a gentlemen of property in Croydon, than the neice of an old woman who threw herself away on an Irish Captain.—Robert was carelessly kind, as became a prosperous Man and a brother; more intent on settling with the Post-Boy, inveighing against the Exorbitant advance in Posting,[2] and pondering over a doubtful halfcrown,[3] than on welcoming a Sister, who was no longer likely to have any property for him to get the direction of.—"Your road through the village is infamous, Elizabeth, said he; worse than ever it was. By Heaven! I would endite it if I lived near you. Who is Surveyor now?"[4]—There was a little neice at Croydon, to be fondly enquired after by the kind-hearted Elizabeth, who regretted very much her not being of the party.—"You are very good—replied her Mother—and I assure you it went very hard with Augusta to have us come away without her. I was

---

1 Appropriate demeanour, including facial expression.
2 Robert and his wife have evidently travelled "post," that is, by hired carriage. They would probably have hired a carriage to take them to the nearest main posting inn, and then another to bring them to the Watsons' house, so Robert needs to pay for the journey. The post-boy, or postilion, would ride on one of the horses to assist the carriage driver.
3 A possibly counterfeit half-crown. A half-crown was a coin worth two shillings and sixpence (so that there were eight half-crowns in a pound). The counterfeiting of silver coins was a particular problem during the early nineteenth-century war years, because of the scarcity of raw silver.
4 The parish was responsible for local roads, which were maintained on the advice of a Surveyor appointed for the purpose. To endite (now more usually spelt "indict") is to bring a legal prosecution.

forced to say we were only going to Church and promise to come back for her directly.—But you know it would not do, to bring her without her maid, and I am as particular as ever in having her properly attended to." "Sweet little Darling!—cried Margaret—It quite broke my heart to leave her.—" "Then why was you in such a hurry to run away from her?" cried Mrs. Robert—"You are a sad shabby girl.—I have been quarrelling with you all the way we came, have not I?—Such a visit as this, I never heard of!—You know how glad we are to have any of you with us—if it be for months together—and I am sorry, (with a witty smile) we have not been able to make Croydon agreable this Autumn."—"My dearest Jane—do not overpower me with your Raillery.—You know what inducements I had to bring me home.—Spare me, I entreat you—I am no match for your arch sallies."[1]—"Well, I only beg you will not set your Neighbours against the place.—Perhaps Emma may be tempted to go back with us, and stay till Christmas, if you do'nt put in your word."—Emma was greatly obliged. "I assure you we have very good society at Croydon.—I do not much attend the Balls, they are rather too mixed,[2]—but our parties are very select and good.—I had seven Tables[3] last week in my Drawingroom.—Are you fond of the Country? How do you like Stanton?"—"Very much"—replied Emma, who thought a comprehensive answer, most to the purpose.—She saw that her Sister in law despised her immediately.—Mrs. Robert Watson was indeed wondering what sort of a home Emma could possibly have been used to in Shropshire, and setting it down as certain that the Aunt could never have had six thousand pounds.—"How charming Emma is!—" whispered Margaret to Mrs. Robert in her most languishing tone.—Emma was quite distressed by such behaviour;—and she did not like it better when she heard Margaret five minutes afterwards say to Elizabeth in a sharp quick accent, totally unlike the first—"Have you heard from Penelope since she went to Chichester?—I had a letter the other day.—I do'nt find she is likely to make anything of it. I fancy she'll come back 'Miss Penelope' as she went.—"—Such, she feared would be Margaret's common voice, when the novelty

---

1 Margaret's mannered vocabulary and phrasing are strongly reminiscent of eighteenth-century sentimental literary works, which were themselves indebted to the novels of Samuel Richardson.

2 Open to a wide range of people, including some that Mrs. Robert clearly sees as socially undesirable.

3 For cards. Each would accommodate four people, probably for whist.

of her own appearance were over; the tone of artificial Sensibility was not recommended by the idea.—The Ladies were invited upstairs to prepare for dinner. "I hope you will find things tolerably comfortable Jane"—said Elizabeth as she opened the door of the spare bedchamber.—"My good Creature, replied Jane, use no ceremony with me, I intreat you. I am one of those who always take things as they find them. I hope I can put up with a small apartment for two or three nights, without making a peice of work. I always wish to be treated quite 'en famille' when I come to see you—and now I do hope you have not been getting a great dinner for us.—Remember we never eat Suppers."[1]—"I suppose, said Margaret rather quickly to Emma, You and I are to be together; Elizabeth always takes care to have a room to herself."—"No—Elizabeth gives me half her's."[2]—"Oh!—(in a soften'd voice, and rather mortified to find that she was not ill used) "I am sorry I am not to have the pleasure of your company—especially as it makes me nervous to be much alone."

Emma was the first of the females in the parlour again; on entering it she found her brother alone.—"So Emma, said he, you are quite the Stranger at home. It must seem odd enough to you to be here.—A pretty peice of work your Aunt Turner has made of it!—By Heaven! a woman should never be trusted with money. I always said she ought to have settled something on you, as soon as her Husband died." "But that would have been trusting *me* with money, replied Emma, and *I* am a woman too.—" "It might have been secured to your future use, without your having any power over it now.—What a blow it must have been upon you!—To find yourself, instead of Heiress of eight or nine thousand pounds, sent back a weight upon your family, without a sixpence.—I hope the old woman will smart for it." "Do not speak disrespectfully of her—She was very good to me; and if she has made an imprudent choice, she will suffer more from it herself, than *I* can possibly do." "I do not mean to distress you, but you know every body must think her an old fool.—I thought Turner had been reckoned an extraordinary sensible, clever Man.—How the Devil came he to make such a will?"—"My Uncle's Sense is not at all impeached in my opinion, by his attachment to my

---

1 Dinner, the main meal, eaten in the afternoon or early evening, was supplemented by an informal light or cold supper later.
2 Space requirements were at a premium, given the large families of the time. Girls routinely shared a bedroom into adulthood, as JA herself did with her sister Cassandra.

Aunt. She had been an excellent wife to him. The most Liberal and enlightened minds are always the most confiding.—The event has been unfortunate, but my Uncle's memory is if possible endeared to me by such a proof of tender respect for my Aunt."—"That's odd sort of Talking!—He might have provided decently for his widow, without leaving every thing that he had to dispose of, or any part of it, at her mercy."—"My Aunt may have erred—said Emma warmly—she *has* erred—but my Uncle's conduct was faultless. I was her own Neice, and he left to herself the power and the pleasure of providing for me."—"But unluckily she has left the pleasure of providing for you, to your Father and without the power.—That's the long and the short of the business. After keeping you at a distance from your family for such a length of time as must do away all natural affection among us and breeding you up (I suppose) in a superior stile, you are returned upon their hands without a sixpence." "You know, replied Emma struggling with her tears, my Uncle's melancholy state of health.—He was a greater Invalid than my father. He could not leave home." "I do not mean to make you cry—" said Robert rather softened—and after a short silence, by way of changing the subject, he added—"I am just come from my Father's room, he seems very indifferent.[1] It will be a sad break-up when he dies. Pity, you can none of you get married!—You must come to Croydon as well as the rest, and see what you can do there.—I beleive if Margaret had had a thousand or fifteen hundred pounds, there was a young man who would have thought of her." Emma was glad when they were joined by the others; it was better to look at her Sister in law's finery, than listen to Robert, who had equally irritated and greived her.—Mrs. Robert exactly as smart as she had been at her own party, came in with apologies for her dress— "I would not make you wait, said she, so I put on the first thing I met with.—I am afraid I am a sad figure.—My dear Mr. Watson—(to her husband) you have not put any fresh powder in your hair."[2]—"No—I do not intend it.—I think there is powder enough in my hair for my wife and Sisters."—"Indeed you ought to make some alteration in your dress before dinner when you are out visitting, tho' you do not at home." "Nonsense.—" "It is very odd you should not like to do what other gentlemen do. Mr. Mar-

---

1 In poor health.
2 See p. 279, note 2.

shall and Mr. Hemmings change their dress every day of their Lives before dinner. And what was the use of my putting up[1] your last new Coat, if you are never to wear it."—"Do be satisfied with being fine yourself, and leave your husband alone."—To put an end to this altercation, and soften the evident vexation of her Sister in law, Emma (tho' in no Spirits to make such nonsense easy) began to admire her gown.—It produced immediate complacency.—"Do you like it?—said she.—I am very happy.—It has been excessively admired;—but sometimes I think the pattern too large.—I shall wear one tomorrow that I think you will prefer to this.—Have you seen the one I gave Margaret?—"

Dinner came, and except when Mrs. Robert looked at her husband's head, she continued gay and flippant, chiding Elizabeth for the profusion on the Table, and absolutely protesting against the entrance of the roast Turkey—which formed the only exception to "You see your dinner".[2]—"I do beg and entreat that no Turkey may be seen to day. I am really frightened out of my wits with the number of dishes we have already. Let us have no Turkey I beseech you."—"My dear, replied Elizabeth, the Turkey is roasted, and it may just as well come in, as stay in the Kitchen. Besides if it is cut, I am in hopes my Father may be tempted to eat a bit, for it is rather a favourite dish." "You may have it in my dear, but I assure you *I* sha'nt touch it."—

Mr. Watson had not been well enough to join the party at dinner, but was prevailed on to come down and drink tea with them.—"I wish we may be able to have a game of cards tonight," said Elizabeth to Mrs. Robert after seeing her father comfortably seated in his arm chair.—"Not on my account my dear, I beg. You know I am no card player. I think a snug chat infinitely better. I always say Cards are very well sometimes, to break a formal circle, but one never wants them among friends." "I was thinking of its' being something to amuse my father, answered Elizabeth—if it was not disagreable to you. He says his head won't bear Whist—but perhaps if we make a round game[3] he may be tempted to sit down with us.—" "By all means my dear Creature. I am quite at your service. Only do not oblige me to chuse the

---

1 Packing to bring.
2 Dishes were usually served together (see p. 300, note 1); evidently the turkey, as a special treat, was to be brought in separately.
3 A game, usually of cards and with fairly simple rules, in which any number of players could play individually.

game, that's all. *Speculation*[1] is the only round game at Croydon now, but I can play any thing.—When there is only one or two of you at home, you must be quite at a loss to amuse him—why do not you get him to play at Cribbage?[2]—Margaret and I have played at Cribbage, most nights that we have not been engaged."—A sound like a distant Carriage was at this moment caught; every body listened, it became more decided; it certainly drew nearer.—It was an unusual sound in Stanton at any time of the day, for the Village was on no very public road, and contained no gentleman's family but the Rector's.—The wheels rapidly approached;—in two minutes the general expectation was answered; they stopped beyond a doubt at the garden gate of the Parsonage. "Who could it be?—it was certainly a postchaise.[3]— Penelope was the only creature to be thought of. She might perhaps have met with some unexpected opportunity of returning."—A pause of suspense ensued.—Steps were distinguished, first along the paved Footway which led under the windows of the house to the front door, and then within the passage. They were the Steps of a man. It could not be Penelope. It must be Samuel.—The door opened, and displayed Tom Musgrave in the wrap of a Travellor.—He had been in London and was now on his way home, and he had come half a mile out of his road merely to call for ten minutes at Stanton. He loved to take people by surprise, with sudden visits at extraordinary seasons; and in the present instance had had the additional motive of being able to tell the Miss Watsons, whom he depended on finding sitting quietly employed after tea, that he was going home to an eight o'clock dinner.—As it happened however, he did not give more surprise than he received, when instead of being shewn into the usual little Sitting room, the door of the best parlour a foot larger each way than the other was thrown open, and he beheld a circle of smart people whom he could not immediately recognize arranged with all the honours of visiting round the fire, and Miss

---

1   A card game involving the trading of trump cards with "fish," or coun-
    ters. It was simple, popular with families, and could be noisy. In *Mans-
    field Park*, the Bertrams and their guests enjoy a lively game of Specula-
    tion (Vol. 2, ch. 7).

2   A game, usually for two players, in which cards attract varying number
    of points depending on the way they are collected and grouped. It is rel-
    atively quiet, and requires some skill and concentration.

3   A travelling carriage, possibly hired, in which the occupants might travel
    long distances.

Watson sitting at the best Pembroke Table,[1] with the best Tea things before her. He stood a few seconds, in silent amazement.—"Musgrave!"—ejaculated Margaret in a tender voice.—He recollected himself, and came forward, delighted to find such a circle of Friends, and blessing his good fortune for the unlooked-for Indulgence.—He shook hands with Robert, bowed and smiled to the Ladies, and did everything very prettily; but as to any particularity of address or Emotion towards Margaret, Emma who closely observed him, perceived nothing that did not justify Elizabeth's opinions tho' Margaret's modest smiles imported that she meant to take the visit to herself.—He was persuaded without much difficulty to throw off his great coat, and drink tea with them. "For whether he dined at eight or nine, as he observed, was a matter of very little consequence"—and without seeming to seek, he did not turn away from the chair close to Margaret which she was assiduous in providing him.—She had thus secured him from her Sisters—but it was not immediately in her power to preserve him from her Brother's claims, for as he came avowedly from London, and had left it only four hours ago, the last current report as to public news, and the general opinion of the day must be understood, before Robert could let his attention be yeilded to the less national, and important demands of the Women.—At last however he was at liberty to hear Margaret's soft address, as she spoke her fears of his having had a most terrible, cold, dark dreadful Journey.—"Indeed you should not have set out so late.—" "I could not be earlier, he replied. I was detained chatting at the Bedford,[2] by a friend.—All hours are alike to me.—How long have you been in the Country Miss Margaret?"—"We came only this morning—My kind Brother and Sister brought me home this very morning.—'Tis singular is not it?" "You were gone a great while, were not you? a fortnight I suppose?"—"*You* may call a fortnight a great while Mr. Musgrave, said Mrs. Robert smartly—but *we* think a month very little. I assure you we bring her home at the end of a month, much against our will." "A month! have you really been gone a Month! 'tis amazing how Time flies.—" "You may imagine, said Margaret

---

1 A small table with a hinged drop-leaf on each side, useful in a limited space because it could be expanded for use and then folded away.

2 Bedford Coffee House, operating since the early eighteenth century on a site adjoining the Covent Garden Theatre. John Thorpe, aspiring to fashion, claims to have met General Tilney "for ever" at the Bedford (*Northanger Abbey*, Vol. 1, ch. 12).

in a sort of Whisper, what are my Sensations in finding myself once more at Stanton. You know what a sad visitor I make.—And I was so excessively impatient to see Emma;—I dreaded the meeting, and at the same time longed for it.—Do not you comprehend the sort of feeling?"—"Not at all, cried he aloud. I could never dread a meeting with Miss Emma Watson,—or any of her Sisters." It was lucky that he added that finish.—"Were you speaking to me?—"said Emma, who had caught her own name.—"Not absolutely—he answered—but I was thinking of you,—as many at a greater distance are probably doing at this moment.—Fine open[1] weather Miss Emma!—Charming season for Hunting." "Emma is delightful, is not she?—whispered Margaret. I have found her more than answer my warmest hopes.— Did you ever see any thing more perfectly beautiful?—I think even *you* must be a convert to a brown complexion."—He hesitated; Margaret was fair herself, and he did not particularly want to compliment her; but Miss Osborne and Miss Carr were likewise fair, and his devotion to them carried the day. "Your Sister's complexion, said he at last, is as fine as a dark complexion can be, but I still profess my preference of a white skin. You have seen Miss Osborne?—She is my model for a truly feminine complexion, and she is very fair."—"Is she fairer than me?"—Tom made no reply.—"Upon my Honour Ladies, said he, giving a glance over his own person, I am highly endebted to your Condescension for admitting me, in such Dishabille[2] into your Drawingroom. I really did not consider how unfit I was to be here, or I hope I should have kept my distance. Lady Osborne would tell me that I were growing as careless as her son, if she saw me in this condition."—The Ladies were not wanting in civil returns; and Robert Watson stealing a veiw of his own head in an opposite glass,—said with equal civility, "You cannot be more in dishabille than myself.—We got here so late, that I had not time even to put a little fresh powder in my hair."—Emma could not help entering into what she supposed her Sister in law's feelings at that moment.—When the Tea things were removed, Tom began to talk of his Carriage—but the old Card Table being set out, and the fish and counters[3] with a tolerably clean pack brought forward

---

1 Mild, frost-free.
2 Informal dress, with a hint of carelessness in style.
3 Fish were small flat pieces of bone or ivory, sometimes, though not always, shaped like fish, used instead of money.

from the beaufit[1] by Miss Watson, the general voice was so urgent with him to join their party, that he agreed to allow himself another quarter of an hour. Even Emma was pleased that he would stay, for she was beginning to feel that a family party might be the worst of all parties; and the others were delighted.—"What's your Game?"—cried he, as they stood round the Table.—"Speculation I beleive, said Elizabeth—My Sister recommends it, and I fancy we all like it. I know *you* do, Tom."—"It is the only round game played at Croydon now, said Mrs. Robert—we never think of any other. I am glad it is a favourite with you."—"Oh! me! cried Tom. Whatever you decide on, will be a favourite with *me*.—I have had some pleasant hours at Speculation in my time—but I have not been in the way of it now for a long while.—Vingt-un is the game at Osborne Castle; I have played nothing but Vingt-un[2] of late. You would be astonished to hear the noise we make there.—The fine old, lofty Drawing-room rings again. Lady Osborne sometimes declares she cannot hear herself speak.—Lord Osborne enjoys it famously and he makes the best Dealer without exception that I ever beheld—such quickness and spirit! he lets nobody dream over their cards.—I wish you could see him overdraw himself on both his own cards[3]—it is worth any thing in the World!"—"Dear me!—cried Margaret why should not we play at vingt un?—I think it is a much better game than Speculation. I cannot say I am very fond of Speculation." Mrs. Robert offered not another word in support of the game.—She was quite vanquished, and the fashions of Osborne-Castle carried it over the fashions of Croydon.—"Do you see much of the Parsonage-family at the Castle, Mr. Musgrave?—" said Emma, as they were taking their seats.—"Oh! yes—they are almost always there. Mrs. Blake is a nice little good-humoured Woman, She and I are sworn friends; and Howard's a very Gentlemanlike good sort of fellow!—You are not forgotten I

---

1 Buffet; a sideboard or sidetable.
2 Vingt-et-un, now also known as Black Jack or pontoon, is a simple game of chance played with a full pack of cards by any number of players up to ten. The game was therefore appropriate to social groups, and could certainly be noisy.
3 If, on receiving two cards, a player holds a pair, he or she can split them and use each as the basis of two separate hands. Lord Osborne is described as finding himself with more than the desired twenty-one points on both the hands he is playing, and is therefore overdrawn and out of the game.

assure you by any of the party. I fancy you must have a little Cheek-glowing now and then Miss Emma. Were not you rather warm last Saturday about nine or ten o'clock in the Evening—? I will tell you how it was.—I see you are dieing to know.—Says Howard to Lord Osborne——" At this interesting moment he was called on by the others, to regulate the game and determine some disputable point; and his attention was so totally engaged in the business and afterwards by the course of the game as never to revert to what he had been saying before;—and Emma, tho' suffering a good deal from Curiosity, dared not remind him.—He proved a very useful addition at their Table; without him, it would have been a party of such very near relations as could have felt little Interest, and perhaps maintained little complaisance, but his presence gave variety and secured good manners.—He was in fact excellently qualified to shine at a round Game; and few situations made him appear to greater advantage. He played with spirit, and had a great deal to say, and tho' with no wit himself, could sometimes make use of the wit of an absent friend; and had a lively way of retailing a commonplace, or saying a mere nothing, that had great effect at a Card Table. The ways, and good Jokes of Osborne Castle were now added to his ordinary means of Entertainment; he repeated the smart sayings of one Lady, detailed the oversights of another and indulged them even with a copy of Lord Osborne's stile of overdrawing himself on both cards.—The Clock struck nine, while he was thus agreably occupied; and when Nanny came in with her Master's Bason of Gruel,[1] he had the pleasure of observing to Mr. Watson that he should leave him at supper, while he went home to dinner himself.—The Carriage was ordered to the door—and no entreaties for his staying longer could now avail,—for he well knew, that if he staid he must sit down to supper in less than ten minutes—which to a Man whose heart had been long fixed on calling his next meal a Dinner, was quite insupportable.—On finding him determined to go, Margaret began to wink and nod at Elizabeth to ask him to dinner for the following day; and Elizabeth at last not able to resist hints, which her own hospitable, social temper more than half-seconded, gave the invitation. "Would he give Robert the meeting,[2] they should be very

---

1 Basin, or bowl, of gruel, a light liquid food chiefly consumed by invalids, made by boiling oatmeal in water or milk, sometimes with the addition of sugar or spices.
2 A formal invitation to dine in honour of Robert's visit, but a homely grammatical construction.

happy." "With the greatest pleasure"—was his first reply. In a moment afterwards—"That is if I can possibly get here in time—but I shoot with Lord Osborne, and therefore must not engage—You will not think of me unless you see me."—And so, he departed, delighted with the uncertainty in which he had left it.—

———

Margaret in the joy of her heart under circumstances, which she chose to consider as peculiarly propitious, would willingly have made a confidante of Emma when they were alone for a short time the next morning; and had proceeded so far as to say—"The young man who was here last night my dear Emma and returns to day, is more interesting to me, than perhaps you may be aware—" but Emma pretending to understand nothing extraordinary in the words, made some very inapplicable reply, and jumping up, ran away from a subject which was odious to her feelings.—As Margaret would not allow a doubt to be repeated of Musgrave's coming to dinner, preparations were made for his Entertainment much exceeding what had been deemed necessary the day before;—and taking the office of superintendance intirely from her Sister, she was half the morning in the Kitchen herself directing and scolding.—After a great deal of indifferent Cooking, and anxious Suspense however, they were obliged to sit down without their Guest.—Tom Musgrave never came, and Margaret was at no pains to conceal her vexation under the disappointment, or repress the peevishness of her Temper—. The Peace of the party for the remainder of that day, and the whole of the next, which comprised the length of Robert and Jane's visit, was continually invaded by her fretful displeasure, and querulous attacks.—Elizabeth was the usual object of both. Margaret had just respect enough for her Brother and Sister's opinion, to behave properly by *them,* but Elizabeth and the maids could never do any thing right—and Emma, whom she seemed no longer to think about, found the continuance of the gentle voice beyond her calculation short. Eager to be as little among them as possible, Emma was delighted with the alternative of sitting above, with her father, and warmly entreated to be his constant Companion each Evening—and as Elizabeth loved company of any kind too well, not to prefer being below, at all risks as she had rather talk of Croydon to Jane, with every interruption of Margaret's perverseness, than sit with only her father, who frequently could not endure Talking at all, the affair was so settled, as soon as she could be persuaded to beleive it no sacrifice on her Sister's part.—To Emma, the Exchange was most acceptable, and delightful. Her father, if ill, required little more than gentleness and silence; and, being a man of Sense and Education, was if able to converse, a welcome companion.—In *his* chamber, Emma was at peace from the dreadful mortifications of unequal Society, and family Discord—from the immediate endurance of Hard-hearted prosperity, low-minded Conceit, and wrong-headed folly, engrafted on an untoward Disposition.—She still suffered from them in the Contemplation of their existence, in memory and in prospect, but for the moment, she ceased to be tortured by their effects.—She was at leisure, she could read and think,—tho' her situation was hardly such as to make reflection very soothing. The Evils arising from the loss of her Uncle were neither trifling, nor likely to lessen; and when Thought had been freely indulged, in contrasting the past and the present, the employment of mind, the dissipation of unpleasant ideas which only reading could produce, made her thankfully turn to a book.—The change in her home society and stile of Life in consequence of the death of one friend and the imprudence of another had indeed been striking.—From being the first object of Hope and Solicitude to an Uncle who had formed her mind with the care of a Parent, and of Tenderness to an Aunt whose amiable temper had delighted to give her every indulgence, from being the Life and Spirit of a House, where all had been comfort and Elegance, and the expected Heiress of an easy Independance,[1] she was become of importance to no one, a burden on those, whose affection she could not expect, an addition in an house, already overstocked, surrounded by inferior minds with little chance of domestic comfort, and as little hope of future support.—It was well for her that she was naturally chearful;—for the Change had been such as might have plunged weak spirits in Despondence.—

She was very much pressed by Robert and Jane to return with them to Croydon, and had some difficulty in getting a refusal accepted; as they thought too highly of their own kindness and situation, to suppose the offer could appear in a less advantageous light to anybody else.—Elizabeth gave them her interest,

---

1 If Robert's assessment of Mrs. Turner's wealth is correct, Emma could have expected to inherit £8,000 or £9,000. With such an income, she could have lived comfortably if she remained unmarried, without being dependent on her family for subsistence, or had sufficient fortune in her own right to have attracted a husband.

tho' evidently against her own, in privately urging Emma to go—
"You do not know what you refuse Emma—said she—nor what
you have to bear at home.—I would advise you by all means to
accept the invitation; there is always something lively going on at
Croydon. You will be in company almost every day, and Robert
and Jane will be very kind to you.—As for me, I shall be no worse
off without you, than I have been used to be; but poor Margaret's
disagreable ways are new to *you*, and they would vex you more
than you think for, if you stay at home.—" Emma was of course
un-influenced, except to greater esteem for Elizabeth, by such
representations—and the Visitors departed without her.—

Sanditon[1]

---

1 There was an Austen family tradition that JA had intended the novel to
   be called "The Brothers." Letters between JA's niece and nephew, Anna
   Lefroy and James Edward Austen Leigh, written in the 1860s as Austen
   Leigh was making arrangements for the publication of his *Memoir*
   (1871), refer to the manuscript as "Sanditon," and it has become known
   by that name. However, in the *Memoir* itself, Austen Leigh refers only to
   "The Last Work."

A Gentleman and Lady travelling from Tunbridge towards that part of the Sussex Coast which lies between Hastings and East Bourne,[1] being induced by Business to quit the high road, and attempt a very rough Lane, were overturned in toiling up its' long ascent half rock, half sand. The accident happened just beyond the only Gentleman's House near the Lane—a House, which their Driver on being first required to take that Direction, had conceived to be necessarily their object, and had with most unwilling Looks been constrained to pass by—. He had grumbled and shaken his Shoulders so much indeed, and pitied and cut his Horses so sharply, that he might have been open to the suspicion of over-turning them on purpose[2] (especially as the Carriage was not his Masters) if the road had not indisputably become considerably worse than before, as soon as the premises of the said House were left behind—expressing with a most intelligent portentous counte-nance that beyond it no wheels but cart wheels could safely pro-ceed. The severity of the fall was broken by their slow pace and the narrowness of the Lane, and the Gentleman having scrambled out and helped out his companion, they neither of them at first felt more than shaken and bruised. But the Gentleman had in the course of the extrication sprained his foot—and soon becoming sensible of it was obliged in a few moments to cut short, both his remonstrance to the Driver and his congratulations to his wife and himself—and sit down on the bank, unable to stand.—

"There is something wrong here, said he—putting his hand to his ancle—But never mind, my Dear—(looking up at her with a smile)—It could not have happened, you know, in a better place.—Good out of Evil—. The very thing perhaps to be wished for. We shall soon get releif.—*There*, I fancy lies my cure"—point-ing to the neat-looking end of a Cottage, which was seen roman-tically situated among wood on a high Eminence at some little Distance[3]—"Does not *that* promise to be the very place?—" His

---

1 Tonbridge is about thirty miles south of London, on a main coach road to the south coast. After the spa town of Tunbridge Wells, the road divides, one branch going on to Eastbourne and the other to Hastings, about fifteen miles east, both on the south coast.

2 Carriage accidents were common in fact and in fiction, partly because of the poor state of the roads. See p. 305, note 4.

3 Mr. Parker is reflecting ideas of beauty newly popular in the late eighteenth and early nineteenth centuries. The fashion for the pictur-

wife fervently hoped it was—but stood, terrified and anxious, neither able to do or suggest anything—and receiving her first real comfort from the sight of several persons now coming to their assistance. The accident had been discerned from a Hayfield adjoining the House they had passed—and the persons who approached, were a well-looking Hale, Gentlemanlike Man, of middle age, the Proprietor of the Place, who happened to be among his Haymakers at the time, and three or four of the ablest of them summoned to attend their Master—to say nothing of all the rest of the field, Men, Women and Children—not very far off.—Mr. Heywood, such was the name of the said Proprietor, advanced with a very civil salutation—much concern for the accident—some surprise at any body's attempting that road in a Carriage—and ready offers of assistance. His courtesies were received with Goodbreeding and gratitude and while one or two of the Men lent their help to the Driver in getting the Carriage upright again, the Travellor said—"You are extremely obliging Sir, and I take you at your word.—The injury to my Leg is I dare say very trifling, but it is always best in these cases to have a Surgeon's opinion[1] without loss of time; and as the road does not seem at present in a favourable state for my getting up to his house myself, I will thank you to send off one of these good People for the Surgeon." "The Surgeon Sir!—replied Mr. Heywood—I am afraid you will find no Surgeon at hand here, but I dare say we shall do very well without him."—"Nay Sir, if *he* is not in the way his Partner will do just as well[2]—or rather better—. I would rather see his Partner indeed—I would prefer the attendance of his Partner.—One of these good people can be with him in three minutes I am sure. I need not ask whether I see the House (looking towards the Cottage); for excepting your own, we have passed none in this place, which can be the Abode of a Gentleman."—Mr. Heywood looked very much astonished and replied—"What Sir! are you expecting to find a Surgeon in that Cottage?—We have neither Surgeon nor Partner in the Parish I assure you."—"Excuse me Sir—replied the other. I am sorry to

---

esque was popularised by William Gilpin (1724-1804), whose travel writings did much to mould genteel taste.

1 See p. 278, note 1.
2 Just as only a licensed surgeon could legally perform surgical operations, so only a licensed apothecary could dispense drugs. It was therefore common for surgeons and apothecaries to practise in partnership.

have the appearance of contradicting you—but though from the extent of the Parish or some other cause you may not be aware of the fact,—Stay—Can I be mistaken in the place?—Am I not in Willingden?—Is not this Willingden?" "Yes Sir, this is certainly Willingden." "Then Sir, I can bring proof of your having a Surgeon in the Parish—whether you may know it or not. Here Sir— (taking out his Pocket book—) if you will do me the favour of casting your eye over these advertisements, which I cut out myself from the Morning Post and the Kentish Gazette, only yesterday morning in London[1]—I think you will be convinced that I am not speaking at random. You will find it an advertisement Sir, of the dissolution of a Partnership in the Medical Line——in your own Parish—extensive Business—undeniable Character—respectable references—wishing to form a separate Establishment—you will find it at full length Sir"—offering him the two little oblong extracts.—"Sir—said Mr. Heywood with a good humoured smile—if you were to shew me all the Newspapers that are printed in one week throughout the Kingdom, you would not persuade me of there being a Surgeon in Willingden,—for having lived here ever since I was born, Man and Boy fifty-seven years, I think I must have *known* of such a person, at least I may venture to say that he has not *much Business*;—To be sure, if Gentlemen were to be often attempting this Lane in Post-chaises, it might not be a bad speculation for a Surgeon to get a House at the top of the Hill.—But as to that Cottage, I can assure you Sir that it is in fact—(inspite of its spruce air at this distance—) as indifferent a double Tenement[2] as any in the Parish, and that My Shepherd lives at one end, and three old women at the other." He took the peices of paper as he spoke—and having looked them over, added—"I beleive I can explain it Sir.—Your mistake is in the place.—There are two Willingdens in this Country[3]—and your advertisements refer to the other—which is Great Willingden, or Willingden Abbots, and lies seven miles off, on the other side of Battel[4]—quite down in the

---

1 *The Morning Post*, issued daily, was the most important newspaper for the monied and fashionable in London. The *Kentish Gazette* came out twice weekly, with a catchment area of Kent and nearby counties, including Sussex. Both newspapers contained advertisements of the kind mentioned here.
2 A house divided and let to two separate tenants.
3 County or local area.
4 Battle is a small town eight miles inland from Hastings, both named after the Battle of Hastings (1066), which was fought nearby.

Weald.[1] And *we* Sir—(speaking rather proudly) are not in the Weald."—"Not *down* in the Weald I am sure Sir, replied the Travellor, pleasantly. It took us half an hour to climb your Hill.—Well Sir—I dare say it is as you say, and I have made an abominably stupid Blunder.—All done in a moment;—the advertisements did not catch my eye till the last half hour of our being in Town—; when everything was in the hurry and confusion which always attend a short stay there—One is never able to complete anything in the way of Business you know till the Carriage is at the door—and accordingly satisfying myself with a breif enquiry, and finding we were actually to pass within a mile or two of a *Willingden* I sought no farther.—My Dear—(to his wife) I am very sorry to have brought you into this Scrape. But do not be alarmed about my Leg. It gives me no pain while I am quiet,—and as soon as these good people have succeeded in setting the Carriage to rights and turning the Horses round, the best thing we can do will be to measure back our steps into the Turnpike road and proceed to Hailsham,[2] and so Home, without attempting anything farther.—Two hours take us home, from Hailsham—And when once at home, we have our remedy at hand you know.—A little of our own Bracing Sea Air will soon set me on my feet again.—Depend upon it my Dear, it is exactly a case for the Sea. Saline air and immersion[3] will be the very thing.—My Sensations[4] tell me so already."—In a most friendly manner Mr. Heywood here interposed, entreating them not to think of proceeding till the ancle had been examined, and some refreshment taken, and very cordially pressing them to make use of his House for both purposes.—"We are always well stocked, said he, with all the common remedies for Sprains and Bruises—and I will answer for the pleasure it will give my Wife and daughters to be of service to you

---

1 A stretch of southern England, formerly woodland ("weald" is the Old English word for "forest"), that lies between the two ranges of chalk uplands known as the North and South Downs.

2 See p. 278, note 2. Hailsham is a market town thirteen miles south west of Battle and ten miles north of Eastbourne.

3 Sea air and salt water were both regarded as having healing properties. "Were I to enumerate half the diseases which are every day cured by sea-bathing, you might justly say you had received a treatise," writes Jery Melford (Tobias Smollett, *The Expedition of Humphry Clinker* [3 vols, 1771], Vol. 2, p. 136). "Immersion" could be in the sea, or in sea-water baths.

4 Instinctive feelings, rather than rational thoughts.

and this Lady, in every way in their power.—" A twinge or two, in trying to move his foot disposed the Travellor to think rather more as he had done at first of the benefit of immediate assistance—and consulting his wife in the few words of "Well my Dear, I beleive it will be better for us—" turned again to Mr. Heywood—and said—"Before we accept your Hospitality Sir,—and in order to do away any unfavourable impression which the sort of wild goose-chase you find me in, may have given rise to—allow me to tell you who we are. My name is Parker.—Mr. Parker of Sanditon;—this Lady, my wife Mrs. Parker. We are on our road home from London;—*My* name perhaps—tho' I am by no means the first of my Family, holding Landed Property in the Parish of Sanditon, may be unknown at this distance from the Coast—but Sanditon itself—everybody has heard of Sanditon,—the favourite—for a young and rising Bathing-place, certainly the favourite Spot of all that are to be found along the Coast of Sussex;[1] the most favoured by Nature, and promising to be the most chosen by Man."—"Yes—I have heard of Sanditon, replied Mr. Heywood.—Every five years, one hears of some new place or other starting up by the Sea, and growing the fashion.—How they can half of them be filled, is the wonder! *Where* People can be found with Money or Time to go to them!—Bad things for a Country;—sure to raise the price of Provisions and make the Poor good for nothing[2]—as I dare say you find, Sir." "Not at all Sir, not at all—cried Mr. Parker eagerly. Quite the contrary I assure you.—A common idea—but a mistaken one. It may apply to your large, overgrown Places, like Brighton, or Worthing, or

---

1 The development of seaside resorts was a natural extension to the eighteenth-century fashion for seeking medical attention and social occupation in spa towns such as Bath. Numbers increased, especially along the south coast, which had the sunniest weather. They were greeted with some cynicism: "In process of time, should the present taste continue, it is not improbable but that every paltry village on the Sussex coast which has a convenient beach for bathing will rise to a considerable town," wrote the anonymous author of *A Guide to All the Watering and Sea Bathing Places* (London, 1803), p. 202.

2 Mr. Heywood follows the influential economic thinking of Adam Smith: "When the quantity of any commodity which is brought to market falls short of the effectual demand ... the market price will rise more or less above the natural price," and one of the results might well be that "the interests of the labourers ... will prompt them to withdraw a part of their labour" (Adam Smith, *An Inquiry into the Nature and Causes of the Wealth of Nations* [2 vols, 1776], Vol. 1, Bk 1, ch. 7).

East Bourne[1]—but *not* to a small Village like Sanditon, precluded by its size from experiencing any of the evils of Civilization, while the growth of the place, the Buildings, the Nursery Grounds,[2] the demand for every thing, and the sure resort of the very best Company, those regular, steady, private[3] Families of thorough Gentility and Character, who are a blessing every where, excite the industry of the Poor and diffuse comfort and improvement among them of every sort.—No Sir, I assure you, Sanditon is not a place—"

"I do not mean to take exceptions to *any* place in particular Sir, answered Mr. Heywood—I only think our Coast is too full of them altogether—But had we not better try to get you"—

"Our Coast too full"—repeated Mr. Parker—"On that point perhaps we may not totally disagree;—at least there are *enough*. Our Coast is abundant enough; it demands no more.—Everybody's Taste and every body's finances may be suited—And those good people who are trying to add to the number, are in my opinion excessively absurd, and must soon find themselves—the Dupes of their own fallacious Calculations.—Such a place as Sanditon Sir, I may say was wanted, was called for.—Nature had marked it out—had spoken in most intelligible Characters—The finest, purest Sea Breeze on the Coast—acknowledged to be so—Excellent Bathing—fine hard Sand—Deep Water ten yards from the Shore—no Mud—no Weeds—no slimey rocks—Never was there a place more palpably designed by Nature for the resort of the Invalid—the very Spot which Thousands seemed in need of—The most desirable distance from London! One complete, measured mile nearer than East Bourne. Only conceive Sir, the advantage of saving a whole Mile, in a long Journey.[4] But Brinshore Sir, which I dare say you have in your eye—the attempts of two or three speculating People about Brinshore, this last Year, to raise

---

1 All seaside resorts on the south coast, with Eastbourne about twenty miles east and Worthing about fourteen miles west of Brighton. Brighton was by far the largest of the three, and the most popular with fashionable tourists.

2 The fields where vegetables and fruits were cultivated.

3 Not maintaining a public position, and therefore not of the highest social status, but with an implication of domesticity and respectability.

4 Access from London was a strong selling point for tourist resorts. The *Guide to All the Watering and Sea Bathing Places*, regularly reprinted, gives prominence to distances from London in the description of each resort it mentions.

that paltry Hamlet, lying, as it does between a stagnant marsh, a bleak Moor and the constant effluvia of a ridge of putrifying Sea weed,[1] can end in nothing but their own Disappointment. What in the name of Common Sense is to *recommend* Brinshore?—A most insalubrious Air—Roads proverbially detestable—Water Brackish beyond example, impossible to get a good dish of Tea within three miles of the place—and as for the Soil—it is so cold and ungrateful that it can hardly be made to yeild a Cabbage.— Depend upon it Sir, that this is a faithful Description of Brinshore—not in the smallest degree exaggerated—and if you have heard it differently spoken of—"

"Sir, I never heard it spoken of in my Life before, said Mr. Heywood. I did not know there was such a place in the World."— "You did not!—There my Dear—(turning with exultation to his Wife)—you see how it is. So much for the Celebrity of Brinshore!—This Gentleman did not know there was such a place in the World.—Why, in truth Sir, I fancy we may apply to Brinshore, that line of the Poet Cowper in his description of the religious Cottager, as opposed to Voltaire—"*She*, never heard of half a mile from home."[2]—"With all my Heart Sir—Apply any Verses you like to it—But I want to see something applied to your Leg—and I am sure by your Lady's countenance that she is quite of my opinion and thinks it a pity to lose any more time—And here come my Girls to speak for themselves and their Mother (two or three genteel looking young Women followed by as many Maid

---

1 According to William Buchan, whose book of medical advice went through many editions and was regarded as essential in many households, "effluvia from putrid stagnating water" and "vegetable effluvia" were causes of malignant fevers (William Buchan, *Domestic Medicine: Or, A Treatise on the Prevention and Cure of Diseases by Regimen and Simple Medicines*, 17th ed. [1800], pp. 148, 195).

2 A reference to William Cowper's poem, "Truth," in which the early eighteenth-century writer, wit, and iconoclast Voltaire is contrasted with a simple peasant woman

who weaves at her own door,
Pillow and bobbins all her little store ...
Just knows, and knows no more, her bible true,
A truth the brilliant Frenchman never knew ...
Oh happy peasant! Oh unhappy bard!
His the mere tinsel, her's the rich reward;
He prais'd perhaps for ages yet to come,
She never heard of half a mile from home.
(*Poems by William Cowper* [London: Johnson, 1782], pp. 89-90)

Servants, were now seen issueing from the House)—I began to wonder the Bustle should not have reached *them.*—A thing of this kind soon makes a Stir in a lonely place like ours.—Now Sir, let us see how you can be best conveyed into the House."—The young Ladies approached and said every thing that was proper to recommend their Father's offers; and in an unaffected manner calculated to make the Strangers easy—and as Mrs. Parker was exceedingly anxious for relief—and her Husband by this time, not much less disposed for it—a very few Civil Scruples were enough—especially as the Carriage being now set up, was Discovered to have received such Injury on the fallen side as to be unfit for present use.—Mr. Parker was therefore carried into the House, and his Carriage wheeled off to a vacant Barn.—

Chapter 2.—

The acquaintance, thus oddly begun, was neither short nor unimportant. For a whole fortnight the Travellors were fixed at Willingden; Mr. Parker's sprain proving too serious for him to move sooner.—He had fallen into very good hands. The Heywoods were a thoroughly respectable family, and every possible attention was paid in the kindest and most unpretending manner, to both Husband and wife. *He* was waited on and nursed, and *she* cheared and comforted with unremitting kindness—and as every office of Hospitality and friendliness was received as it ought—as there was not more good will on one side than Gratitude on the other—nor any deficiency of generally pleasant manners on either, they grew to like each other in the course of that fortnight, exceedingly well.—Mr. Parker's Character and History were soon unfolded. All that he understood of himself, he readily told, for he was very openhearted;—and where he might be himself in the dark, his conversation was still giving information, to such of the Heywoods as could observe.—By such he was perceived to be an Enthusiast;[1]—on the subject of Sanditon, a complete Enthusiast.—Sanditon,—the success of Sanditon as a small, fashionable Bathing Place was the object, for which he seemed to live. A very few years ago, and it had been a quiet Village of no pretensions; but some natural advantages in its position and some accidental circumstances having suggested to himself, and the other principal Land Holder, the probability of its' becoming a profitable Speculation, they had engaged in it, and planned and built, and

---

1 Carrying the sense of visionary, or self-deluded.

praised and puffed,[1] and raised it to a something of young Renown—and Mr. Parker could now think of very little besides.—The Facts, which in more direct communication, he laid before them were that he was about five and thirty—had been married,—very happily married seven years—and had four sweet Children at home;—that he was of a respectable Family, and easy though not large fortune;—no Profession[2]—succeeding as eldest son to the Property which two or three Generations had been holding and accumulating before him;—that he had two Brothers and two Sisters—all single and all independant—the eldest of the two former indeed, by collateral Inheritance,[3] quite as well provided for as himself.—His object in quitting the high road, to hunt for an advertising Surgeon, was also plainly stated;—it had not proceeded from any intention of spraining his ancle or doing himself any other Injury for the good of such Surgeon—nor (as Mr. Heywood had been apt to suppose) from any design of entering into Partnership with him—; it was merely in consequence of a wish to establish some medical Man at Sanditon, which the nature of the Advertisement induced him to expect to accomplish in Willingden.—He was convinced that the advantage of a medical Man at hand would very materially promote the rise and prosperity of the Place—would in fact tend to bring a prodigious influx;—nothing else was wanting. He had *strong* reason to beleive that *one* family had been deterred last year from trying Sanditon on that account—and probably very many more—and his own Sisters who were sad Invalids, and whom he was very anxious to get to Sanditon this Summer, could hardly be expected to hazard themselves in a place where they could not have immediate medical advice.—Upon the whole, Mr. Parker was evidently an amiable, family-man, fond of Wife, Children, Brothers and Sisters—and generally kind-hearted;—Liberal, gentlemanlike, easy to please;—of a sanguine turn of mind, with more Imagination than Judgement. And Mrs. Parker was as evidently a gentle, amiable, sweet tempered Woman, the properest

---

1 Advertised with exaggerated praise.
2 A normal situation for the eldest son of a gentleman's family, since he would expect to inherit the family estate and its income. Younger sons, who could expect little or no inheritance, might enter professions considered genteel: the law, the church, the army, or the navy.
3 Possessing some form of assured income, through inheritance willed from a relative with no direct heir, and therefore not reliant on other family members for income.

wife in the World for a Man of strong Understanding, but not of capacity to supply the cooler reflection which her own Husband sometimes needed, and so entirely waiting to be guided on every occasion, that whether he were risking his Fortune or spraining his Ancle, she remained equally useless.—Sanditon was a second wife and four Children to him—hardly less Dear—and certainly more engrossing.—He could talk of it for ever.—It had indeed the highest claims;—not only those of Birth place, Property, and Home,—it was his Mine, his Lottery, his Speculation and his Hobby Horse; his Occupation his Hope and his Futurity.[1]—He was extremely desirous of drawing his good friends at Willingden thither; and his endeavours in the cause, were as grateful and disinterested, as they were warm.—He wanted to secure the promise of a visit—to get as many of the Family as his own house would contain, to follow him to Sanditon as soon as possible—and healthy as they all undeniably were—foresaw that every one of them would be benefited by the sea.—He held it indeed as certain, that no person could be really well, no person, (however upheld for the present by fortuitous aids of exercise and spirits in a semblance of Health) could be really in a state of secure and permanent Health without spending at least six weeks by the Sea every year.—The Sea Air and Sea Bathing together were nearly infallible, one or the other of them being a match for every Disorder, of the Stomach, the Lungs or the Blood; They were anti-spasmodic, anti-pulmonary, anti-sceptic anti-bilious and anti-rheumatic.[2] Nobody could catch cold by the Sea, Nobody

---

1   Much money had been made from mining in Britain in the eighteenth
    century. A variety of lotteries operated, including a state lottery, but the
    practice was always controversial. In June 1816, Parliament debated
    whether lotteries should continue; the government defended the practice
    against many detractors on the grounds that the income could be used
    for major projects. A hobby-horse was originally a popular children's toy
    consisting of a long stick with a horse's head at one end of it, and so by
    extension both a favourite and a delusional pastime; no early nine-
    teenth-century reader would be like to miss an allusion to Uncle Toby's
    obsession with the siege of Namur (referred to as his "hobby-horse") in
    Laurence Sterne's *Tristram Shandy* (1760-67). The usual meaning of
    "futurity" is simply "the future," but JA implies a stronger sense of con-
    fidence in future events.
2   JA is satirising the medical jargon of the time, which frequently
    employed words prefixed with "anti." JA's unusual spelling of antiseptic
    may be a deliberate allusion to Mr. Parker's lack of scepticism. "Anti-
    bilious" was an afterthought, added above the line in the manuscript,

wanted appetite by the Sea, Nobody wanted Spirits, Nobody wanted Strength.—They were healing, softing,[1] relaxing—fortifying and bracing—seemingly just as was wanted—sometimes one, sometimes the other.—If the Sea breeze failed, the Sea-Bath was the certain corrective;—and where Bathing disagreed, the Sea Breeze alone was evidently designed by Nature for the cure.—His eloquence however could not prevail. Mr. and Mrs. Heywood never left home. Marrying early and having a very numerous Family, their movements had been long limitted to one small circle; and they were older in Habits than in Age.—Excepting two Journeys to London in the year, to receive his Dividends,[2] Mr. Heywood went no farther than his feet or his welltried old Horse could carry him, and Mrs. Heywood's Adventurings were only now and then to visit her Neighbours, in the old Coach which had been new when they married and fresh lined on their eldest Son's coming of age ten years ago.[3]—They had very pretty Property—enough, had their family been of reasonable Limits to have allowed them a very gentlemanlike share of Luxuries and Change—enough for them to have indulged in a new Carriage and better roads, an occasional month at TunbridgeWells, and symptoms of the Gout and aWinter at Bath;[4]— but the maintenance, Education and fitting out of fourteen Children demanded a very quiet, settled, careful course of Life—and obliged them to be stationary and healthy at Willingden. What Prudence had at first enjoined, was now rendered pleasant by

---

possibly with her own illness in mind: on 24 January 1817 she wrote, "I am more & more convinced that *Bile* is at the bottom of all I have suffered" (*Jane Austen's Letters*, coll. and ed. Deirdre Le Faye [Oxford: Oxford UP, 1995], p. 327). Neither "anti-pulmonary" nor "anti-rheumatic" appears in the *Oxford English Dictionary*.

1 The meaning is clear, and the word does exist, but it is very unusual; possibly JA intended "softening."

2 Methods of money transfer were rudimentary; it would be advisable, if not essential, to go in person to collect dividend payments.

3 "Coach" rather than "carriage" carries the sense of a heavy, old-fashioned vehicle. It would be common to acquire a new coach or carriage on marriage. The vehicle would require regular relining—that is, renewing the cloth covering of the woodwork on the inside of the carriage— and this was expensive.

4 These spa towns were longer-established than the newer seaside resorts. Though both continued to attract invalids and tourists in the early nineteenth century, they no longer had the fashionable cachet of earlier decades.

Habit. They never left home, and they had a gratification in saying so.—But very far from wishing their Children to do the same, they were glad to promote *their* getting out into the World, as much as possible. *They* staid at home, that their Children *might* get out;—and while making that home extremely comfortable, welcomed every change from it which could give useful Connections or respectable acquaintance to Sons or Daughters. When Mr. and Mrs. Parker therefore ceased from soliciting a family-visit, and bounded their veiws to carrying back one Daughter with them, no difficulties were started. It was general pleasure and consent.—Their invitation was to Miss Charlotte Heywood, a very pleasing young woman of two and twenty, the eldest of the Daughters at home, and the one, who under her Mother's directions had been particularly useful and obliging to them; who had attended them most, and knew them best.—Charlotte was to go,—with excellent health, to bathe and be better if she could—to receive every possible pleasure which Sanditon could be made to supply by the gratitude of those she went with—and to buy new Parasols, new Gloves, and new Broches, for her Sisters and herself at the Library,[1] which Mr. Parker was anxiously wishing to support.—All that Mr. Heywood himself could be persuaded to promise was, that he would send everyone to Sanditon, who asked his advice, and that nothing should ever induce him (as far as the future could be answered for) to spend even five Shillings at Brinshore.—

Chapter 3.

Every Neighbourhood should have a great Lady.—The great Lady of Sanditon, was Lady Denham;[2] and in their Journey from Willingden to the Coast, Mr. Parker gave Charlotte a more detailed account of her, than had been called for before.—She had been necessarily often mentioned at Willingden,—for being his Colleague in speculation, Sanditon itself could not be talked

---

1   The library at a spa or seaside resort offered many services beyond the loan of books. At the library at Brighton, Lydia Bennet sees "such beautiful ornaments as made her quite wild" (*Pride and Prejudice*, Vol. 2, ch. 19).

2   As the widow of a baronet, Lady Denham is a rather modest "great lady." A baronetcy is a hereditary title and ranks above a knight, but below the other ranks of aristocracy. Lady Russell, "the widow of only a knight ... gave the dignity of a baronet all its due" (*Persuasion*, Vol. 1, ch. 2).

of long, without the introduction of Lady Denham and that she was a very rich old Lady, who had buried two Husbands, who knew the value of Money, was very much looked up to and had a poor Cousin living with her, were facts already well known, but some further particulars of her history, and her Character served to lighten the tediousness of a long Hill, or a heavy bit of road, and to give the visiting Young Lady a suitable Knowledge of the Person with whom she might now expect to be daily associating.—Lady Denham had been a rich Miss Brereton, born to Wealth but not to Education. Her first Husband had been a Mr. Hollis, a man of considerable Property in the Country, of which a large share of the Parish of Sanditon, with Manor and Mansion House[1] made a part. He had been an elderly Man when she married him;—her own age about thirty.—Her motives for such a Match could be little understood at the distance of forty years, but she had so well nursed and pleased Mr. Hollis, that at his death he left her everything—all his Estates, and all at her Disposal.[2] After a widowhood of some years, she had been induced to marry again. The late Sir Harry Denham, of Denham Park in the Neighbourhood of Sanditon had succeeded in removing her and her large Income to his own Domains, but he could not succeed in the veiws of permanently enriching his family, which were attributed to him. She had been too wary to put anything out of her own Power—and when on Sir Harry's Decease she returned again to her own House at Sanditon, she was said to have made this boast to a friend "that though she had *got* nothing but her Title from the Family, still she had *given* nothing for it."[3]—For the Title, it was to be supposed that she had married—and Mr. Parker acknowledged there being just such a degree of value for it apparent now, as to give her conduct that natural explanation. "There is at times said he—a little self-importance—but it is not

---

1 Since medieval times, many rural settlements had been structured with the local church, houses, and agricultural land under the ownership of the lord of the manor. The lord of the manor gradually lost his formal responsibilities, but the legalistic term "manor and mansion house" continued to suggest extensive control over the village.

2 Somewhat unusually, Mr. Hollis's property was not entailed on male heirs, and he has made an active choice to leave it to his widow without conditions.

3 When a women married, her property usually became part of her husband's estate, but a legal arrangement could be made by which she could retain it. The widow of a baronet would keep her title unless she married again.

offensive;—and there are moments, there are points, when her Love of Money is carried greatly too far. But she is a goodnatured Woman, a very goodnatured Woman—a very obliging, friendly Neighbour; a chearful, independant, valuable Character—and her faults may be entirely imputed to her want of Education. She has good natural Sense, but quite uncultivated.—She has a fine active mind, as well as a fine healthy frame for a Woman of seventy, and enters into the improvement of Sanditon with a spirit truly admirable—though now and then, a Littleness *will* appear. She cannot look forward quite as I would have her—and takes alarm at a trifling present expence, without considering what returns it *will* make her in a year or two.

That is—we think *differently*, we now, and then, see things *differently*, Miss Heywood.—Those who tell their own Story you know must be listened to with Caution.—When you see us in contact, you will judge for yourself."—Lady Denham was indeed a great Lady beyond the common wants of Society—for she had many Thousands a year to bequeath, and three distinct sets of People to be courted by; her own relations, who might very reasonably wish for her Original Thirty Thousand Pounds[1] among them, the legal Heirs of Mr. Hollis, who must hope to be more endebted to *her* sense of Justice than he had allowed them to be to *his*, and those Members of the Denham Family, whom her second Husband had hoped to make a good Bargain for.—By all of these, or by Branches of them, she had no doubt been long, and still continued to be, well attacked;—and of these three divisions, Mr. Parker did not hesitate to say that Mr. Hollis' Kindred were the *least* in favour and Sir Harry Denham's the *most*.—The former he beleived, had done themselves irremediable harm by expressions of very unwise and unjustifiable resentment at the time of Mr. Hollis's death;—the Latter, to the advantage of being the remnant of a Connection which she certainly valued, joined those of having been known to her from their Childhood and of being always at hand to preserve their interest by reasonable attention. Sir Edward, the present Baronet, nephew to Sir Harry, resided constantly at Denham Park; and Mr. Parker had little doubt, that he and his Sister Miss Denham who lived with him, would be principally remembered in her Will. He sincerely hoped it.—Miss Denham had a very small provision—and her Brother was a poor Man for his rank in Society. "He is a warm friend to

---

1 A substantial sum. Emma Woodhouse, heiress of £30,000, is considered
   to be significantly wealthy (*Emma*, Vol. 1, ch. 16).

Sanditon—said Mr. Parker—and his hand would be as liberal as his heart, had he the Power.—He would be a noble Coadjutor![1]—As it is, he does what he can—and is running up a tasteful little Cottage Ornèe,[2] on a strip of Waste Ground Lady Denham has granted him—, which I have no doubt we shall have many a Candidate for, before the end even of *this* Season."[3] Till within the last twelvemonth, Mr. Parker had considered Sir Edward as standing without a rival, as having the fairest chance of succeeding to the greater part of all that she had to give—but there was now another person's claims to be taken into the account, those of the young female relation, whom Lady Denham had been induced to receive into her Family. After having always protested against any such addition, and long and often enjoyed the repeated defeats she had given to every attempt of her relations to introduce this young Lady, or that young Lady as a Companion[4] at Sanditon House, she had brought back with her from London last Michaelmas[5] a Miss Brereton, who bid fair by her merits to vie in favour with Sir Edward, and to secure for herself and her family that share of the accumulated Property which they had certainly the best right to inherit.—Mr. Parker spoke warmly of Clara Brereton, and the interest of his story increased very much with the introduction of such a Character. Charlotte listened with more than amusement now;—it was solicitude and Enjoyment, as she heard her described to be lovely, amiable, gentle, unassuming, conducting herself uniformly with great good sense, and evidently gaining by her innate worth, on the affections of her Patroness.—Beauty, Sweetness, Poverty and Dependance, do not want the imagination of a Man to operate upon. With due exceptions—Woman feels for Woman very promptly

1 Helper.
2 A mock-rustic house designed to be picturesque, and for genteel occupation; the fashion had become established in the 1780s and continued well into the nineteenth century.
3 The usual summer holiday season would end in October.
4 Wealthy families, and particularly wealthy women living alone, often took into their households a gentlewoman in poverty, perhaps a less fortunate family member, who was expected to provide company and companionship in return for her keep. The arrangement was open to abuse. See Appendix D.
5 The feast day of St Michael, 29 September, was one of the four "quarter days" of the year, on which many regular legal and financial transactions took place. Lady Denham's visit to London might have concerned her financial affairs.

and compassionately. He gave the particulars which had led to Clara's admission at Sanditon, as no bad exemplification of that mixture of Character, that union of Littleness with Kindness with Good Sense with even Liberality which he saw in Lady Denham. After having avoided London for many years, and principally on account of these very Cousins who were continually writing, inviting and tormenting her, and whom she was determined to keep at a distance, she had been obliged to go there last Michaelmas with the certainty of being detained at least a fortnight.— She had gone to an Hotel—living by her own account, as prudently as possible, to defy the reputed expensiveness of such a home, and at the end of three Days calling for her Bill, that she might judge of her state.—Its' amount was such as determined her on staying not another hour in the House, and she was preparing in all the anger and perturbation which a beleif of very gross imposition *there*, and an ignorance of *where* to go for better usage, to leave the Hotel at all hazards, when the Cousins, the politic and lucky Cousins, who seemed always to have a spy on her, introduced themselves at this important moment, and learning her situation, persuaded her to accept such a home for the rest of her Stay as their humbler house in a very inferior part of London, could offer.—She went; was delighted with her welcome and the hospitality and attention she received from every body—found her good Cousins the Breretons beyond her expectation worthy people—and finally was impelled by a personal knowledge of their narrow Income and pecuniary difficulties, to invite one of the girls of the family to pass the Winter with her. The invitation was to *one*, for six months—with the probability of another being then to take her place;—but in *selecting* the one, Lady Denham had shewn the good part of her Character—for passing by the actual *daughters* of the House, she had chosen Clara, a Neice—, more helpless and more pitiable of course than any— and dependant on Poverty—an additional Burthen on an encumbered Circle—and one, who had been so low in every worldly veiw, as with all her natural endowments and powers, to have been preparing for a situation little better than a Nursery Maid.[1]—Clara had returned with her—and by her good sense and merit had now, to all appearance secured a very strong hold in Lady Denham's regard. The six months had long been over—

---

1 The nursery maid, whose task was to look after the young children of the family and keep their nursery clean, was among the lowest of the female domestic servants.

and not a syllable was breathed of any change, or exchange.—She was a general favourite;—the influence of her steady conduct and mild, gentle Temper was felt by everybody. The prejudices which had met her at first in some quarters, were all dissipated. She was felt to be worthy of Trust—to be the very companion who would guide and soften Lady Denham—who would enlarge her mind and open her hand.—She was as thoroughly amiable as she was lovely—and since having had the advantage of their Sanditon Breezes, that Loveliness was complete.

Chapter 4.

"And whose very snug-looking Place is this?"—said Charlotte, as in a sheltered Dip within two miles of the Sea, they passed close by a moderate-sized house, well fenced and planted, and rich in the Garden, Orchard and Meadows which are the best embellishments of such a Dwelling. "It seems to have as many comforts about it as Willingden."—"Ah!—said Mr. Parker.—This is my old House—the house of my Forefathers—the house where I and all my Brothers and Sisters were born and bred—and where my own three eldest Children were born—where Mrs. Parker and I lived till within the last two years—till our new House was finished.— I am glad you are pleased with it.—It is an honest old Place—and Hillier keeps it in very good order. I have given it up you know to the Man who occupies the cheif of my Land. *He* gets a better House by it—and I, a rather better situation!—one other Hill brings us to Sanditon—modern Sanditon—a beautiful Spot.— Our Ancestors, you know always built in a hole.[1]—Here were we, pent down in this little contracted Nook, without Air or Veiw, only one mile and three quarters from the noblest expanse of Ocean between the Southforeland and the Land's end,[2] and without the smallest advantage from it. You will not think I have made a bad exchange, when we reach Trafalgar House—which by the bye, I almost wish I had not named Trafalgar—for Waterloo is more the thing now.[3] However, Waterloo is in reserve—and if we

---

1 The traditional reason for building settlements "in a hole" would be for shelter and protection. The hilltop situation of modern Sanditon gives priority to the sea view and increases exposure to bad weather.

2 The full length of England's south coast from the South Foreland, around Dover, in the east, to Land's End at the tip of Cornwall, to the west.

3 At the Battle of Trafalgar, fought on 21 October 1805 off the coast of Spain, the combined French and Spanish fleets were defeated by

have encouragement enough this year for a little Crescent[1] to be ventured on—(as I trust we shall) then, we shall be able to call it Waterloo Crescent—and the name joined to the form of the Building, which always takes, will give us the command of Lodgers—. In a good Season we should have more applications than we could attend to."—"It was always a very comfortable House—said Mrs. Parker—looking at it through the back window with something like the fondness of regret.—And such a nice Garden—such an excellent Garden." "Yes, my Love, but *that* we may be said to carry with us.—*It* supplies us, as before, with all the fruit and vegetables we want; and we have in fact all the comfort of an excellent Kitchen Garden, without the constant Eyesore of its formalities;[2] or the yearly nuisance of its decaying vegetation.—Who can endure a Cabbage Bed in October?" "Oh! dear—yes.—We are quite as well off for Gardenstuff as ever we were—for if it is forgot to be brought at any time, we can always buy what we want at Sanditon-House.—The Gardiner there, is glad enough to supply us—. But it was a nice place for the Children to run about in. So Shady in Summer!" "My dear, we shall have shade enough on the Hill and more than enough in the course of a very few years—. The Growth of my Plantations[3] is a general astonishment. In the mean while we have the Canvas Awning, which gives us the most complete comfort within doors—and you can get a Parasol at Whitby's for little Mary at any time, or a large Bonnet at Jebbs'—And as for the Boys, I must say I would rather *them* run about in the Sunshine than not. I am sure we agree my dear, in wishing our Boys to be as hardy as pos-

---

the British under the command of Lord Nelson, effectively ending the naval war in Britain's favour. Its impact at home, enhanced by the news of Nelson's death on the day of the battle, was immense. On 18 June 1815, the Anglo-Dutch army under the Duke of Wellington, assisted by the Prussian army, defeated Napoleon at the Battle of Waterloo.

1 First used in the name of the Royal Crescent in Bath (1767-75), a curved terrace of houses was associated with superior accommodation in a spa town. It did, in fact, require a substantial number of houses to make its effect.

2 Outward form or appearance, but possibly referring also to the planting of fruit and vegetables in formal rows and squares. Contemporary ideas of the picturesque favoured the removal of unsightly details in order to provide a beautiful aspect.

3 Areas deliberately planted up with trees, sometimes for commercial use.

sible."—"Yes indeed, I am sure we do—and I will get Mary a little Parasol, which will make her as proud as can be. How Grave she will walk about with it, and fancy herself quite a little Woman.—Oh! I have not the smallest doubt of our being a great deal better off where we are now. If we any of us want to bathe, we have not a quarter of a mile to go.—But you know, (still looking back) one loves to look at an old friend, at a place where one has been happy.—The Hilliers did not seem to feel the Storms last Winter at all.—I remember seeing Mrs. Hillier after one of those dreadful Nights, when *we* had been literally rocked in our bed, and she did not seem at all aware of the Wind being anything more than common." "Yes, yes—that's likely enough. *We* have all the Grandeur of the Storm,[1] with less real danger, because the Wind meeting with nothing to oppose or confine it around our House, simply rages and passes on—while down in this Gutter—nothing is known of the state of the Air, below the Tops of the Trees—and the Inhabitants may be taken totally unawares by one of those dreadful Currents which should do more mischief in a Valley, when they *do* arise than an open Country ever experiences in the heaviest Gale.—But my dear Love—as to Gardenstuff;—you were saying that any accidental omission is supplied in a moment by Lady Denham's Gardiner—but it occurs to me that we ought to go else where upon such occasions—and that old Stringer and his son have a higher claim. I encouraged him to set up—and am afraid he does not do very well—that is, there has not been time enough yet.—He *will* do very well beyond a doubt—but at first it is Up hill work; and therefore we must give him what Help we can—and when any Vegetables or fruit happen to be wanted,—and it will not be amiss to have them often wanted, to have something or other forgotten most days;—Just to have a nominal supply you know, that poor old Andrew may not lose his daily Job—but in fact to buy the cheif of our consumption of the Stringers.—" "Very well my Love, that can be easily done—and Cook will be satisfied—which will be a great comfort, for she is always complaining of old Andrew now, and says he never brings her what she wants.—There—now the old House is

---

1 Novelists and poets had just begun to explore the artistic possibilities of the sea-storm. In his novel, *The Antiquary*, which JA read on publication in 1816, Walter Scott describes his heroine and her father, caught by a sudden storm, becoming stranded "between two of the most magnificent, yet most dreadful objects of nature—a raging tide and an insurmountable precipice" (*The Antiquary* [1816], Vol. 1, ch. 7).

quite left behind.—What is it, your Brother Sidney says about its' being a Hospital?"

"Oh! my dear Mary, merely a Joke of his. He pretends to advise me to make a Hospital of it. He pretends to laugh at my Improvements. Sidney says any thing you know. He has always said what he chose of and to us, all. Most Families have such a member among them I beleive Miss Heywood.—There is a someone in most families privileged by superior abilities or spirits to say anything.—In ours, it is Sidney; who is a very clever Young Man, and with great powers of pleasing.—He lives too much in the World to be settled; that is his only fault.—He is here and there and every where. I wish we may get him to Sanditon. I should like to have you acquainted with him.—And it would be a fine thing for the Place!—Such a young Man as Sidney, with his neat equipage[1] and fashionable air,—You and I Mary, know what effect it might have: Many a respectable Family, many a careful Mother, many a pretty Daughter, might it secure us, to the prejudice of East Bourne and Hastings."—They were now approaching the Church and real village of Sanditon, which stood at the foot of the Hill they were afterwards to ascend—a Hill, whose side was covered with the Woods and enclosures[2] of Sanditon House and whose Height ended in an open Down where the new Buildings might soon be looked for. A branch only, of the Valley, winding more obliquely towards the Sea, gave a passage to an inconsiderable Stream, and formed at its mouth, a third Habitable Division, in a small cluster of Fisherman's Houses.—The Village contained little more than Cottages, but the Spirit of the day had been caught, as Mr. Parker observed with delight to Charlotte, and two or three of the best of them were smartened up with a white Curtain and "Lodgings to let"—, and farther on, in the little Green Court of an old Farm House, two Females in elegant white were actually to be seen with their books and camp stools—and in turning the corner of the Baker's shop, the sound of a Harp[3] might be heard through the upper Casement.—Such

---

1 Carriage, horses, and related accessories, together with the servants necessary to keep them in order.

2 Strictly speaking, enclosures were areas of common land taken into private ownership and fenced off for cultivation, a controversial process that had become widespread in the eighteenth century, but Mr. Parker may intend the more general sense of "enclosed land."

3 For many fashionable young women of the early nineteenth century, the harp had replaced the pianoforte as the most favoured musical instru-

sights and sounds were highly Blissful to Mr. Parker.—Not that he had any personal concern in the success of the Village itself; for considering it as too remote from the Beach, he had done nothing there—but it was a most valuable proof of the increasing fashion of the place altogether. If the *village* could attract, the Hill might be nearly full.—He anticipated an amazing Season.—At the same time last year, (late in July) there had not been a single Lodger in the Village!—nor did he remember any during the whole Summer, excepting one family of children who came from London for sea air after the hooping Cough, and whose Mother would not let them be nearer the Shore for fear of their tumbling in.—"Civilization, Civilization indeed!—cried Mr. Parker, delighted—. Look my dear Mary—Look at William Heeley's windows.—Blue Shoes, and nankin Boots!¹—Who would have expected such a sight at a Shoemaker's in old Sanditon!—This is new within the Month. There was no blue Shoe when we passed this way a month ago—Glorious indeed!—Well, I think I *have* done something in my Day.—Now, for our Hill, our health-breathing Hill.²—" In ascending, they passed the Lodge-Gates of Sanditon House, and saw the top of the House itself among its Groves. It was the last Building of former Days in that line of the Parish. A little higher up, the Modern began; and in crossing the Down, a Prospect House, a Bellevue Cottage, and a Denham Place³ were to be looked at by Charlotte with the calmness of

---

ment. The harp was "calculated ... to show a fine figure to advantage. The contour of the whole form, the turn and polish of a beautiful hand and arm, the richly-slippered and well-made foot on the pedal stops, the gentle motion of a lovely neck, and, above all, the sweetly-tempered expression of an intelligent countenance; these are shown at one glance, when the fair performer is seated unaffectedly, yet gracefully, at the harp" (*The Mirror of the Graces; or, The English Lady's Costume* [1811], p. 194).

1 From the 1790s, blue shoes had become fashionable for women, replacing more serviceable black. Nankin boots were ladies' light half-boots with uppers made of nankeen, a yellow-coloured cotton originally from Nanking in China; they were worn by women for walking and riding, but were regarded as more fashionable than practical. See p. 301, note 3.

2 A much-anthologised song attributed to George, Lord Lyttelton (1709-73) includes the lines "Adieu! thou sweet health-breathing hill, / Thou canst not my comfort restore."

3 By their names, the new houses proclaim either their exposed situation (privileging the view) or the achievements of contemporary speculators.

amused Curiosity, and by Mr. Parker with the eager eye which hoped to see scarcely any empty houses.—More Bills at the Window[1] than he had calculated on;—and a smaller shew of company on the Hill—Fewer Carriages, fewer Walkers. He had fancied it just the time of day for them to be all returning from their Airings to dinner.[2]—But the Sands and the Terrace always attracted some—and the Tide must be flowing—about half-Tide now.—He longed to be on the Sands, the Cliffs, at his own House, and every where out of his House at once. His Spirits rose with the very sight of the Sea and he could almost feel his Ancle getting stronger already.—Trafalgar House on the most elevated spot on the Down was a light elegant Building, standing in a small Lawn with a very young plantation round it, about an hundred yards from the brow of a steep, but not very lofty Cliff—and the nearest to it, of every Building, excepting one short row of smart-looking Houses, called the Terrace, with a broad walk in front, aspiring to be the Mall of the Place.[3] In this row were the best Milliner's shop and the Library—a little detached from it, the Hotel and Billiard room[4]—Here began the Descent to the Beach, and to the Bathing Machines[5]—and this was therefore the favourite spot for Beauty and Fashion.—At Trafalgar House, rising at a little distance behind the Terrace, The Travellors were safely set down, and all was happiness and Joy between Papa and Mama and their Children; while Charlotte having received possession of her apartment, found amusement enough in standing

---

1 Notices are posted in house windows advertising accommodation to let.
2 Dinner, the main meal of the day, would have been served in a spa around 3:00 p.m., earlier than would have been usual for fashionable families in their town homes. It marked the dividing line between outdoor and health pursuits during the earlier part of the day and social events in the evening.
3 The terrace, much favoured in the new seaside and spa resorts, was a line of attached houses raised up from natural street level in order to provide a wide walkway outside as a formal promenade. The Mall in St. James's Park was London's most fashionable promenade.
4 A milliner's would sell lace, ribbons, accessories, and knick-knacks as well as hats; billiard-rooms were popular in the new seaside resorts.
5 Even the smallest resorts would offer bathing machines to facilitate seabathing. They were closed wooden compartments on wheels that were pulled into the sea by a horse. The bather would change in the compartment and then bathe from its steps; when he or she was finished, the machine would be pulled back onto dry land.

at her ample, venetian window,[1] and looking over the miscellaneous foreground of unfinished Buildings, waving Linen, and
tops of Houses, to the Sea, dancing and sparkling in Sunshine
and Freshness.—

Chapter 5.

When they met before dinner, Mr. Parker was looking over Letters.—"Not a Line from Sidney!—said he.—He is an idle fellow.—I sent him an account of my accident from Willingden, and
thought he would have vouchsafed me an answer.—But perhaps
it implies that he is coming himself.—I trust it may.—But here is
a Letter from one of my Sisters. *They* never fail me.—Women are
the only Correspondents to be depended on.—Now Mary, (smiling at his Wife)—before I open it, what shall we guess as to the
state of health of those it comes from—or rather what would Sidney say if he were here?—Sidney is a saucy fellow, Miss Heywood.—And you must know, he will have it there is a good deal
of Imagination in my two Sisters' complaints—but it really is not
so—or very little—They have wretched health, as you have heard
us say frequently and are subject to a variety of very serious Disorders.—Indeed, I do not beleive they know what a day's health
is;—and at the same time, they are such excellent useful Women
and have so much energy of Character that, where any Good is
to be done, they force themselves on exertions which to those
who do not thoroughly know them, have an extraordinary
appearance.—But there is really no affectation about them. They
have only weaker constitutions and stronger minds than are often
met with, either separate or together.—And our Youngest Brother
who lives with them, and who is not much above twenty, I am
sorry to say, is almost as great an Invalid as themselves.—He is so
delicate that he can engage in no Profession.—Sidney laughs at
him—but it really is no Joke—tho' Sidney often makes me laugh
at them all inspite of myself.—Now, if he were here, I know he
would be offering odds, that either Susan, Diana or Arthur would
appear by this letter to have been at the point of death within the
last month.—" Having run his eye over the Letter, he shook his
head and began—: "No chance of seeing them at Sanditon I am
sorry to say.—A very indifferent account of them indeed. Seri-

---

1   A window with three openings, the central one being arched and larger
    than those on either side, designed to allow as much light and air into
    the room as possible.

ously, a *very* indifferent account.—Mary, you will be quite sorry to hear how ill they have been and are.—Miss Heywood, if you will give me leave, I will read Diana's Letter aloud.—I like to have my friends acquainted with each other—and I am afraid this is the only sort of acquaintance I shall have the means of accomplishing between you.—And I can have no scruple on Diana's account—for her Letters shew her exactly as she is, the most active, friendly, warmhearted Being in existence, and therefore must give a good impression." He read.—"My dear Tom, We were all much greived at your accident, and if you had not described yourself as fallen into such very good hands, I should have been with you at all hazards the day after the receipt of your Letter, though it found me suffering under a more severe attack than usual of my old greivance, Spasmodic Bile[1] and hardly able to crawl from my Bed to the Sofa.—But how were you treated?—Send me more Particulars in your next.—If indeed a simple Sprain, as you denominate it, nothing would have been so judicious as Friction,[2] Friction by the hand alone, supposing it could be applied *instantly.*—Two years ago I happened to be calling on Mrs. Sheldon when her Coachman sprained his foot as he was cleaning the Carriage and could hardly limp into the House—but by the immediate use of Friction alone, steadily persevered in, (and I rubbed his Ancle with my own hand for six Hours without Intermission)—he was well in three days.—Many Thanks my dear Tom, for the kindness with respect to us, which had so large a share in bringing on your accident—But pray: never run into Peril again, in looking for an Apothecary on our account, for had you the most experienced Man in his Line Settled at Sanditon, it would be no recommendation to us. We have entirely done with the whole Medical Tribe.[3] We have consulted Physician after Physician in vain, till we are quite convinced that they can do nothing for us and that we must trust to our own knowledge of our own wretched Constitutions for any relief.—But if you think it advisable for the interest of the *Place*, to get a Medical Man there, I will undertake the commission with pleasure, and have no doubt of succeeding.—I could soon put the necessary Irons in the fire.—As for getting to Sanditon myself, it is quite an Impos-

---

1 Bile is the bitter fluid secreted by the liver; an excess or an obstruction causes pain, nausea, and, in Diana's case, spasms.

2 Chafing or rubbing, a recognised treatment for various ailments, though not usually for sprains or strains.

3 Clichéd description for a group of doctors.

sibility. I greive to say that I dare not attempt it, but my feelings tell me too plainly that in my present state, the Sea air would probably be the death of me.—And neither of my dear Companions will leave me, or I would promote their going down to you for a fortnight. But in truth, I doubt whether Susan's nerves would be equal to the effort. She has been suffering much from the Headache and Six Leaches a day for ten days together[1] releived her so little that we thought it right to change our measures—and being convinced on examination that much of the Evil lay in her Gum, I persuaded her to attack the disorder there. She has accordingly had three Teeth drawn,[2] and is decidedly better, but her Nerves are a good deal deranged. She can only speak in a whisper—and fainted away twice this morning on poor Arthur's trying to suppress a cough. He, I am happy to say is tolerably well—tho' more languid than I like—and I fear for his Liver.[3]—I have heard nothing of Sidney since your being together in Town, but conclude his scheme to the Isle of Wight[4] has not taken place, or we should have seen him in his way.—Most sincerely do we wish you a good Season at Sanditon, and though we cannot contribute to your Beau Monde[5] in person, we are doing our utmost to send you Company worth having; and think we may safely reckon on securing you two large Families, one a rich West Indian from Surry,[6] the other, a most respectable Girls Boarding School,

---

1 In cases of headache, believed to be caused by excess of blood or a bilious constitution, it was thought to be beneficial to apply leeches to the temples or behind the ears.

2 A traumatic procedure, since there were no effective means of dulling the pain involved. A dentist of the time wrote that extraction was only used if all other ways of dealing with toothache failed: "But," he added, "persons are in general terrified at the thoughts, and strive by all possible means to avoid it"—an understandable response in the light of his account of everything that could go wrong, including extracting the wrong tooth (F.B. Spilsbury, *Every Lady and Gentleman Their Own Dentist, as Far as the Operations Will Allow* [London, 1791), pp. 33-36).

3 It was believed that sedentary or languid habits could be both cause and symptom of liver problems.

4 An island off the south coast of England, accessible from Southampton and Portsmouth, and visible from many towns and villages along the coast.

5 The French phrase had been used since the early eighteenth century to describe the fashionable world.

6 This would be the family of an English merchant who had made his fortune in the West Indies, or an English gentleman who had been living

or Academy, from Camberwell.[1]—I will not tell you how many People I have employed in the business—Wheel within wheel.— But Success more than repays.—Yours most affecly—&c" "Well—said Mr. Parker as he finished.—Though I dare say Sidney might find something extremely entertaining in this Letter and make us laugh for half an hour together I declare *I* by myself, can see nothing in it—but what is either very pitiable or very creditable.—With all their sufferings, you perceive how much they are occupied in promoting the Good of others!—So anxious for Sanditon! Two large Families—One, for Prospect House probably, the other, for No. 2 Denham Place—or the end house of the Terrace,—and extra Beds at the Hotel.—I told you my Sisters were excellent Women, Miss Heywood." "And I am sure they must be very extraordinary ones.—said Charlotte. I am astonished at the chearful style of the Letter, considering the state in which both Sisters appear to be.—Three Teeth drawn at once!—frightful!—Your Sister Diana seems almost as ill as possible, but those three Teeth of your Sister Susan's, are more distressing than all the rest.—" "Oh!—they are so used to the operation—to every operation—and have such Fortitude!—" "Your Sisters know what they are about, I dare say, but their Measures seem to touch on Extremes.—I feel that in any illness, *I* should be so anxious for Professional advice, so very little venturesome for myself, or any body I loved!—But then, *we* have been so healthy a family, that I can be no Judge of what the habit of self-doctoring may do.—" "Why to own the truth, said Mrs. Parker— I *do* think the Miss Parkers carry it too far sometimes—and so do you my Love, you know.—You often think they would be better, if they would leave themselves more alone—and especially Arthur. I know you think it a great pity they should give *him* such a turn for being ill.—" "Well, well—my dear Mary—I grant you, it *is* unfortunate for poor Arthur, that, at his time of Life he should be encouraged to give way to Indisposition. It *is* bad;—it *is* bad that he should be fancying himself too sickly for any Profession—and sit down at one and twenty, on the interest of his

---

on his West Indian plantations. Because of the large profits to be made in trade from the West Indies, such families would be assumed to be very wealthy. Surrey, then a rural county, lies between London and the south coast.

1   Then a village three miles south of the Thames, one of a series of small settlements within reach of the capital, but offering healthier air and surroundings.

own little Fortune, without any idea of attempting to improve it, or of engaging in any occupation that may be of use to himself or others.—But let us talk of pleasanter things.—These two large Families are just what we wanted—But—here is something at hand, pleasanter still—Morgan, with his "Dinner on Table."—

Chap. 6

The Party were very soon moving after Dinner. Mr. Parker could not be satisfied without an early visit to the Library, and the Library Subscription book,[1] and Charlotte was glad to see as much, and as quickly as possible, where all was new. They were out in the very quietest part of a Watering-place Day, when the important Business of Dinner or of sitting after Dinner was going on in almost every inhabited Lodging;—here and there a solitary Elderly Man might be seen, who was forced to move early and walk for health—but in general, it was a thorough pause of Company, it was Emptiness and Tranquillity on the Terrace, the Cliffs, and the Sands.—The Shops were deserted—the Straw Hats and pendant Lace seemed left to their fate both within the House and without, and Mrs. Whilby at the Library was sitting in her inner room, reading one of her own Novels, for want of employment.— The List of Subscribers was but commonplace. The Lady Denham, Miss Brereton, Mr. and Mrs. Parker—Sir Edward Denham and Miss Denham, whose names might be said to lead off the Season,[2] were followed by nothing better than—Mrs. Mathews— Miss Mathews, Miss E. Mathews, Miss H. Mathews.—Dr. and Mrs. Brown—Mr. Richard Pratt.—Lieutenant Smith RN.[3] Captain Little,—Limehouse.[4]—Mrs. Jane Fisher. Miss Fisher. Miss Scroggs.—Rev. Mr. Hankins. Mr. Beard—Solicitor, Grays Inn.[5]—Mrs. Davis. And Miss Merryweather.—Mr. Parker could

---

1 Since every genteel visitor to a resort would be expected to subscribe to the library, the subscription book acted as a kind of social register.

2 The resident gentry would naturally be the first names on the list, but, significantly, none of the visitors matches the residents in rank.

3 Lieutenant was a very modest rank in the Royal Navy. JA's two naval brothers, Frank and Charles, were promoted from lieutenant to captain at ages twenty-four and twenty-five respectively.

4 An area on the north bank of the Thames where many of London's port facilities were located.

5 One of the Inns of Court in London that formed the heart of the English legal system.

not but feel that the List was not only without Distinction, but less numerous than he had hoped. It was but July however, and August and September were the Months;[1]—And besides, the promised large Families from Surry and Camberwell, were an ever-ready consolation.—Mrs. Whitby came forward without delay from her Literary recess, delighted to see Mr. Parker again, whose manners recommended him to every body, and they were fully occupied in their various Civilities and Communications, while Charlotte having added her name to the List as the first offering to the success of the Season, was busy in some immediate purchases for the further good of Everybody, as soon as Miss Whitby could be hurried down from her Toilette,[2] with all her glossy Curls and smart Trinkets to wait on her.—The Library of course, afforded every thing; all the useless things in the World that could not be done without, and among so many pretty Temptations, and with so much good will for Mr. Parker to encourage Expenditure, Charlotte began to feel that she must check herself—or rather she reflected that at two and Twenty there could be no excuse for her doing otherwise—and that it would not do for her to be spending all her Money the very first Evening. She took up a Book; it happened to be a volume of *Camilla*.[3] She had not *Camilla's* Youth, and had no intention of having her Distress,—so, she turned from the Drawers of rings and Broches, repressed farther solicitation and paid for what she bought.—For her particular gratification, they were then to take a Turn on the Cliff—but as they quitted the Library they were met by two Ladies whose arrival made an alteration necessary, Lady Denham and Miss Brereton.—They had been to Trafalgar House, and been directed thence to the Library, and though Lady Denham was a great deal too active to regard the walk of a mile as anything requiring rest, and talked of going home again directly, the Parkers knew that to be pressed into their House, and obliged to take her Tea with them, would suit her best,—and

1 The summer holiday season extended from May to October, but was at its height in September.
2 The process of preparing her dress and appearance for public view.
3 *Camilla, or, a Picture of Youth* (5 vols, 1796), by Frances Burney. Camilla is just seventeen for the major part of the novel; her distresses include various social embarrassments caused by her impetuosity and inexperience. She is tempted to overspend a small allowance in the purchase of "little keep-sakes" at the beginning of a visit to the fashionable spa of Tunbridge Wells (Bk 6, ch. 2).

therefore the stroll on the Cliff gave way to an immediate return home.—"No, no, said her Ladyship—I will not have you hurry your Tea on my account.—I know you like your Tea late.—My early hours are not to put my Neighbours to inconvenience. No, no, Miss Clara and I will get back to our own Tea.—We came out with no other Thought.—We wanted just to see you and make sure of your being really come—, but we get back to our own Tea."—She went on however towards Trafalgar House and took possession of the Drawing room very quietly—without seeming to hear a word of Mrs. Parker's orders to the Servant as they entered, to bring Tea directly. Charlotte was fully consoled for the loss of her walk, by finding herself in company with those, whom the conversation of the morning had given her a great curiosity to see. She observed them well.—Lady Denham was of middle height, stout,[1] upright and alert in her motions, with a shrewd eye, and self-satisfied air—but not an unagreable Countenance— and tho' her manner was rather downright and abrupt, as of a person who valued herself on being free-spoken, there was a goodhumour and cordiality about her—a civility and readiness to be acquainted with Charlotte herself, and of a heartiness of wel- come towards her old friends, which was inspiring the Good will, she seemed to feel;—And as for Miss Brereton, her appearance so completely justified Mr. Parker's praise that Charlotte thought she had never beheld a more lovely, or more Interesting young Woman.—Elegantly tall, regularly handsome, with great delicacy of complexion and soft Blue eyes, a sweetly modest and yet nat- urally graceful Address, Charlotte could see in her only the most perfect representation of whatever Heroine might be most beau- tiful and bewitching, in all the numerous volumes they had left behind them on Mrs. Whilby's shelves.—Perhaps it might be partly oweing to her having just issued from a Circulating Library—but she could not separate the idea of a complete Hero- ine from Clara Brereton. Her situation with Lady Denham so very much in favour of it!—She seemed placed with her on pur- pose to be ill-used.—Such Poverty and Dependance joined to such Beauty and Merit, seemed to leave no choice in the busi- ness.—These feelings were not the result of any spirit of Romance in Charlotte herself. No, she was a very sober-minded young Lady, sufficiently well-read in Novels to supply her Imag- ination with amusements, but not at all unreasonably influenced by them; and while she pleased herself in the first five minutes

1 Strong; robust.

with fancying the Persecutions which *ought* to be the Lot of the interesting Clara, especially in the form of the most barbarous conduct on Lady Denham's side, she found no reluctance to admit from subsequent observation, that they appeared to be on very comfortable Terms.—She could see nothing worse in Lady Denham, than the sort of oldfashioned formality of always calling her *Miss Clara*—nor anything objectionable in the degree of observance and attention which Clara paid.—On one side it seemed protecting kindness, on the other grateful and affectionate respect.—The Conversation turned entirely upon Sanditon, its present number of Visitants[1] and the Chances of a good Season. It was evident that Lady Denham had more anxiety, more fears of loss, than her Coadjutor. She wanted to have the Place fill faster, and seemed to have many harassing apprehensions of the Lodgings being in some instances under-let.—Miss Diana Parker's two large Families were not forgotten. "Very good, very good, said her Ladyship.—A West Indy Family and a school. That sounds well. That will bring Money."—"No people spend more freely, I beleive, than West Indians,"[2] observed Mr. Parker.— "Aye—so I have heard—and because they have full Purses, fancy themselves equal, may be, to your old Country Families. But then, they who scatter their Money so freely, never think of whether they may not be doing mischeif by raising the price of Things—And I have heard that's very much the case with your West-ingines—and if they come among us to raise the price of our necessaries of Life, we shall not much thank them Mr. Parker."—"My dear Madam, they can only raise the price of consumeable Articles, by such an extraordinary Demand for them and such a diffusion of Money among us, as must do us more Good than harm.[3]—Our Butchers and Bakers and Traders in

---

1 A form of "visitors" becoming archaic in the early nineteenth century.

2 The wealthy West Indian merchants and their families were regarded as prone to temperamental and emotional extremes because of the hot climate (a belief still prevalent when Charlotte Brontë wrote of mad Bertha Mason in *Jane Eyre* [1847]).

3 Unstable market conditions resulting from the end of war with France in 1815 give this discussion particular resonance in 1817. The phenomenon on which Mr. Parker and Lady Denham express such different views had been influentially explored by Adam Smith, who favoured the working of the marketplace and concluded that even in case of sudden increase in demand, the price of commodities would maintain their "natural price" (*Wealth of Nations*, Vol. 1, p. 70).

general cannot get rich without bringing Prosperity to *us.*—If *they* do not gain, our rents must be insecure—and in proportion to their profit must be ours eventually in the increased value of our Houses." "Oh!—well.—But I should not like to have Butcher's meat raised, though—and I shall keep it down as long as I can.—Aye—that young Lady smiles I see;—I dare say she thinks me an odd sort of a Creature,—but *she* will come to care about such matters herself in time. Yes, yes, my Dear, depend upon it, you will be thinking of the price of Butcher's meat in time—tho' you may not happen to have quite such a Servants Hall to feed, as I have.—And I do beleive *those* are best off, that have fewest Servants.—I am not a Woman of Parade, as all the World knows, and if it was not for what I owe to poor Mr. Hollis's memory, I should never keep up Sanditon House as I do;—it is not for my own pleasure.—Well Mr. Parker—and the other is a Boarding school, a French Boarding School,[1] is it?—No harm in that.—They'll stay their six weeks.—And out of such a number, who knows but some may be consumptive and want Asses milk—and I have two Milch asses[2] at this present time.—But perhaps the little Misses may hurt the Furniture.—I hope they will have a good sharp Governess to look after them."—Poor Mr. Parker got no more credit from Lady Denham than he had from his Sisters, for the Object which had taken him to Willingden. "Lord! my dear Sir, she cried, how could you think of such a thing? I am very sorry you met with your accident, but upon my word you deserved it.—Going after a Doctor!—Why, what should we do with a Doctor here? It would be only encouraging our Servants and the Poor to fancy themselves ill, if there was a Doctor at hand.—Oh! pray, let us have none of the Tribe at Sanditon. We go on very well as we are. There is the Sea and the Downs and my Milch-asses—and I have told Mrs. Whilby that if any body enquires for a Chamber-Horse,[3] they may be supplied at a fair rate—(poor Mr. Hollis's Chamber Horse, as good as new)—and what can People

---

1 A boarding school run by a Frenchwoman or a woman purporting to be French. In the 1780s, JA and her sister Cassandra attended a school run by "Mrs. La Tournelle" (whose real name was Sarah Hackett).

2 Asses' milk was considered to resemble human milk, and therefore to be superior to other milk. It was seen as particularly suitable for asthmatics and consumptives.

3 An early exercise machine that simulated the experience of riding a horse. The word appears twice in this sentence; on the first occasion, JA writes "chamber-house," which seems to be a slip.

want for more?—Here have I lived seventy good years in the world and never took Physic above twice—and never saw the face of a Doctor in all my Life, on my *own* account.—And I verily beleive if my poor dear Sir Harry had never seen one neither, he would have been alive now.—Ten fees, one after another, did the Man take who sent *him* out of the World.—I beseech you Mr. Parker, no Doctors here."—

The Tea things were brought in.—"Oh! my dear Mrs. Parker—you should not indeed—Why would you do so? I was just upon the point of wishing you good Evening. But since you are so very neighbourly, I beleive Miss Clara and I must stay."—

Chapter 7.

The popularity of the Parkers brought them some visitors the very next morning;—amongst them, Sir Edward Denham and his Sister, who having been at Sanditon House drove on to pay their Compliments; and the duty of Letter-writing being accomplished, Charlotte was settled with Mrs. Parker in the Drawing room in time to see them all.—The Denhams were the only ones to excite particular attention. Charlotte was glad to complete her knowledge of the family by an introduction to them, and found them, the better half at least—(for while single the *Gentleman* may sometimes be thought the better half, of the pair)—not unworthy notice.—Miss Denham was a fine young woman, but cold and reserved, giving the idea of one who felt her consequence with Pride and her Poverty with Discontent, and who was immediately gnawed by the want of an handsomer Equipage than the simple Gig[1] in which they travelled, and which their Groom was leading about still in her sight.—Sir Edward was much her superior in air and manner;—certainly handsome, but yet more to be remarked for his very good Address and wish of paying attention and giving pleasure.—He came into the room remarkably well, talked much—and very much to Charlotte, by whom he chanced to be placed—and she soon perceived that he had a fine Countenance, a most pleasing gentleness of Voice, and a great deal of Conversation. She liked him.—Sober-minded as she was, she thought him agreable, and did not quarrel with the suspicion of his finding her equally so, which *would* arise, from his evidently disregarding his Sister's motion to go, and persisting in

---

1 A two-wheeled open carriage drawn by a single horse, designed to carry two people.

his station and his discourse.—I make no apologies for my Heroine's vanity.—If there are young Ladies in the World at her time of Life, more dull of Fancy and more careless of pleasing, I know them not, and never wish to know them.—At last, from the low French windows of the Drawing room which commanded the road and all the Paths across the Down, Charlotte and Sir Edward as they sat, could not but observe Lady Denham and Miss Brereton walking by—and there was instantly a slight change in Sir Edward's countenance—with an anxious glance after them as they proceeded—followed by an early proposal to his Sister—not only merely for moving, but for walking on together to the Terrace—which altogether gave an hasty turn to Charlotte's fancy, cured her of her halfhour's fever, and placed her in a more capable state of judging, when Sir Edward was gone, of *how* agreable he had actually been.—"Perhaps there was a good deal in his Air and Address; And his Title did him no harm." She was very soon in his company again. The first object of the Parkers, when their House was cleared of morning visitors was to get out themselves;—the Terrace was the attraction to all;—Every body who walked, must begin with the Terrace, and there, seated on one of the two Green Benches by the Gravel walk, they found the united Denham Party;—but though united in the Gross,[1] very distinctly divided again—the two superior Ladies being at one end of the bench, and Sir Edward and Miss Brereton at the other.—Charlotte's first glances told her that Sir Edward's air was that of a Lover.—There could be no doubt of his Devotion to Clara.—How Clara received it, was less obvious—but she was inclined to think not very favourably; for tho' sitting thus apart with him (which probably she might not have been able to prevent) her air was calm and grave.—That the young Lady at the other end of the Bench was doing Penance, was indubitable. The difference in Miss Denham's countenance, the change from Miss Denham sitting in cold Grandeur in Mrs. Parker's Drawing-room to be kept from silence by the efforts of others, to Miss Denham at Lady Denham's Elbow, listening and talking with smiling attention or solicitous eagerness, was very striking—and very amusing—or very melancholy, just as Satire or Morality might prevail.—Miss Denham's Character was pretty well decided with Charlotte. Sir Edward's required longer Observation. He surprised her by quitting Clara immediately on their all joining and agreeing to walk, and by addressing his attentions

---

1 In a general way.

entirely to herself.—Stationing himself close by her, he seemed to mean to detach her as much as possible from the rest of the Party and to give her the whole of his Conversation. He began, in a tone of great Taste and Feeling, to talk of the Sea and the Sea shore—and ran with Energy through all the usual Phrases employed in praise of their Sublimity,[1] and descriptive of the *undescribable* Emotions they excite in the Mind of Sensibility.— The terrific[2] Grandeur of the Ocean in a Storm, its glassy surface in a calm, it's Gulls and its Samphire,[3] and the deep fathoms of it's Abysses, it's quick vicissitudes, it's direful Deceptions, it's Mariners tempting it in Sunshine and overwhelmed by the sudden Tempest, all were eagerly and fluently touched;—rather commonplace perhaps—but doing very well from the Lips of a handsome Sir Edward,—and she could not but think him a Man of Feeling[4]—till he began to stagger her by the number of his Quotations, and the bewilderment of some of his sentences.—"Do you remember, said he, Scott's beautiful Lines on the Sea?—Oh! what a description they convey!—They are never out of my Thoughts when I walk here.—That Man who can read them unmoved must have the nerves of an Assassin![5]—Heaven defend me from meeting such a Man un-armed.—" "What description do you mean?—said Charlotte. I remember none at this moment,

---

1   Edmund Burke defined the sublime: "Whatever is fitted in any sort to excite the ideas of pain, and danger, that is to say, whatever is in any sort terrible, or is conversant about terrible objects, or operates in a manner analogous to terror, is a source of the *sublime*; that is, it is productive of the strongest emotion which the mind is capable of feeling" (*A Philosophical Enquiry into the Origin of Our Ideas of the Sublime and the Beautiful* [1757, 2nd ed., Section 7]).

2   Causing terror.

3   An aromatic plant that grows in rocks by the sea, the fleshy leaves of which are gathered for culinary purposes.

4   There may be a specific allusion here to the popular novel, *The Man of Feeling* (1771), by Henry Mackenzie, in which the eponymous hero Harley is so sensitive as to be debilitated from all meaningful action in the world, but the phrase had a more general application.

5   A word much beloved of Gothic novelists. In the lurid opening scene of *The Italian* (1797), Ann Radcliffe depicts English tourists in an Italian church encountering a figure with "an eye of uncommon ferocity" who turns out to be an assassin: "assassinations are so frequent," comments a local friar, "that our cities would be half depopulated" if sanctuary were not offered to the perpetrators (Vol. 1, ch. 1).

of the Sea, in either of Scott's Poems.—"[1] "Do not you indeed?
—Nor can I exactly recall the beginning at this moment—But—
you cannot have forgotten his description of Woman.—'Oh!
Woman in our Hours of Ease'[2]——Delicious! Delicious!—Had
he written nothing more, he would have been Immortal. And
then again, that unequalled, unrivalled Address to Parental affection—

> 'Some feelings are to Mortals given
> With less of Earth in them than Heaven' &c[3]

But while we are on the subject of Poetry, what think you Miss
Heywood of Burns Lines to his Mary?"[4]—
"Oh! there is Pathos to madden one!—If ever there was a
Man who *felt*, it was Burns.—Montgomery has all the Fire of

---

1 At this date, Walter Scott, the most popular poet of the time, was best
   known for *Marmion* (1808) and *The Lady of the Lake* (1810). In neither
   of these poems are there prominent "lines on the sea," though in
   Marmion, during an account of a voyage, "The whitening breakers
   sound so near / Where, boiling through the rocks they roar" (*Marmion:
   A Tale of Flodden Field* [3rd ed., 1808], Canto 2, verse 8).
2 The quotation comes from a moment of high drama in *Marmion*. Marmion has been fatally wounded and the maiden Clara comes to his aid:
     O, Woman! in our hours of ease,
     Uncertain, coy, and hard to please,
     And variable as the shade
     By the light quivering aspen made;
     When pain and anguish wring the brow,
     A ministering angel thou!—   (Canto 6, verse 30)
3 The lines come from *The Lady of the Lake* (1810, Canto 2, verse 22);
   they celebrate the selfless love of a father for his daughter. The quoted
   lines are followed by:
     And if there be a human tear
     From passion's dross refined and clear,
     A tear so limpid and so meek,
     It would not stain an angel's cheek,
     'Tis that which pious fathers shed
     Upon a duteous daughter's head!
4 Robert Burns became famous in the late 1780s as a rustic genius.
   "Mary" is likely to be Mary Campbell, known as "Highland Mary," with
   whom he planned, for a brief, intense period before her sudden death in
   1786, to share his life. He wrote several poems to her, including an elegy
   that was much anthologised. The poem finished:

Poetry,[1] Wordsworth has the true soul of it[2]—Campbell in his pleasures of Hope has touched the extreme of our Sensations— 'Like Angel's visits, few and far between.'[3] Can you conceive any thing more subduing, more melting, more fraught with the deep Sublime than that Line?—But Burns—I confess my sense of his Pre-eminence Miss Heywood.—If Scott *has* a fault, it is the want of Passion.—Tender, Elegant, Descriptive—but *Tame*.[4]—The Man who cannot do justice to the attributes of Woman is my contempt.—Sometimes indeed a flash of feeling seems to irradiate him—as in the Lines we were speaking of—'Oh! Woman in our hours of Ease'—. But Burns is always on fire.—His Soul was the Altar in which lovely Woman sat enshrined, his Spirit truly breathed the immortal Incence which is her Due.—" "I have read several of Burn's Poems with great delight, said Charlotte as soon

---

O pale, pale now, those rosy lips,
　I aft hae kiss'd sae fondly!
And clos'd for ay, the sparkling glance,
　That dwalt on me sae kindly!
And mouldering now in silent dust,
　That heart that lo'ed me dearly!
But still within my bosom's core,
　Shall live my Highland Mary.
(*The Works of Robert Burns* [4 vols, 1800], Vol. 4, p. 18.)

1　James Montgomery (1771-1854) was considered a dangerous radical in the 1790s. He later wrote narrative poetry on political themes, including *The West Indies*, marking the abolition of the slave trade (1807).

2　William Wordsworth (1770-1850) had by the 1810s outgrown the radicalism that had influenced the early volume of poems he wrote with Samuel Taylor Coleridge, *Lyrical Ballads* (1798), and had consolidated his poetic reputation with *Poems in Two Volumes* (1807) and *The Excursion* (1814).

3　Thomas Campbell (1777-1844) had his first success with the much-reprinted "The Pleasures of Hope," a lengthy meditation on hope in a world of war and injustice, which includes the lines:
　　Cease, every joy, to glimmer on my mind,
　　But leave—oh! leave—the light of Hope behind;
　　What though my winged hours of bliss have been,
　　Like angel visits, few and far between ... ("The Pleasures of Hope," Part 2, lines 221-24, in *The Pleasures of Hope: in Two Parts and Other Poems* [1799])

4　Scott reached the height of his popularity as a poet around 1810; in the 1810s, his romantic tales of the English and Scottish past began to seem tame in comparison with the obsessive characters, exotic locations, racy situations, and pyrotechnic poetic style of Lord Byron's mature poems.

as she had time to speak, but I am not poetic enough to separate a Man's Poetry entirely from his Character;—and poor Burns's known Irregularities, greatly interrupt my enjoyment of his Lines.—I have difficulty in depending on the *Truth* of his Feelings as a Lover. I have not faith in the *sincerity* of the affections of a Man of his Description. He felt and he wrote and he forgot."[1] "Oh! no no—exclaimed Sir Edward in an extasy. He was all ardour and Truth!—His Genius and his Susceptibilities might lead him into some Aberrations—But who is perfect?—It were Hyper-criticism, it were Pseudo-philosophy to expect from the soul of high toned Genius, the grovellings of a common mind.— The Coruscations[2] of Talent, elicited by impassioned feeling in the breast of Man, are perhaps incompatible with some of the prosaic Decencies of Life;—nor can you, loveliest Miss Heywood—(speaking with an air of deep sentiment)—nor can any Woman be a fair Judge of what a Man may be propelled to say, write or do, by the sovereign impulses of illimitable ardour." This was very fine;—but if Charlotte understood it at all, not very moral—and being moreover by no means pleased with his extraordinary stile of compliment, she gravely answered "I really know nothing of the matter.—This is a charming day. The Wind I fancy must be Southerly." "Happy, happy Wind, to engage Miss Heywood's Thoughts!—" She began to think him downright silly.—His chusing to walk with her, she had learnt to understand. It was done to pique Miss Brereton. She had read it, in an anxious glance or two on his side—but why he should talk so much Nonsense, unless he could do no better, was un-intelligible.—He seemed very sentimental, very full of some Feelings or other, and very much addicted to all the newest-fashioned hard words—had not a very clear Brain she presumed, and talked a good deal by rote.—The Future might explain him further—but

---

1   Aspects of Robert Burns's turbulent life were well known through a number of published biographies, and were regarded as closely allied to the power of his poetry. Robert Heron, for example, wrote that Burns "sings what he had himself ... felt with keen emotions of pain or pleasure. You actually see what he describes: you more than sympathise with his joys; your bosom is inflamed with all his fire: your heart dies away within you, infected by the contagion of his despondency" (*A Memoir of the Life of the Late Robert Burns* [Edinburgh, 1797], pp. 48-50). Byron praised Burns among poets who "Feel as they write, and write but as they feel" (*English Bards and Scotch Reviewers* [1809], line 817).

2   Quivering flashes of light, such as those sparking from stars.

when there was a proposition for going into the Library she felt that she had had quite enough of Sir Edward for one morning, and very gladly accepted Lady Denham's invitation of remaining on the Terrace with her.—The others all left them, Sir Edward with looks of very gallant despair in tearing himself away, and they united their agreableness—that is, Lady Denham like a true great Lady, talked and talked only of her own concerns, and Charlotte listened—amused in considering the contrast between her two companions.—Certainly, there was no strain of doubtful Sentiment, nor any phrase of difficult interpretation in Lady Denham's discourse. Taking hold of Charlotte's arm with the ease of one who felt that any notice from her was an Honour, and communicative, from the influence of the same conscious Importance or a natural love of talking, she immediately said in a tone of great satisfaction—and with a look of arch sagacity—"Miss Esther wants me to invite her and her Brother to spend a week with me at Sanditon House, as I did last Summer—But I sha'nt.—She has been trying to get round me every way, with her praise of this, and her praise of that; but I saw what she was about.—I saw through it all.—I am not very easily taken-in my Dear." Charlotte could think of nothing more harmless to be said, than the simple enquiry of—"Sir Edward and Miss Denham?"—"Yes, my Dear. *My young Folks*, as I call them sometimes, for I take them very much by the hand. I had them with me last Summer about this time, for a week; from Monday to Monday; and very delighted and thankful they were.—For they are very good young People my Dear. I would not have you think that I *only* notice them, for poor dear Sir Harry's sake. No, no; they are very deserving themselves, or trust me, they would not be so much in *my* Company.—I am not the Woman to help any body blindfold.—I always take care to know what I am about and who I have to deal with, before I stir a finger.—I do not think I was ever over-reached in my Life; and that is a good deal for a Woman to say that has been married twice.—Poor dear Sir Harry (between ourselves) thought at first to have got more—But (with a bit of a sigh) He is gone, and we must not find fault with the Dead. Nobody could live happier together than us—and he was a very honourable Man, quite the Gentleman of ancient Family.—And when he died, I gave Sir Edward his Gold Watch.—" She said this with a look at her Companion which implied its' right to produce a great Impression—and seeing no rapturous astonishment in Charlottes countenance, added quickly—"He did not bequeath it to his Nephew, my dear—It was no bequest. It was not in the Will. He only told me, and *that* but once, that he should wish his Nephew to have his Watch; but it need not have been binding, if I had not chose it."—"Very kind indeed! very Handsome!"— said Charlotte, absolutely forced to affect admiration.—"Yes, my dear—and it is not the *only* kind thing I have done by him.— I have been a very liberal friend to Sir Edward. And poor young Man, he needs it bad enough;—For though I am *only* the *Dowager*[1] my Dear, and he is the *Heir*, things do not stand between us in the way they commonly do between those two parties.— Not a shilling do I receive from the Denham Estate. Sir Edward has no Payments to make *me*. He don't stand uppermost, beleive me.—It is *I* that help *him*." "Indeed!—He is a very fine young Man;—particularly Elegant in his Address."—This was said cheifly for the sake of saying something—but Charlotte directly saw that it was laying her open to suspicion by Lady Denham's giving a shrewd glance at her and replying—"Yes, yes, he is very well to look at—and it is to be hoped some Lady of large fortune will think so—for Sir Edward *must* marry for Money.—He and I often talk that matter over.—A handsome young fellow like him, will go smirking and smiling about and paying girls compliments, but he knows he *must* marry for Money.—And Sir Edward is a very steady young Man in the main, and has got very good notions." "Sir Edward Denham, said Charlotte, with such personal Advantages may be almost sure of getting a Woman of fortune, if he chuses it."—This glorious sentiment seemed quite to remove suspicion. "Aye my Dear—That's very sensibly said, cried Lady Denham. And if we could but get a young Heiress to Sanditon! But Heiresses are monstrous scarce! I do not think we have had an Heiress here, or even a Co[2]—since Sanditon has been a public place. Families come after Families, but as far as I can learn, it is not one in an hundred of them that have any real Property, Landed or Funded.[3]—An Income perhaps, but no Property. Clergymen may be, or Lawyers from Town, or Half pay officers, or Widows

---

1 A woman whose husband is dead but who has a title or property that has come to her from him.

2 I.e., a co- or joint-heiress.

3 Income deriving from ownership of land, or money invested in government stocks or funds, the chief sources of the wealth of the aristocracy and gentry.

with only a Jointure.[1] And what good can such people do anybody?—except just as they take our empty Houses—and (between ourselves) I think they are great fools for not staying at home. Now, if we could get a young Heiress to be sent here for her health—(and if she was ordered to drink asses milk I could supply her)—and as soon as she got well, have her fall in love with Sir Edward!"—"That would be very fortunate indeed." "And Miss Esther must marry somebody of fortune too—She must get a rich Husband. Ah! young Ladies that have no Money are very much to be pitied!—But—after a short pause—if Miss Esther thinks to talk me into inviting them to come and stay at Sanditon House, she will find herself mistaken.—Matters are altered with me since last Summer you know—. I have Miss Clara with me now, which makes a great difference." She spoke this so seriously that Charlotte instantly saw in it the evidence of real penetration and prepared for some fuller remarks—but it was followed only by—"I have no fancy for having my House as full as an Hotel. I should not chuse to have my two Housemaids Time taken up all the morning, in dusting out Bed rooms.—They have Miss Clara's room to put to rights as well as my own every day.—If they had hard Places, they would want Higher wages.—" For objections of this Nature, Charlotte was not prepared, and she found it so impossible even to affect simpathy, that she could say nothing.— Lady Denham soon added, with great glee—"And besides all this my Dear, am I to be filling my House to the prejudice of Sanditon?—If People want to be by the Sea, why dont they take Lodgings?—Here are a great many empty Houses—three on this very Terrace; no fewer than three Lodging Papers staring in the face at this very moment, Numbers 3, 4 and 8. 8, the Corner House may be too large for them, but either of the two others are nice little snug Houses, very fit for a young Gentleman and his sister—And so, my dear, the next time Miss Esther begins talking about the Dampness of Denham Park, and the Good Bathing always does her, I shall advise them to come and take one of these Lodgings for a fortnight.—Don't you think that will be very fair?—Charity begins at home you know."—Charlotte's feelings were divided between amusement and indignation—but indigna-

---

1 Officers in the army and navy not on active service had their income reduced to what was usually called "half pay," though the actual figure could be a little more. Jointure was that part of an estate willed from husband to wife, usually a small proportion since the main part of the estate would go to the heir.

tion had the larger and the increasing share.—She kept her Countenance and she kept a civil Silence. She could not carry her forbearance farther; but without attempting to listen longer, and only conscious that Lady Denham was still talking on in the same way, allowed her Thoughts to form themselves into such a Meditation as this.—"She is thoroughly mean. I had not expected anything so bad.—Mr. Parker spoke too mildly of her.—His Judgement is evidently not to be trusted.—His own Goodnature misleads him. He is too kind hearted to see clearly.—I must judge for myself.—And their very *connection* prejudices him.—He has persuaded her to engage in the same Speculation—and because their object in that Line is the same, he fancies she feels like him in others.—But she is very, very mean.—I can see no Good in her.—Poor Miss Brereton!—And she makes every body mean about her.—This poor Sir Edward and his Sister,—how far Nature meant them to be respectable I cannot tell,—but they are *obliged* to be Mean in their Servility to her.—And I am Mean too, in giving her my attention, with the appearance of coinciding with her.—Thus it is, when Rich People are Sordid."—

Chapter 8.

The two Ladies continued walking together till rejoined by the others, who as they issued from the Library were followed by a young Whilby running off with five volumes[1] under his arm to Sir Edward's Gig—and Sir Edward approaching Charlotte, said "You may perceive what has been our occupation. My Sister wanted my Counsel in the selection of some books.—We have many leisure hours, and read a great deal.—I am no indiscriminate Novel-Reader. The mere Trash of the common Circulating Library, I hold in the highest contempt. You will never hear me advocating those puerile Emanations which detail nothing but discordant Principles incapable of Amalgamation, or those vapid tissues of ordinary Occurrences from which no useful Deductions can be drawn.[2]—In vain may we put them into a literary

---

1 Possibly Burney's *Camilla*, which Charlotte had already seen on Mrs. Whilby's counter and which was among the relatively few novels of the time published in as many as five volumes.

2 Circulating libraries offered books for loan in return for an annual subscription or fee; although they carried a wide range of fiction and non-fiction, circulating-library novels were a byword for trash. Sir

Alembic;—we distil nothing which can add to Science.[1]—You understand me I am sure?" "I am not quite certain that I do.—But if you will describe the sort of Novels which you *do* approve, I dare say it will give me a clearer idea." "Most willingly, Fair Questioner.[2]—The Novels which I approve are such as display Human Nature with Grandeur—such as shew her in the Sublimities of intense Feeling—such as exhibit the progress of strong Passion from the first Germ of incipient Susceptibility to the utmost Energies of Reason half-dethroned,—where we see the strong spark of Woman's Captivations elicit such Fire in the Soul of Man as leads him—(though at the risk of some Aberration from the strict line of Primitive[3] Obligations)—to hazard all, dare all, atchieve all, to obtain her.—Such are the Works which I peruse with delight, and I hope I may say, with Amelioration. They hold forth the most splendid Portraitures of high Conceptions, Unbounded Veiws, illimitable Ardour, indomptible Decision—and even when the Event is mainly anti-prosperous to the high-toned Machinations of the prime Character, the potent, pervading Hero of the Story, it leaves us full of Generous Emotions for him;—our Hearts are paralized—. T'were Pseudo-Philosophy to assert that we do not feel more enwraped by the brilliancy of his Career, than by the tranquil and morbid[4] Virtues

---

Edward's declaration forms a neat companion-piece to the famous description of the novel in *Northanger Abbey* (published at the end of 1817, but largely written much earlier) as a work "in which the greatest powers of the mind are displayed, in which the most thorough knowledge of human nature, the happiest delineation of its varieties, the liveliest effusions of wit and humour are conveyed to the world in the best chosen language" (Vol. 1, ch. 5). Throughout the eighteenth century, novelists claimed that their work offered a combination of instruction and entertainment. In the 1790s, fiction was often used to explore political ideas related to the French Revolution, while, in the early nineteenth century, many novels were either Gothic romances or domestic fiction, exploring moral issues more or less seriously through the presentation of day-to-day life.

1 An alembic is a glass vessel with a top, traditionally used for the distilling of chemicals, but acquiring a figurative meaning towards the end of the eighteenth century. "Science" meant general knowledge.

2 In *Camilla*, Miss Margland, trying to cajole the pretty, vain, and vacuous Indiana Lynmere, "began a negociation with the fair questioner" (Vol. 1, Bk 2, ch. 13).

3 Basic.

4 The traditional meaning is gloomy, brooding, but it here seems to have the implication of dullness.

of any opposing Character. Our approbation of the Latter is but Eleemosynary.[1]—These are the Novels which enlarge the primitive Capabilities of the Heart, and which it cannot impugn the Sense or be any Dereliction of the character, of the most anti-peurile Man, to be conversant with."—

"If I understand you aright—said Charlotte—our taste in Novels is not at all the same." And here they were obliged to part—Miss Denham being too much tired of them all, to stay any longer.—The truth was that Sir Edward whom circumstances had confined very much to one spot had read more sentimental Novels than agreed with him. His fancy had been early caught by all the impassioned, and most exceptionable parts of Richardsons;[2] and such Authors as have since appeared to tread in Richardson's steps, so far as Man's determined pursuit of Woman in defiance of every opposition of feeling and convenience is concerned,[3] had since occupied the greater part of his literary hours, and formed his Character.—With a perversity of Judgement, which must be attributed to his not having by Nature a very strong head, the Graces, the Spirit, the Ingenuity, and the Perseverance, of the Villain of the Story outweighed all his absurdities and all his Atrocities with Sir Edward. With him, such Conduct was Genius, Fire and Feeling.—It interested and inflamed him; and he was always more anxious for its Success and mourned over its Discomfitures with more Tenderness than could ever have been contemplated by the Authors.—Though he owed many of his ideas to this sort of reading, it were unjust to say that

---

1   Given or received as an act of charity; the word was mostly used in legal documents and social commentaries.

2   Richardson's novels attracted controversy because they seemed to wallow in their explorations of virtue in peril. *Clarissa* (1747-48) tells, at immense length and in the protagonists' own words, of the aristocratic Robert Lovelace's determination to seduce the virtuous Clarissa and her determination not to be seduced, despite finding herself in his power. The struggle ends in rape and Clarissa's death, and Richardson intended Lovelace's own subsequent death in a duel to be seen as punishment for his transgressions. However, to Richardson's consternation, Lovelace, endowed with wit, inventiveness, and humour, proved attractive to readers, and he took his place in a literary tradition of the (possibly) reformed rake.

3   The Lovelace figure was much copied by later novelists. Most of them replaced Richardson's subtleties with a much cruder representation of a predatory male, possibly appropriate in a melodramatic plot, but completely out of place in a realistic representation of contemporary life.

he read nothing else, or that his Language were not formed on a more general Knowledge of modern Literature.—He read all the Essays, Letters, Tours and Criticisms of the day—and with the same ill-luck which made him derive only false Principles from Lessons of Morality, and incentives to Vice from the History of it's overthrow, he gathered only hard words and involved sentences from the style of our most approved Writers.—

Sir Edward's great object in life was to be seductive.—With such personal advantages as he knew himself to possess, and such Talents as he did also give himself credit for, he regarded it as his Duty.—He felt that he was formed to be a dangerous Man—quite in the line of the Lovelaces.—The very name of Sir Edward he thought, carried some degree of fascination with it.—To be generally gallant and assiduous about the fair, to make fine speeches to every pretty Girl, was but the inferior part of the Character he had to play.—Miss Heywood, or any other young Woman with any pretensions to Beauty, he was entitled (according to his own veiws of Society) to approach with high Compliment and Rhapsody on the slightest acquaintance; but it was Clara alone on whom he had serious designs; it was Clara whom he meant to seduce.—Her seduction was quite determined on. Her Situation in every way called for it. She was his rival in Lady Denham's favour, she was young, lovely and dependant.—He had very early seen the necessity of the case, and had now been long trying with cautious assiduity to make an impression on her heart, and to undermine her Principles.—Clara saw through him, and had not the least intention of being seduced—but she bore with him patiently enough to confirm the sort of attachment which her personal Charms had raised.—A greater degree of discouragement indeed would not have affected Sir Edward—. He was armed against the highest pitch of Disdain or Aversion.—If she could not be won by affection, he must carry her off. He knew his Business.—Already had he had many Musings on the subject. If he *were* constrained so to act, he must naturally wish to strike out something new, to exceed those who had gone before him—and he felt a strong curiosity to ascertain whether the Neighbourhood of Tombuctoo might not afford some solitary House adapted for Clara's reception;[1]—but the Expence alas! of

---

1 Lovelace abducted Clarissa and took her to London; later novelists chose more exotic destinations. For instance, the obsessive Colonel Hargrave in Mary Brunton's *Self-Control* (1811) has the heroine carried off to a hut in the wilds of Canada. Little was known about Timbuctoo, an

Measures in that masterly style was ill-suited to his Purse, and Prudence obliged him to prefer the quietest sort of ruin and disgrace for the object of his Affections, to the more renowned.—

Chapter 9.

One day, soon after Charlotte's arrival at Sanditon, she had the pleasure of seeing just as she ascended from the Sands to the Terrace, a Gentleman's Carriage with Post Horses standing at the door of the Hotel, as very lately arrived, and by the quantity of Luggage taking off, bringing, it might be hoped, some respectable family determined on a long residence.—Delighted to have such good news for Mr. and Mrs. Parker, who had both gone home some time before, she proceeded for Trafalgar House with as much alacrity as could remain, after having been contending for the last two hours with a very fine wind blowing directly on shore; but she had not reached the little Lawn, when she saw a Lady walking nimbly behind her at no great distance; and convinced that it could be no acquaintance of her own, she resolved to hurry on and get into the House if possible before her. But the Stranger's pace did not allow this to be accomplished;— Charlotte was on the steps and had rung, but the door was not opened, when the other crossed the Lawn;—and when the Servant appeared, they were just equally ready for entering the House.—The ease of the Lady, her "How do you do Morgan?—" and Morgan's Looks on seeing her, were a moment's astonishment—but another moment brought Mr. Parker into the Hall to welcome the Sister he had seen from the Drawing room, and she was soon introduced to Miss Diana Parker. There was a great deal of surprise but still more pleasure in seeing her.—Nothing could be kinder than her reception from both Husband and Wife. "How did she come? and with whom?—And they were so glad to find her equal to the Journey!—And that she was to belong to *them*,[1] was a thing of course." Miss Diana Parker was about four and thirty, of middling height and slender;—delicate looking rather than sickly; with an agreable face, and a very animated eye;—her manners resembling her Brother's in their ease and frankness, though with more decision and less mildness in her Tone. She began an account of herself without delay—Thanking

---

ancient city on the southern edge of the African Sahara, and it was often used to signify the most distant place imaginable.

1 Be their guests.

them for their Invitation, but "*that* was quite out of the question, for they were all three come, and meant to get into Lodgings and make some stay."—"All three come!—What!—Susan and Arthur!—Susan able to come too!—This was better and better." "Yes—we are actually all come. Quite unavoidable.—Nothing else to be done.—You shall hear all about it.—But my dear Mary, send for the Children;—I long to see them."—"And how has Susan born the Journey?—and how is Arthur?—and why do not we see him here with you?"—

"Susan has born it wonderfully. She had not a wink of sleep either the night before we set out, or last night at Chichester,[1] and as this is Not so common with her as with *me*, I have had a thousand fears for her—but she has kept up wonderfully, had no Hysterics of consequence till we came within sight of poor old Sanditon—and the attack was not very violent—nearly over by the time we reached your Hotel—so that we got her out of the Carriage extremely well, with only Mr. Woodcock's assistance—and when I left her she was Directing the Disposal of the Luggage, and helping old Sam uncord the Trunks.—She desired her best Love, with a thousand regrets at being so poor a Creature that she could not come with me. And as for poor Arthur, he would not have been unwilling himself, but there is so much Wind that I did not think he could safely venture,—for I am *sure* there is Lumbago hanging about him—and so I helped him on with his great Coat and sent him off to the Terrace, to take us Lodgings.—Miss Heywood must have seen our Carriage standing at the Hotel.—I knew Miss Heywood the moment I saw her before me on the Down.—My dear Tom I am glad to see you walk so well. Let me feel your ancle.—That's right; all right and clean. The play of your Sinews a *very* little affected;—barely perceptible.—Well—now for the explanation of my being here.—I told you in my Letter, of the two considerable Families, I was hoping to secure for you—the West Indians, and the Seminary.[2]—" Here Mr. Parker drew his Chair still nearer to his Sister, and took her hand again most affectionately as he answered "Yes, Yes;—How active and how kind you have been!"—"The Westindians, she continued, whom I look upon as

---

1 A small town five miles inland from the south coast. See p. 274, note 1.

2 In the eighteenth century, a general synonym for "school," but by the early nineteenth century, particularly applied to a school for young ladies. In *Emma*, JA contrasts Mrs. Goddard's "real, honest, old-

the *most* desirable of the two—as the Best of the Good—prove to be a Mrs. Griffiths and her family. I know them only through others.—You must have heard me mention Miss Capper, the particular friend of *my* very particular friend Fanny Noyce;—now, Miss Capper is extremely intimate with a Mrs. Darling, who is on terms of constant correspondence with Mrs. Griffiths herself.— Only a *short* chain, you see, between us, and not a Link wanting. Mrs. Griffiths meant to go to the Sea, for her Young People's benefit—had fixed on the coast of Sussex, but was undecided as to the where, wanted something Private, and wrote to ask the opinion of her friend Mrs. Darling.—Miss Capper happened to be staying with Mrs. Darling when Mrs. Griffiths's Letter arrived, and was consulted on the question; *she* wrote the same day to Fanny Noyce and mentioned it to her—and Fanny all alive for *us*, instantly took up her pen and forwarded the circumstance to me—except as to *Names*—which have but lately transpired.— There was but *one* thing for *me* to do.—I answered Fanny's Letter by the same Post and pressed for the recommendation of Sanditon. Fanny had feared your having no house large enough to receive such a Family.—But I seem to be spinning out my story to an endless length.—You see how it was all managed. I had the pleasure of hearing soon afterwards by the same simple link of connection that Sanditon *had been* recommended by Mrs. Darling, and that the Westindians were very much disposed to go thither.—This was the state of the case when I wrote to you;— but two days ago;—yes, the day before yesterday—I heard again from Fanny Noyce, saying that *she* had heard from Miss Capper, who by a Letter from Mrs. Darling understood that Mrs. Griffiths has expressed herself in a letter to Mrs. Darling more doubtingly on the subject of Sanditon.—Am I clear?—I would be anything rather than not clear."—"Oh! perfectly, perfectly. Well?"—"The reason of this hesitation, was her having no connections in the place, and no means of ascertaining that she should have good accomodations on arriving there;—and she was particularly careful and scrupulous on all those matters more on account of a certain Miss Lambe a young Lady (probably a Neice) under her care, than on her own account or her Daugh-

---

fashioned Boarding-school" with "a seminary, or an establishment, or any thing which professed, in long sentences of refined nonsense, to combine liberal acquirements with elegant morality upon new principles and new systems—and where young ladies for enormous pay might be screwed out of health and into vanity" (Vol. 1, ch. 3).

ters.—Miss Lambe has an immense fortune—richer than all the rest—and very delicate health.—One sees clearly enough by all this, the *sort* of Woman Mrs. Griffiths must be—as helpless and indolent, as Wealth and a Hot Climate are apt to make us. But we are not all born to equal Energy.—What was to be done?—I had a few moments indecision;—whether to offer to write to *you*,—or to Mrs. Whitby to secure them a House?—but neither pleased me.—I hate to employ others, when I am equal to act myself—and my conscience told me that this was an occasion which called for me. Here was a family of helpless Invalides whom I might essentially serve.—I sounded Susan—the same Thought had occurred to her.—Arthur made no difficulties—our plan was arranged immediately, we were off yesterday morning at six—, left Chichester at the same hour to day—and here we are.—"

"Excellent!—Excellent!—cried Mr. Parker.—Diana, you are unequal'd in serving your friends and doing Good to all the World—I know nobody like you.—Mary, my Love, is not she a wonderful Creature?—Well—and now, what House do you design to engage for them?—What is the size of their family?—"

"I do not at all know—replied his Sister—have not the least idea;—never heard any particulars;—but I am very sure that the largest house at Sanditon cannot be *too* large. They are more likely to want a second.—I shall take only one however, and that, but for a week certain.—Miss Heywood, I astonish you.—You hardly know what to make of me.—I see by your Looks, that you are not used to such quick measures."—The words "Unaccountable officiousness!—Activity run mad!"—had just passed through Charlotte's mind—but a civil answer was easy. "I dare say I do look surprised, said she—because these are very great exertions, and I know what Invalides both You and Your Sister are." "Invalides indeed.—I trust there are not three People in England who have so sad a right to that appellation.—But my dear Miss Heywood, we are sent into this World to be as extensively useful as possible, and where some degree of Strength of Mind is given, it is not a feeble body which will excuse us—or incline us to excuse ourselves.—The World is pretty much divided between the weak of Mind and the Strong—between those who can act and those who can not and it is the bounden Duty of the Capable to let no opportunity of being useful escape them.—My Sister's Complaints and mine are happily not often of a Nature, to threaten Existence *immediately*—and as long as we *can* exert ourselves to be of use of others, I am convinced that the Body is the better, for the refreshment the Mind receives in doing its' Duty.—While I have been travelling, with this object in veiw, I have been perfectly well."—The entrance of the Children ended this little panegyric on her own Disposition—and after having noticed and caressed them all,—she prepared to go.— "Cannot you dine with us?—Is not it possible to prevail on you to dine with us?" was then the cry; and *that* being absolutely negatived, it was "And when shall we see you again? and how can we be of use to you?"—and Mr. Parker warmly offered his assistance in taking the house for Mrs. Griffiths.—"I will come to you the moment I have dined, said he, and we will go about together."—But this was immediately declined.—"No, my dear Tom, upon no account in the World, shall you stir a step on any business of mine.—Your Ancle wants rest. I see by the position of your foot, that you have used it too much already.—No, I shall go about my House-taking directly. Our Dinner is not ordered till six—and by that time I hope to have completed it. It is now only half past four.—As to seeing *me* again today—I cannot answer for it; the others will be at the Hotel all the Evening, and delighted to see you at any time, but as soon as I get back I shall hear what Arthur has done about our own Lodgings, and probably the moment Dinner is over, shall be out again on business relative to them, for we hope to get into some Lodgings or other and be settled after breakfast tomorrow.—I have not much confidence in poor Arthur's skill for Lodging-taking, but he seemed to like the commission.—" "I think you are doing too much, said Mr. Parker. You will knock yourself up. You should not move again after Dinner." "No, indeed you should not, cried his wife, for Dinner is such a mere *name* with you all, that it can do you no good.—I know what your appetites are."— "My appetite is very much mended I assure you lately. I have been taking some Bitters of my own decocting,[1] which have done wonders. Susan never eats—I grant you—and just at present *I* shall want nothing; I never eat for about a week after a Journey—but as for Arthur, he is only too much disposed for Food. We are often obliged to check him."—"But you have not told me any thing of the *other* Family coming to Sanditon, said Mr. Parker as he walked with her to the door of the House—the Camberwell Seminary; have we a good chance of *them*?"

---

1 Either quinine or bitter native herbs such as camomile or tansy, made into a medicine by boiling them down in water to a concentrate. Bitters were used against a wide range of ailments, including fevers and upset stomachs.

"Oh! Certain—quite certain.—I had forgotten them for the moment, but I had a letter three days ago from my friend Mrs. Charles Dupuis which assured me of Camberwell. Camberwell will be here to a certainty, and very soon.—*That* good Woman (I do not know her name) not being so wealthy and independant as Mrs. Griffiths—can travel and chuse for herself.—I will tell you how I got at *her*. Mrs. Charles Dupuis lives almost next door to a Lady, who has a relation lately settled at Clapham, who actually attends the Seminary and gives lessons on Eloquence and Belles Lettres[1] to some of the Girls.—I got that Man a Hare[2] from one of Sidney's friends—and he recommended Sanditon;—Without *my* appearing however—Mrs. Charles Dupuis managed it all."—

Chapter 10.

It was not a week, since Miss Diana Parker had been told by her feelings, that the Sea Air would probably in her present state, be the death of her, and now she was at Sanditon, intending to make some Stay, and without appearing to have the slightest recollection of having written or felt any such thing.—It was impossible for Charlotte not to suspect a good deal of fancy in such an extraordinary state of health.—Disorders and Recoveries so very much out of the common way, seemed more like the amusement of eager Minds in want of employment than of actual afflictions and releif. The Parkers, were no doubt a family of Imagination and quick feelings—and while the eldest Brother found vent for his superfluity of sensation as a Projector,[3] the Sisters were perhaps driven to dissipate theirs in the invention of odd complaints.—The *whole* of their mental vivacity was evidently not so employed; Part was laid out in a Zeal for being useful.—It should seem that they must either be very busy for the Good of others, or else extremely ill themselves. Some natural delicacy of Constitution in fact, with an unfortunate turn for medecine, especially quack Medecine, had given them an early tendency at various

---

1 Both subjects that formed a usual part of the curriculum for this kind of school. *Belles lettres* denotes elegant or polite literature.
2 At a time when animals and birds were shot on country estates or common land, they were often given or sold in this informal way rather than through butchers.
3 Someone who forms a project or enterprise, with some implication that the venture is misguided or foolish.

times, to various Disorders;—the rest of their Suffering was from Fancy, the love of Distinction and the love of the Wonderful.— They had charitable hearts and many amiable feelings—but a spirit of restless activity, and the glory of doing more than anybody else, had their share in every exertion of Benevolence—and there was Vanity in all they did, as well as in all they endured.—

Mr. and Mrs. Parker spent a great part of the Evening at the Hotel; but Charlotte had only two or three veiws of Miss Diana posting[1] over the Down after a House for this Lady whom she had never seen, and who had never employed her. She was not made acquainted with the others till the following day, when, being removed into Lodgings and all the party continuing quite well, their Brother and Sister and herself were entreated to drink tea with them.—They were in one of the Terrace Houses—and she found them arranged for the Evening, in a small neat Drawing room, with a beautiful veiw of the Sea if they had chosen it,— but though it had been a very fair English Summer-day,—not only was there no open window, but the Sopha and the Table, and the Establishment[2] in general was all at the other end of the room by a brisk fire.—Miss Parker whom, remembering the three Teeth drawn in one day, Charlotte approached with a peculiar degree of respectful Compassion, was not very unlike her Sister in person or manner—tho' more thin and worn by Illness and Medecine, more relaxed in air, and more subdued in voice. She talked however, the whole Evening as incessantly as Diana—and excepting that she sat with salts in her hand, took Drops two or three times from one, out of the several Phials already at home on the Mantlepeice,[3]—and made a great many odd faces and contortions, Charlotte could perceive no symptoms of illness which she, in the boldness of her own good health, would not have undertaken to cure, by putting out the fire, opening the Window, and disposing of the Drops and the Salts by means of one or the other. She had had considerable curiosity to see Mr. Arthur Parker; and having fancied him a very puny, delicate-looking young Man, the smallest very materially of not a robust Family, was astonished to find him quite as tall as his Brother and a great deal Stouter—Broad made and Lusty—and with no other look of

---

1 Hurrying (alluding to the swift movement of a post-chaise).
2 Arrangement, of both people and furniture.
3 Smelling salts, consisting usually of ammonium carbonate, were used to combat faintness; drops would usually be either laudanum (an opiate), or elixir of vitriol, taken to combat hysteria and flatulence.

an Invalide, than a sodden complexion.[1]—Diana was evidently the cheif of the family; principal mover and actor;—she had been on her Feet the whole Morning, on Mrs. Griffiths's business or their own, and was still the most alert of the three.—Susan had only superintended their final removal from the Hotel, bringing two heavy Boxes herself, and Arthur had found the air so cold that he had merely walked from one House to the other as nimbly as he could,—and boasted much of sitting by the fire till he had cooked up a very good one.—Diana, whose exercise had been too domestic to admit of calculation, but who, by her own account, had not once sat down during the space of seven hours, confessed herself a little tired. She had been too successful however for much fatigue; for not only had she by walking and talking down a thousand difficulties at last secured a proper House at eight guineas per week[2] for Mrs. Griffiths; she had also opened so many Treaties with Cooks, Housemaids, Washerwomen and Bathing Women,[3] that Mrs. Griffiths would have little more to do on her arrival, than to wave her hand and collect them around her for choice.—Her concluding effort in the cause, had been a few polite lines of Information to Mrs. Griffiths herself—time not allowing for the circuitous train of intelligence which had been hitherto kept up,—and she was now regaling in the delight of opening the first Trenches of an acquaintance with such a powerful discharge of unexpected obligation.[4] Mr. and Mrs. Parker and Charlotte had seen two Post chaises crossing the Down to the Hotel as they were setting off,—a joyful sight—and full of speculation.—The Miss Parkers and Arthur had also seen something;—they could distinguish from their window that there *was* an arrival at the Hotel, but not its amount. Their visitors answered for two Hack-Chaises.[5]—Could it be the Camberwell Seminary?—No—No.—Had there been a third carriage, perhaps

---

1   The modern meaning of "stout"—plump, corpulent—was just coming into use in the early nineteenth century; JA may intend this, or the earlier use of well- or strongly-made. "Lusty": large, or substantial. "Sodden": characterised by heaviness or dullness.
2   A substantial rent for the period.
3   Women employed to assist bathers to change and get in and out of the sea or seawater-bath.
4   Unusual use of the military metaphors, including the term for digging of hollows or ditches in the ground.
5   A "hack" or "hackney-chaise," like a post chaise, was a coach available for hire.

it might; but it was very generally agreed that two Hack chaises could never contain a Seminary.—Mr. Parker was confident of another new Family.—When they were all finally seated, after some removals to look at the Sea and the Hotel, Charlotte's place was by Arthur, who was sitting next to the Fire with a degree of Enjoyment which gave a good deal of merit to his civility in wishing her to take his Chair.—There was nothing dubious in her manner of declining it, and he sat down again with much satisfaction. She drew back her Chair to have all the advantage of his Person as a screen, and was very thankful for every inch of Back and Shoulders beyond her pre-conceived idea. Arthur was heavy in Eye as well as figure, but by no means indisposed to talk;—and while the other four were cheifly engaged together, he evidently felt it no penance to have a fine young Woman next to him, requiring in common Politeness some attention—as his Brother, who felt the decided want of some motive for action, some Powerful object of animation for him, observed with considerable pleasure.—Such was the influence of Youth and Bloom that he began even to make a sort of apology for having a Fire. "We should not have one at home, said he, but the Sea air is always damp. I am not afraid of any thing so much as Damp.—" "I am so fortunate, said Charlotte as never to know whether the air is damp or dry. It has always some property that is wholesome and invigorating to me.—" "*I* like the air too, as well as anybody can; replied Arthur, I am very fond of standing at an open window when there is no Wind—but unluckily a Damp air does not like *me*.—It gives me the Rheumatism.—You are not rheumatic I suppose?—" "Not at all." "That's a great blessing.—But perhaps you are nervous." "No—I beleive not. I have no idea that I am."—"*I* am very nervous.—To say the truth—Nerves are the worst part of my Complaints in *my* opinion.[1]—My Sisters think me Bilious, but I doubt it.—" "You are quite in the right, to doubt it as long as you possibly can, I am sure.—" "If I were Bilious, he continued, you know Wine would disagree with me, but it always does me good.—The more Wine I drink (in moderation) the better I am.—I am always best of an Evening.—If you had seen me today

---

1 "Of all diseases incident to mankind, those of the nervous kind are the most complicated and difficult to cure. A volume would not be sufficient to point out their various appearances. They imitate almost every disease; and are seldom alike in two different persons, or even the same person at different times" (George Buchan, *Domestic Medicine*, p. 420).

before Dinner, you would have thought me a very poor Creature.—" Charlotte could beleive it—. She kept her countenance however, and said—"As far as I can understand what nervous complaints are, I have a great idea of the efficacy of air and exercise for them:—daily, regular Exercise;—and I should recommend rather more of it to *you* than I suspect you are in the habit of taking.—" "Oh! I am very fond of exercise myself—he replied—and mean to walk a great deal while I am here, if the Weather is temperate. I shall be out every morning before breakfast—and take several turns upon the Terrace, and you will often see me at Trafalgar House."—"But you do not call a walk to Trafalgar House much exercise?—" "Not, as to mere distance, but the Hill is so steep!—Walking up that Hill, in the middle of the day, would throw me into such a Perspiration!—You would see me all in a Bath by the time I got there!—I am very subject to Perspiration, and there cannot be a surer sign of Nervousness.—" They were now advancing so deep in Physics,[1] that Charlotte veiwed the entrance of the Servant with the Tea things, as a very fortunate Interruption.—It produced a great and immediate change. The young Man's attentions were instantly lost. He took his own Cocoa from the Tray,—which seemed provided with almost as many Tea-pots &c as there were persons in company, Miss Parker drinking one sort of Herb-Tea and Miss Diana another, and turning completely to the Fire, sat coddling and cooking it to his own satisfaction and toasting some Slices of Bread, brought up ready-prepared in the Toast rack—and till it was all done, she heard nothing of his voice but the murmuring of a few broken sentences of self-approbation and success.— When his Toils were over however, he moved back his Chair into as gallant a Line as ever, and proved that he had not been working only for himself, by his earnest invitation to her to take both Cocoa and Toast.—She was already helped to Tea—which surprised him—so totally self-engrossed had he been.—"I thought I should have been in time, said he, but cocoa takes a great deal of Boiling."—"I am much obliged to you, replied Charlotte—but I *prefer* Tea." "Then I will help myself, said he.—A large Dish of rather weak Cocoa every evening, agrees with me better than any thing."—

It struck her however, as he poured out this rather weak Cocoa, that it came forth in a very fine, dark coloured stream—

---

1 The scientific study of human beings and of the laws that govern the
  human body.

and at the same moment, his Sisters both crying out—"Oh! Arthur, you get your Cocoa stronger and stronger every Evening"—, with Arthur's somewhat conscious reply of "*Tis* rather stronger than it should be tonight"—convinced her that Arthur was by no means so fond of being starved as they could desire, or as he felt proper himself.—He was certainly very happy to turn the conversation on dry Toast, and hear no more of his Sisters.—"I hope you will eat some of this Toast, said he, I reckon myself a very good Toaster; I never burn my Toasts—I never put them too near the Fire at first—and yet, you see, there is not a Corner but what is well browned.—I hope you like dry Toast.—" "With a reasonable quantity of Butter spread over it, very much—said Charlotte—but not otherwise.—" "No more do I—said he exceedingly pleased—We think quite alike there.—So far from dry Toast being wholesome, *I* think it a very bad thing for the Stomach. Without a little butter to soften it, it hurts the Coats of the Stomach.[1] I am sure it does.—I will have the pleasure of spreading some for you directly—and afterwards. I will spread some for myself.—Very bad indeed for the Coats of the Stomach—but there is no convincing *some* people.—It irritates and acts like a nutmeg grater.—" He could not get the command of the Butter however, without a struggle; His Sisters accusing him of eating a great deal too much, and declaring he was not to be trusted;—and he maintaining that he only eat enough to secure the Coats of his Stomach;—and besides, he only wanted it now for Miss Heywood.—Such a plea must prevail, he got the butter and spread away for her with an accuracy of Judgement which at least delighted himself; but when her Toast was done, and he took his own in hand, Charlotte could hardly contain herself as she saw him watching his Sisters, while he scrupulously scraped off almost as much butter as he put on, and then seize an odd moment for adding a great dab just before it went into his Mouth.—Certainly, Mr. Arthur Parker's enjoyments in Invalidism were very different from his Sisters—by no means so spiritualized.—A good deal of Earthy Dross[2] hung about him. Char-

---

1 "Coats" are the protective layers of membrane lining the stomach. Butter was seen as potentially harmful to health: because it went rancid easily, it upset the stomach, and bread without butter was recommended on health grounds.

2 "Dross" was the scum thrown off from metals in the process of melting; the phrase is used more generally to mean impure materiality compared with a purer spirituality, similar to "common clay."

lotte could not but suspect him of adopting that line of Life, principally for the indulgence of an indolent Temper—and to be determined on having no Disorders but such as called for warm rooms and good Nourishment.—In one particular however, she soon found that he had caught something from *them*.—"What! said he—Do you venture upon two dishes of strong Green Tea in one Evening?—What Nerves you must have!—How I envy you.—Now, if *I* were to swallow only one such dish—what do you think it's effect would be upon me?—" "Keep you awake perhaps all night"—replied Charlotte, meaning to overthrow his attempts at Surprise, by the Grandeur of her own Conceptions.—"Oh! if that were all!—he exclaimed.—No—it would act on me like Poison and entirely take away the use of my right side, before I had swallowed it five minutes.—It sounds almost incredible—but it has happened to me so often that I cannot doubt it.—The use of my right Side is entirely taken away for several hours!" "It sounds rather odd to be sure—answered Charlotte coolly—but I dare say it would be proved to be the simplest thing in the World, by those who have studied right sides and Green Tea scientifically[1] and thoroughly understand all the possibilities of their action on each other."—Soon after Tea, a Letter was brought to Miss Diana Parker from the Hotel.—"From Mrs. Charles Dupuis—said she.—some private hand."[2]—And having read a few lines, exclaimed aloud "Well, this is very extraordinary! very extraordinary indeed!—That both should have the same name.—Two Mrs. Griffiths!—This is a Letter of recommendation and introduction to me, of the Lady from Camberwell—and *her* name happens to be Griffiths too."—A few lines more however, and the colour rushed into her Cheeks, and with much Perturbation she added—"The oddest thing that ever was!—a Miss Lambe too!—a young Westindian of large Fortune.—But it *cannot* be the same.—Impossible that it should be the same."—She read the Letter aloud for comfort.—It was merely to "introduce the Bearer, Mrs. Griffiths from Camberwell, and the three young Ladies under her care, to Miss Diana Parker's notice.—Mrs. Griffiths being a stranger at Sanditon, was anxious for a respectable Introduction—and Mrs. Charles Dupuis therefore, at

---

1 A number of eighteenth-century treatises assessed the health benefits of tea, both black and green. Buchan felt that the real problem was the "imprudent use" of it; he particularly advised against drinking tea in the morning (*Domestic Medicine*, pp. 66-67).

2 A personal letter, delivered by private carrier.

the instance of the intermediate friend, provided her with this Letter, knowing that she could not do her dear Diana a greater kindness than by giving her the means of being useful.—Mrs. Griffiths's cheif solicitude would be for the accomodation and comfort of one of the young Ladies under her care, a Miss Lambe, a young West Indian of large Fortune, in delicate health."—"It was very strange!—very remarkable!—very extraordinary" but they were all agreed in determining it to be *impossible* that there should not be two Families; such a totally distinct set of people as were concerned in the reports of each made that matter quite certain. There *must* be two Families.—Impossible to be otherwise. "Impossible" and "Impossible", was repeated over and over again with great fervour.—An accidental resemblance of Names and circumstances, however striking at first, involved nothing really incredible—and so it was settled.—Miss Diana herself derived an immediate advantage to counterbalance her Perplexity. She must put her shawl over her shoulders, and be running about again. Tired as she was, she must instantly repair to the Hotel, to investigate the truth and offer her Services.—

Chapter 11.

It would not do.—Not all that the whole Parker race could say among themselves, could produce a happier catastrophée[1] than that the Family from Surry and the Family from Camberwell were one and the same.—The rich Westindians, and the young Ladies Seminary had all entered Sanditon in those two Hack chaises. The Mrs. Griffiths who in her friend Mrs. Darling's hands, had wavered as to coming and been unequal to the Journey, was the very same Mrs. Griffiths whose plans were at the same period (under another representation) perfectly decided, and who was without fears or difficulties.—All that had the appearance of Incongruity in the reports of the two, might very fairly be placed to the account of the Vanity, the Ignorance, or the blunders of the many engaged in the cause by the vigilance and caution of Miss Diana Parker. *Her* intimate friends must be officious like herself, and the subject had supplied Letters and Extracts and Messages enough to make everything appear what it was not. Miss Diana probably felt a little awkward on being first obliged to admit her mistake. A long Journey from Hamp-

---

1   The denouement, the action that produces the resolution and conclusion of a dramatic piece.

shire taken for nothing—a Brother disappointed—an expensive House on her hands for a week, must have been some of her immediate reflections—and much worse than all the rest, must have been the sort of sensation of being less clear-sighted and infallible than she had beleived herself.—No part of it however seemed to trouble her long. There were so many to share in the shame and the blame, that probably when she had divided out their proper portions to Mrs. Darling, Miss Capper, Fanny Noyce, Mrs. Charles Dupuis and Mrs. Charles Dupuis's Neighbour, there might be a mere trifle of reproach remaining for herself.—At any rate, she was seen all the following morning walking about after Lodgings with Mrs. Griffiths—as alert as ever.—Mrs. Griffiths was a very well behaved, genteel kind of Woman, who supported herself by receiving such great girls and young Ladies, as wanted either Masters for finishing their Education, or a home for beginning their Displays.[1]—She had several more under her care than the three who were now come to Sanditon, but the others all happened to be absent.—Of these three, and indeed of all, Miss Lambe was beyond comparison the most important and precious, as she paid in proportion to her fortune.—She was about seventeen, half-mulatto,[2] chilly and tender, had a maid of her own, was to have the best room in the Lodgings, and was always of the first consequence in every plan of Mrs. Griffiths.—The other Girls, two Miss Beauforts were just such young Ladies as may be met with, in at least one family out of three, throughout the Kingdom; they had tolerable complexions, shewey figures, an upright decided carriage and an assured Look;—they were very accomplished and very Ignorant, their time being divided between such pursuits as might attract admiration, and those Labours and Expedients of dexterous Ingenuity, by which they could dress in a stile much beyond what they *ought* to have afforded; they were some of the first in every change of fashion—and the object of all, was to captivate some Man of much better fortune than their own.—Mrs. Griffiths had preferred a small, retired place, like Sanditon, on Miss Lambe's account—and the Miss Beauforts, though naturally preferring

---

1 Acquiring and learning how to show off the accomplishments.

2 A mulatto was the child of a black and a white person, often a female slave and male slave owner; the term was used more generally for someone of mixed race. See, for example, "Miss Swartz, the rich woolly-haired mulatto from St. Kitts" (William Thackeray, *Vanity Fair* [London, 1847], Vol. 1, ch. 1); the novel is set in the 1810s.

any thing to Smallness and Retirement, yet having in the course of the Spring been involved in the inevitable expence of six new Dresses each for a three days visit, were constrained to be satisfied with Sanditon also, till their circumstances were retreived. There, with the hire of a Harp for one, and the purchase of some Drawing paper for the other and all the finery they could already command, they meant to be very economical, very elegant and very secluded; with the hope on Miss Beaufort's side, of praise and celebrity from all who walked within the sound of her Instrument, and on Miss Letitia's, of curiosity and rapture in all who came near her while she sketched—and to Both, the consolation of meaning to be the most stylish Girls in the Place.—The particular introduction of Mrs. Griffiths to Miss Diana Parker, secured them immediately an acquaintance with the Trafalgar House-family, and with the Denhams;—and the Miss Beauforts were soon satisfied with "the Circle in which they moved in Sanditon" to use a proper phrase, for every body must now "move in a Circle",—to the prevalence of which rotatory Motion, is perhaps to be attributed the Giddiness and false steps of many.— Lady Denham had other motives for calling on Mrs. Griffiths besides attention to the Parkers.—In Miss Lambe, here was the very young Lady, sickly and rich, whom she had been asking for; and she made the acquaintance for Sir Edward's sake, and the sake of her Milch asses. How it might answer with regard to the Baronet, remained to be proved, but as to the Animals, she soon found that all her calculations of Profit would be vain. Mrs. Griffiths would not allow Miss Lambe to have the smallest symptom of a Decline,[1] or any complaint which Asses milk could possibly releive. "Miss Lambe was under the constant care of an experienced Physician;—and his Prescriptions must be their rule—" and except in favour of some Tonic Pills, which a Cousin of her own had a Property in,[2] Mrs. Griffiths did never deviate from the strict medecinal page.—The corner house of the Terrace was the one in which Miss Diana Parker had the pleasure of settling her new friends, and considering that it commanded in front the favourite Lounge[3] of all the Visitors at Sanditon, and on one side, whatever might be going on at the Hotel, there could not have

---

1 Not merely a general failure of health, but a more specific disease, such as tuberculosis, in which bodily strength gradually fails.
2 Mrs. Griffiths's cousin had invested in the company or concern that produced the tonic pills.
3 Place for strolling or lounging about.

been a more favourable spot for the seclusions of the Miss Beauforts. And accordingly, long before they had suited themselves with an Instrument, or with Drawing paper, they had, by the frequency of their appearance at the low Windows upstairs,[1] in order to close the blinds, or open the Blinds, to arrange a flower pot on the Balcony, or look at nothing through a Telescope,[2] attracted many an eye upwards, and made many a Gazer gaze again.—A little novelty has a great effect in so small a place; the Miss Beauforts, who would have been nothing at Brighton, could not move here without notice;—and even Mr. Arthur Parker, though little disposed for supernumerary exertion, always quitted the Terrace, in his way to his Brothers by this corner House, for the sake of a glimpse of the Miss Beauforts, though it was half a quarter of a mile roundabout, and added two steps to the ascent of the Hill.

Chapter 12.

Charlotte had been ten days at Sanditon without seeing Sanditon House, every attempt at calling on Lady Denham having been defeated by meeting with her beforehand. But now it was to be more resolutely undertaken, at a more early hour, that nothing might be neglected of attention to Lady Denham or amusement to Charlotte.—"And if you should find a favourable opening my Love, said Mr. Parker (who did not mean to go with them)—I think you had better mention the poor Mullins's situation, and sound her Ladyship as to a Subscription for them.[3] I am not fond of charitable subscriptions in a place of this kind—It is a sort of tax upon all that come—Yet as their distress is very great and I almost promised the poor Woman yesterday to get something

---

1 In Georgian houses, the living rooms were often above ground level, with a balcony outside, and large or full-length windows through which the occupants could see and be seen.

2 In the early years of the nineteenth century, the astronomical work of brother and sister, William and Caroline Herschel, did much to make astronomy popular as a pastime for both men and women.

3 At a time when there was little organised poor relief, the responsibility for assisting the poor was usually a matter of private charity. A subscription was an arrangement whereby people signed up to make a specific contribution to a worthy cause, and the participation of prominent people encouraged others to contribute. In the hard times following the war in 1815, the number of charitable subscriptions increased rapidly, and they were regarded with increasing ambivalence as a result.

done for her, I beleive we must set a subscription on foot and therefore the sooner the better,—and Lady Denham's name at the head of the List will be a very necessary beginning.—You will not dislike speaking to her about it, Mary?—" "I will do whatever you wish me, replied his Wife—but you would do it so much better yourself. I shall not know what to say."—"My dear Mary, cried he, it is impossible you can be really at a loss. Nothing can be more simple. You have only to state the present afflicted situation of the family, their earnest application to me, and my being willing to promote a little subscription for their releif, provided it meet with her approbation."—"The easiest thing in the World—cried Miss Diana Parker who happened to be calling on them at the moment—. All said and done, in less time than you have been talking of it now.—And while you are on the subject of subscriptions Mary, I will thank you to mention a very melancholy case to Lady Denham, which has been represented to me in the most affecting terms.—There is a poor Woman in Worcestershire, whom some friends of mine are exceedingly interested about, and I have undertaken to collect whatever I can for her.[1] If you would mention the circumstance to Lady Denham!—Lady Denham *can* give, if she is properly attacked—and I look upon her to be the sort of Person who, when once she is prevailed on to undraw[2] her Purse, would as readily give ten guineas as five.[3]—And therefore, if you find her in a Giving mood, you might as well speak in favour of another Charity which I and a few more, have very much at heart—the establishment of a Charitable Repository at Burton on Trent.[4]—And then,—there is the family of the poor Man who was hung last assizes at York,[5] tho' we really *have* raised

---

1 Worcestershire is a rural county north west of London, about two hundred miles from Sanditon. Charitable intervention was usually very local.

2 Unfasten.

3 Either of these sums would be a substantial charitable donation.

4 Burton on Trent was a manufacturing town in Staffordshire, about two hundred miles north of the Sussex coast. A charitable repository was a place where donated goods were sold for the benefit of the poor, the precursor of the modern-day charity shop.

5 A town fully three hundred miles north of Sanditon. The assizes were local court sessions, held periodically, with lawyers travelling from one location to the next to participate. Crimes carrying the death penalty included forgery, theft of goods of relatively small value, and—particularly relevant to York as a major staging post on the Great North Road between London and Edinburgh—highway robbery.

the sum we wanted for putting them all out,[1] yet if you *can* get a Guinea from her on their behalf, it may as well be done.—" "My dear Diana! exclaimed Mrs. Parker—I could no more mention these things to Lady Denham than I could fly."—"Where's the difficulty?—I wish I could go with you myself—but in five minutes I must be at Mrs. Griffiths's—to encourage Miss Lambe in taking her first Dip. She is so frightened, poor Thing, that I promised to come and keep up her Spirits, and go in the Machine[2] with her if she wished it—and as soon as that is over, I must hurry home, for Susan is to have Leaches at one oclock which will be a three hours business,[3]—therefore I really have not a moment to spare—besides that (between ourselves) I ought to be in bed myself at this present time, for I am hardly able to stand—and when the Leaches have done, I dare say we shall both go to our rooms for the rest of the day."—"I am sorry to hear it, indeed; but if this is the case I hope Arthur will come to us."—"If Arthur takes my advice, he will go to bed too, for if he stays up by himself, he will certainly eat and drink more than he ought;—but you see Mary, how impossible it is for me to go with you to Lady Denham's."—"Upon second thoughts Mary, said her husband, I will not trouble you to speak about the Mullins's.—I will take an opportunity of seeing Lady Denham myself.—I know how little it suits you to be pressing matters upon a Mind at all unwilling."—*His* application thus withdrawn, his sister could say no more in support of hers, which was his object, as he felt all their impropriety and all the certainty of their ill effect upon his own better claim.—Mrs. Parker was delighted at this release, and set off very happy with her friend and her little girl, on this walk to Sanditon House.—It was a close, misty morning, and when they reached the brow of the Hill, they could not for some time make out what sort of Carriage it was, which they saw coming up. It appeared at different moments to be everything from the Gig to the Phaeton,—from one horse to four; and just as they were concluding in favour of

---

1 Setting them up in apprenticeships or other jobs, which would require the payment of an initial premium.
2 See p. 342, note 5.
3 Applying leeches was a delicate operation: they were usually pressed against the skin in a small glass until they fastened on to the flesh. Once they were pulled away, pressure had to be applied to the wound to stop the flow of blood.

a Tandem,[1] little Mary's young eyes distinguished the Coachman and she eagerly called out, "T'is Uncle Sidney Mama, it is indeed." And so it proved.—Mr. Sidney Parker driving his Servant in a very neat Carriage was soon opposite to them, and they all stopped for a few minutes. The manners of the Parkers were always pleasant among themselves—and it was a very friendly meeting between Sidney and his Sister in law, who was most kindly taking it for granted that he was on his way to Trafalgar House. This he declined however. "He was just come from Eastbourne, proposing to spend two or three days, as it might happen, at Sanditon—but the Hotel must be his Quarters—He was expecting to be joined there by a friend or two."—The rest was common enquiries and remarks, with kind notice of little Mary, and a very well-bred Bow and proper address to Miss Heywood on her being named to him—and they parted, to meet again within a few hours.—Sidney Parker was about seven or eight and twenty, very good-looking with a decided air of Ease and Fashion, and a lively countenance.—This adventure afforded agreable discussion for some time. Mrs. Parker entered into all her Husband's joy on the occasion, and exulted in the credit which Sidney's arrival would give to the place. The road to Sanditon House was a broad, handsome, planted approach[2] between fields, and conducting at the end of a quarter of a mile through second Gates into the Grounds, which though not extensive had all the Beauty and Respectability which an abundance of very fine Timber[3] could give.—These Entrance Gates were so much in a corner of the Grounds or Paddock, so near one of its Boundaries, that an outside fence was at first almost pressing on the road—till an angle *here*, and a curve there threw them to a better distance. The Fence was a proper Park paling in excellent condition; with clusters of fine Elms, or rows of old Thorns following its line almost every where.[4]—*Almost* must be

---

1 A gig is a light two-wheeled carriage drawn by a single horse. A phaeton is a slightly more substantial four-wheeled open carriage drawn by a pair of horses. A tandem is a two-wheeled carriage drawn by two horses harnessed one behind the other.

2 The drive to the house is formally planted with trees on either side for an aesthetic effect becoming slightly outmoded by the 1810s.

3 Large quantities of mature trees, a valuable asset for a country estate, took many years to grow; their presence indicated good and thoughtful management over several generations.

4 A paling was a solid fence, another sign of good management of the estate. Elm was traditionally grown for its timber. Hawthorn is a prickly shrub traditional to the English countryside.

stipulated—for there were vacant spaces—and through one of these, Charlotte as soon as they entered the Enclosure, caught a glimpse over the pales of something White and Womanish, in the field on the other side;—it was a something which immediately brought Miss Brereton into her head—and stepping to the pales, she saw indeed—and very decidedly inspite of the Mist, Miss Brereton seated, not far before her, at the foot of the bank which sloped down from the outside of the Paling and which a narrow Path seemed to skirt along;—Miss Brereton seated, apparently very composedly—and Sir Edward Denham by her side.—They were sitting so near each other and appeared so closely engaged in gentle conversation, that Charlotte instantly felt she had nothing to do but to step back again, and say not a word.—Privacy was certainly their object.—It could not but strike her rather unfavourably with regard to Clara;—but hers was a situation which must not be judged with severity.—She was glad to perceive that nothing had been discerned by Mrs. Parker. If Charlotte had not been considerably the tallest of the two, Miss Brereton's white ribbons might not have fallen within the ken of *her* more observant eyes.—Among other points of moralising reflection which the sight of this Tete a Tete produced, Charlotte could not but think of the extreme difficulty which secret Lovers must have in finding a proper spot for their Stolen Interveiws.—Here perhaps they had thought themselves so perfectly secure from observation!—the whole field open before them—a steep bank and Pales never crossed by the foot of Man at their back—and a great thickness of air, in aid.—Yet here, she had seen them. They were really ill-used.—The House was large and handsome; two Servants appeared, to admit them, and every thing had a suitable air of Property and Order.—Lady Denham valued herself upon her liberal Establishment, and had great enjoyment in order and the Importance of her style of living.—They were shewn into the usual[1] sitting room, well-proportioned and well-furnished;—tho' it was Furniture rather originally good and extremely well kept, than new or shewey—and as Lady Denham was not there, Charlotte had leisure to look about, and to be told by Mrs. Parker that the whole-length Portrait of a stately Gentleman, which placed over the Mantlepeice, caught the eyes immediately, was the picture of Sir Harry Denham—and that one among many minia-

---

1 Ordinary; everyday.

tures in another part of the room, little conspicuous, represented Mr. Hollis.—Poor Mr. Hollis!—It was impossible not to feel him hardly used; to be obliged to stand back in his own House and see the best place by the fire constantly occupied by Sir Harry Denham.[1]

---

1 The manuscript ends here, and JA wrote the date "March 18," in a firm hand, immediately beneath the last line. On 23 March she wrote to her niece Fanny Knight that "about a week ago I was very poorly," and she never recovered her health. She died on 18 July 1817.

Appendix A: Austen's Letters about Fiction

[In the summer of 1814, Jane Austen's niece, Anna (1793-1872), was writing a novel, and sent instalments to Jane, Jane's mother, and Jane's sister Cassandra, then living at Chawton. Jane's comments on Anna's work, delivered in a series of letters from July to November 1814, provide insight into her own priorities as a writer, and in particular her care over social and geographical detail, as these extracts show. Anna's marriage to Ben Lefroy in November 1814 and subsequent, almost immediate, pregnancy seem to have interrupted her work, and her daughter later recollected that the manuscript of "Which is the Heroine?" was eventually thrown on to the fire in the late 1820s: "In later years when I expressed my sorrow that she had destroyed it, she said she could never have borne to finish it, but incomplete as it was Jane Austen's criticisms would have made it valuable" (Fanny Lefroy, "Family History," Hampshire Record Office, 23M93/85/2). The letters were kept within the family and were eventually given to St. John's College Oxford, where they are now held.]

1. To Anna Austen, Wednesday 10-Thursday 18 August 1814

My dear Anna

...

Wednesday 17.—We have just finished the 1st of the 3 Books I had the pleasure of receiving yesterday; *I* read it aloud—and we are all very much amused, & like the work quite as well as ever.—I depend upon getting through another book before dinner, but there is really a great deal of respectable reading in your 48 Pages. I was an hour about it.— I have no doubt that 6 will make a very good sized volume.—You must be quite pleased to have accomplished so much.—I like Lord P.— and his Brother very much;—I am only afraid that Lord P.—'s good nature will make most people like him better than he deserves.—The whole Portman Family are very good—and Lady Anne, who was your great dread, you have succeeded particularly well with.—Bell Griffin is just what she should be.—My Corrections have not been more important than before;—here & there, we have thought the sense might be expressed in fewer words—and I have scratched out Sir Tho: from walking with the other Men to the Stables &c the very day after his breaking his arm—for though I find that your Papa *did* walk out immediately after *his* arm was set, I think it can be so little usual as to *appear* unnatural in a book—& it does not seem to be material that Sir Tho: should go with them.—Lyme will not do. Lyme is towards 40 miles distance from Dawlish & would not be talked of there.—I have put Starcross indeed.—If you prefer *Exeter*, that must be always safe.—I have also scratched out the Introduction between Lord P. & his Brother, & Mr. Griffin. A Country Surgeon (dont tell Mr C. Lyford) would not be introduced to Men of their rank.—And when Mr. Portman is first brought in, he w^d not be introduced as *the Honble*—*That* distinction is never mentioned at such times;—at least I believe not.— Now, we have finished the 2^d book—or rather the 5th.—I *do* think you had better omit Lady Helena's postscript;—to those who are acquainted with P. & P. it will seem an Imitation.—And your Aunt C. & I both recommend you making a little alteration in the last scene between Devereux F. & Lady Clanmurray & her Daughter. We think they press him too much—more than sensible Women or well-bred Women would do. *Lady C.* at least, should have discretion enough to be sooner satisfied with his determination of not going with them.—I am very much pleased with Egerton as yet.—I did not expect to like him, but I do; & Susan is a very nice little animated Creature—but St Julian is the delight of one's Life. He is quite interesting.—The whole of his Break-off with Lady H. is very well done.—

Yes—Russel Square is a very proper distance from Berkeley S^t.— We are reading the last book.—They must be *two* days going from Dawlish to Bath; They are nearly 100 miles apart.

Thursday. We finished it last night, after our return from drinking tea at the G^t House.—The last chapter does not please us quite so well, we do not thoroughly like the *Play*; perhaps from having had too much of Plays in that way lately.—And we think you had better not leave England. Let the Portmans go to Ireland, but as you know nothing of the manners there, you had better not go with them. You will be in danger of giving false representations. Stick to Bath & the Foresters. There you will be quite at home.—Your Aunt C. does not like desultory novels, & is rather fearful yours will be too much so, that there will be too frequent a change from one set of people to another, & that circumstances will be sometimes introduced of apparent consequence, which will lead to nothing.—It will not be so great an objection to *me*, if it does. I allow much more Latitude than She does—& think Nature & Spirit cover many sins of a wandering story—and People in general do not care so much about it—for your comfort. I should like to have had more of Devereux. I do not feel enough acquainted with him.— You were afraid of meddling with him I dare say.—I like your sketch of Lord Clanmurray, and your picture of the two poor young girls enjoyments is very good.—I have not yet noticed St Julian's serious conversation with Cecilia, but I liked it exceedingly;—what he says about the madness of otherwise sensible Women, on the subject of their Daughters coming out, is worth it's weight in gold.—I do not see that the language sinks.—Pray go on.

Yours very affec:^{ly} J. Austen

[Postscript]
Twice you have put Dorsetshire for Devonshire. I have altered it.— Mr Griffin must have lived in Devonshire; Dawlish is half way down the County.—

2. To Anna Austen, Friday 9-Sunday 18 September 1814

My dear Anna

We have been very much amused by your 3 books, but I have a good many criticisms to make—more than you will like.—We are not satisfied with Mrs F.'s settling herself as Tenant & near Neighbour to such a Man as Sir T. H. without having some other inducement to go there; she ought to have some friend living thereabouts to tempt her. A woman, going with two girls just growing up, into a Neighbourhood where she knows nobody but one Man, of not very good character, is an awkwardness which so prudent a woman as M^{rs} F would not be likely to fall into. Remember, she is very prudent;—you must not let her act inconsistently.—Give her a friend, & let that friend be invited to meet her at the Priory, & we shall have no objection to her dining there as she does; but otherwise, a woman in her situation would hardly go there, before she had been visited by other Families.—I like the scene itself, the Miss Lesleys, Lady Anne, & the Music, very much.—Lesley *is* a noble name.—Sir T. H. you always do very well; I have only taken the liberty of expunging one phrase of his, which would not be allowable. "Bless my Heart."—It is too familiar & inelegant. Your G. M. is more disturbed at Mrs F.'s not returning the Egertons visit sooner, than anything else. They ought to have called at the Parsonage before Sunday.—

You describe a sweet place, but your descriptions are often more minute than will be liked. You give too many particulars of right hand & left.—

Mrs F. is not careful enough of Susan's health;—Susan ought not to be walking out so soon after Heavy rains, taking long walks in the dirt. An anxious Mother would not suffer it.—I like your Susan very much indeed, she is a sweet creature, her playfulness of fancy is very delightful. I like her as she is *now* exceedingly, but I am not so well satisfied with her behaviour to George R. At first she seemed all over attachment & feeling, & afterwards to have none at all; she is so extremely composed at the Ball, & so well satisfied apparently with Mr Morgan. She seems to have changed her Character.—You are now collecting your People delightfully, getting them exactly into such a spot as is the delight of my life;—3 or 4 Families in a Country Village is the very thing to work on—& I hope you will write a great deal more, & make full use of them while they are so very favourably arranged. You are but *now* coming to the heart & beauty of your book; till the heroine grows up, the fun must be imperfect—but I expect a great deal of entertainment from the next 3 or 4 books, & I hope you will not resent these remarks by sending me no more.—We like the Egertons very well, we see no Blue Pantaloons, or Cocks & Hens;—there is nothing to *enchant* one certainly in Mr L. L.—but we make no objection to him, & his inclination to like Susan is pleasing.—The Sister is a good contrast—but the name of Rachael is as much as I can bear.—They are not so much like the Papillons as I expected. Your last chapter is very entertaining—the conversation on Genius &c. Mr St J.—& Susan both talk in character & very well.—In some former parts, Cecilia is perhaps a little too solemn & good, but upon the whole, her disposition is very well opposed to Susan's—her want of Imagination is very natural.—I wish you could make Mrs F. talk more, but she must be difficult to manage & make entertaining, because there is so much common sence & propriety about her that nothing can be very *broad*. Her Economy & her Ambition must not be staring.—The Papers left by Mrs Fisher is very good.—Of course, one guesses something.—I hope when you have written a great deal more you will be equal to scratching out some of the past.—The scene with Mrs Mellish, I should condemn; it is prosy & nothing to the purpose—& indeed, the more you can find in your heart to curtail between Dawlish & Newton Priors, the better I think it will be.—One does not care for girls till they are grown up.—Your Aunt C. quite enters into the exquisiteness of that name. Newton Priors is really a Nonpareil.—Milton w^d have given his eyes to have thought of it.—Is not the Cottage taken from Tollard Royal?—

...

—Y^rs affec:^ly

J. Austen

Appendix B: Continuations of "Evelyn" and "Catharine" by James Edward Austen and Anna Lefroy

["Evelyn" and "Catharine," written in 1792, were both left unfinished. In about 1815-16, James Edward Austen (1798-1874), the son of Austen's brother, James, attempted to complete both stories. Then aged seventeen or eighteen, he visited Jane Austen and her family at Chawton quite frequently and could have received his aunt's permission to continue stories that she too had written when she was about seventeen. He succeeded in completing "Evelyn" (number 1, below), but did not get far with his attempt to finish "Catharine" (number 3, below). Much later, probably after he had changed his name to Austen Leigh in 1837 and after Cassandra Austen's death in 1845, he attempted, unsuccessfully, to complete "Catharine" once again (number 4, below). In addition, Austen's niece, Anna Lefroy (1793-1872), made her own attempt to complete "Evelyn" (number 2, below). Anna, the daughter of James Austen and the half-sister of James Edward Austen, married Benjamin Lefroy in November 1814. Since she initialled her continuation "JAEL" (Jane Anna Elizabeth Lefroy), she must have written it either at the end of 1814 or later. Her attempt breaks off abruptly without much advancing the story.]

1. James Edward Austen, Continuation of "Evelyn," c. 1815-16

On his return home, he rang the housebell, but no one appeared, a second time he rang, but the door was not opened, a third and a fourth with as little success, when observing the dining parlour window open he leapt in, and persued his way through the house till he reached Marias' Dressingroom, where he found all the servants assembled at tea. Surprized at so very unusual a sight, he fainted, on his recovery he found himself on the Sofa, with his wife's maid kneeling by him, chafing his temples with Hungary water—.[1] From her he learned that his beloved Maria had been so much grieved at his departure that she died of a broken heart about 3 hours after his departure.

He then became sufficiently composed to give necessary orders for her funeral which took place the Monday following this being the Saturday—When Mr Gower had settled the order of the procession he set out himself to Carlisle, to give vent to his sorrow in the bosom of his

---

1 An alcohol-based perfume, thought to have restorative properties.

family—He arrived there in high health and spirits, after a delightful journey of 3 days and a 1/2—What was his surprize on entering the Breakfast parlour to see Rosa his beloved Rosa seated on a Sofa; at the sight of him she fainted and would have fallen had not a Gentleman sitting with his back to the door, started up and saved her from sinking to the ground—She very soon came to herself and then introduced this gentleman to her Brother as her Husband a Mr Davenport—

But my dearest Rosa said the astonished Gower, I thought you were dead and buried. Why my dr Frederick replied Rosa I wished you to think so, hoping that you would spread the report about the country and it would thus by some means reach —— Castle—By this I hoped some how or other to touch the hearts of its inhabitants. It was not till the day before yesterday that I heard of the death of my beloved Henry which I learned from Mr D—— who concluded by offering me his hand. I accepted it with transport, and was married yesterday—Mr Gower, embraced his sister and shook hands with Mr Davenport, he then took a stroll into the town—As he passed by a public house he called for a pot of beer, which was brought him immediately by his old friend Mrs Willis—

Great was his astonishment at seeing Mrs Willis in Carlisle. But not forgetful of the respect he owed her, he dropped on one knee, and received the frothy cup from her, more grateful to *him* than Nectar— He instantly made her an offer of his hand and heart, which she graciously condescended to accept, telling him that she was only on a visit to her cousin, who kept the *Anchor* and should be ready to return to Evelyn, whenever he chose—The next morning they were married and immediately proceeded to Evelyn—When he reached home, he recollected that he had never written to Mr and Mrs Webb to inform them of the death of their daughter, which he rightly supposed they knew nothing of, as they never took in any newspapers—He immediately dispatched the following Letter—

Evelyn—Augst 19th—1809—

Dearest Madam,

How can words express the poignancy of my feelings! Our Maria, our beloved Maria is no more, she breathed her last, on Saturday the 12th of Augst—I see you now in an agony of grief lamenting not your own, but my loss—Rest satisfied I am happy, possessed of my lovely Sarah what more can I wish for?—

I remain

respectfully Yours

Fr. Gower—

Generous, best of Men

how truly we rejoice to hear of your present welfare and happiness! and how truly grateful are we for your unexampled generosity in writing to condole with us on the late unlucky accident which befel our Maria—I have enclosed a draught on our banker for 30 pounds, which Mr Webb joins with me in entreating you and the amiable Sarah to accept—

Your most grateful

Anne Augusta Webb

Mr and Mrs Gower resided many years at Evelyn enjoying perfect happiness the just reward of their virtues. The only alteration which took place at Evelyn was that Mr and Mrs Davenport settled there in Mrs Willis's former abode and were for many years the proprietors of the White horse Inn—

2. Anna Lefroy, Continuation of "Evelyn," c. 1814-15

On re entering his circular domain, his round-Robin of perpetual peace; where enjoyment had no End; and calamity no commencement, his spirits became wonderfully composed, and a delicious calm extended itself through every nerve—With his pocket hankerchief (once hemmed by the genius of the too susceptible Rosa) he wiped the morbid moisture from his brow;—then flew to the Boudoir of his Maria—And, did she not fly to meet her Frederick? Did she not dart from the Couch on which she had so gracefully reclined, and, bounding like an agile Fawn over the intervening Foot stool, precipitate herself into his arms? Does she not, though fainting between every syllable, breathe forth as it were by installments her Frederick's adored name? Who is there of perception so obtuse as not to realize the touching scene? Who, of ear so dull as not to catch the soft murmur of Maria's voice? Ah! Who? The heart of every sympathetic reader repeats, Ah, Who? Vain Echo! Vain sympathy! There is no Meeting—no Murmur—No Maria—It is not in the power of language however potent; nor in that of style, however diffuse to render justice to the astonishment of Mr. Gower—Arming himself with a mahogany ruler which some fatality had placed on Maria's writing table, and calling repeatedly on her beloved Name, he rushed forward to examine the adjacent apartments—In the Dressing room of his lost one he had the melancholy satisfaction of picking up a curl paper, and a gust of wind, as he re entered the Boudoir, swept from the table, and placed at his feet a skein of black sewing silk—These were the only traces of Maria!! Carefully locking the doors of these now desolate rooms, burying the key deep in his Waistcoat pocket, and the mystery of Maria's disappearance yet deeper in his heart of hearts, Mr. Gower left his once happy home, and sought a supper, and a Bed, at the house of the hospitable Mrs Willis —— There was an oppression on his chest which made him extremely uncomfortable; he regretted that instead of the skein of silk carefully wrapped up in the curl paper and placed beneath his pillow, he had not rather swallowed Laudanum—It would have been, in all probability, more efficacious—At last, Mr Gower slept a troubled sleep, and in due course of time he dreamt a troubled dream—He dreamed of Maria, as how could he less? She stood by his Bed side, in her Dressing Gown—one hand held an open book, with the forefinger of the other she pointed to this ominous passage—"Tantôt c'est un vide; qui nous ennuie; tantôt c'est un poids qui nous oppresse"—[1] The unfortunate Frederick uttered a deep groan—and as the vision closed the volume he observed these characters strangely imprinted on the Cover—Rolandi—Berners Street. *Who* was this dangerous Rolandi? Doubtless a Bravo or a Monk—possibly both—and what was he to Maria? Vainly he would have dared the worst, and put the fatal question—the semblance of Maria raised her monitory finger, and interdicted speech—Yet, some words she spoke, or seemed to speak her self; Mr. Gower could distinguish only these—Search—Cupboard—Top shelf—Once more he essayed to speak, but it was all bewilderment—He heard strange Demon-like Sounds; hissing and spitting—he smelt an unearthly smell the agony became unbearable, and he awoke—Maria had vanished; the Rush light was expiring in the Socket; and the benevolent Mrs. Willis entering his room, threw open the shutters, and in accordance with her own warmth of heart admitted the full blaze of a Summer morning's Sun—

JAEL

3. James Edward Austen, first continuation of "Catharine," c. 1815-16

Kitty continued in this state of satisfaction during the remainder of the Stanley's visit—Who took their leave with many pressing invitations to visit them in London, when as Camilla said, she might have an opportunity of becoming acquainted with that sweet girl Augusta Hallifax— Or Rather (thought Kitty,) of seeing my dr Mary Wynn again—Mrs Percival in answer to Mrs Stanley's invitation replied—That she

---

1 French: "Sometimes it is a void that worries us; sometimes it is a burden that oppresses us."

looked upon London as the hot house of Vice where virtue had long been banished from Society and wickedness of every description was daily gaining ground—that Kitty was of herself sufficiently inclined to give way to, and indulge in vicious inclinations—and therefore was the last girl in the world to be trusted in London, as she would be totally unable to withstand temptation ——

After the departure of the Stanleys Kitty returned to her usual occupations, but Alas! they had lost their power of pleasing. Her bower alone retained its interest in her feelings, and perhaps that was oweing to the particular remembrance it brought to her mind of Edwd Stanley.

4. James Edward Austen Leigh, second continuation of "Catharine," post-1845

The Summer passed away unmarked by any incident worth narrating, or any pleasure to Catharine save one, which arose from the receipt of a letter from her friend Cecilia now Mrs Lascelles, announcing the Speedy return of herself and Husband to England.

A correspondance productive indeed of little pleasure to either party had been established between Camilla and Catharine. The latter had now lost the only Satisfaction she had ever received from the letters of Miss Stanley, as that young Lady having informed her Friend of the departure of her Brother to Lyons now never mentioned his name—Her letters seldom contained any Intelligence except a description of some new Article of Dress, an enumeration of various engagements, a panegyric on Augusta Halifax and perhaps a little abuse of the unfortunate Sir Peter ——

The Grove, for so was the Mansion of Mrs. Percival at Chetwynde denominated was situated wthin. five miles from Exeter, but though that Lady possessed a carriage and horses of her own, it was seldom that Catharine could prevail on her to visit that town for the purpose of shopping, on account of the many officers perpetually Quartered there and infested the principal Streets—A company of strolling players in their way from some Neighbouring Races having opened a temporary Theatre there, Mrs. Percival was prevailed on by her Niece to indulge her by attending the performance once during their stay—Mrs. Percival insisted on paying Miss Dudley the compliment of inviting her to join the party, when a new difficulty arose, from the necessity of having Some Gentleman to attend them—

Appendix C: "Love and Freindship" (1790) and Frances Burney's Evelina (1778)

[Among the most memorable scenes in "Love and Freindship" is that in Letter 11th, in which Laura beseeches her grandfather, Lord St. Clair, to acknowledge her. Their spectacularly overwrought encounter is followed in quick succession by meetings with three more long-lost grandchildren: Sophia, Philander, and Gustavus. The passage parodies two famous scenes in Frances Burney's epistolary novel *Evelina* (Vol. 3, Letters 17 and 19), in which the heroine is at last acknowledged by her father, Sir John Belmont. Thanks to the machinations of a nurse, who had exchanged her own baby, Polly, for Evelina, Sir John had been tricked into believing that Polly was his daughter. After being brought up in a convent in France, Polly returns to England and is initially accepted by Sir John as his child, born to his late wife Caroline Evelyn. When Sir John is told that Evelina is his daughter, in Letter 17, he at first rejects her claim. Only in Letter 19, the second excerpt below, does he finally recognize that Evelina, not Polly, is indeed his daughter, and thus the heiress to his estate. Like Evelina, Laura, in "Love and Freindship," falls on her knees, and like Sir John, Lord St. Clair exclaims "Acknowledge thee!" There is also a parallel between Sir John's interjection, "Oh dear resemblance of thy murdered mother!" and that of Lord St. Clair, "Yes dear resemblance of my Laurina."]

1. From *Evelina*, ed. Susan Kubica Howard (Peterborough: Broadview, 2000), 515

The voice of a *father*—Oh dear and revered name!—which then, for the first time, struck my ears, affected me in a manner I cannot describe, though it was only employed to give orders to a servant as he came down stairs.

Then, entering the parlour, I heard him say, "I am sorry, Madam, I made you wait, but I have an engagement which now calls me away: however, if you have any commands for me, I shall be glad of the honour of your company some other time."

"I am come, Sir," said Mrs. Selwyn, "to introduce your daughter to you."

"I am infinitely obliged to you," answered he, "but I have just had the satisfaction of breakfasting with her. Ma'am, your most obedient."

"You refuse, then, to see her?"

"I am much indebted to you, Madam, for this desire of encreasing my family, but you must excuse me if I decline taking advantage of it. I have already a daughter, to whom I owe every thing; and it is not three days since, that I had the pleasure of discovering a son; how many more sons and daughters may be brought to me, I am yet to learn, but I am, already, perfectly satisfied with the size of my family."

2. From *Evelina*, ed. Susan Kubica Howard (Peterborough: Broadview, 2000), 529-31

I then took from my pocket-book her last letter, and, pressing it to my lips, with a trembling hand, and still upon my knees, I held it out to him.

Hastily snatching it from me, "Great Heaven!" cried he, "'tis her writing—Whence comes this?—who gave it you—why had I it not sooner?"

I made no answer; his vehemence intimidated me, and I ventured not to move from the suppliant posture in which I had put myself.

He went from me to the window, where his eyes were for some time rivetted upon the direction of the letter, though his hand shook so violently he could hardly hold it. Then, bringing it to me, "Open it,"—cried he,—"for I cannot!"

I had, myself, hardly strength to obey him; but, when I had, he took it back, and walked hastily up and down the room, as if dreading to read it. At length, turning to me, "Do you know," cried he, "its contents?"

"No, Sir," answered I; "it has never been unsealed."

He then again went to the window, and began reading. Having hastily run it over, he cast up his eyes with a look of desperation; the letter fell from his hand, and he exclaimed, "Yes! thou art sainted!—thou art blessed!—and I am cursed for ever!" He continued some time fixed in this melancholy position; after which, casting himself with violence upon the ground, "Oh wretch," cried he, "unworthy life and light, in what dungeon canst thou hide thy head?"

I could restrain myself no longer; I rose and went to him; I did not dare speak, but with pity and concern unutterable, I wept and hung over him.

Soon after, starting up, he again seized the letter, exclaiming, "Acknowledge thee, Caroline!—yes, with my heart's best blood would I acknowledge thee!—Oh that thou couldst witness the agony of my soul!—Ten thousand daggers could not have wounded me like this letter!"

Then, after again reading it, "Evelina," he cried, "she charges me to receive thee;—wilt thou, in obedience to her will, own for thy father the destroyer of thy mother?"

What a dreadful question! I shuddered, but could not speak.

"To clear her fame, and receive her child," continued he, looking stedfastly at the letter, "are the conditions upon which she leaves me her forgiveness: her fame, I have already cleared;—and oh how willingly would I take her child to my bosom,—fold her to my heart,—call upon her to mitigate my anguish, and pour the balm of comfort on my wounds, were I not conscious I deserve not to receive it, and that all my affliction is the result of my own guilt!"

It was in vain I attempted to speak; horror and grief took from me all power of utterance.

He then read aloud from the letter, "*Look not like thy unfortunate mother!*—Sweet soul, with what bitterness of spirit hast thou written?—Come hither, Evelina: Gracious Heaven!" looking earnestly at me, "never was likeness more striking!—the eye,—the face,—the form,—Oh my child, my child!" Imagine, Sir,—for I can never describe my feelings, when I saw him sink upon his knees before me! "Oh dear resemblance of thy murdered mother!—Oh all that remains of the most injured of women! behold thy father at thy feet!—bending thus lowly to implore you would not hate him;—Oh, then, thou representative of my departed wife, speak to me in her name, and say that the remorse which tears my soul, tortures me not in vain!"

"Oh rise, rise, my beloved father," cried I, attempting to assist him, "I cannot bear to see you thus;—reverse not the law of nature, rise yourself, and bless your kneeling daughter!"

"May Heaven bless thee, my child!—" cried he, "for *I* dare not." He then rose, and embracing me most affectionately, added, "I see, I see that thou art all kindness, softness, and tenderness; I need not have feared thee, thou art all the fondest father could wish, and I will try to frame my mind to less painful sensations at thy sight. Perhaps the time may come, when I may know the comfort of such a daughter,—at present, I am only fit to be alone: dreadful as are my reflections, they ought merely to torment myself.—Adieu, my child;—be not angry,— I cannot stay with thee,—oh Evelina! thy countenance is a dagger to my heart!—just so, thy mother looked,—just so—"

Appendix D: From Mary Wollstonecraft's Thoughts on the Education of Daughters *(1787): "Unfortunate Situation of Females, fashionably educated, and left without a Fortune"*

[Mary Wollstonecraft (1759-97) was a feminist author whose most famous work was *A Vindication of the Rights of Woman* (1792). Born into a genteel but increasingly impecunious family, she experienced at first-hand the very limited options available to women who did not attract moneyed husbands and thus needed to support themselves. She spent periods as a companion, a teacher, and a governess in an aristocratic household before deciding to try to earn her living as a professional writer. While still influenced by orthodox religion and before coming into contact with radical thinkers, she used her experiences in the workplace as the basis of her first book, *Thoughts on the Education of Daughters*.]

I have hitherto only spoken of those females, who will have a provision made for them by their parents. But many who have been well, or at least fashionably educated, are left without a fortune, and if they are not entirely devoid of delicacy, they must frequently remain single.

Few are the modes of earning a subsistence, and those very humiliating. Perhaps to be an humble companion to some rich old cousin, or what is still worse, to live with strangers, who are so intolerably tyrannical, that none of their own relations can bear to live with them, though they should even expect a fortune in reversion. It is impossible to enumerate the many hours of anguish such a person must spend. Above the servants, yet considered by them as a spy, and ever reminded of her inferiority when in conversation with the superiors. If she cannot condescend to mean flattery, she has not a chance of being a favorite; and should any of the visitors take notice of her, and she for a moment forget her subordinate state, she is sure to be reminded of it.

Painfully sensible of unkindness, she is alive to every thing, and many sarcasms reach her, which were perhaps directed another way. She is alone, shut out from equality and confidence, and the concealed anxiety impairs her constitution; for she must wear a cheerful face, or be dismissed. The being dependant on the caprice of a fellow-creature, though certainly very necessary in this state of discipline, is yet a very bitter corrective, which we would fain shrink from.

A teacher at a school is only a kind of upper servant, who has more work than the menial ones.

A governess to young ladies is equally disagreeable. It is ten to one if they meet with a reasonable mother; and if she is not so, she will be continually finding fault to prove she is not ignorant, and be displeased if her pupils do not improve, but angry if the proper methods are taken to make them do so. The children treat them with disrespect, and often with insolence. In the mean time life glides away, and the spirits with it; "and when youth and genial years are flown," they have nothing to subsist on; or, perhaps, on some extraordinary occasion, some small allowance may be made for them, which is thought a great charity.

The few trades which are left, are now gradually falling into the hands of the men, and certainly they are not very respectable.

It is hard for a person who has a relish for polished society, to herd with the vulgar, or to condescend to mix with her former equals when she is considered in a different light. What unwelcome heart-breaking knowledge is then poured in on her! I mean a view of the selfishness and depravity of the world; for every other acquirement is a source of pleasure, though they may occasion temporary inconveniences. How cutting is the contempt she meets with!—A young mind looks round for love and friendship; but love and friendship fly from poverty: expect them not if you are poor! The mind must then sink into meanness, and accommodate itself to its new state, or dare to be unhappy. Yet I think no reflecting person would give up the experience and improvement they have gained, to have avoided the misfortunes; on the contrary, they are thankfully ranked amongst the choicest blessings of life, when we are not under their immediate pressure.

How earnestly does a mind full of sensibility look for disinterested friendship, and long to meet with good unalloyed. When fortune smiles they hug the dear delusion; but dream not that it is one. The painted cloud disappears suddenly, the scene is changed, and what an aching void is left in the heart! A void which only religion can fill up— and how few seek this internal comfort!

A woman, who has beauty without sentiment, is in great danger of being seduced; and if she has any, cannot guard herself from painful mortifications. It is very disagreeable to keep up a continual reserve with men she has been formerly familiar with; yet if she places confidence, it is ten to one but she is deceived. Few men seriously think of marrying an inferior; and if they have honor enough not to take advantage of the artless tenderness of a woman who loves, and thinks not of the difference of rank, they do not undeceive her until she has anticipated happiness, which, contrasted with her dependant situation, appears delightful. The disappointment is severe; and the heart receives a wound which does not easily admit of a compleat cure, as the good that is missed is not valued according to its real worth: for fancy drew the picture, and grief delights to create food to feed on.

If what I have written should be read by parents, who are now going on in thoughtless extravagance, and anxious only that their daughters may be *genteelly educated*, let them consider to what sorrows they expose them; for I have not over-coloured the picture.

Though I warn parents to guard against leaving their daughters to encounter so much misery; yet if a young woman falls into it, she ought not to be discontented. Good must ultimately arise from every thing, to those who look beyond this infancy of their being; and here the comfort of a good conscience is our only stable support. The main business of our lives is to learn to be virtuous; and He who is training us up for immortal bliss, knows best what trials will contribute to make us so; and our resignation and improvement will render us respectable to ourselves, and to that Being, whose approbation is of more value than life itself. It is true, tribulation produces anguish, and we would fain avoid the bitter cup, though convinced its effects would be the most salutary. The Almighty is then the kind parent, who chastens and educates, and indulges us not when it would tend to our hurt. He is compassion itself, and never wounds but to heal, when the ends of correction are answered.

Appendix E: From Walter Scott, Quarterly Review *14 (issue for October 1815, appeared March 1816, pp. 188-201)*

[Jane Austen's fourth novel, *Emma*, was published by John Murray in December 1815. This was the first time she had been published by Murray, widely regarded as the leading London publisher, and it was Murray, in his capacity as owner of the *Quarterly*, who asked Walter Scott, one of the most famous writers of the day, to review the novel. Scott's appreciative review, which took into account at least some of Austen's earlier writings, is the most substantial criticism of her work to appear in her lifetime.]

The author is already known to the public by the two novels announced in her title-page,[1] and both, the last especially, attracted, with justice, an attention from the public far superior to what is granted to the ephemeral productions which supply the regular demand of watering-places and circulating libraries. They belong to a class of fictions which has arisen almost in our own times, and which draws the characters and incidents introduced more immediately from the current of ordinary life than was permitted by the former rules of the novel. In its first appearance, the novel was the legitimate child of the romance; and though the manners and general turn of the composition were altered so as to suit modern times, the author remained fettered by many peculiarities derived from the original style of romantic fiction. These may be chiefly traced in the conduct of the narrative, and the tone of sentiment attributed to the fictitious personages. On the first point, although

> The talisman and magic wand were broke,
> Knights, dwarfs, and genii vanish'd into smoke,[2]

---

1 In fact, the title page of *Emma* states "By the author of 'Pride and Prejudice' &c &c." Scott refers in his review to *Sense and Sensibility* (1811) and *Pride and Prejudice* (1813), but not to *Mansfield Park* (1814).

2 From the prologue to George Colman's *Polly Honeycombe, a Dramatic Novel of One Act* (1761), which describes successive forms of imaginative

still the reader expected to peruse a course of adventures of a nature more interesting and extraordinary than those which occur in his own life, or that of his next-door neighbours. The hero no longer defeated armies by his single sword, clove giants to the chine, or gained kingdoms. But he was expected to go through perils by sea and land, to be steeped in poverty, to be tried by temptation, to be exposed to the alternate vicissitudes of adversity and prosperity, and his life was a troubled scene of suffering and achievement. Few novelists, indeed, adventured to deny to the hero his final hour of tranquillity and happiness, though it was the prevailing fashion never to relieve him out of his last and most dreadful distress until the finishing chapters of his history; so that although his prosperity in the record of his life was short, we were bound to believe it was long and uninterrupted when the author had done with him. The heroine was usually condemned to equal hardships and hazards. She was regularly exposed to being forcibly carried off like a Sabine virgin by some frantic admirer.[1] And even if she escaped the terrors of masked ruffians, an insidious ravisher, a cloak wrapped forcibly around her head, and a coach with the blinds up driving she could not conjecture whither, she had still her share of wandering, of poverty, of obloquy, of seclusion, and of imprisonment, and was frequently extended upon a bed of sickness, and reduced to her last shilling before the author condescended to shield her from persecution.[2] In all these dread contingencies the mind of the reader was expected to sympathize, since by incidents so much beyond the bounds of his ordinary experience, his wonder and interest ought at once to be excited. But gradually he became familiar with the land of fiction, the adventures of which he assimilated not with those of real life, but with each other. Let the distress of the hero or heroine be ever so great, the reader reposed an imperturbable confidence in the talents of the author, who, as he had plunged them into

---

narrative. The "dread Sorceress" Romance is said to have cast a spell over common sense until

This Fiend to quell, his sword Cervantes drew,

A trusty Spanish Blade, Toledo true:

Her Talismans and Magick Wand he broke—

Knights, Genii, Castles——vanish'd into smoke.

1 Alluding to the famous legend of the early days of Rome, when a group of young Roman men abducted the unmarried daughters of their Sabine neighbours.

2 Jane Austen's burlesque "Plan of a Novel" identifies similar novelistic features. For example, a typical heroine is "often reduced to support herself & her Father by her Talents, & work for her Bread;—continually cheated & defrauded of her hire, worn down to a skeleton, & now & then starved to death" (*Later Manuscripts*, p. 228).

distress, would in his own good time, and when things, as Tony Lumkin says, were in a concatenation accordingly,[1] bring his favourites out of all their troubles. Mr. Crabbe has expressed his own and our feelings excellently on this subject.

> For should we grant these beauties all endure
> Severest pangs, they've still the speediest cure;
> Before one charm be withered from the face,
> Except the bloom which shall again have place,
> In wedlock ends each wish, in triumph all disgrace.
> And life to come, we fairly may suppose,
> One light bright contrast to these wild dark woes.[2]

In short, the author of novels was, in former times, expected to tread pretty much in the limits between the concentric circles of probability and possibility; and as he was not permitted to transgress the latter, his narrative, to make amends, almost always went beyond the bounds of the former....

We return to the second broad line of distinction between the novel, as formerly composed, and real life,—the difference, namely, of the sentiments. The novelist professed to give an imitation of nature, but it was, as the French say, *la belle nature*. Human beings, indeed, were presented, but in the most sentimental mood, and with minds purified by a sensibility which often verged on extravagance. In the serious class of novels, the hero was usually

> A knight of love, who never broke a vow.[3]

... The heroine was, of course, still more immaculate; and to have conferred her affections upon any other than the lover to whom the reader had destined her from their first meeting, would have been a crime

---

1 Tony Lumpkin is a character in Oliver Goldsmith's popular play, *She Stoops to Conquer* (1773). It is one of Tony's drunken comrades rather than Tony himself who says that "The genteel thing is the genteel thing at any time. If so be that a gentleman bees in a concatenation accordingly" (Act 1, Scene 2). A concatenation is a linked chain or union (of events), though its meaning here is unclear.

2 From "The Borough," Letter 20, in George Crabbe, *Works* (1834), Vol. 4, p. 11.

3 Alluding to John Dryden's description of true lovers: "those, who wear the woodbine on their brow, / Were knights of love, who never broke their vow," in "The Flower and the Leaf," *The Miscellaneous Works of John Dryden Esq.* (4 vols, 1767), Vol. 3, p. 117.

against sentiment which no author, of moderate prudence, would have hazarded, under the old *régime*.

Here, therefore, we have two essentials and important circumstances, in which the earlier novels differed from those now in fashion, and were more nearly assimilated to the old romances. And there can be no doubt that, by the studied involution and extrication of the story, by the combination of incidents new, striking and wonderful beyond the course of ordinary life, the former authors opened that obvious and strong sense of interest which arises from curiosity; as by the pure, elevated, and romantic cast of the sentiment, they conciliated those better propensities of our nature which loves to contemplate the picture of virtue, even when confessedly unable to imitate its excellences.

But strong and powerful as these sources of emotion and interest may be, they are, like all others, capable of being exhausted by habit. The imitators who rushed in crowds upon each path in which the great masters of the art had successively led the way, produced upon the public mind the usual effect of satiety. The first writer of a new class is, as it were, placed on a pinnacle of excellence, to which, at the earliest glance of a surprised admirer, his ascent seems little less than miraculous. Time and imitation speedily diminish the wonder, and each successive attempt establishes a kind of progressive scale of ascent between the lately deified author, and the reader, who had deemed his excellence inaccessible. The stupidity, the mediocrity, the merit of his imitators, are alike fatal to the first inventor, by showing how possible it is to exaggerate his faults and to come within a certain point of his beauties.

Materials also (and the man of genius as well as his wretched imitator must work with the same) become stale and familiar. Social life, in our civilized days, affords few instances capable of being painted in the strong dark colours which excite surprise and horror; and robbers, smugglers, bailiffs, caverns, dungeons, and mad-houses, have been all introduced until they ceased to interest. And thus in the novel, as in every style of composition which appeals to the public taste, the more rich and easily worked mines being exhausted, the adventurous author must, if he is desirous of success, have recourse to those which were disdained by his predecessors as unproductive, or avoided as only capable of being turned to profit by great skill and labour.

Accordingly a style of novel has arisen, within the last fifteen or twenty years, differing from the former in the points upon which the interest hinges; neither alarming our credulity nor amusing our imagination by wild variety of incident, or by those pictures of romantic affection and sensibility, which were formerly as certain attributes of fictitious characters as they are of rare occurrence among those who actually live and die. The substitute for these excitements, which had lost much of their poignancy by the repeated and injudicious use of them, was the art of copying from nature as she really exists in the common walks of life, and presenting to the reader, instead of the splendid scenes of an imaginary world, a correct and striking representation of that which is daily taking place around him.

In adventuring upon this task, the author makes obvious sacrifices, and encounters peculiar difficulty. He who paints from *le beau idéal*, if his scenes and sentiments are striking and interesting, is in a great measure exempted from the difficult task of reconciling them with the ordinary probabilities of life: but he who paints a scene of common occurrence, places his composition within that extensive range of criticism which general experience offers to every reader. The resemblance of a statue of Hercules we must take on the artist's judgment; but every one can criticize that which is presented as the portrait of a friend, or neighbour. Something more than a mere sign-post likeness is also demanded. The portrait must have spirit and character, as well as resemblance; and being deprived of all that, according to Bayes, goes "to elevate and surprize,"[1] it must make amends by displaying depth of knowledge and dexterity of execution.

---

1 Bayes is a character in the play, *The Rehearsal* (1671), by George, Duke of Buckingham. The phrase "elevate and surprize" is first used by Johnson and Smith in Act 1, Scene 1, just before Bayes comes onstage, but, later in the play, Bayes claims that "the chief Art in Poetry, is to elevate your expectation, and then bring you off in some extraordinary way" (4.1).

Select Bibliography

Works

Austen, Jane. *Catharine and Other Writings*. Ed. Margaret Anne Doody and Douglas Murray. Oxford: Oxford UP, 1993.

———. *Catharine, or The Bower*. Ed. Juliet McMaster et al. Edmonton, AB: Juvenilia P, 1996.

———. *Emma* (1816). Ed. Richard Cronin and Dorothy McMillan. Cambridge: Cambridge UP, 2005.

———. *Jane Austen's Fiction Manuscripts: A Digital Edition*. Ed. Kathryn Sutherland. 2010. http://www.janeausten.ac.uk.

———. *Jane Austen's Letters*. Ed. Deirdre Le Faye. 4th ed. Oxford: Oxford UP, 2011.

———. *Juvenilia*. Ed. Peter Sabor. Cambridge: Cambridge UP, 2006.

———. *Lady Susan*. Ed. Christine Alexander and David Owen. Sydney, Australia: Juvenilia P, 2005.

———. *Lady Susan, The Watsons, Sanditon*. Ed. Margaret Drabble. Harmondsworth: Penguin, 1974.

———. *Later Manuscripts*. Ed. Janet Todd and Linda Bree. Cambridge: Cambridge UP, 2008.

———. *Lesley Castle*. Ed. Jan Fergus et al. Edmonton, AB: Juvenilia P, 1998.

———. *Love & Freindship*. Ed. Juliet McMaster et al. Edmonton, AB: Juvenilia P, 1995.

———. *Mansfield Park* (1814). Ed. John Wiltshire. Cambridge: Cambridge UP, 2005.

———. *Northanger Abbey* (1817). Ed. Barbara M. Benedict and Deirdre Le Faye. Cambridge: Cambridge UP, 2006.

———. *Persuasion* (1817). Ed. Janet Todd and Antje Blank. Cambridge: Cambridge UP, 2006.

———. *Pride and Prejudice* (1813). Ed. Pat Rogers. Cambridge: Cambridge UP, 2006.

———. *Sense and Sensibility* (1811). Ed. Edward Copeland. Cambridge: Cambridge UP, 2006.

———. *Three Mini-Dramas*. Ed. Juliet McMaster, Lesley Peterson, et al. Sydney, Australia: Juvenilia P, 2006.

Biographies

Austen Leigh, James Edward. A *Memoir of Jane Austen*. London: Richard Bentley and Son, 1870.

——. *A Memoir of Jane Austen*. 2nd ed. London: Richard Bentley and Son, 1871.

Honan, Park. *Jane Austen: Her Life*. London: Weidenfeld and Nicolson, 1987.

Le Faye, Deirdre. *A Chronology of Jane Austen and Her Family*. Cambridge: Cambridge UP, 2006.

——. *Jane Austen: A Family Record*. 2nd ed. Cambridge: Cambridge UP, 2004.

Nokes, David. *Jane Austen: A Life*. New York: Farrar, Straus, and Giroux, 1997.

Tomalin, Claire. *Jane Austen: A Life*. London: Viking, 1997.

Critical Studies

Alexander, Christine, and David Owen. "*Lady Susan*: A Re-Evaluation of Jane Austen's Epistolary Novel." *Persuasions* 27 (2005): 54-68.

Byrne, Paula. *Jane Austen and the Theatre*. London: Hambledon; NY: Palgrave, 2002.

Chapman, R.W. *Jane Austen: Facts and Problems*. Oxford: Clarendon P, 1948.

Copeland, Edward and Juliet McMaster, eds. *The Cambridge Companion to Jane Austen*. 2nd ed. Cambridge: Cambridge UP, 2011.

Doody, Margaret Anne. "Jane Austen, that Disconcerting 'Child.'" In *The Child Writer from Austen to Woolf*. Ed. Christine Alexander and Juliet McMaster. Cambridge: Cambridge UP, 2005. 101-21.

Gilbert, Sandra M., and Susan Gubar. *The Madwoman in the Attic: The Woman Writer and the Nineteenth-Century Literary Imagination*. New Haven: Yale UP, 1979.

Gilson, David. *A Bibliography of Jane Austen*. Revised ed. Winchester: St. Paul's Bibliographies; New Castle, DE: Oak Knoll P, 1997.

Grey, J. David, ed. *Jane Austen's Beginnings: The Juvenilia and Lady Susan*. Ann Arbor, MI: UMI Research P, 1989.

Hill, Constance. *Jane Austen: Her Homes and Her Friends*. London; NY: John Lane, 1902.

Knox-Shaw, Peter. *Jane Austen and the Enlightenment*. Cambridge: Cambridge UP, 2004.

Leavis, Q.D. "A Critical Theory of Jane Austen's Writings." *Scrutiny* 10 (1941): 61-87. Reprinted in *Collected Essays*. Vol. 1. Ed. G. Singh. Cambridge: Cambridge UP, 1983.

Litz, A. Walton. *Jane Austen. A Study of Her Artistic Development*. London: Chatto & Windus, 1965.

McMaster, Juliet. "'God gave us our relations': The Watson Family." *Persuasions* 8 (1986): 60-72.

———. "The Juvenilia: Energy Versus Sympathy." In *A Companion to Jane Austen Studies*. Ed. Laura Cooner Lambdin and Robert Thomas Lambdin. Westport, CT: Greenwood P, 2000. 173-89.

———. "Young Jane Austen: Author." In *A Companion to Jane Austen*. Ed. Claudia Johnson and Clara Tuite. Oxford: Blackwell, 2009. 81-90.

Mudrick, Marvin. *Jane Austen: Irony as Defense and Discovery*. Princeton: Princeton UP, 1952. Reprint, Berkeley; Los Angeles: U of California P, 1968.

Roberts, Warren. *Jane Austen and the French Revolution*. London: Macmillan, 1979. Reprint, London: Athlone P, 1995.

Sabor, Peter. "Brotherly and Sisterly Dedications in Jane Austen's Juvenilia." *Persuasions* 31 (2009): 33-46.

Southam, B.C. *Jane Austen's Literary Manuscripts: A Study of the Novelist's Development through the Surviving Papers*. Rev. ed. London; NY: Athlone P, 2001.

———. *Jane Austen: A Students' Guide to the Later Manuscripts*. London: Concord, 2007.

Sutherland, Kathryn, ed. *J.E. Austen-Leigh: A Memoir of Jane Austen and Other Family Recollections*. Oxford: Oxford UP, 2002.

———. *Jane Austen's Textual Lives: From Aeschylus to Bollywood*. Oxford: Oxford UP, 2005.

Todd, Janet. *An Introduction to Jane Austen*. Cambridge: Cambridge UP, 2008.

———, ed. *Jane Austen in Context*. Cambridge: Cambridge UP, 2005.

Tuite, Clara. *Romantic Austen: Sexual Politics and the Literary Canon*. Cambridge: Cambridge UP, 2002.

Waldron, Mary. *Jane Austen and the Fiction of Her Time*. Cambridge: Cambridge UP, 1999.

Wiesenfarth, Joseph. "*The Watsons* as Pretext." *Persuasions* 8 (1986): 101-11.

Wiltshire, John. "Sickness and Silliness in *Sanditon*." *Persuasions* 19 (1997): 93-102.

———. *Jane Austen and the Body*. Cambridge: Cambridge UP, 1992.

Woolf, Virginia. "Jane Austen Practising." *New Statesman*, 15 July 1922. Reprinted in *The Essays of Virginia Woolf. Vol. 3, 1919-1924*. Ed. Andrew McNeillie. London: Chatto & Windus, 1988. 331-35.

From the Publisher

A name never says it all, but the word "Broadview" expresses a good deal of the philosophy behind our company. We are open to a broad range of academic approaches and political viewpoints. We pay attention to the broad impact book publishing and book printing has in the wider world; for some years now we have used 100% recycled paper for most titles. Our publishing program is internationally oriented and broad-ranging. Our individual titles often appeal to a broad readership too; many are of interest as much to general readers as to academics and students.

Founded in 1985, Broadview remains a fully independent company owned by its shareholders—not an imprint or subsidiary of a larger multinational.

For the most accurate information on our books (including information on pricing, editions, and formats) please visit our website at www.broadviewpress.com. Our print books and ebooks are also available for sale on our site.

broadview press
www.broadviewpress.com

This book is made of paper from well-managed FSC® - certified forests, recycled materials, and other controlled sources.